TRANSFORMATION PROTOCOL

Joe Ballen, Book Three

David M. Kelly

Nemesis Press

Transformation Protocol : Joe Ballen, Book Three

ISBN-13: 978-1-9991150-1-2

ISBN-10: 1-9991150-1-5

First Published 2019

Nemesis Press
Wahnapitae, Ontario

www.nemesispress.com

Printed in U.S.A

Dedication

To my wife, Hilary, for the continued support, care, and love. Without whom none of this would be possible. May you always be by my side.

Chapter One

On a bad day, I hate everyone. On a good day, I only hate myself. Today was somewhere in between.

We get sold an idea when we're young. Call it a group indoctrination or maybe propaganda to keep the masses quiet. I'm sure you've heard it—perhaps you even believe it. The idea that things get better. With time, even the biggest tragedies and screw-ups are replaced with happier, more positive experiences and memories.

That's bullshit. Nothing but a contemptuous lie that seeps inside you like venom, and the worst of it is that you *want* it to be true. We all want it to be true because if it isn't, then what the hell's the point of existing? For a while I'd almost believed it too. Things had been looking up. I had a wife, possibly a family. Then it all fell apart in an instant, leaving an emptiness that gnawed at me from the inside—a blanket of shadow that hated the light.

"Help! Help! The sky is falling!"

Hardrock Harry was stuck again. He'd dug a tunnel fifty meters deeper into the asteroid than he'd previously managed, which made it his best run so far. Despite that, it was well short of the performance levels needed to pass the field trials. As usual, he'd failed while executing a turn, the trickiest part of the operation but one his design specs said he should have been capable of.

"Sorry, Joe." Harry's soft voice had a doleful quality that wasn't part of his general programming. "My progress rate is 0.00 meters per second, my cutters are bound up, and I've switched off to prevent overheating."

I pulled out my flask, poured a cup of strong whiskey-laced coffee, and swallowed a mouthful. "Don't worry, Harry. You'll get it next time. Can you back out?"

There was a short delay, which gave the impression that Harry was thinking about it, but in reality, that was simply the time it took for my message to reach him. Harry was operating inside the KG-643 asteroid test site, while I was in an office in the bustling new-tech area of Carney, Baltimore.

I was running the gang through a testing program that was supposed to prove the value of autonomous mining and construction robots, designed to construct a habitat from suitable asteroids without supervision. The trials weren't going well.

"Harry's in the way again, the dumbass. I can't set the RokFrac unless he moves."

The new voice was sharper with a heavy New York accent. Blasting Bob was another member of the team. He was designed to follow behind Harry, planting rock-splitting charges in the holes drilled by Harry. The debris would then be collected by several Muckout Mikes, units that shipped the rocks to the processing station where they would get crushed and treated to form the basis of an airtight astrocrete used to line the tunnels.

The drilling and charges had to be precise. If not, the explosions could trap the robots, possibly damaging them but certainly ending their ability to work on their own. The project had ambitious goals, which so far seemed about as remote as Proxima Centauri, where the robots were destined to operate under field trials in a few months.

I checked Harry's remote cameras. Bob floated a few meters behind him, his arms twitching as if impatient to get on with his work.

"Keep your powder dry, Bobby," I muttered. "You'll get your chance to blow something up soon."

Harry, Bob, and the Mikes formed a new system designed to give us an advantage in developing off-world bases. Once the details of the Jump drive were released, there'd been a push to expand, and not only in the United States and Provinces. The PanAsian Confederation, the Atolls, and several of the Corporate States had launched ships to the closer stars. It was like the ancient land rushes after the Europeans invaded North America, but on an interstellar scale.

We knew planetary systems were common, but habitable worlds didn't appear to be. And so far, all habitats had been built using Earth, or lunar, resources, an unsustainable proposition even in the short-term.

We needed a way of creating habitats on site from local materials. Sure, we could drill out asteroids, which we'd found in every star system we'd visited, but that wasn't a long-term solution either. Those annoying creatures known as humans were biologically adapted to work in a one-g environment and suffered from all sorts of problems when operating in microgravity.

Special drugs and tailored exercise routines could only do so much. Although I agreed that we desperately needed to expand outside the solar system, this wasn't the answer, and knowing it was the wrong approach made me hate the project.

"Ballen?" I recognized the clipped tones of Giles Palmer without looking around. "What's going on? Those damned 'bots have stopped again."

Palmer was well-qualified as a project manager, bringing the perfect mix of ignorance and over-optimistic self-belief that guaranteed failure. He had no ZeeGee experience and limited knowledge of remote operations, but that didn't stop him from telling everyone else how to do their jobs.

"Harry ran into some tough deposits as he was turning." I took another swig of coffee. Luckily for Palmer, the alcohol was having a soothing effect. "The cutter units overheated, and he shut down to protect them."

"The H4-RR1 unit is supposed to do what we tell it, not decide what *it* wants to do. Cutters can be replaced easily enough."

Palmer was the only person involved in the project who insisted on using the bots' official designations. He was also the only one apparently unable to comprehend that a cutting bit might be disposable while in Earth's orbit, but when the bots were several light-years from the nearest replacement, it could mean complete project failure.

"The units are programmed to be independent. They're designed to protect themselves and avoid damage." I'd explained this so many times I was considering setting up a special "Palmer" button to trigger one of a selection of canned messages.

He frowned, the florid skin on his forehead wrinkling above his bushy unibrow. "We need an external code review."

I ignored the dig. My code was good, and he knew it.

"The units worked perfectly during simulations," he continued.

"They always do." I swallowed more of the spiked coffee. "If you'll let me get back to work, I'll clear this up and diagnose the problem."

He gave a couple of exaggerated sniffs. "Have you been drinking?"

"Mother Shaughnessy's patent health elixir." I coughed theatrically then drained the rest of the cup. "Got a bit of a chill. Wouldn't want to be the cause of any project delays."

"We can't have any delays. The schedule is fixed, you know that."

"Exactly." I screwed the cap back on my flask. "So why don't you run along and cook up some more of those imaginary resources you're so fond of?"

"You have a bad attitude, Ballen."

I didn't need his supercilious tone. Not today. "It's a talent that's taken years to develop. I'm glad it's not going to waste."

"You are intolerable. Impossible to work with. I'll have to report this to the project board. I'm sure they'll be happy to take the appropriate steps when they hear of your continuous obstructionism."

"Joe... I think we've got a problem."

I turned to the console to find Logan staring at me from the com screen. He was in a Hopper out at the ore-processing station a few hundred kilometers from the asteroid, clearing a blockage.

A shrill warble sounded, and I checked the readouts. It took a few seconds to make sense of the displays. This was nothing to do with Harry or Bob. After the tunneling was done, Mudslapper Moses was programmed to follow behind to spray seamless astrocrete and finish off with a quick-dry polymer coating. This was designed to make the tunnel airtight and waterproof, while another unit—Wiring Willie—followed behind Moses installing standard power cabling, water lines, and life-support ducting.

Willie's sensors struggled in the cloud of polymer spray, so he was supposed to stay well back, but the logjam meant he'd caught up with Moses, with disastrous results. Moses' spray arms were interlocked with Willie's wiring and tubing spools, while Willie's barrel-like body had a gray splash of the quick-dry polymer across the middle.

"Get off me. Geez. Is this a square dance?" Willie growled through the speakers. "I don't need this kind of disrespect."

"What have you done, Ballen?" Palmer leaned over my shoulder to study the displays. He couldn't understand them, but that didn't stop him from trying. "You've screwed up again, haven't you?"

"I've detected an explosion risk in the area, Joe. I'm scared," Harry yelped. "I'm sorry. I'm going to have to do a reset."

I thumbed the comms button knowing it was too late. "Harry, don't—" The displays showing Harry's readouts turned dark as he switched himself off. It would be three minutes before he finished rebooting.

"Some schmucks are blocking my path. I'm trapped. I'm trapped," Bob called out belatedly.

I should have put them on standby at the first sign of trouble and would have if Palmer hadn't stuck his nose in. "Take it easy, Bob." I hit the override.

"This is all your fault, Ballen." Palmer stabbed his finger at the console and then at me. "If I have anything to do with it, you're off this job."

"I'm quaking in my boots." I looked back at the readouts. "You don't have to work so hard at being an asshole, Palmer. You've got it down pat."

He hesitated then thought better of it and left.

I directed Moses to edge backward, and he extricated himself with a minimal amount of wrenching. The robots were built to take a pounding, so the damage was messy but largely superficial. Bob was easier to deal with, and I triggered his reset, giving time for Harry to finish rebooting.

"Sorry, Joe," Logan mumbled. "I should have put them on suspend right away. I thought I could clear the blockage before they got into trouble."

I poured more coffee and toasted him via the screen. "Another wonderful day in the blessed life of Joe Ballen."

"None of it was your fault." Logan didn't comment on my

drink—he knew better. "Proper AI development costs millions, and even then it's flaky. They've nickel-and-dimed this project from the start."

"Joe, I think the heat sinks aren't working right on my left-side cutting arms." Harry was back from robot zombie land.

I rewound the diagnostic trace to the point he'd run into trouble. There'd been a rise in temperature, but it was within acceptable tolerances. Harry was the front man in the whole system, so his programming gave bigger priority to avoiding damage, but it made him look like a whining hypochondriac. I needed to dampen the hysteresis curves to make him a little less risk-averse, but that would mean going deep into his core programming—something I wasn't supposed to do. The proper procedure was to request a software specialist to do the work, but that would take two weeks to process, followed by another four of familiarization before the code would even get touched. Software people didn't understand the concept of either urgency or deadlines.

"Okay, take a break, guys." I swallowed the final dregs of my coffee. "I need to have a talk with Harry."

"You've got that look in your eyes." Logan stared at me suspiciously. "What are you planning?"

It was close to check-out time for me, and I didn't want to stay late, especially today. I didn't owe the project that. The trouble was my stupid professional pride got in the way of dropping everything. I switched my console to connect to Harry's service interface and logged into a back door I wasn't supposed to know about. "I'm making sure I log enough project time. Wouldn't want to let the side down."

"And I suppose I get to cover for you again?" Logan shook his head. "I'll be down in three hours. How about coming over for dinner? Aurore would love to see you again."

Aurore Vergari was Logan's wife. She was a technician who'd worked with him on the secret *Shokasta* project, and they'd enjoyed each other's company so much, they'd continued the relationship after returning to Earth. I knew Logan's family wasn't one hundred percent in favor of it, as she wasn't from the Nations, so they shared a small place in the packed suburb of Woodlawn and kept things low-key. Eventually, he'd bring them around. Logan was that type of person, quietly determined, and Aurore was so sweet, it was impossible for anyone to dislike her.

I'd have been happy to meet with them usually, but seeing them together only reminded me how alone I was. Something else I didn't need today.

As I worked on Harry's programming, I thought more about the job. Certainly we could tunnel out an asteroid, and if this project worked, we'd be able to do that faster and more predictably. But it wouldn't solve the world's problems. We were like Neanderthals dreaming of having a bigger cave when what we needed was a high-rise.

Even though the Atolls were no longer blocking Earth's development in space, they still had the upper hand in terms of expansion. With their super-secret crystalline growth technology, they were able to seed a new Atoll and create a habitat capable of holding hundreds of people in a matter of weeks—and thousands within months.

We were able to do pretty fast constructions on asteroids and assemble stations from expandable units, but they were only suitable for researchers and the military. To avoid physiological problems in ZeeGee, ordinary people needed something big, and Earth was too inexperienced in that type of work.

The PAC had a better idea with their Taikong Gaogu project. They'd developed a massive 3-D printer that would create a giant drum of astrocrete reinforced with nano-fiber. The drums would have a radius of one kilometer with basic habitation levels printed in place. Theoretically, they could be any length, but the immediate plan was to produce standard two-kilometer-long sections. These would be docked together to produce bigger living areas as needed.

It was ambitious but likely the closest we'd get to the self-assembly process the Atolls used, unless they released their secret—and there was more chance of the Baltimore Bulls winning the GlydeBall playoffs. Each finished drum would have twenty levels at one-g and provide about one-hundred and eighty square kilometers total habitable space. The PAC's public plans called for each drum to sustain a population of three-quarters of a million people and, most importantly, they had the political will to achieve this.

I'd devoured every write-up I could find on the project. If the Remote units were able to keep up a steady diet of raw materials—efficiently mined from asteroids or comets—the basic construction could be completed and ready to pressurize in as little as six weeks. With the population pressure caused by the equatorial Zone of Death, the PAC was desperate. The "Big Drums" looked like a good solution and more practical than the rather pathetic asteroid tunneling I was working on for the USP.

I'd have offered myself for sale on the VoyPorn network for a chance to work on their project, but I wouldn't have gotten anywhere near it. Like everyone else, the PAC was looking to get their own head start on colonization and, in their eyes, I'd be nothing but a foreign spy.

Besides, I'd probably struggle to make a buck.

When I finally left the tomb-like office building, it was past nine. I was heading back to my rat hole of an apartment and shuffled onto the MagTrans with a late stream of commuters. I didn't have an aeromobile and couldn't afford to use a cab on the miserly salary the Off-World Development Project paid—especially as I was still picking up my share of the bills from Dollie's cab company. She didn't want me to, but if I hadn't, the whole thing would have sunk without a trace. Business had nose-dived once the off-world projects started up. The last update I'd seen showed she was down to four drivers, and that wasn't nearly enough to pay the rent. Dollie had offered to buy back my share in one of her friendlier moments, but I knew she didn't have the money.

The MagTrans was crowded despite the hour, but I managed to find a seat. As always, the compartment smelled of old sweat and tired people, mixed with a metallic tang of ozone drifting up from the maglev inductors. While the technology was clean, people weren't.

I thought about hopping off one stop early and making my way to the Evil Banker, an L3 bar on the Eastern Parkway that specialized in loud music, cheap booze, and not much in the way of conversation. But instead I hit the automated twenty-four-hour liquor store and picked up a liter of Strelka, a cheap one hundred and seventy proof rotgut that I'd become addicted to. It was supposedly imported from Russia, though I found it hard to believe someone would pay to ship industrial degreaser all that way.

I slapped my key over the lock, and the door to my apartment slid open. Howard's Lofts was an exclusive three-by-seven-meter slumber pad on fortieth, frequented by traveling business people, hookers, junkies, drop-outs on universal wag, and people like me who didn't much care where they slept. At least I wasn't selling my body parts... yet.

"Hi, honey, I'm home," I called out to the refrigerator that was bolted to the countertop. My words bounced around the cold, gray concrete walls. The tight confines of the apartment didn't worry me—no one who's worked or lived in space could ever be claustrophobic. What bothered me was how big it was in its emptiness. I slumped in the meager dining area—in reality a half-meter plastic table attached to a pair of equally plastic chairs—also bolted down—and littered with empty bottles from previous nights. I needed to clean house but switched on the 3V instead.

The seal on the vodka broke with a crack, and I threw the first shot down in a single gulp. It didn't taste of anything, but after the second swallow, who cared? Drinking alone was always considered unhealthy, but what's the alternative when you're on your own and don't want new friends? Loneliness can't be cured by other people—it's on the inside, and no one can make you feel less lonely, except yourself—something that was beyond me.

So, yeah, things get better? It was a lie long before we poisoned the environment that gave us life. It died out long before the petty bickering and onslaught of imagined slights tore nations apart, pitting generation against generation, old against young, one race against another and, always, rich against poor, strong against weak. The have's against the have-nots. Perhaps things *do* get better for some people, but I've never met one.

Dollie had left me one hundred and sixty-three days and fourteen hours ago. Not that I was counting. Today was also her birthday, though I never knew how she figured that out—her early background was as murky as mine. I poured another shot and threw it down my throat to join the first. "Happy birthday, Dollie."

13

Technically, I suppose you could say I left her. In the sense that we'd been sharing an apartment at the time, and after six months of bitter recriminations, arguments, sniping, and more arguments, I'd left and checked myself into this dump. Dollie blamed me for what happened to our unborn child, even though the Geneium doctors said they couldn't have saved the baby. She also blamed me for letting them save her.

And the worst of it was, I agreed with her. I blamed myself too.

Chapter Two

I should never have let Dollie go into space with me. I should have left her on the High-Rig when we transferred to the *Sarac*. I should have knocked her out cold. Or tied her up. Reported her to SecOps for security violations. Anything to prevent her making the trip that had cost us our unborn child. Of course, stopping Dollie from doing anything was like trying to persuade a hydrogen-rich white dwarf not to go nova.

I poured another drink, looking for something—anything—on the 3V to distract me from my thoughts but the universe didn't want to play ball. Every channel was full of the same news. I was already half-buzzed by the cheap booze and had trouble focusing on the tiny display. Sure, 3V service was one of our Universal Access Rights, but nobody said it had to be comfortable to use. I flopped down on the Lilliputian couch, laughingly described in the room advert as a "two-person love seat." It might have been, if one of the people was a long-extinct spider monkey, which would push the concept of love into unfathomable and potentially illegal depths.

"...ADF vessel *Yukawa* returned from its trial flight today. The ship first made a Jump to the Marduk Atoll at Alpha Centauri B, then stopped at the O'Connell Outpost at Ross 154, followed by the fledgling Wright Atoll at Wolf 1061 before finally visiting Rhoda Station, the research base orbiting Barnard's star. The flight has been successfully completed and proves the new design to be viable. Congratulations were sent to Captain Brackeen over the outcome of the trials—"

The *Yukawa* was an AF-11, one of the new generation of ships coming from the Atoll shipyards since the release of the Ananta data. The Atolls initially tried to adapt their regular cruisers to work with the Jump drive, but the design severely restricted the length of the Jump, even after major structural changes. The *Yukawa's* layout was closer to the *Shokasta* and *Ananta*, though as was often the case with the Atolls, there were a number of different design features. There were no doubt good reasons for the configuration choices, but they were kept under wraps—the Atolls had a distinctly one-way concept of sharing.

"…the station was no longer intact. Unofficially sourced reports say there are no survivors."

"What? Wait." I fumbled with the controls, winding the broadcast back a few minutes.

"In news that has shocked not only the Atoll community but the nation-states of Earth, Captain Brackeen reported that the Wright Atoll at Wolf 1061 had been destroyed. Communications regarding the destruction were transmitted directly to the Atoll council but were intercepted. Our information suggests that debris was found at the location, but the station was no longer intact. Unofficially-sourced reports say there are no survivors.

"Speculation around the cause of the destruction is widespread among the security, political, and scientific circles, but it is too early to suggest any nefarious cause, and no one was willing to make an official statement. Although the Atolls seeded the station, it was considered a neutral scientific base, and while most of the staff were Atoll citizens, there were dozens of scientists from all the nation-states and no consensus—"

It might be "too early" to speculate, but in time-honored tradition, that was exactly what they were about to do. There's nothing more rampant than a bunch of journalists with a juicy story and no answers. Even in my somewhat lubricated state, I was shocked. Although exploration beyond the solar system was in its infancy, the technology of survival in space had a solid track record for over a century and a half—stations didn't typically blow up on their own, especially Atolls. The fact that it was so far away didn't change that—it just made direct communication and rescue practically impossible. If we were lucky, we might get a clue in around six years—if Wright Station had broadcast anything.

Assuming they even knew what was about to happen.

I paused the report, lifted the bottle, and took a deep drink of the caustic vodka. Since the *Ananta* data release, everyone had gone space nuts—and not only in the form of official Earth projects. I'd heard several stories of orbital ships being retrofitted with cobbled together Jump drives and shooting for the stars, usually leaving nothing to show for their grand plans except a swarm of orbital debris for the clean-up squads.

My Scroll buzzed. It was Logan, and I picked up, though I probably shouldn't have.

"You've seen the news?" His face looked grim.

"Just caught it. A lot of people will be looking for answers. And I'm guessing our Atoll friends won't be very cooperative."

He nodded, the camera-tracking making it look as though the walls behind him were bouncing up and down in an earthquake. "There's more, Joe. Don't ask me how I know. But one of our ships, the *Sacagawea*, is overdue."

I'd never heard of it, but that didn't surprise me given the fact I was exiled from working space-side. And besides, Logan had his own special connections. "MilSec or SecOps?"

"You drunk, Joe?" He pantomimed sniffing the air. "I wouldn't know anything about that."

"Right..." I toasted him, despite his frown. "I'm higher than the Oort cloud right now."

"They were on long-range reconnaissance—operating as far out as five parsecs."

"That's a long way, even with the Jump. Maybe they got held up sight-seeing."

"They're under strict orders. They should have been back two months ago. The authorities have been keeping a tight lid on it, but with this latest news it's bound to come out."

He was right. Regardless of whatever deals they'd done to hide the news, the press would be all over the story like guano at a bird sanctuary.

"I'm sure they'll send out ships to investigate." I tilted the bottle in a bitter salute. "Good luck to them."

"It could have been an engineering failure, but it might be more."

Logan paused. "They want me to take a look."

"That's a dangerous journey, my friend." I felt a pang of jealousy. Despite what had happened on my last journey, I still yearned to head out and boldly go where generations before me had only dreamed of. "Watch your back."

The remains of my vodka disappeared in a single swallow. I didn't care if it upset Logan. He was leaving, and I was staying behind. After everything else that had happened, it was just one more miserable entry in Ballen's Bad Luck Journal.

My ears fizzled as the vodka burned, and I didn't hear Logan's next words clearly. "Say again?"

"Come with me." Logan spoke deliberately. "I can pick my own crew. You could be one of them."

I was about to say "hell, yes," when I skidded to a halt. "What's the catch?"

Logan's eyes dropped, and his head turned away a little. This was a first—Logan Twofeathers embarrassed.

"It would have to be a package deal. You… and the *Shokasta*."

Suddenly it made sense. I'd left the ship at the High-Rig with a random Jump programmed, her systems locked with an encrypted biometric key. SecOps couldn't risk losing the ship by breaking the lock, so it stayed there, floating above the Earth like a lost puppy waiting for my return. While the technology wasn't a hundred percent, it would take a lot to break it. It was my bargaining chip. Originally put in place in case of fallout from my rather unorthodox return to Earth with Dollie. But since then, it had taken on a much greater significance.

I refilled my glass. "I'll be happy to unlock the ship. You know the conditions as well as they do."

Logan nodded. "You've seen the news?"

"About the Atoll Station? Yes."

Logan's grim expression provided all the clue I needed. I scrambled for the 3V controls, punching up my solitary pro-grammed search—labeled "Paek."

While the search ran in the background, the news came up focusing on the other issues of the day. Krystal Bliss had announced plans to marry her long-time companion of two weeks, Robert Romney III. The wedding was to take place on Heaven, the luxury orbital station famous as the tax-free residence of the richest corporate heads. The couple were reportedly "finding the time" in between him filming his latest action flick, *Hard Stud 5*, its two sequels, and her extensive concert tour of Luna.

The search results for Paek came up in a few seconds, and I punched the play button on the newest.

"In other news, Xselsia Corporation announced the appointment of its new off-world development director, Ewin Paek. Unusually, the former Atoller has renounced his citizenship to take up his new role. CEO Garth Hump-Inge said this appointment demonstrated the corporation's commitment to equal opportunities and heralded a new era..."

I'd stopped listening as soon as Paek's face appeared. His narrow jaw and high cheekbones were engraved on my brain as permanently as if etched by a laser cutter—the man who had killed our unborn child through his racist-inspired attack on the *Shokasta* at the very edge of the solar system.

The glass of vodka splintered against the corner of the screen, and the display flickered several times, the bottom left corner blacking out.

"Paek announced plans to establish a new processing plant to develop the rich Anglada asteroid fields around Proxima Centauri. Commercial development of the fields is estimated to be worth over seventy billion credits annually.

The image switched to a broadcast of Paek at the press conference.

"This is a historic moment for myself and for Earth-centered space development. I'm humbled to have been chosen by Xselsia to lead their diversification program and feel sure this will initiate a new era of cooperation. Working together, I believe we can create a future of greater collaboration between—"

The screen exploded as I hurled an empty vodka bottle into it. "When did you find out?"

"On my way down the Elevator. At the same time I read about the Yukawa." Logan's long face looked more somber than usual. "We tried to get him, Joe."

"Not hard enough. Not by a long shot." A volcano five seconds from eruption felt like it was burning in my gut. My fists clenched, and I pulled away from the Scroll pickup. "Maybe Earth doesn't care what happened. But I do."

"They tried, Joe. *We* tried. There's no extradition between Earth and the Atolls. You know that. The Atolls handled it internally."

"A demotion doesn't feel like justice. What happened to working collectively? I see that shit all the time in the newsfeeds."

"It's a political game. We asked them to turn him over to face charges in the USP—they refused."

"He's a criminal. And now he's with the Corporates, so still untouchable."

"Even more so than before. They're arranging an All-Parties Conference. Everybody will be there: Atolls, USP, PAC, Old Europe, United Africa—even the goddamn Muscat Alliance. They're deciding the ground rules for carving up space itself."

"And screw Joe Ballen and the Charter of Justice."

A tremble ran through my legs and arm, as if a series of electric shocks were galvanizing the muscles. Neuralgic shock. It had been happening more frequently recently. Alcohol interfered with the neural bridges, breaking them down—a good reason to bite the bullet. I fought to suppress the shakes, not wanting to let Logan see me flopping around on the floor like a choking fish.

"This is bigger than one person."

I held Logan's stare. "Nothing is."

"I can't cover you anymore, Joe. You've seen it—it's moving too fast. The Corporates, Atolls, PAC, and here too. Everyone's trying to grab as big a piece of space as they can. It's like an explosion. The brass wants *Shokasta* in action, and they're ready to throw away the Charter to get it."

"The lock on the ship might be tougher than they realize."

"Grandfather used to say locks only keep honest people honest. SecOps isn't going to play straight anymore. And you're vulnerable."

"Yeah. SecOps could withhold my alcohol supply."

"They're talking about canceling your medical credits."

Without the drugs I was getting through the medical system, the neuralgia would cripple me, and my drinking habits were hastening the process. I'd have months if I was lucky, more likely weeks, before my body started failing from stress-induced neural failure. I was about to tell Logan to go to hell anyway when he held up his hand.

"They also mentioned Dollie."

I stopped, not knowing what to say. I doubted the Geneium would stop treating her, but the authorities could make things very difficult for her as an individual and for her business. "You people are scum."

Logan held his hands apart. "I'm only the messenger."

"Lie down with dogs..."

My Scroll beeped, indicating an incoming message. I had no idea what it was, but I saw Dollie's name attached to it, and put Logan on hold while I opened it.

It was the final decree on my marriage.

I hadn't contested the divorce. There hadn't been much point, legally or otherwise. But that didn't mean I welcomed it. I'd committed to Dollie when we got married, and my feelings hadn't changed. After losing our child, our relationship had fractured. I'd tried to hold things together, but that's hard in those circumstances, and hard becomes impossible when only one person was making an effort.

Dollie had withdrawn, like a light shutting off. I tried to understand what she was going through and support her, but it seemed the more I tried, the more she resented me. By the time I moved out to the temporary quarters I was in now, she was almost a stranger.

I switched back to Logan. "Message from Dollie."

His face brightened. "You're talking again?"

"Sure, if you count getting the big shaft as a form of communication." I forwarded the divorce notification to him.

Logan slumped. "Sorry, Joe. I know that must hurt."

"Six months ago it would have. Now, all it means is I'm free to chase the slitches again."

Logan knew me better than that. "What about this job? It would be good for you to have a break."

"Let me sleep on it, okay?"

The background behind Logan changed, and I realized his Elevator carriage had arrived at the Earth terminus.

"I've got a connection to make. I'll call you tomorrow. And Joe?" He paused. "Stay away from Dollie, okay? It wouldn't be good for either of you right now."

"Do I look stupid?"

"I'm not going to answer that one." Logan grinned, and a second later ended the call.

I filled a new tumbler with vodka and swallowed it in one gulp, then opened my Scroll and called a cab.

Maybe Logan should have answered.

Dollie's place was a thirty-minute hop, which gave me plenty of time to figure out what I was going to say. My plan was a combination of emotional blackmail mixed with as much pleading as she'd let me get in before throwing me out, or calling the cops. Not very dignified, but it was the best I could come up with under the circumstances.

The cab driver didn't say a word. I knew the detectors in the passenger cabin would pick up the alcohol on my breath, so he no doubt dismissed me as a typical YAD—Yet Another Drunk—which I couldn't really argue with.

After paying the inflated fare, I hopped out on the L7 landing pad and made my way across the balcony walkway to Dollie's apartment. Taking a deep breath, I pushed the announcer and waited, not sure if she'd answer when she saw it was me. But a few minutes later, the door slid open. She was looking the other way and giggling, holding out her credit chip.

"Take ten for yourself," she said.

She looked as beautiful as ever, and all I wanted to do was gather her up in my arms. "You'd be overpaying."

Dollie spun around and momentarily her face lit up, then quickly hardened. "What are you doing here?"

"Everything I shouldn't be."

Dollie sniffed the air between us. "You've been drinking."

"Not nearly enough." All my preparations had evaporated the moment I saw her, and all that remained was a sense of bitterness. "I'm glad you're having fun. Celebrating the big day, I imagine."

"Big day?"

I laughed harshly. "Drop the pretense. You owe me more than

that."

"I don't *owe* you anything."

"Not anymore." I crumpled the divorce eFlimsy in my hand and tossed it to her. "It could have been different. If you'd tried."

"Tried what? Crawling inside a bottle with you?" Her face darkened. "Or subjecting myself to fertility treatments in the hope I could satisfy your chauvinistic urges?"

My hands clenched and my head swam from the booze I was carrying in my bloodstream. After Dollie lost the baby, she was warned not to try again. The stress on her biological systems would have been too great and most likely end in another failure. Stupidly, I'd asked if Geneering might help, thinking she still wanted children. But she'd twisted it around, making it seem like I was forcing her into becoming a brood mare. "All I wanted was to make a family with you. Is that so—"

"*All you wanted* was for me to risk my life so you could prove you were a complete man."

"Dollie, that's not—" I reached out to take her hand in mine, but that was another mistake.

"Touch me, and I'll break your arm, Joe." Her voice had shifted to its lower male register, telling me she was deadly serious.

"What's taking so long, Dollie? Are you seducing the pizza guy?"

I recognized the voice. It was Sigurd, Dollie's one-time lover. She poked her head around the door and froze. She wasn't wearing her usual complete isolation alt-real suit, and I saw her face for the first time. She was at least fifteen years older than Dollie with a pixie-ish face under a tight shock of gray hair.

"Neck off, Ballen. No one wants you around here, this is girls only."

"Ballen?" Another voice sounded from inside the apartment, and seconds later, Sarah, Dollie's alternate dispatcher, appeared. "Hey, Joe! Good to see you again We were just ta—" She stopped when Sigurd nudged her. "Why don't you come in and have a drinky?"

Sigurd ushered Sarah back inside. "Come on, you need a refill."

Sarah sounded pretty inebriated, even to me. "Seducing the help now? You used to be better than that."

Dollie slapped me across the cheek, the blow hard enough to

jar my alcohol-sozzled brain, and my vision blacked out momentarily.

"It's none of your business." She breathed heavily several times. "*I'm* not your business."

"Divorce doesn't have to be forever." I was blabbering, but only part of my brain knew it, and it wasn't the part in charge of my mouth. "We could make it work. All we need to do is try."

"I'm not going to be here anymore." Dollie looked away as if embarrassed, which she never was. "There's no point coming here again."

"I still love you, Dollie. You know that, don't you?" I saw her jawline soften a little. "Tell me you don't feel the same."

Dollie hesitated, and I felt I'd reached her. Then she sighed. "I'm going away, Joe. I don't know when I'll be back, maybe never."

Her words didn't sink in. "Going where? That's stupid. You can't leave. What will I do if you—"

Dollie snarled. "For once, try thinking of someone other than yourself. I'm leaving, and you can't follow me."

"Are you joining a nunnery or a private sex retreat?"

"Not everything is about sex."

"It is with you." My mouth was leading a life of its own.

Dollie pulled her hand back to slap me again, and I waited almost eagerly for the blow to land. "If you must know, I've got a new job."

"Job?" That was crazy—she had the cab company to run.

"I've got more taxis than drivers qualified to fly them and too many bills to pay. With everyone going space happy, most of my guys are heading off-world."

I knew that and would have been out there myself, if I wasn't barred for refusing to hand over the *Shokasta*. A job was simply another way for her to leave me behind. "That's stupid, you—"

"StriPizza for Buntin," a voice called from behind me.

I turned to see a young guy carrying pizza boxes, wearing nothing but a pair of crotch-hugging gold shorts and matching gold running shoes. His body was oiled and glistening from his bulging biceps to his perfect six-pack. How I'd have looked fifteen years ago—if I'd spent all my earnings on Geneering instead of pounding my way through engineering school.

"Who gets the special sauce?" The guy gave me a dubious glance then turned to Dollie more hopefully.

Dollie reddened and pushed her credit chip at him. "Take ten for yourself."

"What about the show?" Oily-guy asked.

"Just take your money and go," Dollie hissed.

Dollie glared at me over the pizza boxes. "I didn't arrange that, Joe. One of the others must ha—"

"Yeah… not everything is about sex," I snarled. "Sorry I interfered with your *delivery*."

Dollie slammed the door, and I turned to leave, my blood boiling inside my veins. At the Jump-Off, I pulled out my Scroll and was about to call a cab, then stopped to peer over the drop. L7 was over one-hundred meters up, plenty high enough to do the job. I edged closer, feeling the wind buffet my torso as if goading me to do it.

My Scroll beeped. I had a message directing me to report to the Off-World Testing Center for pre-departure induction. I guessed a certain engineer with the name of Logan had filed an application on my behalf.

The following morning came all too soon, and I woke with a headache like two black holes colliding. While my brain might not be creating gravity waves, the surges of nausea were all too real. My Scroll was beeping despite the fact that I remembered switching it to "only in the event of death," which meant it could only be one of two people who knew the override code. I hoped it was Dollie. I owed her an apology for last night, but I was less surprised when Logan appeared.

He took me in with one glance. "You look like crap, my friend."

"That's appropriate."

I rubbed my hand over my face, feeling my eyes crunch under my fingers. I'd carried on with the vodka after returning home and had a vague memory of calling out to order a second bottle. A fact that was confirmed when I rolled over and let my feet drop, kicking away an empty that matched the one on the floor between the bed

25

and the miniature dining area.

"You have an appointment this afternoon."

"I couldn't pass a field sobriety test, let alone an entrance exam for the space eligibility program."

"You confirmed your acceptance last night. The least you can do is show up."

Again, I had a hazy recollection of marking my thumbprint angrily against my Scroll to accept the invitation. I had the crazy, drunken idea of showing Dollie I still had it, mixed with the equally delusional thought that if I returned to space she'd miss me so much she'd want me back. Neither was going to happen, and the test was a rather sad joke.

"You know I can't pass. Not with my issues and not in my current state."

"Get your ass down there. And don't disappoint me."

I shook my head. It hurt and I stopped. "Sure. I don't mind wasting my time. But what about the asteroid project?"

"Palmer has been notified of our indefinite absence. I'm sure he's reworking his schedule as we speak and cursing both our names."

"Great." So regardless of what happened, I was out of a job again. "You sure enjoy making my life difficult."

Logan grinned. "When you need me to."

I ended the call and staggered over to the shower cubicle, grabbed a handful of nerve-tranq from a stash I kept especially for days like this, and punched the Max button for the coffin-like shower. I wanted to login to the net and check the employment registry. If Dollie had taken a job, it would confirm it. But, first, I needed to try and put myself back together, or at least reach a passable facsimile.

The Lofts didn't run to luxuries like a high pressure drier in the rudimentary stall, and I was still dripping when I opened the infosite and logged in—hoping Dollie hadn't changed her access codes. The screen flashed red with an Access Denied message, and I cursed. This was looking set to be yet another perfect day.

Chapter Three

The Testing Center was in Greenbelt, Maryland on the site of the former NASA Goddard Space Flight Center. It was now a major center for space flight and research in the USP and hosted the newly formed Extra-Solar Expansion Coordination Center—with the aim of managing new activity arising from the Jump drive. Based on what I saw in the news feeds and the inside stories I heard from Logan, that was a task comparable to a blind man herding black cats, in ZeeGee, in the dark.

There was no direct transport link from where I was living, but Logan had made sure that I couldn't use this as an excuse. There was a notification on my Scroll telling me that a pre-paid aeromobile would be at my apartment block to pick me up at 1.30 PM.

The driver made good use of the SkyWays to deliver me to the Center by the appointed time. I hesitated by the towering glassite doors, my hands shaking with a combination of the DTs and neural degradation. I swallowed another mouthful of nerve-tranq pills. My pride wouldn't allow me to do less than my best, even though I had no chance of succeeding in my current state. Whether I was able to pass the reaction response tests or not, the blood work would show huge amounts of 'tranq in my system.

I marched through the entrance on legs like week-old celery stalks, trying not to display the limp that had recently returned. A bored-looking receptionist checked my ID without comment except to direct me to room three-zero-seven where I was scheduled to meet my personal testing agent.

The room itself was stark white and antiseptic. The only color came from animated promotional posters on the walls, advertising the work done at the center. The tumble of images made my head hurt, and I dropped into a chair, waiting for my tester to arrive. I took several deep breaths, hoping it would help but knowing it wouldn't and silently cursed Logan for dragging me into this.

"Joe Ballen?" A voice like gravel sliding over rock came from the door.

Logan Twofeathers was standing there with a sheaf of eFlimsies in one hand and a big grin plastered across his face.

"What's going on?" To say I was confused would be an understatement. "You're my examiner?"

"By special arrangement."

It wasn't hard to guess who'd made that happen. "When do I start the tests?"

"You already passed." Logan laughed. "All I need is a biometric imprint from you to make it legal."

"You could have told me." I felt stupid and relieved at the same time. "Why did you put me through all this?"

Logan tapped a thick finger against my chest. "I needed to know there was still some of the old Joe in there."

"What now?"

Logan dropped the eFlimsies on the table in front of me and waited until I'd pressed my thumb against the bottom of the topmost sheet.

"There's an MRT AstroFreighter waiting to take us to the High-Rig. I assume you don't have any reason to go back to town."

His words stung, reminding me that the last time I'd done anything like this I'd said goodbye to Dollie. The AstroFreighter was new though.

The data crystal I'd been given by GaTanHa had a complete record of all the information the Ananta had collected on its travels. This included space maps and details of extra-terrestrial races we had yet to make contact with. It also included a large cache of data on physics and engineering beyond our current knowledge that had spawned a research niche of its own, with thousands of scientists poring over the data. Everyone from the USP to Old Europe, the PAC, and United Africa, along with the Atolls and Corporates was in a race to decipher what they could. But the concepts were obscure, and progress was slow. The AstroFreighter was one of the first practical developments to emerge.

"So, are you in?" Logan raised an eyebrow and held out his hand.

"I don't appear to have a choice."

"I didn't intend giving you one." He grabbed the eFlimsies and filed them into a reader by the wall. "You're registered. All licenses restored."

"I'm not handing over the *Shokasta* until Paek is brought to justice."

"That's your call. In the meantime, we have some investigation to do."

I stood and looked him square in the face. "Tell me again why you're my friend."

Logan's laugh rattled the partition walls in the tiny office. "Because I'm the only son-of-a-bitch dumb enough to put up with you."

I followed him, and we turned to the right, away from where I'd entered. "We're walking to the ship? I expected a secret conveyor belt at the very least."

"Budget cuts." Logan called over his shoulder.

The AstroFreighter was bigger than I'd expected. It looked like a giant arrowhead pointing at the sky, as tall as an L50 high-rise. An array of thrusters was clustered on either side of the lower superstructure, and in the center a large circular elevator provided loading access to the main payload bays. Lift capacity was up to eighty thousand kilograms, more than enough for just about any large-scale project. As it used nothing but water as a propellant, it was perfect as a launch freighter to Earth's orbit, but it could also work as an intra-system heavy carrier depending on the configuration and requirements.

We were lifted on a smaller personnel elevator—almost fulfilling my joke of a secret conveyor belt—like ants getting drawn into a skyscraper. I looked down as we climbed, the height alarming even for an old hand like me. I felt a pang deep inside and wished Dollie were somewhere out there waving me goodbye, but it was too late for that. Instead, I whispered goodbye to her.

"Things turn around." Logan seemed to almost read my mind. "You'll see."

The cockpit was the standard dual control setup, and we clambered awkwardly into the seats that were rotated ninety degrees. As I strapped in, I looked over at Logan. "One day, somebody needs to do something about this. I'm getting tired of being a space monkey."

"Yeah, and the day that happens is the day you'll retire permanently. You taking her up?"

I wrapped my hands around the controls, feeling a flood of adrenaline. For what must have been the first time in months, I genuinely smiled. "If you think I'm capable."

"Aren't you the guy who boasts he can fly anything?"

"I think you're confusing me with some arrogant jerk."

Logan leaned back in his seat, hands nowhere near the controls. "Time you began earning your pay."

The launch sequence was already programmed into the flight computer. I checked air-traffic control, and they opened a corridor for us. We'd pass out of reach of any local traffic in short order, so it wasn't difficult for them to make room, and having a military clearance didn't hurt.

"I don't see why they needed to send a boat like this. The Space Elevator or a regular military launcher would have been plenty," I said, as we waited for the clock to tick down.

"Under normal circumstances, you'd be right. But we're piggy-backing on a delivery of military ordnance. People are worried about recent events—they want us to be more prepared."

"This thing could carry enough weaponry to resupply the entire High-Rig."

"We're loaded up with a few gadgets to help make *our* job easier, including some detection equipment upgrades. They'll be fitted to the *Shokasta* before we leave."

"They're going to a lot of trouble."

"No one knows what we might be up against out there."

Space flight might be relatively routine, but interstellar travel was new, with almost every journey a leap into the unknown. Theoretically, the danger was no greater than a regular space operation, but the vast distances made everything more difficult. Keeping exo-bases resupplied was a big problem, which was why so many people were being pushed through crash-courses in JumpShip training.

I checked the countdown—three minutes until lift. Our status was green, and the injector sequence was building to full pressure. Then I tested the manual flight systems in case of an abort, and all the indicators lit up with go signals.

There's an old saying in engineering that says every time you overcome one set of issues, you run face-first into another, and interstellar travel did nothing to change that. The Jump bypassed the speed of light limit for the ship and its contents, peeling open a fissure in the manifold of space-time and allowing instantaneous, at least from a human perspective, travel to anywhere within range. But once at the destination, Einstein still ruled. Communication back home would take years and left us in a situation more like seventeenth century sea travel where the fastest route for information and news was the ships themselves. And where "out there" was lonelier than anything in human experience.

Even quantum links didn't work. Whatever physics we tapped into when we popped through the inter-dimensional rifts fractured quantum entanglements like glass, making high-speed communication between stars just as impossible as it was before the Jump.

Logan interrupted my thoughts. "We're also carrying several CASTOR units. *Shokasta* is getting a refit."

The CASTOR engine was a revolution in Casimir power that could turn almost any liquid into a superheated plasma steam inside a star chamber. The steam was then focused into a jet to provide higher levels of thrust. That would be an extensive refit for the ship though. "How long is that expected to take?"

Logan shrugged. "You'll have to ask the guy in charge."

That put me on edge. We were about to take a long trip into the depths of interstellar space. The idea of hastily installed systems bolted in by no-name engineers didn't help my confidence. "Do we know who that is?"

"Some crazy bastard named Ballen."

The launch warning sounded, and I put my hands on the

31

controls in case of a problem. The autopilot kicked in, and it felt like a nuclear bomb detonated behind us, punching the ship upward. Despite the mass of the AstroFreighter, we were pulling over five-g, and as our speed increased, the engines throttled back to stay within safety parameters. We hit Max Q, the point of maximum pressure on the ship, in under a minute, and the engines throttled up bringing us to just under seven-g.

I controlled my breathing and croaked to Logan, "So we're basically guinea pigs?"

"The phrase you're looking for is *talented pioneers*."

The AstroFreighter was a single-stage-to-orbit ship despite its size, and there was none of the discontinuity from booster separation or other finessing. It was a display of brute strength lifting that made you feel like you were riding Mjolnir to the stars.

The acceleration decreased, and I breathed easier. "How do we know the CASTOR system will work with the *Shokasta*?"

"We don't, but dozens of people have been working hard for several months to make it happen."

"Let's hope they did their homework."

Once we achieved Low Earth Orbit we had the tricky business of maneuvering to meet the High-Rig, but the flight computer took care of the details, leaving Logan and me to speculate on the Atoll research station and our missing ship.

"I know the captain of the *Sacagawea*." He ran his fingers through his hair. "Leonard Begay. He's Anishinàbe. When great-grandfather moved east after the Big Shake, Begay's people helped ours to settle. They made room for us on their land. We're like family, and family sticks together."

I'd visited the ranch and knew there were other people there, but I hadn't realized the connection. "You must be close."

"Leonard is like a brother to me. When he joined MilSec, everybody came out to give him a good send off." He paused. "He had a fire in him, a spirit that couldn't be quenched. We knew he was destined for great things."

Captaining a USP interstellar cruiser certainly qualified as great things. "His family must be very proud."

"He made us all proud." Logan's voice was like a rasp working a steel block.

His emotion seemed to fill the small control room, and for several minutes I wrestled with the feeling that I should say something but not knowing what.

"Do you think the loss of Wright Station and the *Sacagawea* being overdue is connected?"

Logan didn't answer immediately and then took a breath. "I don't see how that's possible. But everything about deep space is new to us. Leo knew the risks. Any problem that comes along leaves you a long way from help and all too close to death. Even a routine malfunction can kill you at that distance—and nothing ever works one hundred percent."

I didn't believe in luck, good or bad, but sometimes even the most thorough planning isn't enough. As the ache from my arm and legs reminded me all too often.

"Where was the *Sacagawea*?"

Logan shrugged. "Hard to say for sure, but they were a long way from Wright Station and Wolf 1061. If they followed their planned route, they'd have been over twenty light-years away. It's hard to see a connection."

"Not a natural one perhaps."

"You think there's more behind it?" Logan's eyebrow lifted. "Something antagonistic?"

"It seems unlikely, I know. But it would be a hell of a coincidence if two of Earth's exo-missions independently developed problems at almost the same time."

"A common technology problem?" Logan pulled a 3V screen in front of him, bringing up the USP tech archives. "The Jump is still very new."

"That might affect the ship. But the station wasn't equipped with a Jump drive was it?"

Logan looked up engineering reports on the ship and station then waved them on to the main screen. The comparator highlighted the common systems almost immediately.

"The life support and solar generators are well-proven," I said.

"The only thing I can see on that list that looks relatively untested is the Casimir generators."

The Casimir system generated power from the constant seething mass of quantum foam produced by virtual particles springing into life and then vanishing again. In a sense, it was energy from nothing, though in truth it was only borrowed temporarily until the quantum flux took it away again. But we could harness it in the microscopic amount of time it was there. Each individual fluctuation was almost nothing, but as it happened everywhere and constantly, the generators could focus that to produce effectively limitless usable power.

The system was somewhat exotic, but there were no moving parts, and even the constraining field that condensed and focused the quantum foam wasn't critical. If the field collapsed, the virtual particles would dissipate and go about their business, popping in and out of existence harmlessly. Despite the energy levels involved, it wouldn't explode and would be snuffed out like a match.

Logan pointed to one of the subsystem lists for the Wright Atoll. "Why did they arm a research station?"

"You don't know?"

"What can I say? I'm a small cog in the SecOps machine. I have as much idea as you on the mindset of the Atolls."

The weapons system on the base was minimal—a missile system backed by point defense railguns and lasers. I wasn't familiar with the military codes, but it sounded like a relatively small package with a big punch.

"Could be precautionary. You of all people know how paranoid security types can be."

"That's true," Logan mused. "But it looks out of place."

A proximity alarm sounded, and the lights in the control room flashed several times. We were at the point of entry to the High-Rig's traffic control field, and they wanted to take control of the AstroFreighter's controls to bring us in.

I checked we'd been assigned a large enough docking berth then released the maneuvering system to their control. A few minutes later, a docking tube clanked against us, and my ears popped as the air pressure between the ship and station equalized.

As we swam into the tube, Logan operated his wrist interface, and the airlock was open when we got there.

"The Remotes are moving equipment over to bay 17E," Logan said. "You need to get up to speed on the modifications. We're scheduled to leave in twenty-four hours."

The timeline would have been insane if it weren't for the Remotes that could do much of the heavy work. With their assistance, it *might* be possible, as long as we hit no snags. But when did that ever happen?

I headed to the *Shokasta* while Logan disappeared to "make some calls." I hoped they didn't involve any changes to our schedule—we'd be pushing things to leave on time as it was. The ship's airlock opened when I pressed my palm against the lock, and I entered the familiar interior.

It was as brightly lit as I remembered, with color-coded guidelines on the floor directing people to various specialized areas. It seemed superfluous considering there were only two corridors, with all the rooms arranged in the central spine.

I found *our* cabin the way it was when I'd last been here, though the thought of it being mine alone made my stomach tingle, and I swallowed hard. I settled at the large desk display and opened the files on the planned conversion.

The plans were detailed and, for once, had been well thought-out. The new CASTOR system was designed as a drop-in replacement for the original energy collectors and made use of waste energy to superheat liquid fed to it. This came from a series of new tanks to be fitted around the exterior. They added to the ship's bulk, but the clever design maintained the sleek profile of the hull, enabling easy passage through the space-time fissure during the Jump.

The tanks weren't especially clever and neither was the plumbing. The real genius was in the design, and I was rather envious of whoever had come up with it. Somebody outside of the typical workmanlike government engineer bureaucrats—that was certain.

"Nice to see someone around here is earning their paycheck," I said to myself.

The CASTOR system effectively added a turbo-boost to the

Casimir drive. Although the regular drive was a fantastic achievement, it operated at relatively low thrusts. Certainly, that thrust could be maintained almost indefinitely if necessary, but the acceleration wasn't high enough for tactical maneuvering, and that was what the new system was supposed to provide.

The modifications would theoretically enable the ship to make high accelerations of up to twenty-g, though in human terms it was limited to around eight for short durations. And at that level, the tanks gave the ship around twenty minutes of boost. More impressively, the boost could be stepped up and down to whatever level' was needed and replenished anywhere water or ice was available by making use of an extension unit that could plug into regular resupply ports, making it perfect for deep-space operations.

I switched over to the maintenance monitoring display and checked progress. The Remotes were attaching the extra tanks and had moved the CASTOR units to a position floating off the starboard hull. Removal of the existing collectors and installation of the new units were too complicated for the Remote Units, and a team of piloted Hoppers was flocking into place to work on the upgrade. I may have been in charge, but no one had been waiting for me to take over.

It was time I got involved, though. So far, I was feeling more like a spare wrench in the tool chest than a part of the operation. I headed to the main airlock and grabbed my suit, ready to join in the fun. The size of the team at work reinforced the importance the USP was placing on the mission.

Seven exhausting hours later, we'd pulled out the standard collectors and tethered them to the High-Rig bulkhead for safety. Now the CASTOR units were being nudged into place by the Hopper crews, but my stomach was complaining about a lack of input, so I headed to the airlock. As I entered, someone followed me in.

I read the tag on their suit, but I didn't recognize the name Maliska. The guy was slightly built rather than the usual assembly crew heavyweight. I nodded, hit the cycle button, and the pressure built.

Maliska unlocked his helmet, the fogged visor impenetrable.

"Hello, Joe. I hear you're lonely these days, and we have some unfinished business."

It was Gabriella.

Chapter Four

"Are you part of this operation?" I doubted it given Logan's involvement.

She'd reverted back to her shaved head, but her full lips were still as inviting and no doubt as deadly as ever. She blew me a kiss before answering. "Not in the least."

"Then you better not let him catch you here."

"I'm not afraid of that old man." She put her hands behind her back and pouted. "Besides, you'd protect me, wouldn't you, Joe?"

Logan had a scar running the length of his torso from their first encounter. I doubted I could stop him even if I had a mind to-which I didn't. "This is a secure operation. If you're not authorized, you need to leave. I should report you just for being here."

"Since when did Joe Ballen become a Regulation Charlie? I'm sure you could get me added to the mission, if you wanted." Other than her helmet, she hadn't taken off any more of her suit, but she sidled close enough that I could smell her perfume. "You know how... useful I can be."

"I don't want anything to do with you-dead or alive." I moved my hand over the airlock controls. "You've got two minutes to put your helmet on."

"Don't send me away, Joe."

There was something in her voice I couldn't identify. Something I hadn't heard from her before, almost as though she were pleading. I unfastened my p-suit and squirmed out of it. "Why are you here?"

Gabriella bit her lip. "Would you believe me if I said I was looking for work?"

"I wouldn't believe you if you told me the sun was hot."

She slipped out of her suit too, revealing a black skin-tight bodysuit. I was dressed similarly-you needed something inside a p-suit to protect your skin and wick away moisture-but where mine fit me like a pair of old work gloves, hers showed every line and curve and looked almost sprayed on.

I'd had enough of this. I needed to replenish some calories and headed for the wardroom, not caring if she followed or not. If she got annoyed and left, I wasn't going to lose sleep over it. Unluckily, she trailed me all the way.

I grabbed an energy bar and heated a tube of coffee, angrily sucking in a large mouthful and burning my mouth. "What do you want?"

"Too hot for you?" She smirked, then it faded again. "A coffee would be nice."

"That's not what I mean." I was standing by the heating unit and moved out of the way so she could help herself.

Gabriella tutted. "You used to be much more gallant than this, Joe."

"Sorry. Someone trying to murder me multiple times always leaves me grouchy. Can't think why."

She heated a coffee. "I heard you're a free-agent again."

"My marital status is no business of yours." I took another cautious sip of my drink, followed by a bite on the chewy bar. "Why don't we stop dancing around and get to the point?"

Gabriella moved over and took my hand, then pressed it against her chest. "I couldn't agree more."

Her heartbeat sent tingles through my fingertips, and I snatched my hand away. "I'm not in the market for that."

"But I am." She flashed her angelic smile. "You like me, Joe-always have. You just don't want to admit I'm the perfect woman for you."

"Psychotic and murderous isn't my style."

"No?" She reached down and grabbed me. "What's this then? Or did marriage to Dollie turn you into a eunuch?"

I pushed her away. Certainly, she could trigger my male response, but it was a primitive sexual urge, not something I could always control. I'd rather carry an aggravated cobra around in my shorts than get involved with her.

"Don't you have someone to torture or kill? Or did you find yourself unexpectedly short of potential corpses?"

Gabrielle pulled back, and for a moment her face seemed to cloud over. "Sorry, Joe. I just thought that... maybe... That is, do you think that there could ever be hope for something between you and me?"

She sounded so sincere for a moment that I almost believed she wasn't playing her usual head games. Then I mentally slapped myself in the face. "Sure. About the same time we learn how to time-travel."

Gabriella grimaced. "Do you ever wish you could go back and change things?"

Only about every minute of every day since Dollie had left me. "No. I always have a total ball living in the now."

"You're a bad liar. There are things I wish I hadn't done. Or done differently." She looked away. "Especially with you."

"What were you saying about lying?"

Gabriella pulled herself upright. "I really am looking for work."

"I don't have anyone on my hit list right now. Besides, I couldn't pay you even if I did."

"Payment doesn't have to be in money." She winked. The old Gabriella seemed to be back.

"I don't imagine you have problems finding work. With the way the world is, there can't be any shortage of people looking for your... skills."

A trace of sadness flickered across her face. "I've got a contract on the table."

I shook my head. "So this was bullshit after all?"

She hesitated. "I don't want the job I've been offered. I thought perhaps you..."

I finished the bar and washed it down with the last of my coffee, pushing both in the garbage chute. "I don't operate in those circles. Thank bog."

"You could use me for personal protection on your mission."

I laughed. "You don't know what my mission is."

"You're going to look for the Sacagawea."

I stopped. As far as I knew, the information about our operation was secret-Gabriella shouldn't have known about it. I suppose she had to have contacts in order to keep operating the way she did, but it shook me to be faced by the fact that our mission wasn't so covert after all. "If you know that, then you also know I don't need a babysitter."

She smirked at me, putting on a fake coyness. "I have the costume…"

"I don't need that kind either."

Her bravado seemed to falter again. "I know we haven't always seen eye to eye. But it's not been all bad. I helped out on your last trip, remember?"

"Sure… right up until you tried to blow up the ship and everyone in it."

Gabriella glared at me hard enough I could almost feel the blades hitting me. "Look, you're a nice guy, Joe. Aren't I worth a second chance? You could use your contacts… put in a good word for me perhaps. And who knows, if we're around each other, you might get to like me. That wouldn't be too hard, would it?"

I laughed. Not because what she'd said was particularly funny, but because she'd already used up more chances than Bastet, the ancient Egyptian cat goddess. "I have to give it to you-you're good. Really good. The way you put that slight tremor in your voice. And how you drop your chin just so to look vulnerable. I guess I'm supposed to get all chivalrous here and take you into my arms to protect you?"

She stiffened, and for a moment I thought she was going to slap me. She'd done it before more than once, and I wasn't about to let it happen again. But then that sad expression reappeared. "I should have expected that."

I checked the time. "Why don't you leave? Before Logan gets here. Because then you really would have a bad day."

Gabriella's perfect eyebrows furrowed slightly. "You need me, Joe. More than you think."

"I don't need anybody."

"Keep telling yourself that. Maybe one day you'll believe it."

"You've got one minute. Then I'll carry you to the airlock."

"I came here to help." She sighed. "To warn you."

"I don't need a warning to stay away from you."

She nodded and turned to leave, and I followed her toward the airlock to keep an eye on her.

"This mission isn't what you think." Gabriella wriggled back into her p-suit. "You don't know what's going on here."

"So, why don't you tell me?"

She wrinkled her nose. "You know me. I don't share secrets."

"Unless you're well-paid."

Gabriella's dark eyes narrowed into harsh slits and she pulled her helmet down, twisting to lock it into place. I could still hear her, though. "Time I was leaving."

"What's the job you're trying to get out of?"

"See? You do care, after all. It's nothing." She smiled through her visor. "Working on some... transformation protocols."

"What does that mean?"

"Bye, Joe. Miss me." She raised her glove and blew me another kiss.

I stepped clear of the airlock and closed the inner hatch behind me. The atmosphere indicator clicked down to zero and the light came on, indicating the outer door had opened. Despite what I'd said, I almost regretted it. Gabriella might have been a psychopath and as unstable as a pocketful of quarks, but I'd been a boy scout for a long time.

The light on the airlock changed. The outer door had closed again, and the atmospheric cycling had activated. Somebody was coming in, and a very small part of me hoped Gabriella had changed her mind. When the cycle finished, I opened the door to see the diminutive space-suited figure. She turned, and I spotted the name badge.

I reached out and took her helmet as she unzipped her suit. "Aurore? What brings you up here?"

"Just checking you slabs of meat haven't screwed up my project."

I did a double-take. "Yours? You designed the upgrades?"

"Not all of them." Aurore grinned. "It was a family effort."

I winced. Family wasn't a word that sat well with me.

Aurore reached out and put her hand in mine. "Sorry, Joe. That's probably a sore spot right now."

I shrugged. Sore or not, it wasn't about to change, so I had to get used to it. "You guys did a great job. I'd take my hat off to you if I had one."

Aurore grinned, her chiseled ebony cheeks blossoming. "That's high praise coming from you."

"Credit where it's due. That was a lot of work to make everything fit together."

She slipped through the inner door and stowed her gear in the suit locker. "Tell me that after we test it."

Her "we" had a decisiveness about it. "You're coming with us?"

Aurore grinned. "You think I'd let that big Indian out of my sight?"

Her possessiveness reminded me of Dollie's insistence on staying with me on the last trip, and I couldn't help but remember its tragic outcome. I hoped for both their sakes that history wouldn't repeat.

She followed me to the wardroom, and I ducked into the locker to grab some food packs, the energy bar having failed in its mission. When I came out, my saliva glands went into overdrive, and it was nothing to do with what I was carrying. Logan was standing next to Aurore holding a large VacSack with steam rising out of the open top. As I followed my nose, he pulled a giant slice of pizza from the sack and handed it to Aurore.

"If that's pepperoni, I'll kiss you," I said, forgetting the food packs.

"You'll have to settle for a fake meat-feast." Logan grabbed another slice and lofted it in my direction, giving the plate a slow spin to stabilize it.

"I've heard about you lonely space bums," Aurore said. "Forget the kissing. That's my prerogative."

I caught the plate and slipped into a chair in one movement.

"The work records showed you've been busy. I thought you might enjoy something more substantial than space rations." He sat next to Aurore, opposite me. "Plus, I have to maintain my reputation as the great hunter for my lady here."

"Don't worry, your reputation is safe," Aurore said, in-between mouthfuls. "For now, anyway."

"What do you think of the modifications?" Logan demolished his pizza slice and reached for another.

"The design is brilliant. I was congratulating Aurore as she came in. I understand the credit is shared."

"Seventy-thirty," Aurore said, digging Logan in the ribs with her elbow.

"To me." Logan took another bite.

Aurore pulled back in mock insult. "You wish."

"Sixty-forty?" Logan added another slice to her plate.

"Do you remember why I agreed to marry him, Joe?"

"No way. Leave me out of this. I'm lining up for more pizza."

"Fifty-fifty," Aurore said. "Take it or leave it."

Logan laughed, his bellows echoing around the room. "Who cares about the credit? As long as you're one hundred percent mine."

I accepted another slice and folded it along the middle, sliding out of my seat and drifting over to the large display screen on the next table. I'd set it up for ZHexChess tournaments on our previous journey. Now, I used it to pull up the work schedule and checked the progress on the refits. I also needed to escape Logan and Aurore's casual intimacy. It struck too close to home for comfort.

"Will we make it, Joe?" Logan called out.

I analyzed the patterns. The tank fitting was slightly ahead of schedule. The installation of the CASTOR system had slowed, and we'd not started work on the main plumbing and control system yet. "Fourteen hours until we're ready to test."

"Then we're gonna be launching without testing. The guys with the shiny shoulder decorations want us out of here in eight."

"You know launching early won't make any difference to our search?" I looked back at him.

"Sure." He shrugged. "But the brass always confuses start and finish times. Besides, you can bet your next paycheck that the PAC, Atolls, and Corporates will all be out there looking for answers too. You know how it goes."

I knew all too well. My earlier assessment of our status as guinea pigs was looking truer than I'd thought. And if that wasn't enough, it seemed we were also in danger of getting caught in a cross-fire from mutually antagonistic forces.

A second long stint outside the Shokasta ended with the CASTOR systems in place. They weren't functional, but at least we were at a point where we could use the main drive system and make our departure. I hadn't mentioned Gabriella's visit and wasn't sure if I should. She'd only been on the ship briefly, but I knew Logan would be upset. And the longer I held out on him, the worse I felt.

And then there was she'd said. A transformation protocol. What did that mean? A common enough idea in project management-a change in operation for anything beyond the most routine should have a defined set of steps to take you from A to B. But I didn't think she'd used it that way.

"SecOps doesn't know what to believe," Logan said as we finished the pre-flight checks ready to move us away from the High-Rig. "With everyone scrambling to plant their flag on anything within reach, it could be hostile action by one of the other Earth-states, the Atolls, or the Corporates."

"That's not the wildest idea though, is it?" said Aurore from the science terminal.

Logan shook his head but said nothing.

"Come on, give me the worst." I signaled traffic control to update our launch status and received a hold signal in return. "Nothing you can tell me would lower my opinion of the military and political circles."

"The Sacagawea was following a route taking it to star systems located between Sol and known U'gan space," Aurore said.

"They think the U'gani are attacking us?" The distances involved were so large even thinking about it was preposterous. Their nearest known world was three-hundred light-years away. Even with our farthest explorations, we'd barely made a scratch on that distance. And according to the Ananta's data, the U'gani were far ahead of us technologically. I imagined they could wipe us out as easily as we would destroy a termite colony. "Has anyone made contact with them yet?"

"Not that I know of." Logan switched over the power system so that Shokasta was running independently from the station. "But everybody is holding their cards close to their chests. I think SecOps tried sending a remote probe and failed. What little I've seen suggests the PAC tried the same thing. Who knows about the others. Best guess-probably."

I checked the readouts on the Casimir generators to make sure they were operating correctly and the CASTOR units weren't causing problems. We needed some space around us and some velocity too. One discovery since our first Jump was that the process was affected by space-time curvature. Jumping deep inside a gravity well lowered predictability and accuracy, so the recommendation was to have at least one A.U. of separation from anything like a planet.

We were waiting on the all-clear from traffic control when a signal from the main airlock sounded. No one could board because I'd secured the entrance in preparation for departure, but there was someone in the docking tube that connected us to the High-Rig. I triggered the comm screen and saw a uniformed SecOps man at the airlock.

"Mr. Ballen? I'm Sergeant Hernandez. I've been ordered to join you with my squad."

Hernandez was bulky enough to tag him as Geneered, and behind him I saw the blurred shapes of several other uniforms.

"You know about this?" I looked at Logan.

"I thought they didn't want to risk anyone else." He tapped a message into his wrist-com. Barely a minute later, it beeped in response. "They're for real."

I wasn't thrilled with the idea but didn't argue and pressed the controls to unlock the entrance. Given our mission, it might pay to have some grunts with us. "Welcome aboard, Sergeant. We're in the control room. Your people can bunk in any of the unused cabins."

He nodded, a grin spreading over his face. "Cabins? Sounds

better than our usual assignments. Call me Hernandez. Ranks are for officers."

He signed off and when the airlock closed, I secured it once again.

"So, what's the story?" I said to Logan. "If I'd known about this, I'd have thought twice about coming."

"I understand." He gestured at his wrist-com. "But it's not like last time. They're under my command it seems, and we might need them."

I turned to the control station to continue monitoring progress. The last tanks had been fitted, and the crews were filling them.

Ten minutes later, Hernandez arrived, looking bigger in person than he had through the comms. There were three others with him-two men and a woman.

"Mr. Ballen." He nodded and looked across at Logan. "Mr. Twofeathers. Glad to be aboard."

"I'm Logan." He slid out of his seat and held out his hand. Hernandez hesitated, looking from his hand to Logan's. "Your orders please, sergeant?"

They were about the same height, but as tall as Logan was, he couldn't shade the soldier. The others with Hernandez were smaller but not by much, apart from the woman who was solid but slender. Hernandez reached into his uniform pocket and pulled out an eFlimsy.

Logan checked the orders then looked over at me. "Call him Ballen, and this is our science adviser, Aurore Vergari."

Hernandez partly turned to his squad. "Corporal Grant, Private Sullivan, and Private Giotto."

Grant was a tall black guy and similarly built to Hernandez. Sullivan was pasty white and shuffled from one foot to another as if he'd stood on an ant nest, while Giotto was olive-skinned and cute but had a tight, deadly look in her eyes. It was the same expression I'd seen in Gabriella-that of a killer.

Hernandez caught me looking at Giotto and misinterpreted my reaction. "Don't worry, she won't bite so long as you keep your libido in check." He grinned. "Otherwise, she doesn't play nice."

"I'm married. That is, I-"

"Remember that, and you won't have any problems," Giotto called out.

I was going to correct what I'd said but decided it didn't matter. The state of my marriage, or lack of, wasn't any of their business, and I didn't play those kinds of games with people I didn't know. "What's your brief, Sergeant?"

"Please, call me Hernandez." He glanced at Logan. "I've been ordered to place myself at the disposal of Mr... Logan, that is. And we have the broad direction of ensuring the safety of everyone on the mission."

"So, you're on nanny duty?" It seemed a little ridiculous to me, but who could fathom the collective military mind.

Hernandez smiled again. "If you like to think of it that way, feel free. All my team have technical skills, which I understand may be useful on this mission."

I grunted, somewhat relieved to hear that they might be more than the usual gung-ho gorillas MilSec seemed fond of.

"We have one operational detail we'd like to take care of." Hernandez looked embarrassed. "We brought a Transponder Launcher. The brass wants it fitted."

Logan appeared as confused as I was.

"It launches a signal bead after every Jump that broadcasts an ID signal and timestamp." Hernandez shrugged. "The idea is that we can be tracked if something goes wrong."

It seemed pretty dumb. A signal bead wouldn't send out a broadcast strong enough to be picked up at interstellar distances, and even if it did, it would take years for the transmission to crawl back to Earth at light speed. "A deadman's breadcrumb trail? Are they that worried I'm going to run off with the Shokasta?" No one said anything. "Okay. Let's add it to the list."

"I've been advised that they won't clear us for departure until I confirm it's been fitted." Hernandez shrugged. "I guess someone think you're valuable, Ballen."

"More than a cargo ship full of unobtanium." It wasn't me, or anyone onboard, who was valuable. It was the ship itself.

"You'll need a hand installing it," Logan said.

"We better get on it. But they can blame someone else for

missing that departure time." I turned toward the door.

Hernandez rubbed the back of his neck. "One of my team needs to verify the install,"

I turned back. "Who's the lucky winner of the spacewalk lottery?"

He pointed at the woman with the assassin's eyes. "Giotto's our tech specialist."

"Why am I not surprised?" I muttered. "Get suited up. Main airlock in fifteen."

I was in the last stages of sealing my suit when Giotto marched in, dragging a white plastic box about the size of a large suitcase. She was wearing her own suit, a typical MilSec issue, complete with cumbersome armor plating. "Are you going to be able to do the job wearing that?"

"Don't worry about it, Ballen." She twisted her helmet on, but her visor was still open. "I'm planning on letting you do the work. I'm along to make sure you don't screw it up."

She snapped her helmet shut and closed the protective screen so her face was no longer visible.

"Great," I muttered and closed my own helmet. The augmented view screen flickered into life, showing me the inside of the airlock and Giotto and adding a data overlay showing status information. I backed into an EMU unit sitting in the rack by the door, and Giotto did the same. My helmet display changed, confirming the EMU was locked and showed the amount of fuel along with predictions of my remaining delta-v budget. I opened a comm channel to the ship.

"Logan. We're ready for EVA."

"Okay, releasing airlock controls to you."

Logan sounded calm, and I tried to mirror that, though the truth was the soldiers had me on edge. I'd had enough military company to last a lifetime and would have been happy to leave the lot of them behind. I thumbed the airlock cycle controls, and the pumps began removing the air. It was noisy initially but grew silent as we got closer to a vacuum. Once complete, the doors slid open.

We had a view of the High-Rig about five-hundred meters away at the other end of the docking tube, the slab sides of its outer bulkheads bright even with the automatic filtering of my helmet. "Come on. Let's get this done."

I pushed away airlock and let the EMU check my speed while its stabilizing system stopped any spin caused by my exit. Giotto grabbed the transponder case and drifted it through the door, tossing me the safety tether before pushing herself out. It was a cavalier move, but I caught the strap without too much difficulty, feeling the nudge as the line reached maximum and the EMU compensated for the tug.

"You could have lost the transponder," I called to her over the com channel. "You should have kept hold of it or given me the strap before I came out."

"Told you-you do the work, I watch." She maneuvered farther away to get a better view of the High-Rig. "It always looks smaller out here."

Despite her attitude, Giotto's movements demonstrated her experience with ZeeGee. I'd have preferred Logan or Aurore with me, though. Trust was everything in p-suit operations. "Where are we putting this?"

"You can shove it where-"

Her broadcast stopped abruptly. I guessed Hernandez was monitoring us and had overridden her transmission. This was confirmed a few minutes later when his voice came over the channel.

"The directions call for it to be installed near the main accelerators, Ballen." He paused. "There's a built-in detector that will sense the Jump and trigger it to lay an egg."

"Okay. Will do."

I turned toward the rear and told the EMU to head to the first of the giant drum-like accelerators. It brought the boost up slowly and then cut off once we were moving at a decent speed. Giotto's attitude didn't bother me, and Hernandez's intervention wasn't needed. I wasn't there to make friends. Giotto followed about twenty meters back, occasionally floating off to take a closer look at parts of the Shokasta. About two-thirds of the way to the accelerator, the comm opened up again.

51

"Ballen. This is Giotto. We're on private."

The indicator on my visor confirmed that. "What now?"

"This ship is something else. I can see why you don't want to let her go."

I wasn't sure how to take that. If she meant it as an apology, it was obscure to say the least. But if it was something else, it was lost on me. "Enjoy sightseeing while you can."

Ten minutes later, we were by the intersection between the reactor hull and the largest of the accelerator coils. The coils themselves had a textured irregular surface, but the underside of the hull was relatively smooth. I moved the box closer but couldn't see a mount, only a decal that said "Front - Toward Space."

"Does this thing glue on?" I had the usual supplies but had assumed Giotto would take care of the attachment. Though with her attitude, maybe that was supposed to be up to me too. I didn't think adhesive, even astro-stickum, would hold through a Jump. And if I had to go back inside the ship to get some, I might just leave Giotto out there permanently sightseeing.

Giotto floated over, taking her time, and grabbed the box. After aligning it along the ship's central axis, she thumbed an inconspicuous control, and several stubby legs shot out, apparently pegging the transponder in place. I checked the attachment points. They'd penetrated the outer skin of the hull but only to a controlled depth, I hoped. Otherwise, everyone onboard would be eating high-quality vacuum in short order.

"It's self-contained," Giotto called over the comm. "The mounts lock under the surface and pump out a nano-adhesive. It's almost impossible to get off without destroying the unit."

"It might be worth it to stop the snooping," I said, as she pressed another hidden control and a small light flashed green.

"To escape the one thing that might provide a slim chance of rescue? I don't think you're that stupid."

"You don't know me very well."

Giotto ignored me and opened up a channel to the ship. "It's in place, Sarge. Drop a test egg."

Hernandez didn't answer, but a couple of minutes later a small circular opening appeared, and something popped out.

Giotto reached for it but missed, and I managed to grab it before it floated away too far. It looked like a metallic golf ball, and as I held it several transmitter spikes extended out, making it look like a miniature version of the ancient Sputnik design.

"The signal's working," Hernandez said. "Get yourselves back inside."

"Normally they shoot out fast," said Giotto, "three of them spaced out by an hour to give us some redundancy."

I turned and set the EMU to take me back to the airlock. "What's the capacity?"

"It holds two hundred eggs."

That seemed plenty. I couldn't imagine any journey that would take more than sixty Jumps to complete. At maximum range, that would put us over six-hundred light-years away from Earth-which would mean a hell of a lot of dangerous nothing between here and there.

"Thanks for telling me all this before we came out."

"I wanted you to feel useful," Giotto said.

That was the problem-I didn't. She could have handled the job by herself, in the same way that Logan could have handled the ship on his own. I was nothing but a hanger-on, a spare leg, there because I was awkward enough to have commandeered the ship. Maybe I should turn the whole thing over to Logan and crawl back into my hole. I was sure no one would care if I did.

"It's a piss-poor way of tracking us," I said as we approached the airlock. "Barely a step up from chance."

The door slid shut, and the atmosphere refilled. When the green safety lit up, I backed into the rack to leave the EMU to recharge and unlocked my helmet. Giotto had done the same and shrugged inside her armor.

"If you're so smart, come up with a better alternative."

"I'm an engineer, not a physicist." I twisted out of my suit. It was steaming lightly as the moisture in the air condensed around it, but the locker would dry it out.

Like Gabriella, Giotto was wearing a tight-fitting one-piece underneath her suit that only a sterilized sloth could ignore, but I turned away, heading for the inner door.

"You're not so dumb after all, Ballen," she called after me.

She was only partially right. I was escaping before I could do anything to display my own stupidity. But also, she'd got me thinking. My idea wasn't especially smart, but if my hunch was correct, it was within the scope of current engineering.

Chapter Five

I headed to the control room to finish off the launch prep. Logan, Aurore, and Hernandez were clustered around the large 3V display showing clumps of bright stars along with a green glowing "snake" connecting several of the dots.

"Is that the latest MusCat vision of the path to god?" I said.

"Not anything so convoluted." Logan grinned and gestured at Hernandez. "SecOps has provided us with the *Sacagawea's* complete planned route."

The path was roughly circular and looked like someone's halo had fallen off and been mangled in a waste processor unit. It started at our own star system and cut across to the Lalande 21183 system, then dog-legged up to several others that only had catalog numbers. Then it went through the recently explored Learmonth and Buang's star systems before dropping back down through Procyon and Sirius, after which they should have returned to good old Sol. It was one of the most extended routes attempted by a USP ship, involving nine successive Jumps for a total round-trip distance of around ninety light-years.

As the display spun around a big kink poked out on the outward route that looked strangely out of place with the rest of the journey. "Does anyone mind if I take the controls?"

No one raised an objection. "What have you seen, Joe?" said Logan.

"A map through my large intestine."

I zoomed in on two of the projected Jumps until they filled the viewing volume. At that point, the route ran from GL 388 to

GL 382 and then on to GJ 1116A. "See that?"

"The length?" Aurore said.

"According to what we know of Jump theory, the maximum length is three parsecs—around ten light-years. Even with the Casimir generators, we can't generate enough energy to produce a manifold tear that goes farther."

"And these Jumps are longer." Logan wasn't asking.

"The first is over twelve—the second almost fourteen." I pulled up the info displays on the Jump routes.

"You guys are way ahead of me," Hernandez said. "I'm just a grunt who knows how to spin a few wrenches."

"So did they do the journey in two stages or somehow manage it in one?" Aurore said.

That was the question that had leapt into my head the minute I'd seen the long paths. A Jump didn't *have* to be between two stars—it could be to any point in a spherical volume. "Has anyone heard of a ship Jumping into deep space and then continuing?"

Apparently no one had.

There was no reason to avoid Jumping into deep space, but there was also nothing to encourage it. The galaxy was deep, uninviting, and dangerous—why risk a Jump to the middle of nowhere? At least hopping from star to star kept you oriented, no mean trick when you're moving through a three-dimensional space where coordinates are entirely optional.

We were like ancient mariners clinging to the shore for comfort. Back then, they didn't know if their boats were strong enough to survive away from the relative safety of coastal waters. Now we had similar worries about our ships in space. Humans are irrational creatures at best, and when we fear something, it finds unique ways to express itself.

"Maybe the captain wanted to be the first interstellar Columbus?" Hernandez shrugged. "You know. Get in the record books."

"What do we know about the crew?" I looked at Logan.

"Leonard Begay is the captain, and he's an experienced MilSec officer. Like most Earth people, he doesn't have much space experience, but this is his third Jump mission. His crew has mixed levels of experience, so about what you'd expect, given the restrictions we've had to work with in the past." Logan hadn't needed to check the files.

"Not much to go on," Aurore said. "But he doesn't sound like the type who'd take a risk without good reason."

I agreed, but it didn't get us anywhere. I closed the star map and brought up the ship upgrade status. Everything was showing green except the final plumbing and control systems, which we'd have to finish while we were traveling.

"Looks like it's time to ship out," I said.

I strapped myself into the main piloting seat, and the others took their stations. My request to traffic control for clearance was given with almost unseemly haste. "I think they're glad to see us leave," I said.

"They're anxious to get their docking port back with all the activity going on." Logan checked the moorings. "We're clear."

I directed the computer to move us out from the station, keeping our velocity under five meters per second while inside the inner navigation markers, but as soon as we were clear of the general flock of traffic, I lifted the boost until we were at full acceleration. This made things easier as we could walk around and work at a third of a g instead of floating or using the sticky flooring to fake it. I wasn't worried about Logan and Aurore, but other than Giotto, I didn't know what experience the MilSec team had.

As we left Earth's orbit, we moved eastward with the planet's rotation and slid past the Hyasynth orbital platform, still considered the height of Corporate luxury living. We picked up speed, clearing the Atlantic Ocean, and could see Tali Panjang—the PAC space elevator—rising like an impossibly thin spider web strand from its anchor point outside Bengkulu in Indonesia. Tali Panjang had been completed before the High-Rig, with the PAC receiving help from their erstwhile friends in the Atolls. Already, though, we were leaving Earth behind. We crossed lunar orbit four hours later and could relax a little with the ship on autopilot.

My plan was to head toward Mars, completing the work on the CASTOR system and testing it along the way. We'd received reluctant clearance from the Atolls for Mars approach to restock the water tanks—otherwise, our extra boost capability would be depleted during testing. How this had been negotiated, I had no idea. They didn't want us Earthers anywhere near their facilities.

The MilSec people kept mostly to themselves, which was fine by me. But on day three, as I was heading to my room, I found Hernandez and Sullivan blocking the corridor next to an unused cabin. The Sergeant looked up as I approached and waved. "Sorry, Ballen. We'll be out of the way soon."

"Problem?" I said, craning to see through the door.

Hernandez turned to face me, obscuring my view. "We're removing the partition wall to make this a double."

"Yeah?" I caught a glimpse of Giotto. "Who's getting married, and do I get an invite to the bachelor party?"

Hernandez looked at me as if I was speaking in high-Martian then laughed. "We're clearing space to make a combined gym and hand-to-hand practice area. Don't want my guys to get soft. Logan okayed it."

I was puzzled. The ship had an exercise room toward the back of the main corridor. It wasn't much, a basic programmable resistance exoskeleton and some room to work up a sweat. But I couldn't see why they'd need more than that.

Grant appeared down the corridor carrying a crate liberally decorated with MilSec stickers. It was about half a meter on each side and looked too heavy for one person if we'd been on Earth, but his Geneering and the lower gravity made it possible for him to lug it around on his own.

Hernandez pointed through the door. "Anywhere in there."

I'm no expert on military designation codes, so the labels on the crate didn't mean much. But even a grease monkey like me could translate the yellow and black striped "Danger" signs.

"What's in the box?" I said, watching Hernandez for his reaction.

He blinked twice, his smile as stiff as a corpse at a picnic. "Exercise equipment."

Once Grant was inside, Hernandez let me go by, and I made my way to my cabin. It could have been on the level—military types, especially Geneered, have a tendency to think with their gluteus maximus—but maybe it was something else. I knew better than to poke around their operations and would talk to Logan about it the next time we had a quiet moment. Besides, I had other things to worry about.

After throwing on a set of coveralls, it was time to interface the new controls with the ship's main systems. Logan and Aurore were working on the plumbing, while I had the job of ensuring everything could communicate.

At the narrowest section of the main hull was a short antechamber where the forward section of the *Shokasta* joined onto the wider section that contained the main reactors. The control circuits ran behind the inner bulkheads providing a place to patch into the circuitry near the reactor and the star chamber of the CASTOR system. The area was barely big enough for two people to stand in. When I pulled the access panels, I was greeted by a packed array of control circuitry and conduits that looked like the aftermath of an insane HVAC experiment. I sighed. I'd have to isolate and remove several subsystems to gain access, and the computers that design these things never took into account someone having to service or repair them.

I removed the first layer, my hands working on autopilot as I thought about Dollie, wondering what her new job could be. I was surprised. She'd enjoyed running the cab service. Sure, it was tough to recruit drivers right now, but the situation would stabilize eventually, and with her contacts and social skills, I felt sure business would recover.

My mind edged toward her relationship with Sigurd and bounced away again like an accusation of corruption ricocheting off a politician. I hoped she wasn't getting in too deep. From what Dollie had told me, their relationship had been abusive, so it was even more of a surprise to see them together. Despite the divorce, I didn't want her to suffer any more. We'd both been through enough.

I was bouncing between ideas about how I could get back with Dollie, plus other unlikely possibilities, when my comm-set beeped. I was levering a stubborn fitted duct at the time, and the pry bar I was using slipped, slicing across the back of my hand to leave a bloody gash several centimeters long.

"Damn." I shook my hand, sending a splatter of blood across

the wall.

"Hello to you too, Joe." It was Aurore. "You okay?"

"Yeah. Did you get the Jacuzzi plumbed in yet?"

"We've finished the first three sections. That's enough for one morning. I told Logan I'm not doing any more until he comes up with some lunch. You should join us."

"Sounds like good progress. I've downloaded a book called *Teach Yourself Snorkeling Without an Air Supply*. Looks right up my alley." My hand was stinging, and lazy trickles of blood wandered down my fingers. I grabbed a rag and wrapped it around to staunch the flow.

"Don't say things like that, Joe. Come and eat with us."

"I'll be there after I stop in at the MedBay."

"What happened?" I could almost see her eyes rolling.

"I want to loot the isopropyl alcohol supplies before someone else thinks of it." I heard a low grunt in the background, and realized Logan must have heard. "See you in five."

My hand was getting numb as I climbed up to the MedBay, the improvised bandage making it hard to grip the handholds that ran up the wall. Once there, I cleaned it up, then sprayed on a coat of MediSkin to keep it protected and hopefully infection free. It only took a few minutes to dry, then I dragged myself to the wardroom.

After zapping a meal pack for twenty seconds, I grabbed a tube of coffee and sat with the others.

"What happened?" Logan pointed at the patch of MediSkin.

I unpeeled the wrapper from the food and salivated at the smell. It wasn't good quality—I just realized how hungry I was. "Cut myself shaving."

"You holding up okay, Joe?" His dark eyes were wide with concern. "Anything the nerve-tranq can't handle?"

As usual, he managed to cut through everything to the real problem. Since we'd left, I'd been dry and was relying on the 'tranq to control the shakes. But my body still craved the booze and hadn't yet come to a truce with the idea that it had lost on that front, at least for the time being. I tried to recall the moment my hand slipped. I'd been deep in thought, not paying as much attention as

60

I should have. Could I have developed the shakes and not realized? I was enough of a realist to know it was possible. A smart part of me said I should get checked over by a MedTech right away, but that part wasn't calling the shots.

"Let the man eat." Aurore came to my aid. "He needs calories, not an interrogation."

I sighed as the warm caffeine-loaded nectar hit my stomach. Our first trip out, we'd had to deal with the tepid horror of MilSec standard coffee, which had more than a passing resemblance to chlorinated wastewater. But this time, Logan had laid in a supply of freeze-dried Ruiru-AB17. Not a great coffee, but the best mass market bean left on Earth, and a definite step up from stain remover.

"Want to run a diagnostic on my pee?" I chewed on the reheated wrap. "Sorry. I slipped taking down a piece of ducting. You know how cramped everything is in this thing."

"We helped build it, remember?" Aurore laughed. "The construction plans said *pack it tight.*"

"You sure did."

The MilSec team wandered in and snagged some food. They sat down with us, but even with the four of them we only needed a single table.

"How long until Mars?" Sullivan's ears tinged with pink as he looked at me. "I've never seen another planet."

Giotto looked across at him. "If you think you're going to get the chance to lose your virginity, you're SOL. Those Tollers wouldn't even look at a *scroffer* like you."

"Hey, come on." Sullivan grumbled. "I ain't—"

"Knock it off, people," Hernandez said. "And Giotto? Try to behave like you're a lady, even if you've only ever seen one on a 3V screen."

"Sure thing, *Sarge.*" She poked her tongue out. "Going to spank me if I don't?"

"You'd enjoy it too much."

Sullivan and Grant spluttered barely restrained laughs, while Giotto glowered before turning her attention to her food.

"Actually, I'm interested in the answer too," Grant said. His hand was over his wide jaw trying to cover up a grin. "Are we a week away? Two?"

"Depends how the testing goes and how much of a change we make in our velocity," I said. "But if we don't hit too many problems, we should arrive in a little over two days."

The soldiers bumped fists across the narrow table.

"Alright," Giotto mumbled, tapping the table with what looked like a live round of ammunition.

"Didn't realize these things were *that* fast," Hernandez said. "That's kinda crazy."

"What was that first trip like?" Sullivan asked. He was staring at me over his meal with eyes the size of Kohler plates. "Must have been a blast."

I thought about the people we'd lost, Delacort's betrayal, and how Paek's attack had killed our unborn daughter and almost cost Dollie her life. I tried to find the words to describe it all, how it had ripped away everything important in my life, and looked back at him. This was his first space-op, and he looked as excited as a collie pup.

"Yeah... it was a blast," I said, fighting the tension that tightened the back of my neck. "Something I'll never forget." That was true at least, no matter how much I wished I could. Sullivan would learn for himself.

"You should tell them about the time you and Dollie came to the ranch and—" Logan sighed. "Sorry."

I finished my wrap and wiped my fingers. The left ones were tingling from the wound. "No worries. I'm a survivor."

I stood up, and Aurore grabbed my good hand. "You'll be okay, Joe. It takes a while."

"I better finish off the control system. Otherwise, all your hard work will be for nothing."

There was silence as I walked away, but I heard the conversation start up again behind me. I knew Logan hadn't meant any harm, and perhaps Aurore was right—eventually I might be able to think about Dollie and not feel like part of me had died. But that seemed as far off as it had the day I'd moved out.

I got back to work. There's an old saying in engineering, at least as old as the invention of indoor plumbing. Conduit: Everywhere you want to be. The next piece came out relatively easily, and I could almost see the distribution junctions I needed to tap into. I sensed movement and looked up to see Logan shuffling down the ladder toward me.

"To what do I owe this honor?"

"Figured somebody better check your work," he said, dropping the last couple of rungs to land next to me.

"If you came to apologize again, there's no need." It was true, at least in the sense that his apology couldn't make me feel better. I pointed at the open panel. "I'm almost at the control circuits."

Logan ignored my gesture. "Nevertheless, I *am* sorry, Joe. About everything that you've been through."

"How's the weather outside? Still sunny?"

He laughed. "For the next few billion years or so."

"Then we're good."

"Are you sure you're up to this?" Logan's voice was a low growl. "I could arrange transport for you back to Earth from Mars."

He was giving me a chance to walk away. To crawl back into my own little pit and never come out again. Part of me wanted that so badly I could almost taste it, but somewhere buried deep inside, another part of me didn't.

"And miss all the *fun?*" I slapped his shoulder. "Besides, it'd be a shame to waste my newfound sobriety."

Logan didn't laugh this time. He examined my face, his eyes seeming to slice through me as though he could see my very soul. "Only you can decide the journey you take, Joe. That's how it always is. The future's like floating down a river—we never know what's around the next bend."

"With my luck, it'll be straight over a waterfall." I shrugged. "Right now, we need to focus on getting this thing installed, so we can get on with our real journey."

He nodded, apparently satisfied. "Let's do it." He started back up the ladder.

"Hey, Logan?" I remembered my earlier conversation with Hernandez. "Did you okay the MilSec guys to tear up two of the cabins?"

"Sure, why?"

"Nothing, I guess."

He laughed. "You could run a masterclass in suspicion, my friend. They needed some more space. It's not like we're short of it on this run."

He was right. The *Shokasta* was large enough to carry thirty people in relative comfort, or perhaps fifty in a pinch, though it would mean sleeping in shifts or being more than good friends. So far, we hadn't had anywhere near a full complement onboard, and I was happy with that. For all I was used to living in cramped conditions, I enjoyed having the room.

"You better get back to it," I said. "Otherwise I'll be done, while you and Aurora are still playing hide the plumb bob."

"Care to place a bet on that?" He grinned.

I'd never won a bet with Logan in all the years I'd known him, and it was pointless trying. "Sure, loser buys the scotch?"

"Done."

He left me with mixed emotions. It's painful to realize how far you've fallen. I'd hit rock bottom months ago and kept going down. Could I climb back up again with Logan's help? I picked up the pry bar that had gouged my hand. There was a trace of gore on the end, and I wiped it off. I didn't know what might be around that next bend, but I wasn't ready to give in yet.

Chapter Six

Three hours later, I'd dismantled the clutter and installed the new relay controllers. I couldn't do a real test on the system until the others had finished their work, but I made my way back up to the control room to run some preliminary logic checks using simulated data feeds. After that, I'd be able to reinstall the ductwork I'd removed.

While the logic analyzer ran through the different control combinations, I listened to an Earth broadcast. I told myself I was curious if there was further news about the destroyed Atoll station, but in reality I was checking to see if there was more information about Paek.

The main display was running the press conference featuring Porter Seckinger and General Eluise Mkandla, a mixed pair if ever there was and not only in skin color. They were so starkly contrasting they could almost have made a comedy duo. Seckinger was the typical vacuous politician complete with bad jokes and cheap suits. On the other hand, Mkandla always dressed in camo fatigues—usually unbuttoned to reveal both her ample chest and the ever-controversial sloganed t-shirts that were her trademark. Today's had a picture of a military assault rifle and the words "Peace Is Always a Stretch Goal."

"How are off-Earth developments progressing, Minister?" a reporter asked from off-camera. "What's the USP's official position on the loss of the secret Wright Atoll?"

"At the moment, we're working with the Atolls to clarify the details and identify how many of our citizens were there." Seckinger smiled, running his hand nervously through his mop of blond hair. "But it's misguided to suggest their base was a secret. It's a known scientific establishment and has been operating for almost two years."

"Will the USP take action in retaliation for the death of USP citizens?"

"We... that is, the Council of Ministers, have made no decisions on any action or response so far." Seckinger glanced at Mkandla before continuing. "But we are taking advice from MilSec as always in times like these."

"General, are you anticipating any response?" someone else asked. "Will our troops see action?"

Mkandla paused as if filling her lungs with enough breath to blow the entire press contingent out of her way, but when she spoke her voice was controlled and surprisingly gentle. "As Minister Seckinger stated, right now, we're trying to understand the facts. Any discussion of a military response is premature and inflammatory. Who should we respond against? The Atolls? It was their station. The PAC? Old Europe? United Africa? They all had personnel there. At this moment, we have nothing to indicate military action is needed. I suggest that those with calmer heads should advise the more excitable among us."

"Is your shirt a comment on the current situation?" someone called out.

Mkandla waved the question away. "It's a statement of fact. Now as much as any other time."

The press loved needling people to make comments that could be manipulated and sensationalized. No doubt the headlines tomorrow would be full of speculation on Seckinger's "failure" to provide answers. I heard a noise and glanced over my shoulder. It was Hernandez, and I muted the broadcast.

"Your boss looks like one tough lady." I locked the simulator test controls to make sure I didn't screw something up accidentally.

He gestured at the news broadcast on the screen. "Anything new?"

"Just a bunch of journalists blowing off hot air. They were trying to rattle Mkandla and the minister."

"Fat chance of that." Hernandez crossed his arms. "You couldn't rattle her with a fusion bomb."

"You know her?" I waved him to a spare seat.

"Mostly by reputation." He sprawled back, crossing one leg over the other knee. "Came up the hard way. Unconventional, but tough as TiCaLam armor. They call her Carbide Mkandla."

Aurore came in and walked over to her station. "What are you guys plotting?"

"Hernandez was telling me about General Mkandla. Apparently she's a tough cookie and icier than Pluto."

"Why is it that guys always see strong women as cold, while men are ruthless or ambitious?" Aurore said. "She's only doing what's necessary to survive."

Aurore was right—men often characterized women that way. It was probably a defense mechanism because so many felt intimidated by strong women, but Mkandla's square-jawed appearance lent support to Hernandez's assessment.

"Have you met her?" I asked him.

He shook his head. "The only interest she has in guys at my level is gland-to-gland combat."

"This is the best you guys can think of to discuss when I'm around?" Aurore shot us both a withering glance. "Grow up."

"Only saying what I've heard," Hernandez shrugged. "Didn't say I like it. I'm not a saint. But that sort of thing screws up morale."

Aurore finished her checks and marched toward the door. "And I'm sure you'd say the same thing if it was one of the male officers."

She left and Hernandez's face split with a grin. "Sorry, Ballen, I know she's your friend."

"She knows me well enough not to be too disappointed." To be honest, I agreed with him. Relationships like that are poison in an organization—whatever the justification. "Were you looking for me?"

"Logan, actually. We've got two SMPTs we'd like to put together and could use some help." My face must have betrayed my feelings because he held up a hand. "I know—you guys are busy. I only want to get it on the table."

"I'm sure it won't be a problem once we've finished the ship updates." The truth was I was glad to hear we had them onboard. The Space Mobility Personnel Transports were the military equivalent of the Hoppers we used for construction projects but designed to accommodate more than one person. Depending on what we found, they could be invaluable. While the *Shokasta* was a marvel of technology, it wasn't the most maneuverable of ships. They'd give us a much greater range of flexibility in our operations. "I'll talk to Logan about scheduling them in after Mars."

"I better check with him." Hernandez looked embarrassed. "He's the boss on this trip."

His words felt like a slap in the face, but he was right and I tried not to let my annoyance show. "Go ahead."

"There's one more thing."

I waited for him to continue, wondering what else might be going on. As Logan said, I'm a suspicious SOB.

"Do we know where we're going *after* Mars?" He made an all-encompassing sweep with his arm. "It's a big galaxy out there, and I'd like everyone to know what's coming up. Including my team."

I leaned back in my chair. "You're right. Everyone should be in on the decision."

"Huh?"

"The truth is, unless Logan has more information than he's shared with me, we don't know where we're going."

"But..." Hernandez scratched his ear. "I thought you guys had a plan."

"We do. We just haven't figured out what it is yet."

He looked at me as if I were insane, and he might have been right. "We should get everybody together after we finish up today. How about eight, ship's time?"

Hernandez pulled back a little.

"Don't worry. I'll clear it with Logan and get him to confirm it with you."

"I'll make sure my team is on deck."

We were all in the wardroom while I reviewed what little we

knew about the *Sacagawea's* planned journey. I'd spoken to Logan, and he'd pushed me into running the meeting even though he was the one in charge. I got the feeling he was still testing me, but it was hard to tell what was going on behind that hard-edged exterior of his.

"What's the problem?" Grant growled, fingering his black mustache. "We know the planned route, so we follow it until we find them, no?"

"That's one option," I said.

"Not a good one." Logan looked around. "Our ship can't go any faster than the *Sacagawea*. If nothing's happened to them, we'd be on their tail all the way back to Earth. That's a ninety light-year wild goose chase."

"How long?" Sullivan asked.

Logan looked across to me.

"Hard to say." I sucked on my tube of coffee. "A single ship in a star system is a very small needle in a very large haystack."

"They'll have a military transponder," Hernandez said, his voice brashly confident. "That should let us find them pretty easily."

"Assuming it's functioning." I rubbed my hand, trying not to scratch at the MediSkin patch. "If not, then it gets a lot harder. Aurore?"

"If there's no transponder, we have to look for other signals. We'd pick up radio, though there are other sources that occur naturally. Searching for their heat signature is a possibility, but it's time consuming and not necessarily conclusive. Or we could travel a long distance to find them using parallax, but it would be almost impossible to tell the difference between a meteor, a comet, or a ship."

"What's your best guess for checking a complete solar system?" I asked.

"With the detection gear we have onboard and assuming no active signals from the ship"—Aurore looked around, then her confidence seemed to falter and she sighed—"a month, maybe more."

"Their planned route touches eight systems. We can assume they aren't at Sirius. The Atolls have a station there with regular traffic. That leaves us with potentially eight months of searching."

Sullivan groaned, burying his head in his hands. "Man, I had a date lined up."

"The only date you had was with your right hand." Giotto smirked, suppressing a giggle. "What's your suggestion, Ballen?" she asked, ignoring Sullivan.

"We take the reverse route from the *Sacagawea* and hope we find them somewhere along the way."

"That could still make for a long journey." Hernandez sighed. "But I don't have any better suggestions."

"What about those two extra-long Jumps?" Logan held his hands out palm up. "How are we going to tackle those?"

I hadn't forgotten about them, but I didn't have a plan either. Even the thought of Jumping into open space made me shiver. "Let's hope we find out what happened before we get to that point."

There was some general chatter after that, but no one came up with any better suggestions. After about thirty minutes, I decided it was time to call it a night.

"I suggest everyone gets some sleep." I headed toward the door. "We'll be testing the CASTOR system tomorrow, and it might get rough."

My cabin felt especially empty. The warm orange glow from the lights offered a fake promise of comfort that they couldn't fulfill. I heard several of the others pass by, the thin walls letting the noise of footsteps through as I lay on the bed, staring at the featureless ceiling.

I wanted a drink. Several. In fact, what I wanted was a whole skinful. Logan hadn't brought any, though, which I felt sure was a deliberate omission, and I'd been too embarrassed to say anything when I'd realized. I needed it now more than ever. Not to get high but to numb my brain. To switch it off so I didn't have to think about everything that had happened and how screwed up my life was—a mental anesthetic.

Instead, I counted the pop-fasteners on the ceiling in the semi-darkness, imagining each one as another star that we might be visiting. So far, ships had only visited a handful of the closest systems. Even with the Jump drive, moving significant amounts of personnel and materials wasn't easy. The Atolls had set up several research stations, as had the USP. The PAC had their own missions, and nobody knew what the Corporates were up to—they only revealed operational details to their shareholders. No one had discovered a single world that was habitable without significant terraforming, which might be theoretically possible, but not in the near term. All the habitats in other systems were largely provisioned from Earth, except the Atoll ones. Not a very practical solution. The ferrying operations were an enormous undertaking, and even a small misstep could mean disaster.

Again, the Atolls had the advantage. The basics of atmosphere generation and food production were routine with them, so once a new habitat was seeded it became self-sustaining almost right away. But for the USP and the PAC, it was much more involved, making stations dependent on a delicate thread of supply ships for many months.

After a while, I forced myself to move. My thoughts were whirling around in tiny circles, and if I didn't do something to distract myself my head would implode. Either that or I'd fall asleep, and I couldn't let that happen. There was too much to do.

I opened my console and created a new private project area. The transponder I'd installed with Giotto's dubious help had given me some ideas, and I needed to run some simulations to see if they were possible. I started by accessing standard engineering compo- nents, cherry-picking through the listings to provide the function- ality I'd need. It was drudge work, to be sure but was detail-oriented enough to keep my mind busy.

After about an hour, I had the first virtual prototype configured and programmed a set of standard boiler-plate testing routines designed to check basic logic functions. It would take a while for them to run, but that was okay. I'd been keeping myself awake for a reason, and now seemed like a good time to scratch that particular itch.

I slid the door to my cabin aside a few inches and listened. I couldn't hear anything other than the faint hum of background noise. When I felt confident no one was wandering around, I slipped into the corridor and made my way aft.

As I approached the cabins where I'd seen Hernandez and the others working, I slowed, straining for the slightest sounds that might indicate the soldiers were around. Everything was quiet. I felt like a bit of an idiot hanging around in the half-lit corridor, as if I were some sort of pervy Peeping Tom. I *had* to know what they were doing in there, and more importantly what was in that box they didn't want me to get a look at.

I forced my breathing to stay steady, pressing my ear against the cold, textured surface of the door. I couldn't hear anything and grabbed the handle to unlatch it. The lock snapped open, the noise sounding like a gunshot in the night, and I froze. I tried to swallow but couldn't and waited with my pulse banging in my ears like a rivet gun on overdrive.

The door slid open noiselessly and I slipped inside, closing it behind me. The room was lit only by the dim safety lights around the floor, giving everything a ghostly appearance. I peered into the darkened corners of the room. Nothing appeared to be out of place, but that didn't mean anything. Various weight bars crowded one side, and a rack had been attached to one wall that looked like it held wooden swords, which seemed anachronistic considering the weapons they had available. Then I noticed another rack containing short, bulky service rifles more in keeping with what I'd expect. In one corner stood a resistance training exoskeleton similar to the standard ones we had onboard but heavier, and to the left of that I spotted it—the crate I'd seen Grant carrying.

Kneeling next to it, I examined the outside of the crate. Nothing suggested what it held, and I reached out to pop open the locking hasps. The metal was cold against my fingers as I forced the latches up then lifted the lid. It was empty. I slumped. There must have been *something* in it. A weapon? The case was large enough to hold a substantial bomb, but if my suspicion was correct, where was it?

I sensed rather than saw movement behind me and tried to get to my feet. As I turned, something bone-crunchingly hard punched into my back, like someone whipping a steel bar across my neck, and I fell. By instinct I kicked out, catching whoever it was several times with my feet, but my vision was fading. I rolled over, as a blurred shadowy figure jumped forward, and a series of blows smashed into my ribs. I brought my arms up to ward them off, but the attack continued until a final impact caught me just above the eye, and the lights went out.

I heard shouts around me, but my head was so full of mush I couldn't make out any of the words. Lights flashed in my eyes, and I turned away from their intensity. Nothing made any sense. My head felt like it had been removed, and my body like I'd been through a metal crusher—at least three times. My left hand was numb, despite the previous injury, and I wondered if I was waking up after an all-night bender. Maybe I'd dreamed about the mission. Perhaps Dollie hadn't divorced me after all? The pain was deeper than the worst hangover imaginable, though, and somehow I knew it was more physical.

I wanted to roll over, but something, or perhaps someone, held me down. I felt a bed underneath me, but in my current state it felt more like I was lying on a slab of astrocrete.

"Joe?" I didn't identify the voice as Logan's at first. In fact, trying to hear hurt, and the right side of my head felt like I was being attacked with a hammer drill.

Someone was tugging on a piece of rubber attached to my torso, but my body's internal senses told me it must be my arm.

"Can you hear me, Joe?"

It was Logan again, but my answer was a wet mumble. It was similar to sleep paralysis, where your brain is awake but your body is still asleep, but more terrifying and infinitely more excruciating. I screamed but managed nothing but a choked gurgle. The harsh light hit my eyes again, and something momentarily sharp and cold stabbed my neck.

Some of the pain faded, and I could make more sense of my surroundings. We were in the MedBay, which seemed as crowded as the Evil Banker on Twofer-Tuesdays, despite the fact we only had six people onboard. No, seven—I was still here, at least for the

73

moment.

"Everybody out!" That was Aurore, though she seemed to be screaming in my left ear. "Who do you need here, Sullivan?"

"No one." A mixed rabble of voices surrounded me, but I couldn't make them out. "Okay, one person to give me a hand, but that's it."

"That's me." Aurore said. "Everybody else, out. Including you, Logan."

"But—"

"Don't make me repeat myself." Aurore's tone was one I wouldn't want to be on the receiving end of.

The room grew calmer. The pain lessened, and my vision cleared enough to recognize people again. I pushed to sit up but couldn't.

"Tell. Logan," I croaked out. "Tell. I was. Attacked."

Aurore looked down into my eyes and stroked my forehead. "I know. But it…"

She faded again, and I got the feeling I'd missed something. "Did you tell, Logan?"

"He knows."

"He's got several fractured ribs. Severe bruising on his spine." Sullivan sounded as though he was reading a prognosis from the script of *When Good Surgery Goes Bad*. "He's almost certainly suffering from a concussion, and there's damage to his right eye and ear."

"Jesus." Aurore sounded shocked. "You people really screwed up."

The MilSec team had attacked me? That seemed ridiculous, but I hadn't got a clear view of anything after being hit in the neck. There could have been more than one. I faded again momentarily.

"…going to be okay?"

"I can't be one hundred percent sure." Sullivan seemed to be pummeling my ribs, and I winced. "He's hurt but strong enough I think he should recover—with some help."

I was going to offer to change places with him and see how strong he felt. My right eye was still blurry, but the left one had mostly cleared up. I managed to move my hand and grabbed

Aurore's arm with all the strength of a swallowtail butterfly.

"They've got a bomb," I grunted. "They've planted it somewhere. Gonna blow... the ship."

"What?" Aurore sounded panicked, and I couldn't blame her. She obviously had no idea what they were planning.

"I need to sedate him," Sullivan said. "His heart rate is dangerously high."

"No. Listen. They have a bomb..." A thick fog melted through my skull and into my brain. "Bomb, it's going..."

When I came around again, the room was quiet. The lighting was turned down to a dull glow that left the diagnostic lights above the bed the brightest points in the room. I looked at the displays, but they seemed abstract. I could see that the person being monitored was in bad shape, but I didn't connect it with me for several minutes.

My vision hadn't fully cleared, and underneath the drug induced dullness I knew I was badly hurt. I couldn't move and also had a curious sense of weightlessness. I managed to turn my head and saw Logan slumped in a chair by the door. He looked asleep but had a heavy service pistol in his hand.

I whispered his name, not wanting to startle him. His head came up, eyes bright and anxious.

"Joe? Jesus, are you okay?" He stood and moved over to the bed.

"Only slightly better than a dead man." I nodded at the pistol in his hand. "You hunting rabbits or here to put me out of my misery?"

He clipped the gun to his belt. "Making sure nothing happens to you. Aurore said you talked about a bomb."

I thought for several minutes. I hadn't seen a bomb—it could have been a figment of my paranoia. I couldn't imagine what else they'd want to sneak onboard, though. "They've got to be hiding something. Why else would they jump me like this?"

Logan frowned. "What do you remember?"

"I went to their special *training room*. I saw them taking stuff in yesterday and got suspicious. I was poking about, and one, or maybe several, of them came up behind me and put the boot in. They might have been using metal bars, though I couldn't swear to it.

75

They're all Geneered so who knows? It felt like it though. Still does."
My throat cracked. "Is there anything to drink? Water?"

Logan handed me a squeezable bottle of pinkish something.
"An electrolyte solution. It'll help your body heal and rebuild your
strength."

"Have you got those bastards locked up?"

Logan frowned, his eyes narrowing. "Well, your attacker is."

"Thank god for that. Who was it?"

"You should see for yourself." He lifted one thick eyebrow. "Do
you think you can move?"

"I'm pretty hopped up on drugs and floaty. But I'm game to try."

Logan pushed himself up using the edge of the bed, and I heard
the familiar tearing sound as he pulled his feet from the carpet.
Then his feet drifted up. "I killed the engines, so you wouldn't have
to take the gravity. We're moving at a constant speed."

"In that case, I can probably manage." I realized that was why I
hadn't been able to move. I'd been strapped down for safety.
"Unhook me, and I'm with you."

"No way Rocket Ranger." Logan moved around the bed, and I
heard several clicks as he unlatched the cushioned deck. "I'll take
you there."

He unfastened the other side and pulled the deck free with me
on it, the platform now becoming a gurney. Logan punched the
intercom button. "Keep the corridors clear. I'm taking him to the
gym."

He edged the bed through the door—awkward to do in ZeeGee.
Then he dragged me down the corridor toward where I'd been
attacked. Despite the drugs, I felt sweat break out as we approached.

"You okay?" said Logan.

I nodded slightly but it hurt, so I stopped and mumbled a yes.

The door opened ahead of us, and Hernandez swam out,
backing down the corridor so as not to block our path. He glanced
at me, then his eyes darted away and his chin dropped, no doubt
worried about the fall-out from one of his team attacking a civilian.

Logan pulled me inside the compartment, spinning the gurney
so I was upright, almost as though I were standing on the floor.
We weren't the only ones there. At the far end of the room, Private

Sullivan was waiting. His eyes were as big as a pair of small asteroids, and his skin looked even paler than usual.

Hernandez came in behind us, closed the door, and waited there.

"Joe. I want you to meet your attacker."

Logan gestured toward Sullivan, and my head spun. That was crazy. Why would their junior team member and MedTech attack me? And if he had, why had they let him treat me? And besides, Sullivan wasn't anywhere near as heavily Geneered as the others. I doubted he could have caused that much damage on his own, even catching me by surprise. Unless I was right, and he had used a metal bar.

"Throw him out the airlock." I would have done it myself, except even the thought of moving hurt. "Do we know who he's working for?"

I wasn't usually vindictive, but I was willing to make an exception. He'd been out to kill me and sabotage the mission. I didn't care who'd paid him to do it—better to let him die from a vacuum-induced low-calorie diet. I'd had enough of double-dealing traitors on the last trip.

Sullivan opened his mouth a few times but didn't manage to say anything. Then he leaned over, and I noticed the case that had held the bomb. He flicked open the latches, popped up the lid, then reached inside before stepping back.

A metal box rose from the case, lifting up on what looked like two metal struts. It unfolded upward again, and the support struts split, rotating around to lift the expanded box higher. The whole thing was shivering and vibrating as parts unfurled several times more, each time making it taller and wider. It looked like a mechanical refugee from a paranoiac nightmare as it glittered in the light.

When it finished unraveling, it was about the size of a person but with too many limbs. Like a metal stick man crossed with a praying mantis and finished off with a nightmarish set of dentist's equipment. Sullivan pulled out a small box and pressed a control on it. The thing moved forward, demonstrating a number of threatening postures in between bouncing around the walls of the room, finally coming to a rest in front of me and sinking to one knee.

"It's called BRUCE," Hernandez said. "Bi-pedal Responsive Unarmed Combat Educator."

I looked from Hernandez to Logan to Sullivan. "You're telling me a robot kicked the crap out of me?"

Chapter Seven

Logan dragged me back to the MedBay and explained what must have happened. The robot was a new unit, designed to train the MilSec people in advanced unarmed combat techniques in both gravity fields as well as ZeeGee. Sullivan had set it up in test mode and forgotten to disarm it afterward. When I entered the training room it was still active, and I'd inadvertently triggered a session with it. The unit was programmed not to cause significant levels of damage, but it had been set to expect a Geneered opponent, not plain old Ballen of the spaceways.

"Beaten up by a robot? That's pretty embarrassing," The bed felt like it had rocks in it, despite the ZeeGee. I was glad Dollie hadn't been around—she'd have laughed her ass off. Though these days, she'd more likely be cheering the robot on. "What's the outlook for me?"

Logan sat, his face solemn. "According to Sullivan, you need several weeks of recovery time. He can pump you full of military-grade NanoBiotics—that'll cut the healing time down significantly. But you might wish you were dead from the side-effects."

NanoBiotics rebuilt tissues from the inside out. They're insanely expensive, which was why they weren't in more widespread use, but MilSec liked to minimize operational downtime, so soldiers got them no questions asked. The NanoBiotics reproduced in response to the level of damage and self-terminated after a set amount of time. Then they were eliminated using the usual bodily functions—one of the lovely side-effects Logan was referring to.

"Don't they cause mental issues in high doses?" I asked.

"There are rumors to that effect." Logan laughed. "I'm not sure we'd notice the difference in your case."

"Thanks. You're the guy who authorized my pilot's license, remember?"

"Still think there's a bomb?"

I hesitated. "Obviously not. But I couldn't imagine what else they might have been hiding."

"Good, I can lock this cannon away again." He tapped the gun at his waist.

I felt pretty stupid about the whole thing. "So what happens now? Are we going to test the CASTOR system?"

Logan shook his head. "No way. We have no idea what high gravity might do to you. Even for short periods."

I felt a mixture of relief and concern. "We need to get on with the mission."

"And we will. As soon as Sullivan okays it."

My groan bounced around the small ward. "So, the guy responsible for putting me here is going to make me well again? Maybe I should let the psychopathic robot finish me off. It would be a quicker death."

"If that's what you want, I can arrange it." Logan chuckled. "Hell, I'll lock the door to the combat room myself once you're inside."

"Has anyone ever told you your bedside manner sucks?"

Logan shrugged. "What are friends for?"

"I suppose he's in charge of the NanoBiotics?"

Logan nodded.

"Okay. Send him along to poison my system with his self-replicating goo. I don't want to stay in this hole any longer than necessary."

When Sullivan came in, he avoided eye contact. "Mr. Twofeathers said you er... wanted the NanoBiotics."

"Don't let him catch you calling him anything but Logan," I said. "What's the real story on the treatment? Are the side-effects that bad?"

His eyes caught mine but edged away again. "I'd say they've been a little exaggerated to keep demand low. They're expensive."

He was moving around the room like he'd rather be somewhere, anywhere, else and grabbed a packet from the storage cupboard, stripping away the shrink-wrap to reveal a translucent cartridge. It held a pale straw-colored liquid that reminded me of a urine sample, though I hoped I was wrong on that score.

Sullivan pulled a short plastic Biojet injector from another cupboard and tried to load the cartridge into the gun. His hand shook, and the cartridge rattled against the injector's loading port.

"You better settle down. Otherwise you'll end up shooting those things in my ass."

"Sorry, I'm fresh out of basic MedTech training."

Just what I needed. "How many people have you worked on before?"

"Fifty-three. Simulated." He finally managed to load the cartridge. "You're my first live patient."

I wondered if I might be his first dead one too. "Great."

"The medication is delivered to the damage sites directly," he said. "Not to the er... backside."

"That comforts me no end."

He shuffled awkwardly over to the bed. "Look to your left."

The look-away trick was supposed to lower the chance of the patient panicking, but I'd been through enough treatment in the past not to be bothered by it. Besides, I wasn't the nervous one here. "Let's get on with it."

Sullivan pressed the gun to my ribs, and it hissed briefly as the medication was forced through my skin. I knew I'd have a raw spot there for a few days, but considering how beat up I was, it was doubtful I'd notice the extra discomfort.

He repeated the treatments to my arm and the back of my shoulders before one final shot in my neck.

"That's as near as I dare go to the brain," he explained, confirming some of the rumors of possible side-effects.

I rolled onto my back, sucking air through my teeth as the soreness of my wounds melded with the injection pain. "How long till I notice anything?"

"The first signs will hit in about five minutes." Sullivan popped the spent cartridge from the injector and pushed it into the waste disposal. "You'll feel a temperature rise at the wound sites. It'll get painful and itchy as the 'Biotics start rebuilding tissue."

"Oh good… something to look forward to."

"It'll calm down after about thirty minutes. Or at least you'll adjust to it."

"You seem to know a lot for someone who's recently finished basic training."

"I want to be a doctor." Sullivan scratched at his cropped blond hair. "I took lots of pre-med courses in college, but MilSec won't give me further training until I've done two years in the field."

From the military's perspective, it made sense. Not everybody was cut out for medical work, and it was expensive training, so they wanted to get their pound of flesh before investing beyond the basics. "How come you didn't go straight to med school?"

"Couldn't afford it, so I signed up to get qualified."

That was a surprise. Tuition was usually paid for through social funding, as long as you had the grades to qualify, especially for medical and other essential service careers. "What did you do, get caught seducing the Dean's daughter?"

He looked me in the eyes for the first time since he'd come in, and a rueful smile cracked his square face. "Wish that was the case. My parents are the problem."

"They forced you into the military?"

"Too rich." He shrugged. "And too tightfisted. I didn't qualify for funding, and they wouldn't help out."

That had to be rough. I'd never known my parents, but most were plenty willing to help their kids if they could, particularly when it came to supporting them in developing a career. I'd have done the same if… My thoughts ground to a halt, and my stomach churned.

Sullivan must have noticed my change of expression. "The 'Biotics kicking in?"

"It's nothing." As I said it, the injection sites seemed to ignite, and I grunted. "Well, maybe…"

"Whatever you do, don't scratch." Sullivan checked the monitor display above my head. "That can make the nanobots do stupid things, like grow out of control."

"Thanks for the warning."

"I'm sorry about what happened. It was a stupid mistake, leaving—"

I held up my hand to stop him. "It happens. Just try not to make a habit out of it."

A burning sensation bit deep into my tissues, and I gasped louder. "This is fun."

The NanoBiotic Agony Train ran its course as Sullivan said it would, but I was feeling better and worked on my project from my bed. Analysis of the virtual test results suggested the design was viable and could be built almost entirely with off-the-shelf components. I ran several more simulations and took the time while they were completing to document and draw up formal specifications. My idea was patentable, and I wanted to get everything as tight as possible so I could lodge an application before anyone else thought of it. I hadn't told anyone what I was working on, not even Logan. Not that I didn't trust him, but I wanted this to be all mine.

By the third day, I was getting cabin fever and went for a "stroll" around the ship. We were still coasting so there was no gravity, which made it easier on my fragile body. I made my way to the wardroom and found Giotto, Sullivan, and Grant playing poker.

"Look who it is," Giotto said. "The man who would be punch bag."

Grant stared her down then looked back at me. "Good to see you up and about, Ballen. Feeling okay?"

"Yeah, well... better."

"You shouldn't *be* up." Sullivan floated out of his chair and pushed himself over from the table. "I said at least a week."

"I've rested enough." A newscast was running on the 3V. It was Seckinger, making another of his frequent press briefings. Like all politicians, he was in love with the sound of his own voice. I nodded at the display, suppressing a yelp at the pain. "What's the story?"

"Seckinger is pushing his vision of the All-Parties Conference," Grant said. "You know, working together to expand into new-space and all that crap. Wants it to be held on the High-Rig, which no one else is buying into."

New-space was the term people were using to talk about the systems we'd been able to reach so far. It would be great if we could use some brains for once and solve our problems without violence and bloodshed. "Sounds sensible."

"When has *sensible* ever picked a winner?" Giotto grunted.

"Hey, Ballen, I heard you're a Rocket Ranger fan?" Grant said.

"Yeah, well, when I was a kid."

"Me too. I always rooted for Doctor Wingnut though. The Ranger was too much of a do-gooder for my taste."

Giotto hammered her fist on the table with a dull thud, but she was smiling."Do we have a game on, or are you chickens scared of losing more money?"

"Come on, Ballen." Sullivan pointed to the door. "We need to get you back in the MedLab."

"*We* need to back off." I stared at the hand he'd put on my shoulder. "I'm heading upstairs. I'll call if I need you."

I carried on my way, but as I approached I heard raised voices—Logan's deep baritone the loudest.

"Why should they be involved? What have they ever done for us?"

"I get it. All I'm saying is that we'd be better off if we—"

That was Aurore, but she stopped when I clambered through the doorway.

"Joe?" Logan's brow furrowed. "What are you doing here?"

"I came to complain. The flowers haven't been changed in my room in days, and the caviar has gone stale."

"Are you supposed to be up?" Aurore was turned slightly away from Logan, her face tight and expressionless.

"Leave him alone," Logan said. "He wouldn't be here if he didn't feel up to it."

"I'm concerned," Aurore said, breathing deeply. "Aren't you? He's your friend too isn't he?"

"Of course, I am. Why do you twist everything I say?"

I looked across at Hernandez. He was holding on to the bulkhead next to an auxiliary computer station wearing a calculated blank expression. When our eyes locked, he shrugged, as much as to say, "Don't ask me."

"I'm not twisting anything," Aurore said. "You asked what he was doing here. Or am I not supposed to have an opinion on that either?"

I recognized the signs well enough. The storm of couples where both have something to say and neither is listening to the other or themselves. I'd had enough of these with Dollie to spot one from half a galaxy away. They needed to backtrack and regain perspective. Unfortunately, me and Dollie never let go long enough for that to happen, and resentment built like a volcano coming to a slow boil.

"I needed a change of scenery." I floated over and checked out the 3V. Seckinger was again enthusiastically exercising his larynx. "Are they still trying to get everyone to the table to collaborate on new-space development?"

"That's the problem." Logan glared at Aurore. "They're including the Atolls."

"They're human, like the rest of us," she said. "Why shouldn't they be represented?"

So that was what was behind their spat. I had my own reasons to dislike the Atolls—their domination, posturing, and selfish indifference to what happened to people on Earth was well known. Not to mention my personal issues with Paek. I knew Logan didn't like them either, but then again, most Earth people didn't.

"How long until we're ready for testing the CASTOR system?" I said, hoping a change of topic would distract them. "We've got a galaxy to explore."

"Any time really. We're waiting for you to be cleared medically. We've..." Aurore looked at Logan briefly, then back at me. "We've programmed the test patterns into the navigation system. It's only a matter of hitting the *go* button."

"From a MilSec perspective, I'd like to get things moving again." Hernandez spoke quietly but firmly.

I glanced at the controls. "How about we schedule it in six hours? That gives us long enough to make sure everything's secured—plus I get a few more hours of nano-enhanced recovery. I'm sure we'll all be happier to stop drifting through space and get under way."

"I can't allow that."

I turned to see Sullivan floating by the doorway, holding on to a bulkhead grip. "I thought that might be what you had in mind, Ballen. You're not recovered enough. As your de-facto doctor, I won't let you risk your life for the sake of saving a few days."

"You're fired," I said.

His face reddened, and his eyes jumped around everyone in the room. "What?"

"I'm discharging myself. You have no authority over me."

He stared at me for about two minutes then turned and dived back down the corridor.

"That's not a good idea, Joe." Logan tapped the console in front of him. "We don't need to do this."

"There's a ship out there. Lost or in trouble? We don't know." I pointed at the 3V display showing the star map. "But the longer we delay, the lower the odds of finding them alive."

After a short silence, Aurore said, "We all know their chances of survival are close to zero."

"Maybe. But I'm stubborn." I stared at Logan. "Could you take me to the MedBay? I should rest up until we start the maneuvers."

I didn't need any help, but it seemed like a good way of putting some distance between them. Once I strapped myself to the bed, I gestured for Logan to have a seat. He didn't need one in ZeeGee, but I thought it might help to normalize things a little.

"What's with you and Aurore?"

Logan looked away. "Nothing that requires discussion."

"How long have we been friends? How many times have you saved me?" I said. "You might fool other people but not me."

Logan's mouth twitched. "I seem to remember you doing your fair share of saving."

I waited, not saying anything.

"They're including the Atolls in the talks about space development," he said.

"I can't say I'm thrilled with that prospect, but politically it makes sense."

"You know the history of the Atolls? How they came about?"

I'd heard what everyone had but didn't know what Logan was driving at. "Dafazio made the initial breakthrough, didn't he? Came up with the process of engineered crystallization to grow the Atolls. He was a bit of a crazy—felt the destruction of Earth's biosphere had gone too far and the best hope of survival was to establish colonies in space. He persuaded other scientists to join him, and together they created Fibonacci, the first Atoll. Do I pass?"

Logan grunted. "They called the movement the Ninth Adjustment. He manipulated everyone and everything possible to get his own way. Including us."

If you believed history, Dafazio was a cross between Machiavelli and Satan, with a dash of Rasputin for good measure. When the Atolls were first established, it robbed Earth of some of its smartest people and shackled us for decades, but I didn't understand why it seemed so personal to Logan. "We're from Earth—we were blackballed like everyone else, but the genie is out of the bottle now."

Sadness flooded Logan's face. "Not you and me, Joe. I mean the Nations."

"What?" My head seemed to spin momentarily, and it took several seconds for it to register what Logan meant.

"When Dafazio was setting up the Adjustment, he contacted the Nations. He needed somewhere to operate from, away from the spotlight of publicity. In exchange, we were supposed to get access to his new *World of Hope.*"

I'd never heard of this. Not in all the years I'd known Logan. "What happened?"

"What *always* happens—we got screwed, well and truly." He snorted. "The difference was that this time around, the rest of you got it as well."

I didn't know what to say. The history of Logan's people was a long and shameful testament to brutality and painted an appalling picture of what one group of people can do when they justify it through convenient dehumanization. "So how come I don't know about this?"

The cords on his neck stood out as he spoke through clenched teeth. "We kept it quiet, buried it. Do you think we'd want it to get out that we'd been fooled *again*?"

"I'm truly sorry, Logan." It didn't seem enough. "For all of it."

Logan stood and breathed deeply, his powerful chest swelling. "You know the really stupid thing?"

I couldn't imagine anything that could beat what he'd already said, so I stayed quiet, feeling embarrassed and ashamed.

"When everybody else had to deal with Atoll prejudice, people realized how bad it felt to be treated the way my people had been for centuries, and things actually improved. We were finally all in the same damn boat."

"That explains a lot. But I don't see how they can exclude them from the talks. We'd end up in an interstellar war—and for the most part they'd still have the upper hand. Does Aurore know about this?"

"Perhaps war is inevitable." Logan sighed. "I've never told her. Like I said, it's not something openly discussed. You're probably the only one outside the Nations who knows."

It was an honor in some ways, and I felt humbled that Logan had shared it with me. "Maybe you should."

He looked away. "She shouldn't need me to tell her in order to support me."

I smiled at him. "Which would you rather do—fight with her or explain?"

"When did you become a relationship counselor?"

"Once it was too late."

He nodded and zipped through the door like a fish, leaving me feeling tired, confused, and yet strangely hopeful. For him and Aurore but also for humanity's future in space. With enough of us pulling the same way, could we all end up winning for once? I grunted, cinching the safety strap to stop me floating out of bed and put my head down. Those NanoBiotics must be poisoning my brain's natural store of cynicism.

Chapter Eight

I woke to Sullivan pulling my hand, and he wasn't being gentle. It felt like the flesh under the MediSkin was tearing apart. "You still upset because I wouldn't let you keep playing doctor on me?" I growled, struggling to clear my head.

For all the good the NanoBiotics had done, they hadn't helped my hand. They'd been targeted there, but I'd been kind of hoping some would get lost and find their way. Unfortunately, they were all too dutiful, confining their work to the main injury sites.

"There's no cure for stupidity." Sullivan couldn't stop himself from checking the diagnostic readouts above the bed. "You're in poor shape for high-g tests. I strongly suggest we postpone for another two days *at least*."

"How long until we begin?"

"Has anyone ever told you you're a stubborn bastard?" Sullivan let out a sigh. "First sequence in fifteen."

"Both. Many times." I unfastened the restraints and floated off the bed, orienting myself while gripping a handhold. The truth was I wasn't feeling so good. What sleep I'd gotten seemed to make me feel weaker. "I better get upstairs, and you need to get strapped in."

The bunks in the cabins were multi-purpose and could function as acceleration couches as well as beds. The planned maneuvers weren't high enough to turn people to jelly, but anyone who wasn't restrained would be a perfect guinea pig for impact trauma research.

Logan and Aurore were at their stations when I swam through the door, and a large counter was ticking down on the main display.

"How goes the war?" I said looking from one to the other. They both laughed. "Better, thank you," Aurore said.

I strapped myself into the main piloting seat.

"Room for one more?" Hernandez pulled himself into a spare seat. "I made sure the kiddies were tucked away before I came up."

"You'll be disappointed," I said. "There won't be much to see."

"That's what I told my last girlfriend."

My mouth was as dry as Pinocchio's cremated ashes, and I swallowed a mouthful of coffee. It didn't help much, and my leg started quivering. The on-screen counter dropped to zero. I activated the command sequence for the first tests then opened a ship-wide comm channel. "All hands. Prepare for first maneuver in thirty seconds. Four-g deceleration for ten seconds."

"Starting out gently," Hernandez muttered.

"Ten." I counted off the remaining seconds. "Five. Four. Three. Two. One."

We tumbled, as if we'd clipped an asteroid, so fast that it left my brain lurching. It stabilized briefly and then I was kicked in the spine by an invisible elephant.

"Jesus," Aurore whispered.

"Breathe," I called out. Logan gasped next to me, and I heard a groan from Hernandez.

The pressure continued until I thought the seat would drill through my tailbone. Then as fast as it arrived, it was gone. We tumbled again, in a sickening roll that left my head spinning, but the instruments confirmed the move had returned the ship to its original heading.

Hernandez coughed. "What in bog's name was that?"

"Whirling Dervish maneuver," Aurore said. "Rotates the ship to coincide with the thrust axis so the acceleration couches are always *down*."

"That was deliberate?" Hernandez looked incredulous.

Logan grinned. "Be grateful. Otherwise we'd be thrown against the restraints."

"Remember mama's scrambled eggs? Next maneuver in thirty seconds. Six-g deceleration, twenty seconds." I braced myself as I counted down.

Again, I was hit by a wave of nausea as we spun around, and this time the elephant brought along his vindictive brother for good measure. The pressure sent a stab of pain through my injured shoulders. I grunted at the spasm and fought to control my breathing. The lights in the room seemed to darken, and fireflies danced through my field of vision. When the ship lurched back around, I heard someone retch. I wasn't sure who, as I was busy trying not to do the same.

The next test executed, and I struggled to read the screen, announcing it by sheer force of will. This one was a straightforward acceleration sequence without the sickening lurch as a preliminary, but it still had all the crushing g-force.

After that it was a case of maneuver, recover, repeat. The series took almost an hour to complete, and by the time we'd finished, we were all planning on investing heavily in vomit bag shares. The g-force, it turned out, was just the icing. The real puke inducers were the wild tumbles as the ship switched rotations in all three axes to align the thrust.

I felt like a week-old corpse that had been resurrected for the sole purpose of being kicked to death once more. I rubbed my forehead gingerly, and my hand came away slick with blood. Sullivan had been right—it had been too early to try it. Not that I'd ever admit it to him or anyone else—Ballens are made of sterner, and dumber, stuff.

"Everyone okay?" I struggled to look around.

Logan mumbled something that could have been a yes, and Hernandez was coughing.

"Aurore?" I forced my head around.

"Please don't look at me." She unbuckled her seat straps and seconds later was out the door.

Hernandez triggered the ship-wide comm. "Grant? You guys alive down there?"

There was a delay of several minutes before we heard anything.

"Yeah, we're okay." Grant paused. "Sullivan missed the goddamn barf bag."

I finally managed to check the ship's diagnostic readouts. There were several orange and red lights blinking on the screen. "Time to get cleaned up. Looks like we have some patching to do."

The *Shokasta* hadn't been designed to handle such stresses, so we were pushing the structure beyond its design parameters. Thankfully most of the damage was simple to fix. The CASTOR plumbing had sprung leaks at various points, and the control splicing had shaken itself loose, but we had everything patched up and reinforced within a few hours. Hernandez had his team on clean-up duty after Sullivan's disaster in the crew quarters, so even the sour puke smell was mostly gone.

I met back up with Aurore and Logan, feeling hot and sticky after dragging myself awkwardly from one handhold to another. I needed nerve-tranq but wanted to analyze the test performance first.

"Remind me never to be an Aeromobile passenger with you at the wheel," I said to Aurore. "That was vicious."

She laughed. "Do women drivers scare you?"

I stopped, my lighthearted mood evaporating. "Not until recently."

Logan brought up the test logs on the screen. "Analyzing these might let us tune the maneuvers to put less strain on the ship."

"The ship's doing fine," I said. "It's the crew that needs help."

Aurore ignored my feeble attempt at a joke and got straight to the point. "Now we go to Mars?"

I couldn't see any reason not to and programmed the course into the navigation system, then triggered the ship-wide comm. "Prepare for acceleration and gravity in ten minutes."

"I'm heading back to my bunk to rest up some more. To be honest, I'm glad we can't make more than one-third g at the moment."

"Do you want Sullivan to look in on you?" Aurore said.

"Hell, no. I'm suffering enough already."

I slid out of my chair and headed for the exit before the drive kicked in. Every part of me was raw, and my neck felt like I'd been bench testing a guillotine.

I'd been in bed for fourteen hours, which was a record for

me—at least asleep. I felt better. The NanoBiotics worked their magic on my wounds even while I was unconscious. I stumbled to the control room, but it was empty.

After verifying our position and status, I opened the comm. "I know I'm an acquired taste, but did everybody abandon ship while I was asleep?"

The console beeped a few seconds later, and Logan yawned over the speakers. "It's the middle of the night for most people. See you in three hours."

I realized he was right. My internal clock was messed up from the extra sleep, and after a few minutes of mental thumb-twiddling, I headed to the ship's modest fabrication shop to work on my secret project that I'd whimsically named Project RoboPony.

The shop had a large screen that I could use in private, a definite advantage in the design phase. My testing had uncovered some glitches that I wanted to iron out before we reached Mars. Plus, my original simulation was put together using abstract components, with no thought for actual packaging, and I needed to get it as close to a finished deal as I could for the patent application.

I was engrossed in the project when someone knocked on the door. Instinctively, I closed down the design screen then opened the door to find Logan holding several coffee tubes and breakfast pastries.

"Beware engineers bearing gifts." He thrust one of each into my hands. "What's got you hiding away in here, my friend?"

"I'm working on a top-secret project aimed at easing tensions for lonely spacemen."

"Hate to tell you this, but they came up with that one a few thousand years back."

I squeezed the nipple on the tube of coffee and sucked the warm liquid into my mouth, then tried the "pastry." It tasted like a vanilla-flavored block of congealed grease and sugar, which likely wasn't too far from the truth. "Mmmmm... got to love high-density carbs first thing in the morning."

Logan took a bite and grimaced. "Limited supplies and simple storage."

I washed away the taste with another gulp of coffee. "Sometimes you're too damn logical."

"One of us has to be." Logan gestured at the large screen. "Want to tell me about it?"

"Gift shopping. Wouldn't want to spoil your birthday surprise, would you?"

"I'm well-stocked up on knitted socks." He smiled. "Okay, whenever you're ready. But if you're feeling up to it, we could use some help putting together the SMPTs. We might need them at Deimos. Somehow I can't see the 'Tollers helping us out much, despite their promises."

I threw on a set of light coveralls and gracelessly clambered after Logan as we made our way down to the large payload bay on the underbelly of the *Shokasta*. It was the only area big enough to build the SMPTs in, and it was where they'd launch from anyway. Hernandez and his team were waiting with an assortment of crates, the strip lights running the edge of the external doors casting gloomy shadows in all directions.

"Aurore having a lie in?" I said as Logan clambered down the handholds on the large doors.

"When does that ever happen? She's analyzing our aerobatics performance. She could kill the propulsion if you like."

I should have thought of that. Building these things would be a lot easier in ZeeGee—at least for me and Logan. Hernandez's team would be gophers, passing us what we needed. They were soldiers, not construction people, and we'd work faster without them. The stumbling block? I was the only one authorized to pilot the ship.

"Sorry, I'm not prepared to hand over control just yet."

Logan had his hand near a comm panel and lowered it. "You can't go on like this, Joe. At some point you need to trust someone."

"Yeah… look where that's got me." I was thinking about Dollie more than the ship.

Logan clapped his hand on my shoulder. "How about some construction?"

"Back in a few," I said.

I clambered back upstairs and killed the thrust. Aurore was deep into her figures and only looked up momentarily to say hi.

Minutes later, the gravity bled away, leaving us weightless, and I returned to the payload bay.

I floated into the middle of the room to talk to Hernandez. "If your guys unpack the components and pass them to us, we'll handle the assembly."

Logan drifted over, holding out a tool belt for me. He'd already strapped one on and was ready to go.

"Thanks." I snapped the belt around my waist, spinning slowly. "I should have grabbed one myself."

"Don't worry about it. I've got you covered."

I knew Logan would always be there for me, no matter the circumstances. And I was grateful, but at the same time I resented it. Partly because I didn't like feeling so stupid, but also because I knew I wasn't at the top of my game.

I was slipping on a lot of things. Nothing big or obvious to anyone else, perhaps, but I recognized them, and my brain took note. Each additional clumsiness, each moment of forgetfulness, and every instance where my mind wobbled unsure of what to do next was silently recorded and weighed.

I grabbed the first part to move it into position. Was I losing it? I was probably too young for normal dementia, but maybe all the years in space were starting to hit me. *And then there's the booze,* a voice I didn't want to hear whispered inside my head.

The first job was building the SMPT's spine. This was a wide tube that would eventually contain the propellant and air tanks. With Logan's help, we put it together in short order, leaving us with something that resembled a white composite torpedo.

"Let's string it." I floated to the wall.

Logan moved to the front of the cylinder and attached a temporary fitting to it, then pushed himself toward the wall playing out a thin cord behind him.

I did the same at the other end and tied it off to one of the lifting rings dotted around the bay. After we'd attached a few more lines, the tank assembly was anchored in place, making it easier to bolt on the other parts.

"Looks good, Joe," Logan said. "Let's get the rest done."

Most of the parts were flat-packed for easy transport. Giotto and Hernandez pulled several hull panels from their shipping boxes and pushed one into my hands. Now we were working, I seemed to function okay. I'd even been the one to suggest tethering the assembly to make it easier. That made me feel better, but in the dark recesses of my brain, I clung to the fear that I was starting to break down.

I pushed the panel into place and squirmed around to engage the clips that locked it into position, followed up by tightening the bolts that held it in place. Then it was time for the next one. By the time we'd finished, we had something that resembled an origami pufferfish—ugly would have been a compliment.

The second unit went together faster now that we'd been through the process once. And ninety minutes later, we had the two SMPTs floating in the bay. After that, all we had to do was attach the cradle assemblies to the roof so the pair of unlikely looking craft could be secured.

I looked around. Everyone looked flushed—ZeeGee was always hard work. "Time to open a few cold ones, I'd say."

"I wish." Sullivan wiped his forehead then dried his hand on his coveralls. "We should have packed a few cases of Dogrut Dark."

Dogrut looked like a blend of blood and dog piss, and from what I'd heard had a taste to match. At twenty percent alcohol by volume, it wasn't the strongest beer around, but powerful enough—and rough enough—to make you feel like you'd been rutted by a large dog.

"You'd need to put a few hairs on your chest before drinking that." Grant flashed a grin.

"Dogrut would melt the hairs *off* your chest." Hernandez paused then spoke again in a more serious tone. "Besides, on a long op like this, you could find yourself being plied with liquor and wake up with Giotto taking advantage of you. Then it would be my fault."

"Neck off, Sarge." Giotto skewered Hernandez with a look that could have killed and buried the corpse afterward, but she was obviously holding back her own laughter.

"Grab hold, everyone." I left to switch the drive back on.

Gravity settled back on us like a cloak, and by the time I returned, the levity had vanished. The construction of the SMPTs was a victory, but everyone knew the real job had barely begun.

Chapter Nine

The remaining journey to Mars was thankfully routine, and as soon as the planet was in range, I displayed the image on screens throughout the ship. While we weren't heading for Mars itself, Deimos was only twenty-four thousand kilometers away—essentially the same route until we closed enough to set up an approach to the station.

The original base had been destroyed by the Atolls almost five years ago. The new one was smaller and more automated—Atollers didn't like to get their hands dirty if they could help it. It had the water tanks we needed, though, along with a skeleton crew to watch over operations and traffic. I was back in the shop adding the final touches to my plans when the comm opened up.

It was Aurore. "We've got an incoming message from Deimos Station."

I thumbed the comm button. "Logan is in charge, not me."

"He's seen it." She sighed. "Stop pretending you're the last great hermit, and drag yourself up here."

"I like you too."

I didn't know what message could be that important, but Aurore was right—I wouldn't find out hiding in the shop. I secured the console and met Hernandez climbing up the corridor as I left.

"You on the hook too?" I said. "Must be big if Logan wants us both there."

"Let's hope it's not World War Three."

When we got there Logan and Aurore both looked unhappy. Without a word, Logan brought up a recording, and the screen filled with the face of a junior ADF officer.

"Earth-ship *Shokasta*. This is Atoll Station Deimos. You are directed not to approach this facility."

"What?" I spoke at the same time as Hernandez.

"We have permiss—"

The recording continued, interrupting Hernandez. "You will set a course for the Fardosh-Baird Atoll. Any approach to *this* facility will be considered a hostile act, and steps will be taken to prevent any such attempt. Repeat. Make no attempt to approach Atoll Station Deimos.

"You may contact your Earth superiors to confirm the change in directions, but you will find they are fully aware of the situation. A prisoner is being held for your collection at the Atoll. Message ends."

No one spoke for several minutes. Finally, I took a heavy breath to break the silence.

"Is it genuine?" I said.

"I've sent a confirmation request to Earth." Logan shifted in his seat. "But it'll be at least fifteen minutes until we get a response. Something tells me that it is, though."

"Who could they be holding?" Aurore was sitting close to Logan, almost touching him. "All the way out here?"

"Atolls aren't big on prisoner exchanges," Hernandez said.

If they wanted to exchange a hostage, the High-Rig or the PAC Bengkulu elevator would be easier places. To do it out here had to have some significance. Perhaps they were handing over someone they didn't want their own people to know about.

"Paek?" I whispered.

"No way." Logan stared at me as if I were insane. "He's not an Atoller anymore. They'd be declaring war on the Corporates if they took him prisoner now."

"Think about it." I swallowed hard. "They know we want him. They can't hand him over openly, but maybe he's here visiting family or whatever a good little Atoller does. They grab him and lock him up for us."

Logan came over and patted my shoulder. "I know how much you want to get your hands on him, Joe, and I understand. But they wouldn't give him up before, so why would they now? Even if they could."

I felt their collective stares pressing in on me. "There's only one way to find out."

Eventually Aurore spoke. "What are we going to do if it *is* him?"

My arms and shoulders tightened painfully, and I struggled to breathe. "I'm—"

I stopped, not quite sure what to say. My instinct was to throw him through the nearest airlock. Aurore wouldn't like it—she was a gentle soul. And Hernandez would undoubtedly object. His duty would be to get Paek to the proper authorities. I was unsure about Logan. As much as he disliked the Atolls, I couldn't imagine him being okay with a summary execution. But I suspected he wouldn't try and stop me if I decided that's what I had to do.

The intensity of my feelings surprised and scared me. Was I a psychopath? Fixated on destroying another human being because of some crazy mixed-up notion of revenge? I rolled my head to loosen the knots in my neck. I needed to get away from their stares, far enough to give me time to think.

"I'm going to get coffee. Anybody want anything?"

"I'll help." Aurore jumped up.

"I… No, thanks. I'll be back in ten minutes." I headed for the door and clambered down the passage, bloodless hands tight on the handholds.

Giotto was in the wardroom when I arrived. She was wearing a close-fitting bodysuit, and beads of perspiration glistened on her flushed skin. For a few seconds, I couldn't help but admire her lean form, then I forced my brain back to the subject of the prisoner.

"Hey, Ballen. What's happening?" Giotto pulled out a tube of water, the plastic surface misting as the moisture in the air condensed on its cold surface. "Drink?"

"I'll have a whiskey. Neat."

She grinned. "Me too. But back in the real world, what'll it be?"

"Coffee."

"BRUCE can sure give you a hard workout." She tossed me a tube and wiped her head with the towel she had around her neck. She laughed. "But you know that already, huh?"

"Even the memory hurts."

She nodded, a hint of sadness flitting across her face. "They often do."

I heated the tube and gave her a half-assed salute. "Thanks for the coffee."

"What's your story, Ballen? Why are you such a mess?"

I'd started to leave but turned back. "I thought I was fairly buff."

Giotto snorted, almost coughing up the water she was drinking. "Not even close. You look like you'd fall down and break something if someone sneezed next to you."

I knew she was right. Sitting behind a desk all day isn't conducive to staying in shape. And my off-the-job habits didn't help.

"I saw your report. Said you broke up with your wife. Is that it? Shit happens. You need to move on."

"It's a long and not very interesting story."

Her eyes were a bright blue, contrasting with her olive skin. "I have time."

I thought about staying. It was a long time since I'd sat down and talked conversationally with anyone other than Logan. But I needed to get back upstairs. She was right about my general health, though.

"Can that robot do more than beat the crap out of people?" I said.

"It can run you through a whole calisthenics program if you want."

"Could you set me up a timetable?"

She thought for a few moments. "I'd need to adjust the settings to make it suitable for non-Geneered."

"I can program the changes."

"Uh huh… I think I better take care of that." Giotto's eyebrows lifted. "When do we start?"

"No point delaying the pain," I said. "Give me an hour."

Giotto was looking at me strangely, as though she couldn't figure me out. That wasn't too surprising—I often had the same problem.

When I returned, Logan and the others were still at their

stations.

"We received confirmation from SecOps Central on the prisoner pick-up," he said.

Hernandez shrugged. "Guess we got company coming for dinner."

"Does Central know who it is?" I sipped my coffee.

Logan opened his hands wide. "No idea. And what are we going to do with them, if it's someone who needs to be secured?"

That was a good point. "Are we supposed to take them back to Earth before we leave?"

Hernandez drummed his fingers on the console next to him. "The communication said return isn't a priority."

"Then it can't be Paek, surely?" Aurore looked around. "They wouldn't have us pick *him* up and give him a guided space tour for the next few months."

"Not likely." Logan looked at me. "Joe?"

"It doesn't matter what I think." I moved to the main pilot's chair and sat at the controls. "Time for a course correction."

I brought up the orbital characteristics for the Fardosh-Baird Atoll. It was sitting in a synchronous orbit seventeen-thousand kilometers above the surface of Mars making approach a relatively easy task. The navigation system returned several options, and I selected the most direct. There seemed little point hanging around.

"Crew, stand by for course correction in one minute," I said into the comm then looked around. "Has anyone ever been to an Atoll?"

Aurore and Hernandez shook their heads.

"Other than a few high-ranking diplomats, I don't think anybody has in the last sixty years," Logan said.

The maneuvering thrusters kicked in, turning us onto the right course. "Slick back your hair and polish your buttons. We've got an impression to make."

It took us five hours to hit the Fardosh-Baird outer navigation limit, at which point they demanded we hand over control of the *Shokasta* to their traffic control for berthing. None of us were happy doing that, but we either went along with them or lost the chance to replenish the CASTOR system.

I'd spent an hour in the MilSec training room working on an exercise program. It had been relatively lightweight but enough of a strain to feel it in muscles I'd rather not have remembered. Giotto was surprisingly patient, and I'd enjoyed chatting with her. Every conversation I'd had with Dollie for the last year had ended up in shouting and tears, so for me it was a minor achievement to converse with a woman on a somewhat normal level. After we'd finished, we set up an overall plan that would bring me back to what should have been my baseline healthy fitness level and scheduled so it didn't interfere with the team's training.

"I'm gonna hit the shower," I said. "Thanks for the sweat session."

Giotto gave a twisted grin and raised an eyebrow. "You need it. Let me know if you want company."

I wasn't sure how to take her comment. "I'm sure I'll manage now the routine is programmed, but I'll give you a shout if I do."

She seemed about to laugh but held it back, probably to be polite about the sorry state of my fitness. I went to get cleaned up, then headed back to the control room.

"Anything new?" I said. Hernandez had left but the others were there.

"Only that the closer we get, the less I want to be here," said Logan.

"You and me both." I slid into the main pilot's seat and checked the range to the Atoll on the display. "If we give up on replenishing the CASTOR tanks, we could scoot right past them and head to deep space."

"I'm tempted," Logan said. "But I don't want to risk it. The only thing you need in an emergency is whatever you don't have."

"Plus we couldn't pick up the prisoner," Aurore pointed out.

"I could live with that," Logan said. He was peering at the distant Atoll on the screen. "It'll make things more complicated."

He was right, but I was clinging to the idea that they were handing over Paek. And if that was the case, I'd have happily traded the *Shokasta*, down to the last fastener.

"I don't think I ever realized how big they are," I said. Even at a distance, the Atoll was immense. Outside of the main hub, which was two-thousand meters across, the main spokes pushed outward. There were five spokes made up of two main sections each and cross-connected with smaller thruways. The readouts showed each of the main sections was over ten kilometers in diameter and over twenty-five kilometers long. All we could see was the pale gray outer skin, but inside each was a giant O'Neill cylinder forming a multi-level habitable area of almost twenty-thousand square kilometers. I did the math in my head—the Atoll had a total surface area larger than New York state, and about the same size of the old British United Kingdom before it was torn apart by the Euro-schism war. It wasn't purely chance that the Atolls had dominated us for so long.

I spotted an Atoll cruiser docked at another of the outer ports. We had no information on what ship it was, but the last time I'd had a run-in with one of those, things had gotten more than a little hairy.

"Do I hand over control?" I turned to Logan. It was his call, and he nodded.

"Hope we don't regret this," he said.

I felt much the same way as I transferred guidance to their control. "Stand by for remote piloting everyone. Stay secure until otherwise informed."

The main engines died almost instantly then triggered again in short bursts, bringing us parallel with the long face of one of the large cylinders. It wasn't immediately clear, but they'd have to bring us in somewhere on the central hub as that was the only place to easily dock. As we approached, the Atoll filled the display, its size became even more apparent. I switched the view onto the ship-wide screens so everybody could watch.

As we closed, it seemed as though the remote pilot became increasingly confident in handling the ship and the movement smoothed out as we picked up speed once more. The front of the main hub filled the screen, and what had seemed like a solid gray surface from a distance broke up into geometric patterns that looked like an impossibly solid example of fractal geometry swirling down to microscopic levels.

The slab wall was getting near, and I started sweating. I hoped they realized how big *Shokasta* was. We might have been small next to the Atoll, but we weren't a mosquito to an elephant, even if that was how it felt at that moment.

We slid upward, and an area of Atoll hull peeled apart to form an entrance. It was a neat trick because the sections vanished into the rest of the wall as though they'd never been there. I was still trying to figure out how they'd done it when we edged through the opening into the red-lit interior.

It was hard to judge the size of the chamber precisely. The instruments told me the nearest side was five-hundred meters away. The docking bay was large enough to swallow one of their cruisers whole—a sobering thought.

Using the smallest of blasts with the thrusters Atoll Control brought us close to one edge of the bay. I switched pickups to see a mundane docking tube extending out toward us. To be honest, I was half-expecting a weird alien device, and I was reassured seeing something familiar.

The ship reverberated as the tube attached to our airlock and the controls locked in place. The comm system trilled, and a young-looking man in a pale green uniform stared at us. He didn't have that "ideal human" appearance the Atollers typically presented. For one thing, his ears stuck out like a pair of radar dishes, and his chin formed a weak bony point underneath a thick black mustache. Despite that, he looked at us as though we were something he'd unfortunately stepped in.

"I am Lieutenant Kartar Norline of Fardosh Baird Traffic Control. In a few moments, we will unlock the connection between your ship and the station. We will permit only two people to come onboard, one of which must be Joe Ballen. These individuals will undergo a level three decontamination process, during which all clothing must be removed. They will not be returned. No space suits will be needed and will trigger alarms if worn.

"After decon is complete, the individuals will enter the transport tube adjacent to the processing chamber, which will take them to the exchange area. Under no circumstances are these individuals permitted to enter any other part of the Atoll. Is that understood?"

I triggered the comm channel. "This is Joe Ballen. Your instructions have been received and understood. Myself and

another person will be at the airlock in approximately five minutes."
I switched off and looked at Logan. "Who's the lucky one?"

He drummed his fingers on his armrest. "The engineer in me would love to see inside that floating country, but if there's a prisoner involved, you need to take someone from the MilSec team."

Aurore nodded. a gesture that seemed to say "no way is my husband putting himself into the clutches of those Atollers."

Logan activated the comms to Hernandez. "You heard that, Sergeant? Who do you want to send?"

There was only the slightest delay. "I'll send myself. Diplomacy isn't a strong point with these apes of mine."

Jeers and grumbles sounded in the background.

I unfastened my harness and pushed toward the exit. "Meet you at the airlock."

I was putting on a one-piece coverall when Hernandez came in, his usual cheery demeanor absent. He stowed his uniform in a locker and pulled on some slacks and a t-shirt, barely acknowledging my presence.

"Did your pet snail die?" I had no shoes I cared to lose, so pulled on some disposable StickySox. They were designed to go over a set of space boots and fit like long johns on a flea, but some tape took care of that.

"Why no suits?" Hernandez pointed at my feet. "You got some of those for me?"

I opened a storage locker, pulled out a fresh pair of socks, and handed them to him. "No suits is safer—for them."

"'Tollers. After everything, they're still treating us like filthy animals." He followed my example and taped the socks. "Sullivan told me they'll incinerate everything we're wearing and disinfect every room after we leave."

I'd heard of the procedure and didn't like the taste of it anymore than Hernandez, but I understood why they did it. "Hard to believe, but it's not entirely racist. Their environments are cleaner than ours, so they have lower resistance to disease. Plus, some of the dangers on Earth weren't around when their ancestors abandoned the planet. Our bacteria adapted as the climate changed."

"You're defending them after what happened to you? They're a bunch of arrogant bastards that need bringing down several notches." Hernandez pulled a pistol from his uniform and slipped it into his pocket.

"I'm not defending them. But I understand some of their motivations, and they're not all the same." I took a breath. "You better leave the gun here."

"No way." He tapped his chest. "I'm MilSec—no matter what they want to think of us—my job is protection"

I'd not seen him belligerent before—the Atolls sure brought out the best in people—and although I sympathized to an extent, I wasn't stupid. "They won't let you keep it."

"We'll see about that."

I shrugged and handed him a comm-set. I didn't care what he did, as long as he didn't take me with him.

The outer lock beeped, and the indicator light turned green, confirming there was a breathable atmosphere outside. I thumbed the comm button. "Logan, unlock the hatch. We're ready to move out."

"Watch yourself, Joe."

The safety disengaged, and I pressed the button to open the door. Outside, a familiar corrugated tube led into the distance, the lines of hand-loops providing an almost dizzying perspective. We couldn't see outside the tube, but the inside was well lit. I knew there was gravity on Atolls, at least in the habitation cylinders, but here in the central hub, we were weightless. I reached up to grab the first loop, pulling myself out and into the tube, moving forward by batting the loops with my hands.

"Try to keep it smooth," I called over the radio to Hernandez. "It's less tiring that way."

His reply was nothing but a grunt, and I glanced behind to check on him. He was pulling himself hand over hand using the right technique but obviously lacking experience. Even in the short time we'd been underway, he was over fifty meters behind me.

I could see the far end now, the round airlock door lit up with a circle of white lights. I continued, eager to leave the tube but also reluctant to find out what was waiting for us.

"Wait up, Ballen," Hernandez called. "I can't move that fast."

He'd fallen farther back. I didn't want to waste my forward

momentum by stopping. It would make it harder to get going again, but I couldn't leave him to struggle. I grabbed the next loop firmly, holding tight as my momentum tried to push me around and curve me into the sidewall.

It took several minutes for Hernandez to catch up. His face was flushed, and he was grimacing. I grabbed him and guided him to a halt. "Take a break, or you'll have a heart attack before you get there."

After a short break, we set off again, with me bringing up the rear so as not to outpace him. His confidence improved the farther we went, and soon we were at the entrance to the Atoll airlock. It was open, and we squirmed in.

When I closed the outer door, a shrill warbling filled the small airlock, so piercing it made it difficult to think. An artificial voice sounded, almost inaudible against the alarm.

"Illegal weaponry detected. Remove and deposit in compartment B or this chamber will be sterilized. You have sixty standard seconds to comply."

I gave Hernandez an I-told-you-so look that he ignored, but at least he pulled the pistol out of his pocket and placed it in the compartment.

"Think I'll get it back?" he said.

"I hope it's not an heirloom."

The inner door opened, allowing us access to a larger cylindrical room. On one wall was a chute marked "Disposal," and the floor had several red circles painted on it, each about sixty centimeters in diameter. They didn't look decorative.

The voice sounded again. "Remove all clothing and place in the disposal chute then stand in the decontamination spots with arms outstretched. A small screen lit up showing a yellow glowing silhouette to indicate the required position. We did as requested. The sooner this was over the better.

"Stand by for decontamination."

The lights switched from dull to a painful blue-white, and a liquid hit us from all sides. My skin burned intensely for several minutes, and I almost choked on the acrid chlorine-like smell. Another spray blasted us, then the lights returned to normal. I felt like I'd lost several layers of skin, which might not have been far from the truth.

"Now I know what a microwaved chicken dinner feels like," I said.

A panel opened, and I looked inside. I pulled out a one-piece garment with a zipper and hood—the sort of thing you might wear in a clean room environment. The material rustled like dry leaves and felt papery, though I doubted there were any trees involved.

Hernandez frowned. "A necking onesie?"

"You'd rather be naked?"

He muttered a reply that I didn't catch, but I could take a guess. I pulled on my new sartorial statement, and the faceless voice spoke again.

"Cover your heads before proceeding."

My head was shaved as usual, so that seemed pointless. Hernandez on the other hand had a short wiry regulation cut.

"If you're worried about lice," I called out, "we only keep them as pets these days."

"Cover your heads before proceeding."

"I don't want to find there's an actual person behind that voice," Hernandez said. "I might be tempted to tear their arms off."

His Geneered body barely fit the suit when he zipped it up, and it was tight enough to be embarrassing. He'd probably have felt less exposed if he *had* been wearing nothing. He pulled the hood up, looking a bit like an unfinished superhero cartoon.

The door at the other end of the decontamination chamber opened, and we received another instruction.

"Enter the travel tube."

We stepped into a cylindrical elevator car about five meters long with bench seats on both sides. I sat down and found a lap belt that I snugged tight. Hernandez did the same, and the car accelerated at high speed, throwing us sideways. At one point, I felt a strange twisting sensation then the car slowed. When it stopped, we were in a gravity field—the car must have taken us inside one of the Atoll's arms.

The door reopened, and we walked out. It felt like we were in one-g, but I couldn't be sure without doing tests. It was enough to be tiring after the lower force we were used to on the *Shokasta*. We were in a mid-size room that appeared to be a regular office. A large window dominated the far wall showing the surface of Mars far below us, but it must have been a view screen. Not even the Atolls would be crazy enough to put such a large window in a space station.

Hernandez walked toward the screen. "Look at that." He was almost whispering. "Hard to believe people died to keep the Atolls from taking over that desert."

A large desk filled the area by the window with one seat behind it. Other than that, the room was a featureless light blue box without even a hint of decoration. The floor was unusual—it looked like marble tile but almost certainly wasn't. I wanted to take a closer look, but a click alerted us to someone entering.

I turned around, and for a second, I couldn't think of a thing to say.

"Hello, Joe. It's good to see you again."

Her voice was warm and low, and her silver rough-cut hair was all too familiar. Finally I recovered my wits. "McDole?"

Chapter Ten

McDole smiled and sat in the sole chair. "I'm pleased you remember me, Joe."

"Given the circumstances, it would be hard to forget."

A frown touched her lips. "An unfortunate experience. I'm sorry about what happened—then and later."

If it had been anyone else, I'd have walked out. But I knew McDole well enough to understand it was her cultural reticence that kept her words in check rather than any support for Paek. After everything had unfolded, she'd advocated unsuccessfully with the Atoll Archipelago Directorate for him to be handed over.

"You know this… lady?" Hernandez looked at me as though I'd grown a second head. No doubt he expected me to be hostile to all Atollers.

"Commander McDole, this is Sergeant Hernandez, our MilSec representative on this trip."

"Hello, Sergeant. I see you've recovered." McDole pointed at his leg.

Hernandez whistled. "You people sure keep tabs on us, huh?" He laughed and pointed down. "Broken leg. Climbing accident."

"Two years ago, wasn't it?" McDole placed a DataPad on the table.

"This might be a wild guess, but I'm betting you're not our prisoner." I felt awkward standing there, as though I'd been dragged into the principal's office. "Is that the *Goeppert* docked outside?"

She nodded. "I'm still in command of her—just about. We'll get to the matter of the detainee in a while. First, let me apologize for the atrocious cleansing process you've been put through. I assure you it wasn't my choice. The residents of Fardosh-Baird are rather irrational when it comes to matters of hygiene."

She reached down and produced a dark green bottle and a set of glasses. "I remember you enjoyed the Jacobson-Niller, so I'm sure you'll appreciate this. It's a Cabernet Sauvignon from Vin Lustrous on Euler—very palatable with excellent notes of cloves and cinnamon."

McDole poured three glasses and pushed two toward us, lifting the third and sipping from it.

The aroma of fruity alcohol made me salivate. I could cheerfully have guzzled the whole bottle. Not because it smelled delicious, though that was part of it. It was more a self-destructive siren call. Part of my brain wanted—no, needed—the release it knew alcohol could provide. But I didn't touch my glass.

Hernandez was clearly having no such problems. "That's good. Strong finish."

"Surely you're not suspicious, Joe?" The light from McDole's glass created a flickering reflection in her eyes.

"This visit is strictly business." I leaned over the table. "So, how about the prisoner?"

"You've surprised me again, Joe." She took another drink. "We have a USP citizen who has been our *guest* for several years. We'd like to return him to his people, where he belongs."

Hernandez carried on sipping dreamily on the wine, not paying much attention to what was being said.

"That's very enlightened," I said. "What's it going to cost us?"

McDole laughed. "You're always so practical, Joe. That's one of the things I like about you."

"So how about being nice and telling me who the prisoner is—and what you want in return?"

"Easy, Ballen." Hernandez seemed to come out of his daydream. "There's no need for so much hostility." His response was markedly different to his anti-Atoll comments on the way over.

"Do you love the Atollers, Sergeant?"

"Sure do—they serve good booze."

I lifted his glass and sniffed. I couldn't detect anything, but the shift in personality was too much to ignore. "A psychoactive drug in the wine? Are you crazy?"

McDole showed no signs of embarrassment. "Painted on the inside of the glass. Undetectable."

"Mine too?"

She shook her head. "No. Don't worry, it's harmless. In about an hour, he'll be his usual self and won't remember much of this. I wanted him *placid* for a while, so I could talk to you privately. And I knew you wouldn't be allowed to come here without an escort."

"This is a lot of intrigue if all you want to do is hand over a lost tourist."

McDole's smile faltered. "I told you once before. Sometimes I have orders I don't necessarily like. And now my position is... less certain than it was before."

Hernandez had been wandering around the room like a lost puppy, and now he slumped in a corner. He wasn't unconscious but looked dazed.

"Okay. Make it quick."

McDole nodded. "There are many in our community who feel I was too lenient with you. I was supposed to get the Ananta's secrets and destroy your ship, not make a deal to share everything. I also pushed to have Paek handed over for trial at a USP court, so that counted against me too. Now I'm in charge of Atoll Expansion Projects, taking Atoller culture to other solar systems, but the truth is my star is no longer ascending. Most of the senior military would prefer it if I vanished into the depths of space."

"Nobody asked you to do that."

"I'm not looking for sympathy. I did what I thought was right and still believe we should work closer with Earthers." She broke off to sip her wine again. "You heard about Wright Atoll?"

"The rumors that it's been destroyed—yes." I wondered again if my glass had been laced with the psychoactive drug, but I wasn't about to test it. "I hope it's not true. I understand there weren't only Atollers onboard."

"The station was lost, along with all the personnel. We've tried to limit who has the details, but the news slipped out."

"Doesn't sound like the usual Atoll efficiency. Aren't you the space *experts?*"

"Sniping isn't worthy of you, Joe. The reports show that the Atoll research facility suffered a catastrophic failure. Cause unknown. Apparently no warning."

There were any number of reasons I could think of for a failure in space, but given the Atolls' experience, none of them seemed likely. "So what do you want from me? Something tells me you're not interested in my engineering skills, and I turned in my hero outfit at the end of the last *Shokasta* mission."

"I can't tell you everything. But our government has issued orders to inspect all our facilities as soon as possible." McDole stood and moved closer. "We have ships checking on our other stations, but we haven't got a Jump-capable ship available for the Geller Gateway Station at Sirius."

Geller was possibly the smallest of the Atoll research stations. They were studying the binary star and its chaotic system.

"Sirius is our first Jump. If you want us to check in on them, I'll be happy to suggest that."

She hesitated long enough for me to realize she was struggling with what to say next.

"Does it strike you as odd that one of the USP's newest JumpShips has gone missing at almost exactly the same time we lose a station?"

"Possibly." I glanced across at Hernandez, who was busy drooling into his paper coverall. "But they were in vastly different regions of space."

"What if I told you that Wright Atoll is our first such loss"—she raised her glass to her lips—"in the hundred or so years since the first Atoll was established."

That did seem odd. "The only coincidence an engineer believes in is when two points have the same coordinates."

Her smile was weak. "I'd like to go with you. To verify that our station is okay."

I'd have been less surprised if she'd unzipped her skin and turned into a lizard creature. "We could be gone several months."

"I'm not expecting a chauffeur service."

"You alone?"

"If I requested passage for more people, you'd see that as a threat."

I wasn't sure Logan would go for it. "It's not my call. I'm only the pilot on this mission."

"I doubt that but—" She put her glass down and looked at Hernandez in the corner. "Him?"

I shook my head. "I'm sure you remember Logan Twofeathers."

"The rather annoying man from 548-Kressida... interesting."

"I'll need to speak to him. Privately."

McDole nodded. "I'll arrange for the detainee to be brought in while you call."

"You seem confident he'll agree."

"You're very persuasive when you try to be." She paused. "Also, if something is working against the USP and the Atolls, doesn't it make sense to have representatives from both onboard?"

She turned and headed toward the door at the far end of the room. "Say what you want, Joe, and it will be made available."

I waited until she was gone and then spoke out loud, feeling a little stupid. "I'd like a comm channel to my ship."

A soft tone sounded, then a hidden display screen lit up on the wall as though a section of the bulkhead had simply dissolved.

"Joe?" Logan's face appeared on screen. "You okay?"

"I haven't got the prisoner yet, but something else has come up." The view tracked with his face as he sat down. "That doesn't sound promising."

"They want something in exchange." I couldn't think of any way of dressing it up. "Passage for one of their people."

Logan rubbed his jaw. "Why would we go along with that?"

"It's a pre-requisite for getting the prisoner back. And McDole thinks we might be better working together on this one."

"McDole from the *Goeppert*?" Logan pulled back from the camera pick-up. "That's hard to believe."

"She's running their deep space operations. The loss of Wright Station has got the Atolls spooked, it seems."

"What does the sergeant think about it?"

I looked over. Hernandez was playing with his lips and making burbling sounds. "He thinks Atoll wine is excellent."

Logan's eyes widened. "I'm sure you'll explain that to me later. Presumably you think this is a good idea or you wouldn't be asking."

"I think we might need all the allies we can find on this one.

117

And if nothing else, it would be a good move politically."

He snorted. "You don't give a damn about politics."

"I know."

Logan looked away. I could see he was talking to someone off-screen, and I guessed it was Aurore. He must have muted his transmission, as whatever he was saying, I couldn't hear any of it. Then he turned back.

"Okay. Let's do this." He said. "But McDole only, no one else."

"I told her that." I wondered what might be behind all of this and remembered Gabriella's cryptic warning—was there some connection here? What the hell had she meant? From past experience, the only transformation she was expert in was turning live people into dead ones. "We'll be heading back shortly."

"Okay." Logan reached for the disconnect button but hesitated. "And don't forget that prisoner."

The screen went dark, and several minutes later, McDole returned carrying a large tote bag in one hand and a backpack over her shoulder.

"You really *were* confident."

"I believe in being prepared." Her smile was less forced than earlier. "It should be quite an adventure."

"I hope you don't have any weapons."

"Want to frisk me?" She laughed. "I'm not stupid."

"And the prisoner?"

"Bring the detainee in," she said, raising her voice a little.

Two Atoll soldiers entered, leading a man between them. He was bald with a thick gray beard, but I couldn't see his face because his head was tipped down. It wasn't Paek, though. When the trio stopped, the prisoner looked up, his dark eyes full of confusion, which turned to hatred when he saw me.

"Joe Ballen?" he snarled. "I should kill you."

I'd heard that voice over many years when I'd been driving cabs. But it was impossible.

It was Charlie.

His escort stayed close to him, hopefully ready for any hostile moves. The last time I'd seen him was over three years ago, but I recognized him even through the mop of beard. He was wearing the same disposable clothing we were, but his onesie was grimier, as though he'd had it on for quite a while.

"What the hell is this?" I said to McDole then looked back to him. "Charlie's dead."

Charlie lunged forward, and the guards grabbed him none too gently. "You're right, you bastard. And you got him killed."

My mind was tying itself in knots trying to understand what was going on. I'd start a train of thought, but as soon as I came back to Charlie, it would screech to a halt and begin again. He'd been killed by Gabriella's men on Long Island when we'd discovered Harmon's secret hideout. After about the twentieth time of chasing this thought around, it hit me.

"You're *Dan?*"

Dan was Charlie's twin, which didn't make much sense either. Dan had been killed the same day, when the Atolls attacked the original Deimos base.

"Got it in one, you necker. Nobody cared whether old Dan was still alive, did they? Just another forgotten casualty like my brother."

I stepped closer. "But he wasn't forgotten. By me or any of his friends."

"Yeah, right." Dan tensed up, and I thought he was going to try jump me, but he backed off when the guards moved closer.

"What the hell...?" Hernandez was coming out of his daze, struggling to his feet. "Is this... the prisoner?"

McDole nodded. "Daniel Anderson, sole survivor of the Deimos Base incident."

"Incident?" My shoulders tightened. I suppose that was one way of putting it—another way would be the mass slaughter of civilians.

"He's a USP citizen." Henderson was unsteady and wobbled a little as he stood there.

I whispered to McDole, "Did you know about him?"

"Only when I arrived on Fardosh-Baird. The information wasn't widely distributed."

"Grab your gear, citizen. We're leaving." Hernandez's voice was loud enough to echo.

I didn't think it was smart to take along someone as openly

hostile as Dan, but I felt guilty about him. Partly because he'd been locked up for so long, but mostly because Charlie had been killed helping me, so Dan's accusation wasn't far from the mark. What had they been doing to him all this time? Maybe that was why he was so angry. Or perhaps all I was doing was justifying his attitude because he looked like his brother.

"You can leave him here if you like." McDole gestured at Dan. "He'll be quite safe until we return."

I was tempted but didn't know what I'd say to Logan.

"Hey, no." Dan seemed to shrink in size. "You can't leave me with the 'Tollers. They ain't—"

"He's a USP citizen," Hernandez repeated. "Of course he's coming with us."

Dan seemed surprised by this unexpected support. "Yeah, sure. I'm a citizen. I have my rights."

I was less happy with the idea of having Dan onboard than I was with taking along McDole. At least with her, I wouldn't be worrying I'd wake up with a knife in my chest. I couldn't say the same for Dan. Despite that, I realized I couldn't abandon him.

"What's it to be? Come with us and you might not get back to Earth for a year—or not at all, depending what we find. You might live longer if you stay."

Dan glanced at the guards. "Anything's better than being here. Besides, I've lived long enough."

I nodded. "Got any gear?"

Dan snorted. "What you see is what you get."

"What about the resupply?" I asked McDole.

"I ordered it when I left to bring the pris— I mean, Dan. It should be in-progress right now."

"Okay. Let's move."

We entered the transit car. McDole sat on the same bench seat as me, closer than she needed to. Dan was on the opposite side with the somewhat doped-out Hernandez. Dan's eyes never left me, even when the car moved.

Fifteen minutes later, we crossed through the docking tube to the *Shokasta*. As we swung across, McDole moved closer and spoke to me in a low voice.

"Thank you, Joe."

"For what? I told you—Logan is in charge."

"I'm sure he wouldn't have allowed it if you'd been against it."

"Your thanks might be premature. Like I said to Cha—I mean *Dan*—you might live longer if you stay here."

"Possibly. Perhaps you could make it up to me personally."

I snatched a glance at her over my shoulder and banged my head into the airlock door. "What do you mean?"

The door opened and she slid past me, brushing her hand across my arm. "Oh, nothing too unpleasant... Dinner, perhaps?"

She obviously had no idea about the disgusting state of our rations. I wondered briefly about warning her, then a cruel streak in me surfaced—she'd find out soon enough. "Welcome to the *Shokasta*."

Chapter Eleven

The inner door opened, and I showed Dan and McDole to empty quarters. We had plenty of room, though I was concerned about the state of our supplies. More people meant more mouths to feed, and with two new additions, we'd be stretching our resources close to the limit. While we might be able to supplement our stores at the few stations on our planned route, those facilities and options rapidly diminished the farther out we went.

When I let Dan into a cabin, he looked around, as if measuring every millimeter. He didn't say a word, so I couldn't tell whether this was an improvement on his situation on the Atolls or not.

"There are a few ship suits in the supplies. Take a look below bulkhead thirty." I tugged at the paper clothing I was wearing. "Not much, but better than these things."

He nodded, looking like a hamster that had been given a new cage. "The *Shokasta*, huh? Read about her. Hardly seems possible Earth has JumpShips now."

"Ask if you need anything. It's share and share alike here."

McDole followed me along the corridor, handling the ZeeGee with ease. The next couple of rooms were BRUCE's quarters, and I moved by, assuming she'd be happier with a buffer between her and Dan anyway.

"Okay, you can take this one." I slid open the door.

"Thank you." She wedged her bags under the small computer console. "This will be fine."

"I'd better check in with Logan. As I said to Dan, shout if you need anything."

"You have more unused cabins?"

Did she want more space for herself? We'd done it for the exercise room, but I couldn't see us providing her with a luxury suite. "The rest of the rooms up to bulkhead eight are unoccupied. What's on your mind?"

"I'd like to make use of several of them. Is that okay?"

"This isn't a space cruise."

McDole smiled. "I thought it might be prudent to have some supplies delivered. I doubt you're provisioned for extra people. If there's a better place to store them, let me know."

"Make whatever arrangements you need. I have some piloting to do." I moved along the corridor. What she said made perfect sense, but why didn't she say that instead of making me second guess her motives?

After taking the supplies onboard, we headed toward open space. Atoll traffic control managed our departure until we were a thousand kilometers away, but once they released us, I programmed a course at full acceleration. Even at our best speed, it would take a couple of days of cruising until we were one A.U. clear of the planet and at the cautionary safe distance.

On the way, I worked on the documentation for Project RoboPony, so I could send it to Earth before the first Jump. As soon as I finished, I went to set up the transmission.

"You going to share your mystery project or leave us in suspense?" Logan stood next to Aurore while she double-checked the Jump I'd plotted. "Don't you trust your friends?"

I laughed. "I *have* been a little close-mouthed."

"Exactly, and your bluster is almost legendary," Aurore said. "You've had Logan so wound up, I wondered if he was more interested in you than me."

"Right... and on that day, they'll declare world peace." I opened my files on the large display volume.

"Is this a private party?" McDole climbed up from the corridor to the lower decks. "I came to discuss strategy, but I'll leave if you want."

There wasn't much point. What I was doing wasn't meant to be secret, and Fardosh-Baird would pick up and undoubtedly decrypt my transmission before it reached Earth. "Stay. This will affect the Atolls too."

Logan came over. "Interesting. And even more intriguing. What have you got, my friend?"

I opened the first 3-D schematic from my submission. It showed a sphere three meters across, unimpressive at first glance.

Logan laughed. "You're bringing disco lighting to space?"

"Have faith." I hit the controls to show an animation of the sphere opening and each of its components moving away from the main structure, while displaying the subsystem notes. One by one, the simulated parts moved off screen as the layers were peeled back.

"That's a fast pulse communication block," Logan said, as a component drifted away.

"There's a high-precision positioning array there," Aurore said. "Some type of navigation buoy?"

"An adaptive frequency laser generator?" McDole read off another of the components. "I hope you're not going into the weapons design business, Joe."

"We already have more than enough of those," I said.

The last layers peeled away, leaving a smaller sphere and a squared off box wrapped around one side of it.

"That's a Casimir generator." Aurore pointed to the display. "What *is* this thing?"

"What's the biggest challenge facing us *out there* at the moment?"

"Ships?" McDole said.

"We can build more," I said. "Try again."

"Searching for habitable planets." Logan looked expectant.

I shook my head. "We'll find them in time."

"Oh, jeez..." Aurore's eyes were wide. "This thing is a communications relay!"

I gave her a round of applause. "We have a winner."

"Excellent. What's my prize?" Aurore said.

I moved closer to the display screen. "How about a deep-space cruise to the stars?"

Aurore laughed. "I don't think my husband would approve."

"I won't tell him if you don't." I opened another file showing a simulation of the expected use. "We program the relays to Jump back and forth between two systems. Each one has a built-in communications array triggered by a general code. When it detects a suitably tagged transmission, it records it, then after Jumping to its target system it re-transmits it using the same code."

"Unbelievable, yet so simple," Logan said. "They Jump between different stars and give you an interstellar messaging system."

"The selected Casimir generator is small. By my calculations, it can make a Jump about every two hours. Not perfect and far from instantaneous."

"But communication time would be cut dramatically." McDole raised an eyebrow. "That's very impressive."

"Why use standard components?" Logan said. "A custom design would give you a greater hold on the technology."

I shrugged. "I'm registering a patent on it, but I know the design will be bootlegged almost immediately. Custom design would give me greater intellectual property rights, but I want this thing used. And let's face it, neither the PAC"—I looked at McDole—"or the Atolls are very good at recognizing anyone's copyright except their own."

I triggered the transmission and an acknowledgment appeared on screen. "That's it—Project RoboPony is almost official."

"Would this support encrypted channels?" Logan pointed at the screen.

"The Jump kills quantum entanglement, so you'd have to use classical encryption methods, but those are all vulnerable. Anyway... maybe we need more openness. There's been too much deception."

"There may be ways." McDole furrowed her brow. "Sorry, I tend to think of things from a military perspective. It's a remarkable idea, and I'd feel a lot more confident on our current journey if we had them in place now."

The transmission status changed to completed, and I felt a small sense of achievement. "I wish I could offer a toast, but coffee is the strongest drink we have."

I made my excuses and headed back to my room. I felt pleased but also strangely despondent. It was something I'd felt before at the end of a project—a relief that it was finished mixed with a sense of "what now?" This time around, the sense of loss seemed greater than normal, and I wanted to be away from people for a while—I wasn't good at faking amiability.

Sometime later, I heard a knock on the door. McDole was outside, wearing a white patterned kaftan-like garment that was simultaneously floaty and yet seemed to cling to her curves.

"I came to make good on that dinner invite," she said.

"I don't recall making one."

"That's why I thought I should."

She was partly inside the room, stopping me from closing the door, and I got the impression that she wasn't about to make it easy on me. "Okay, give me a minute. The wardroom is that way." I gestured with my thumb.

"My cabin would be more comfortable." Her lips curved into a smile. "And I have something prepared."

I sighed. Sometimes you just have to make it clear. "I'm not interested in company right now."

"Indulge me."

McDole had reprogrammed the lighting in her room into something less harsh than the usual efficient-but-clinical setting. It made it more intimate and somehow cozier than usual. McDole brought out two meal packs. They were steaming, indicating that she'd already put them through a heating unit.

The bed was tucked away, and the table was open with a chair on either side, meaning she'd borrowed one from another cabin. She peeled open the packs, and the room was flooded with the delicious aroma of something spicy. I was certain it wasn't from our stores, and my mouth began watering in an uncontrollable Pavlovian response.

I examined the mixture of yellowed rice and what looked like chicken. Most Atollers were vegan, so I doubted it was real. There were also small pieces of assorted vegetables and what looked like plump raisins stirred in with the rest.

"That looks amazing," I said.

"Wine?" She reached into a drawer and pulled out a plastic bottle.

I eyed it suspiciously. "Help me out here. Are you planning on drugging me or seducing me?"

"How about both?" Her voice was low and sensual as she poured two glasses of wine.

"I've never seen you out of uniform before." I tried to change the subject, feeling a flush reach my ears.

"Do you think it looks good on me?"

"You don't need me to tell you that." I tasted the food and almost fell in love. The dish had a heavenly combination of cumin and turmeric, giving it an Eastern flavor.

"I don't, but it would be nice." She took a bite and washed it down with a sip of wine. "You're rather impressive... for an Earthman."

"Thanks for the qualification. I think."

"We're so culturally conditioned to dismiss Earthers. It makes it difficult to see around that to get to the truth."

I took another mouthful of the delicious food, avoiding the wine. "So, you're all brain-washed by propaganda?"

McDole laughed. "You might see it that way. I think it's more that a culture finds certain things acceptable and society tends to reinforce those ideas. We don't undergo mass indoctrination sessions."

"Okay, so it's *only* unconscious bias?"

"Stop trying so hard to be unpleasant, Joe." She leaned forward. "We're friends, aren't we? I'm pointing out that *all* cultures have ways of looking at things that aren't always rational."

"True—but Atoll biases kill Earth people."

She pulled back, her face hardening momentarily. "Would Earth hold back from doing the same in reverse if they had the opportunity? I seem to recall you attacked the *Bethe*..."

"That's a strangely selective memory. We *defended* ourselves when the *Bethe* tried to illegally board a USP vessel."

McDole's face softened. "Let's not fight. Mistakes have been made on both sides, haven't they?"

It was true, and it was impossible to assign blame. The Atolls had dominated and embargoed Earth for decades, but they'd not left the planet without reason. "This trip is too long to make enemies, but I'll never stop fighting for a fair chance for *all* humans."

She lifted her glass in a toast. "I know that, Joe. And that's another thing I like about you. When you say *all* humans, I know you mean it. There's a way you could do more, though."

I finished my food and put my fork down. "How's that?"

"Join us. Help push for that inside Atoll society. Show us how we're wrong to hate and fear Earthers—isn't that what you want?"

I laughed. "That would be a great suggestion, if Atolls allowed *scroffers* to become citizens, but they haven't for almost a hundred years."

"That's true..." McDole leaned close again. "Unless you conjoin with a citizen."

Her breath was warm against my face. "You're asking me to marry you?"

"Why not? It's happened before."

But not for several decades that I knew of. "You're forgetting, I'm already married."

She shook her head. "Atolls recognize all forms of cohabitation, including polygamy. We're not as narrow-minded as Earthers."

"That's very flattering but—"

"And your marriage has ended, has it not?"

She moved over to me, leaning in close. Her eyes were dark and alive. Her gaze locked with mine and our lips brushed, the touch sending electricity through my skin. My hands instinctively slid around her waist.

"We could be good together," McDole murmured, her lips hungry, seeking my own. "Don't you see—we could do good *things* together."

I felt myself respond and kissed her back, my arms sliding around her and pulling her against me. For a few moments, I felt I could stay wrapped up in the kiss forever—the way I'd always felt I could with Dollie. But with that, the feeling vanished like a wisp of air fluttering away in the vacuum of space.

I tried not to let it show, but McDole pulled back, a sad expression on her face.

"Sorry, Joe. I thought..." Her words faded and she tried again. "I'd *hoped* that maybe you—"

I pressed a finger against her lips. "I'm the one who needs to be sorry."

I headed back to my quarters, confusion running around my head like a particle stream in an accelerator. McDole was an attractive woman, and I enjoyed her company. But despite all that, I was still tied to the past—trapped in the ridiculous delusion that I could somehow persuade Dollie to come back to me. I hated myself for refusing McDole's advances, and at the same time hated Dollie for pushing me out of her life.

I told myself it was better to forget about all that type of thing, that I was better off without those complications in my life. But I wasn't sure I could convince anyone, let alone myself.

Pulling my thoughts back to safer ground, I reviewed the plans for tomorrow. We'd be far enough from Mars' gravity well to risk the first Jump, and my pulse raced. I'd imagined traveling to new star systems since I was a boy and never believed it would ever be real. But here we were, ready to make our first Jump. A chance to see other worlds with our own eyes. I let the idea fill me with excitement, pushing all the emotional confusion away.

Almost.

Chapter Twelve

By midday the following day, we were in a position to make the Jump to Sirius, which at nine light-years was close to our theoretical maximum. I wished we'd had enough time to put together some of my RoboPony relays. It would have been reassuring to leave a communication chain behind us to keep us in touch with what was happening on Earth. But we had our orders.

The last piece of interesting news was coverage of a meeting between Porter Seckinger and Fan Hua Song, the PAC Minister for Deep Space Development. The broadcast was my twisted idea of entertainment while I ate lunch in the wardroom. Seckinger was his usual toadsome self, but Song kept her cards well hidden, despite her outwardly enthusiastic manner. Whatever their politics and personalities, they were both selling the All-Parties Conference like it was the first squirt from the fountain of youth.

"We have communicated with the various governments of Earth, the Archipelago Directorate, and the Corporate Executive, and we have agreed on a tentative meeting to discuss strategic development of deep space." Song spoke with her usual measured tone. "This will take place in August at Lunar Free State and will provide an opportunity to determine best practices for all peoples to effectively use the new resources we now have access to."

Seckinger stepped forward and put his arm around Song's shoulders. He dominated her by several inches and gave her an overly familiar squeeze that made her wince. "Thank you, Minister Song. The USP looks forward to meeting with *everyone* and laying the groundwork for peaceful co-existence as we move into the future."

"Those assholes."

I looked around to see Grant. He must have slipped in while I was eating. He sat a few tables away, which struck me as a little unfriendly, but the tough-as-steel corporal didn't seem the most affable of people at the best of times.

"Don't you believe in avoiding conflict?" I said.

"War's inevitable. Everyone's after the same shit, and from what I see there ain't a lot of it to go around."

"You mean habitable planets?" I gathered up my garbage and pushed it into the recycler. "We'll find them eventually."

"You may be right." Grant chewed on his sandwich. "But no one wants to share. It's all words. You'll see."

I looked back at the screen. Seckinger was shaking hands vigorously with the diminutive Song, who looked as though she was expecting her arm to fall off any minute. Behind them, slightly out of focus, was the hulking figure of General Mkandla. She looked happy with the proceedings, but her t-shirt had the saying "All I need is some quiet time" over the image of a silenced pistol.

"I'm hoping sense will prevail."

"Didn't realize you were an optimist." He took another bite. "You and Giotto been spending time together. Something I should know there?"

I'd done several sessions with BRUCE, and she'd come along to make sure I didn't get hurt again, or maybe she was making sure I didn't mess around with the robot's programming. It was entirely innocent and even if it wasn't, it was none of his business. But I got the feeling it was more than idle curiosity. "She's helping me with an exercise routine."

Grant raised his eyebrows. "That what they call it these days?"

"I'm not sure it's any of your concern, but that's all it is." My fingers clenched. "If that isn't enough, feel free to check with her."

"She's part of the team." Grant leaned back, his chair creaking under the weight of all that Geneered muscle. "I don't like it when my people get messed up. By anyone."

And I didn't like threats, no matter how veiled. But we had a long time together ahead of us, so I swallowed my anger. Without saying anything else, I headed for the control room. It was empty, and I was glad to have some time to let my temper cool. Grant's attitude was as welcome as leeches on a hemophiliac, especially on a journey like this. It reminded me why I hated having anything to do with the military.

As the ship approached our planned Jump point, Logan and Aurore came in and strapped themselves into their seats. I'd suggested everyone be secured for the Jump, remembering how disconcerting it had been the first time I'd experienced it. From what I'd read, the nausea we'd experienced heading back to Earth was due to the fact that we were Jumping into a gravity well from a position where space-time curvature was flatter. Theoretically, our distance from any large mass, plus the fact that we were Jumping to the outer regions of the Sirius system, would limit any bad effects, but I wasn't taking any chances.

"Everything okay, Joe?" said Logan.

"We're on track."

"Not what I meant." He was staring at me. "You're on edge."

I cursed silently. Logan always seemed to look inside me and see what was going on. "Private matter—tell you later."

"I'll remind you."

A message flashed up, indicating we were at the safe Jump point, and I looked over at Logan. "Your call, *Captain*."

He grimaced at the title. "When you're ready."

I was about to broadcast a warning when Hernandez hurried in. He shrugged apologetically. "I felt I should be here, even though there's nothing for me to do."

"There still won't be any green-skinned dancing girls." I pointed to a spare seat. "But pull up a log."

As he fastened himself in, I opened a comm channel. "All hands. Secure for Jump in two minutes."

Logan brought up a front view and piped it throughout the ship. The on-screen counter ticked down. At thirty seconds, I engaged the Jump sequence and let the system follow its pro-grammed directions. There was no turning back now.

"Hang on to your hats, everybody," I called.

The counter hit one, and the Jump drive power readouts shot to maximum. My stomach did flip-flops as though I was going to vomit, and I wasn't sure if that was the effect of the drive or adrenaline. The main screen dissolved into a chaotic polychromatic swirl of patterns, and I had to look away. Then, almost before the sensation was born, it vanished. I blinked hard, and floating whirls filled my sight as if I'd rubbed my eyes too hard. The effect didn't last long, certainly less time than when I'd last tried this.

I scanned the display, but the view seemed unchanged. Not too surprising—nine light-years might be a long way in human terms, but astronomically-speaking we'd hardly moved.

"It didn't work?" Hernandez sounded confused.

I reached for the controls and turned the ship, bringing the nose around to line up with what the instruments told me was the center of the system. I held my breath as the brilliant light of a bloated star drifted onto the screen, the display automatically adjusting to prevent glare. Then, as the sun centered, a second much smaller one appeared, nestled onto the glow of the first.

"That's beautiful," whispered Aurore.

I nodded in agreement. "We made it alright."

Sirius was bigger and hotter than our sun, and its blue-white light was visible even with the image filtering. For all its glory, though, the system itself was sparse from a human perspective. There was one planet close into the main star, named "Tabor" by Atoll scientists, but it was almost as uninhabitable as Mercury. If I remembered correctly, the surface temperature averaged over a hundred and seventy degrees Celsius—a sun worshipper's paradise, for maybe ten seconds.

The proximity of the white dwarf companion made other planetary formations impossible, leaving a number of small plane-toids and an extensive asteroid belt at a considerable distance from the two stars. It was one of the first star systems visited but only because it was relatively close to our own. Geller Station was nothing more than a scientific and resupply base—other than the potential for asteroid mining, the system had little of interest.

I checked our local coordinates. "We're about a hundred-million kilometers from the station. Comms lag is eleven minutes round-trip. Hang on, though." The power reserves were at thirty-five percent. "Looks like we have enough juice to get closer."

"What about the one A.U. limit.?" said Aurore.

"We'd be well outside that distance from Sirius. Presumably the station is small enough not to have to worry about it so much."

Logan rubbed his chin, his eyes fixed on the screen. "How about shooting for ten-million klicks?"

I fed the numbers into the navigation system. It was close energy-wise but looked possible. "I think we're okay." I started programming the Jump into the system.

"What do you think?" Logan looked over at Aurore.

She was running the numbers, making sure I hadn't missed anything. "Looks okay, but it would be safer to go in on the regular drive."

Logan mulled it over for several minutes. "Okay. Go ahead, Joe. Try not to drop us inside a star."

I broadcast another warning and executed the Jump. There was a moment of discomfort but nothing compared to the big Jump. Once the room stopped spinning, I rechecked the distance to Geller.

"We're eight-million kilometers away from the station. Comms lag about thirty seconds."

"Thanks." Logan straightened his shirt. "I guess I better do this."

I set up a transmission and nodded to him.

"Geller Station. This is Captain Twofeathers of the *USN Shokasta*. We're on a search-and-rescue mission, investigating the late arrival of the *USN Sacagawea*. We have several people onboard including ADF Commander McDole and would like to rendezvous with your station. Please advise on your approach requirements."

He gestured cut, and I ended the broadcast.

"How was that?" he said.

"Very dignified." Aurore moved across, put her arms around him, then kissed his head. "You hate this formal stuff, don't you?"

"You should play one of those Space Fleet captains on 3V." I laughed. "Captain Logan, Hero of the Seventh Galaxy!"

Logan growled, but a smile wasn't hidden too far below the surface.

Hernandez confirmed that the transponder had deployed then unstrapped himself. "I'm going to check on my team. We better get ready for escort duty."

He was gone before anyone could respond, and I turned to

Logan. "Do you want that?"

"Unless something suspicious happens, I'd say we keep things low-key." Logan tapped his fingers on his armrest. "McDole should open the door for us."

A few seconds later, the comms system beeped. I opened the transmission, and a grizzled looking man appeared on the screen.

"Greetings, Captain Twofeathers. Flight Lieutenant Gavyn Moriaby here. A little surprised to see a *scroffer* ship, but I suppose I shouldn't be. We have limited facilities, but you're welcome to dock with us—subject to confirmation of Commander McDole's presence, of course. Have to keep everything *by the book*." Moriaby glanced down. "I note your position and am sending our designated traffic control paths. Use approach sixty-delta-one. Our outer traffic marker is at four-thousand kilometers. Approach freely until then. Oh, and welcome to Sirius."

"Not the friendliest of welcomes," muttered Aurore.

"Haven't you heard?" I said. "The most common Geneering in Atollers is to remove their *courtesy* genes."

I programmed the course and started the autopilot. Geller Station was situated on the edge of a vast asteroid belt over twenty-seven A.U. from Sirius and was a combined observation and processing station. Mostly, they were processing the belt for raw materials to resupply Atoll ships, and the station itself was relatively small, which was more than you could say about the huge storage bays floating near the station.

It would take a little over a day to get there. The extra Jump was a big time-saver, and I felt unreasonably elated. We'd made our first Jump—two, in fact—and now we were viewing a new star and other worlds. At least, telescopically. It was a dream I thought would never happen.

I was in the stores area. With the extra people onboard, I was nervous about how long we could stay out here—even with the extra supplies McDole had provided. Once past Sirius, there were only a few small research stations, and I doubted they'd have enough provisions to be of much help.

136

When Logan planned the mission, it was only going to be him, Aurore, and me. Now we had three times that number of people. The MilSec team had been thrown at us last minute, and our schedule hadn't allowed us time to take on the extra rations needed—bureaucrats simply didn't understand space travel. I'd finished the early counts and was doing the math inside my head based on an average of eight thousand kilojoules per day, and we were well short of being able to complete the entire journey.

Water was largely recyclable, and we had plenty of storage space, but we could hardly pull over to Billy Bob's Market and Wholesale to restock.

I was about to head upstairs when I heard a cough. It was Dan. I hadn't seen much of him since he came aboard. I imagined he was adapted to whatever schedule they'd used on Fardosh-Baird, and I worked standard time like the rest of the ship.

He stared at me with a strange look on his face then broke out in a sheepish grin. "Got a question, if you ain't too busy."

He'd cleaned himself up a bit. His remaining hair and beard had been trimmed, and he didn't look quite so much like *The Prisoner of Zenda*. His clean ship suit was a big improvement on the raggedy paper clothes he'd been wearing when we first saw him.

I couldn't quite place his expression—a look of hunger mixed with something else. Maybe it was due to the fact that he'd been locked up so long. "How can I help?"

"Been away so long, I lost touch with so much. Wondered if I could have access to the ship's information library. The 'Tollers never let me see more than garbage game shows and soaps. Be nice to exercise the brain a bit. Do some catch-up."

I felt bad. I'd already activated the console in McDole's room. "Sorry, I should have done that earlier."

"Hell, nothing to be sorry for, Joe." He grinned again, and I saw half his teeth were missing. "I'm your guest. It beats living with those stuck-up bastards on Fardosh-Baird."

"I'll set it up when I'm back at the controls." It was good to see he was trying to move on.

"Hey, that's something else." His dark eyes glistened like a pair of oily bearings. "D'ya think I could *see* the control room, when you have a bit of spare time? I mean, jeez, this is a starship. I thought both me and Earth would be dead before we saw this stuff."

"Sure. Give me a few minutes to finish here, and we can go up together." He reminded me so much of Charlie, both in appearance and speech, that it was hard to remember he wasn't the old friend I'd shared so much coffee with over the years.

"Sounds, great." He smiled, then a frown slipped over his features. "Listen, I owe you an apology, Joe. For when I first met ya. Ya know, saying how you got Charlie killed an' all."

I didn't know what to say. "I'm sorry it happened. He was a good friend, and he saved my life."

"I was talking with Logan a couple of days ago. He told me how it had all gone down. Those hired killers—never knew nothing about that."

An awkward silence fell, then Dan held out his hand. "I hope someday ya might call me a friend. Can we make a fresh start, huh?"

I hesitated only momentarily, then shook his hand. "Don't have a problem with that."

When we arrived, I logged the data I'd found while Dan marveled at the instruments.

"Jeez. This room is bigger than the ship I escaped in when the 'Tollers attacked Deimos." He laughed. "What happened to building 'em small?"

"No need with the new Casimir generators. And to keep the Jump transition smooth, bigger is better in some ways. Easier to generate the field or something."

"Sure is different from the firecrackers I got my wings on." He wandered over to Aurore's station and dragged his hand across the controls. The console was locked, so it didn't respond to him, but even the Access Denied messages made him grin.

"Firecracker" was an old term for a chemical rocket, whether solid-fuel or liquid propellant. It was true—they typically did get much higher acceleration with those systems, but they were pretty much one-shot—a single high-g burn and then you coasted. The Casimir generators allowed *Shokasta*, and other modern ships, the ability to sustain acceleration for days and weeks on end. Although the initial thrust was lower and less dramatic, over time the speeds achieved were much higher, and it also provided a workable pseudo-gravitational field.

"What happened when the Atolls attacked? If you don't mind me asking?"

Dan's forehead wrinkled. "You don't know?"

"Only what was released to the news agencies." I fiddled with the controls.

"Can I see?" Dan shuffled from one foot to another.

I pulled up a historical newscast. It didn't have any real footage—the Atolls had never released any—but it had a half-decent simulation of the attack that had been derived from a mix of remote observation and some dubious hypothesizing. More to the point, it included reports of no survivors.

Dan seemed mesmerized, seeing remotely what he'd somehow lived through. His appearance confused me. He was Charlie's twin brother, which made him about a century old, but he didn't look it and moved like someone several decades younger. Perhaps that could be chalked up to his years in space, but that typically aged people more than preserved them.

"The reports were right. Almost." He didn't look around. "I was working outside—re-calibrating the solar arrays. When the station blew, my Hopper was crunched up and tossed away like an old beer can. The circuits were fried. No thruster control. Tanks were shot. Figured I had maybe twenty minutes of oxygen.

"Then that necking Toller cruiser come out of nowhere. I was sure they were gonna finish the job—no witnesses. But they dragged me onboard and made me a prisoner."

"You were lucky."

"Being held in a Toller cell for six years? Living with people who treated me like an animal? Nothing but a circus freak to frighten their children with." Dan looked back at me, and I caught the flash of anger in his eyes. "You have no idea what they put me through."

I wondered what they'd done to him but didn't want to push him anymore. His reaction went beyond simple anger at being locked up. The Atolls weren't known for their humane treatment of Earth people, but they weren't generally sadists. Then I thought about my plans for Paek. I wasn't usually so harsh, but some people simply deserve death.

Dan pulled a coffee tube out of his pocket and emptied half the tube in one long drink, then smacked his lips. "Neck, I waited six years for a coffee." He took another drink and pointed at the Atoll Cruiser on the news display. "They don't do it. According to the 'Tollers, it's a drug, illegal. They have something they call coffee, but it's Geneered chicory and barley shite. Not worth drinking."

I'd heard about the Atoll's fastidious reputation. Many of them had an extreme pure body-pure mind regime and eliminated many things us *scroffers* took for granted. I suppose it made sense from a scientific perspective, but life without coffee sounded too close to life-after-death. Although with the widespread destruction of coffee growing habitats, substitutes were gaining traction, even on Earth.

I opened the management console and activated the terminal in Dan's quarters. "Okay, you're all set."

Dan grinned and took another gulp of his coffee. "Thanks, Joe. Mighty nice of ya."

"All part of the Ballen Spaceways service."

"If it's okay, I'll go and check it out. Gotta start playing catch-up. I'm behind way too much." He headed for the doorway. I pulled up the provisions system and checked the projections based on the data I'd collected. What came up was worrying.

"Was Dan just here?" Aurore clambered in.

"I forgot to give him access to the information library. He didn't get to view much on Fardosh-Baird."

She swung into her seat and opened up a spectrographic analysis. "Is that what he said?"

"Nothing but garbage 3V, like game shows."

"Weird." Aurore leaned back in her chair. "McDole said he'd read his way through their entire library."

"Their entire *scroffers*-only library, perhaps. Though if he's anything like Charlie, he's probably getting a bit senile." I tapped the console. "Anyway, we have a bigger problem."

"Oh?"

"According to my estimates, we only have enough food to search each star system for two weeks."

"We can't do a thorough survey in that time." Aurore turned to her console and pulled up my data. "It's impossible."

I understood her reaction. Even with the enhanced detection equipment, it would be difficult to detect a ship unless it was actively broadcasting a signal. Thermal signatures would be detectable, but on a Casimir-powered ship, the generators produced much less heat than something like a fusion reactor. It wasn't impossible, but finding something that small in the available search window was unlikely.

"We could head back to Fardosh..."

I didn't finish the thought. I could well imagine the response from Earth if we turned back before we'd really started. Worse still would be the Atoll derision when they found out we'd not provisioned our ship properly for the journey ahead.

Chapter Thirteen

BRUCE was putting me through my fitness program, and my breathing was coming as fast as an aeromobile salesman's lies. The routines were grueling, but I was making progress and feeling less pain. My robotic sadist had driven me through a series of chin-ups and was pacing me as I did several rounds of squat thrusts. I wasn't even halfway done when Giotto walked in.

She stood by the door, watching me with her piercing blue eyes. When I finished my set, I slapped the pause button on BRUCE, grabbed my water bottle, and sat, leaning my back against the wall while I recovered.

"How are things?" I said, wiping my face with a towel then draping it over my shoulders in an attempt to hide the sweat matting my shirt. "Not much going on for you and the guys right now, huh?"

She didn't answer, but carried on staring, her strong jaw set like astrocrete.

"Okay, you're not happy about something—I get that." I swallowed more water. "I'll lend you the infamous Ballen ear of sympathy, if you want to talk."

"Let's see how well you're doing."

"What?"

Giotto crouched, raising her fists in a classic fighter's pose. "Show me what you've got."

I didn't have a chance against her, and we both knew it. She was a fully-trained soldier in her prime, with the benefit of MilSec Geneering. "I'm not crazy. I can't beat you. And don't want to either."

"I'll go easy on you, *old man.*"

It was absurd, but the look on her face told me I wasn't going to easily walk away from this. Whatever was eating her must have really got her pissed. I dropped into a similar position, and we circled each other warily.

She threw a punch at my shoulder, and I dodged away. "Why'd you change your exercise schedule?"

I suddenly realized she was mad at me. We circled each other some more, exchanging a few tentative punches and fakes. "The old one interfered with the approach to Geller Station."

"You're lying." She spat the words out, slamming a right jab into my shoulder that deadened the feeling in that arm.

She was right. The approach wasn't a problem. The navigation system took care of the real work—I only told it what to do occasionally. The truth was, I didn't want any more encounters with Grant. "Would you believe me if I said BRUCE suggested the change would fit better with my biometric charts?"

"No."

I sighed. Sometimes you couldn't avoid things, no matter how you tried. I threw a punch, which she ducked easily. "You don't want to know."

As she came back up, her fist slammed into my stomach, winding me. "Try me."

I staggered back, gasping for air. "Are you trying to finish the job BRUCE started?"

She moved in again and threw another punch at my midriff. I blocked it, swinging my fist at her. Instead of connecting, she avoided the blow, turning to grab my arm and spin me around so my back was to her. She wrapped her muscular arms around my neck and squeezed, none too lightly. "You better tell me."

She let me go, and in between the next few exchanges, I told her about Grant's warning. Her face darkened.

"He has no right to interfere with anything I do off-duty." She slammed her forearm into the side of my neck, and my vision filled with sparks.

"So maybe you should beat the shit out of him instead?"

She spun around, her leg slicing under mine, and I dropped to the floor like a sack of machine parts. She jumped on top of me, straddling my midriff.

"Men are such bastards," she said.

I grunted as she pinned me down. "I'm not in a position to argue."

She jammed her hot lips against mine. After a minute, she pulled back, grinding her pelvis against me.

"I don't want a relationship with you," she said.

"Okay..."

She leaned over and kissed me once more. I felt myself getting warmer.

"I just want to have some fun on this dumb mission." She ripped my shirt open. "Nothing wrong with that, is there?"

"Well..."

"Goddamn regulations."

She moved lower and kissed my chest. My comfort zone felt like it had been vaporized in a nuclear attack, and it wasn't because Giotto was sitting on me. Well, not entirely.

"Giotto..."

"Call me Stacia."

I heard a click. "Joe? Logan said you'd be—"

I looked around. McDole was framed in the doorway, her face an icy mask. She turned abruptly and left.

Giotto stared at me. "You gotta be joking. The 'Toller bitch?"

She didn't resist as I pushed her away and rolled from under her.

"You've got it wrong." I grabbed my water and headed for the door. "I don't want McDole. And I don't want you either. Leave me the hell alone."

I left Giotto kneeling on the floor open-mouthed. There was only one woman I wanted. The problem was that she didn't want me, plus she was around nine light-years away. I still wanted to clear things up with McDole, though, and headed to her cabin.

"Go away, Joe," she called through the composite paneling.

"I know what it looked like. But sometimes appearances are deceptive."

"It's none of my business."

I took a breath. "You're right. But I want to explain anyway."
The door sounded like a gunshot when it hit the stop, and I edged inside. McDole stood with her back to me. "Giotto was looking to fool around on the trip. I didn't realize, and it got a little confused. I'm not choosing her over you. And I'm not choosing you over her, either. I don't want a relationship with anyone. I'm not sure I'll ever want one again, to be honest."

"I thought Earth-men only ever thought about sex?" Her words were sharp. Accusing.

"What?"

"Oh, never mind. One of those silly rumors—a cultural put-down, I suppose."

For the second time in thirty minutes, I was dumbfounded. "I don't have a clue what you're talking about."

McDole turned stiffly to face me."It's said that there are only two things on an Earth-man's mind—food and sex. Base *animalistic* urges. We're all prisoners of our culture sometimes, even me."

"You forgot one."

She frowned. "Sorry?"

"When we're not eating or fucking, we're getting drunk."

I turned and left before she could say another word.

I didn't get drunk. So far as I knew, the only booze on board was McDole's supply—and I guessed I'd be off her friends list now. The MilSec team might have had some stashed away, but I knew it wasn't the answer. Instead I'd gone to my quarters and sprawled on my bunk in the darkness, wondering what Dollie was doing and whether she missed me. Unlikely, if the party I'd witnessed last time I'd seen her was anything to go by. Hell, everything seemed so long ago, she probably didn't remember the good times we'd had.

For once, Logan didn't stop by. He had a habit of knowing when the world was closing in around me, but there was no sign of him. And to be honest, I was grateful. He was no doubt enjoying his time with Aurore, and I didn't blame him for that.

After several hours of fitful sleep, I showered and made my way to the control room. I walked in without a word and sat at the main console, hunching over and nursing my coffee.

Unlike the last stop, our final approach to Geller Station wasn't remotely controlled by the Atoll. Whether they didn't have the ability, or couldn't be bothered, wasn't clear. I was following directions from their traffic controller, bringing the *Shokasta's* speed down to a relative crawl and staying within the designated approach lanes. Our sensors detected the presence of several weapons systems tracking us as we closed, and I tried not to let that worry me.

Geller was smaller than expected—a spinning disk about six-hundred meters across and one-hundred deep. The surface glittered in the harsh light from Sirius making it look like a very fat, semi-metallic pizza.

"That must be the first phase of an Atoll's development," I said.

Logan nodded. "Not as impressive as you'd imagine, is it?"

A few thousand meters beyond the station itself, an array of storage tanks floated in nothing, along with an irregular boxy structure that appeared to be a processing plant. Usually the bones of Atoll operations were hidden from sight by the armored shell around them, but we were getting an unprecedented view of how they worked.

I triggered a detailed scan of the station and the other structures using our full sensor range. It might have been a little rude, but I couldn't see any harm in gathering some intel. As it completed, McDole came in. She showed no obvious signs of embarrassment or hostility. I kept my head down, hoping not to stir up any more bad feelings. I'd already decided to split my time between piloting and staying in my quarters. It seemed like the best thing all around would be to stay out of everyone's way.

After paying her respects to Logan, McDole moved over to me, her eyes fixed on the main view screen.

"I'm sorry, Joe. What I said—well it wasn't very nice." She made no attempt not to be overheard. "I hope you'll accept my apology. I won't bother you again, unless you make it clear your feelings have changed."

She sounded like she was talking about putting the dishes in the recycler or some other mundane chore, and I wondered what the others were making of it. My face and ears reddened, and I tried to focus on the approach.

Logan's eyebrows rose.

"No problem," I muttered, monitoring the ship's deceleration far more closely than necessary.

Geller had no usable docking port. They used an Atoll specific design that would need an adapter to work with the *Shokasta*, and there wasn't a handy docking adapter shop around the corner. We could have gone across on a line, but Logan and Hernandez wanted to test the SMPTs. It was a good opportunity to iron out any bugs, so everyone was at the payload bay waiting for us to finish the approach.

Despite Logan's wishes, Hernandez insisted we had an escort and refused to back down even after a lengthy debate. Logan was usually so calmly persuasive that I was surprised to see him not get his way, but Hernandez played his military trump card for all it was worth. Or perhaps, given Logan's history with the Atolls, he didn't push back as much as he normally would.

We matched velocity with the station a thousand meters away as planned. I activated the drift monitors to make sure the ship wouldn't move then locked the circuits to prevent accidents.

"Okay, time to head down," I said.

We were back in ZeeGee, and the four of us squirmed toward the exit like a school of bizarre fish, with Logan leading the way.

Halfway there we came across Dan outside his quarters. He was fidgeting and had a brief whispered conversation with Logan. Logan waved McDole and Aurore on, holding his hand up to stop me as I floated close. "You need to hear this," he said.

Dan was clasping and unclasping his hands, his eyes not wanting to meet mine or Logan's.

"What's the problem?" I said.

He hesitated, as though not sure what to say. "I don't want to go."

"To the Atoll?"

"I'm scared." Dan hunched up, the top of his bald head catching the light as he lowered his chin. "What if they lock me up again?"

"We won't let them do that." I squeezed his upper arm. He felt surprisingly muscular through his shirt. "It'd do you good to see something other than the inside of the ship."

"No!" His eyes darted around in panic. "They'll put me in a cell and hurt me again."

Logan pulled me to one side, his voice low. "Is there any reason we can't leave him here?"

I thought about it. The controls were locked, so he couldn't take off even if he knew how to fly the ship. I couldn't think of anything else problematic. "Grant is staying behind, so I suppose not. He seems terrified."

"Any idea what they did to him?"

"He's not said much to me. I know he dislikes the Atollers, but I didn't realize he was scared of them."

Logan moved back to Dan. "Okay, you can stay here. Keep an eye on things while we're gone."

"You sure?" He nodded making the loose skin on his neck flap. "It's okay, Joe?

"Of course." I felt uneasy with the idea, but it was Logan's call.

Dan smiled, his eyes closing as he put his hand across his chest. "Thanks. I mean it. You're good guys for sure. Both of you."

He slipped back inside his room like a turtle retreating into its shell, and we made our way to the main airlock.

The journey to the station was short, and the miniature spacecraft functioned without a hitch. It only took a short time to get to the Atoll airlock, and once there, it opened like a cavern. After the outer doors closed, we disembarked the SMPTs in our suits and moved over to a smaller inner airlock to enter the station.

I'd flown over with McDole and Sullivan, while Logan piloted the craft carrying Aurore, Hernandez, and Giotto. I was glad we hadn't taken everyone, or at least one of the small ships would have been packed tight enough to make Siamese twins claustrophobic.

The inner airlock wasn't big enough to hold us all. Logan, McDole, Sullivan, and Hernandez went in first, while those of us in the B team waited. Once the airlock cycled and the doors reopened, the rest of us followed.

We found ourselves in a larger circular vestibule area. The others were stowing their suits in storage lockers, and I noticed Hernandez, Sullivan, and Giotto had bulky pistols strapped across their chests. I wasn't the only one who spotted them.

McDole winced. "You shouldn't have brought those."

"We're on protection duty," Hernandez said. "We can't take care of our people if we can't defend ourselves."

"You have no need for weapons here. Atolls respect life."

I exchanged a look with Logan as I finished taking off my suit.

"Are you telling me there are no weapons on this station?" Hernandez knew we'd detected them on the approach.

"The station is armed, of course," McDole reluctantly admitted.

Hernandez nodded. "But no personal weapons?"

"It's not usual Atoll practice to carry them."

"But not unheard of?"

McDole looked away. "On a station out here, I couldn't say for sure."

"Then I think we'd better hold on to these, ma'am."

I moved over to Logan and spoke in a whisper. "Did you okay that?"

Logan looked grim. "I figured they'd have more sense. This is mostly a social visit for McDole's benefit."

"It may not stay that way for long." I glanced at the soldiers. "I'd have thought Hernandez would have learned after last time."

"He did the same at Fardosh-Baird?" Logan's eyes widened. "Why didn't you tell me?"

"It slipped my mind." Along with meeting Gabriella, I thought guiltily.

A series of high-pitched beeps filled the room, and the lights flashed several times.

"Hold on to the hand rails," McDole called.

I grabbed the closest one. A wave of dizziness hit me, then it vanished and we had gravity. I was trying to work out the mechanics of that trick when the majority of what was now the roof slid away, and a spiral walkway wound its way down to our level. Several armored people ringed the opening, then Moriaby wobbled through the crowd. His smile looked welded on.

"Welcome to Geller Atoll. Please place your weapons in the

storage lockers, or we will be forced to fire."

The people surrounding the opening above us were carrying heavy-looking rifles that looked more than a match for the MilSec team's pistols.

McDole turned to face Logan. "It would be a wise move, Captain Twofeathers."

Logan hesitated for a few seconds then raised his voice. "Sergeant, please instruct your team to rack their weapons. Consider that an order."

Hernandez hesitated, then sighed—a look of disgust on his face. "Okay. Lose the heat."

There was a flurry of movement and rattles as they unclipped the weapons harnesses and stored the guns.

Moriaby tottered down the walkway and shuffled straight to McDole. He was still wearing that smile, but it missed his eyes by several light-years. "Welcome aboard, Commander." He was nodding, his unruly mop of hair bouncing up and down. "It's good to see you, and your... *unusual* friends."

"Thank you, Flight Commander. It's a pleasure to have the opportunity to visit one of our front-line operations. I've heard good things of your work."

"Really?" Moriaby opened his eyes wide. "How interesting. We haven't had a ship visit in two months. My reports are piling up on my computer. I assumed that you'd come to hear first-hand of our achievements. Or am I wrong?"

His voice was verging on insolent, but McDole took it in her stride. "It's unfortunate our remote stations are so difficult to keep in close contact with, but we're as bound by the laws of physics as everyone else."

"Indeed." Moriaby's tone dripped with sarcasm. "And yet, we're only a single Jump from Sol. My staff feel the Directorate doesn't place a very high priority on operations such as ours."

The Directorate was the highest level of government in the Atolls, where representatives of each met every few months to determine their overall strategy and priorities. Its meetings were held in secret locations and rotated between all the Atoll bases. Theoretically, they were McDole's immediate supervisors, but I suspected the Atoll military preferred a looser connection to the political body and filtered any attempts at direct communication.

"It takes a keen interest in all Atolls, as do I. Which is, in part, one of the reasons for my visit." McDole paused. "If you'd care to identify the individuals who feel unrecognized, I'd be more than willing to meet with them one-on-one to address their concerns. Perhaps I can provide them with the inspiration they need."

Moriaby gave a small bow, his good-humored expression looking even more forced. "I don't believe the dissatisfaction has reached the levels that would require such... *interventions*. But I will communicate your generous offer to my staff."

He looked around and, apparently satisfied we were for the most part harmless, gestured toward the stairs. "If you'd care to follow me, I've arranged a modest meal for your enjoyment, much of it grown locally in our solar-nurseries."

McDole caught my eye and winked as she turned to follow him. "It may interest you to know that Mr. Ballen has come up with a solution that will considerably ease communications to stations like Geller."

"You don't say?" Moriaby coughed, and a smile flickered over his lips. "Some dubious faster-than-light communication scheme, I imagine."

McDole ignored the slur. "Not exactly. But once in place, it would give you the ability to contact Sol every few hours."

Moriaby stopped. "You have this *device* with you?"

"The plans were only completed on the way out. Manufacturing and testing has yet to begin, but we're confident of its success."

"Ah... of course. I won't hold my breath then."

It was the type of response I'd expect from an Atoller to anything of Earth origin, and I had to admit I'd love to see his face when the first broadcasts came through.

With Moriaby leading, we were escorted by several guards into the Atoll itself. The interior didn't look anything like the typical pictures we saw of their stations. Usually they showed luscious greenery and beautifully landscaped scenery wrapped around a tubular interior many kilometers across. The overall effect was reminiscent of an earthly paradise from before the time we'd screwed up the planet.

Geller reminded me of Baltimore's urban sprawl mixed with a number of distinctly industrial-looking complexes but turned inside out. There was only one patch of green visible, directly above us as we entered. Not too surprising given the station's relatively small size but at odds with generally-held expectations.

As we moved, I had the sensation of being an ant crawling along the inside of a spinning drainpipe. At the diameter of Geller, rotating the station fast enough to provide a decent artificial gravity effect would be a challenge. This was confirmed when I realized that if I turned my head from side to side too quickly, it was easy to get dizzy.

"You won't have heard the news about the Wright Atoll," McDole said walking beside Moriaby.

"At Wolf 1061?"

"It was destroyed." McDole hissed through clenched teeth. "No survivors."

"That's ridiculous." Moriaby's voice grew strident. "A research station looking for protolife in the planetary system—who'd want to destroy it? Why, even the *scroffers* had people there."

"We don't know the cause yet." McDole glanced at Logan. "That's why I'm out here."

"Well, I'll be damned." Moriaby's words were almost a whisper. "You think we might be in danger too?"

Chapter Fourteen

Moriaby led us to a *modest* dining room, which was large enough to hold a small army—or maybe two—although we were the only ones there other than the guards. To the right, a railed food delivery system took up half the wall, empty but it looked easily capable of serving the missing battalions. Next to that were several ordering terminals set in to the wall, each listing a bewildering array of options. It reminded me of the refectories from my student days—again, unexpected based on what we usually saw of Atoll culture. The more we saw of it, the more Geller Station was starting to resemble the Atoll equivalent of the hind end of space.

We sat at one long table close to the rail system. Moriaby conceded the central seat to McDole, appearing somewhat reluctant to do so. My mind wasn't on the meal or even the station itself. I was still wondering why Dan had stayed behind. What had they done to him that made him so terrified? Although Atollers could be collectively harsh when dealing with people from Earth, they weren't usually that bad individually. He even seemed to avoid McDole onboard the *Shokasta*.

"How many people live here?" Hernandez asked, glancing around the wide hall.

"It varies somewhat," Moriaby said, "but usually we have around two hundred permanent residents."

Hernadez's eyes widened, and I guessed what he was thinking. The room available on the station was immense for so few people. But the Atolls had always valued opulence.

"That seems... under-utilized," Aurore said.

"The station is sized to allow expansion." Moriaby's voice had an edge to it as he stared at McDole. "The migration rates have been somewhat lower than estimated, however."

"Appetite for relocation to underdeveloped Atolls has struggled to gain wider acceptance." McDole looked around, as if explaining it to everybody.

"We're *underdeveloped* because we haven't been allocated the resources. It's a failure of leadership. And it's about time the Directorate tackled that."

"What do you suggest?" McDole looked like she was fighting to keep a neutral expression on her face. "Forced repatriation?"

"Isn't that what the *scroffers* do?"

It was fascinating to see the hostility between them. The Atolls always put on a show of being scientifically driven, cooperative paradises, but apparently paradise had its flaws. It gave me a certain soft spot for Moriaby, though his casual racism grated and I was more than ready to throw a verbal jab of my own.

"Perhaps the Atolls aren't the natural leaders of humanity after all," I said. "It must be hard to inspire people to sacrifice such a lavish existence."

"We have improvements to make." McDole tapped the table. "We're at the beginning of this process. And no one has to struggle. We make thorough use of automation, as you can see."

She nodded at the armored figures standing close by.

"They're robots?" I said.

Rumor had it the early Atollers wanted to escape the limits placed on the use of robots in several Earth societies. The restrictions resulted from fears that automation would replace large numbers of human workers. This was further amplified when the bots started looking more like humans and less like machines. We used robots on Earth, but they were mostly industrial. Humanoid robots were used only in very narrow circumstances.

The ultimate nightmare focused on one very specific fear—armed robots. I glanced at the potential death machines surrounding us, and my hackles rose.

"They're useful for handling tasks Atollers dislike," McDole continued. "And for the purposes of new Atolls, they're good surrogates for developing a community similar enough to existing ones to make them attractive to our people."

The availability of the technology made it a good choice for developing their stations, though I could see some drawbacks. If robots built a community, they might optimize it for other robots, leaving it less-than-optimal for humans. And, if their people were *that* dependent on having the perfect environment, it meant their culture was rigid in an evolutionary sense. A big part of the success of human civilization had been our ability to adapt and thrive, even in the harshest of conditions—and the number of animals that specialized themselves into oblivion littered the textbooks.

"We'll never progress until the priorities from the Directorate are clear," Moriaby sneered, his curved cheeks drawing back from his mouth. "The *scroffers* already have more people out here than we do."

Giotto slammed her hand down on the table, and Hernandez's chair scraped back several inches. Logan had been quiet so far, but now his voice boomed around the hall.

"I'd appreciate it if you'd stop using that term."

Moriaby seemed genuinely surprised. "Pardon me if I've given offense. Don't you people use that term among yourselves?"

As if on cue for a timely interruption, the track behind us rattled, and a number of steaming serving plates and bowls appeared. As the scent of the warm food spread, my mouth watered. When I glanced around, I saw I wasn't alone in my reaction.

"Help yourselves." Moriaby waved his hand toward the food. "We don't have serving people… or robots."

The chatter stopped for the most part as everyone loaded their plates. There was golden sweet corn, steaming Idaho potatoes, all manner of green vegetables, and what appeared to be slices of roast beef in a thick onion gravy. I guessed the beef was some form of processed soy, but that wasn't going to stop me.

McDole and Moriaby were deep in conversation while people were serving themselves. Moriaby's face told me he wasn't enjoying what he was hearing, and I wished I was close enough to make out what they were saying.

I nudged Logan and pointed to the two Atollers. "Are you sure you don't have any clue what happened to the Wright Atoll?"

"Only what was said on the public newscasts." He forked a large potato onto his plate. "If anyone higher up in SecOps knows, they're keeping it quiet."

"Well, Moriaby looks like he's chewing on a diamond-tipped grinding wheel."

Aurore leaned in between us with a mischievous grin on her face. "Perhaps you could use your manly charms on McDole, Joe. I'm sure she wouldn't mind you *pumping her* for information."

"Leave the guy alone," said Logan, fighting back a smirk. "His ego's plenty big enough as it is."

I ignored them. "I'd like to know what went down, wouldn't you?"

"If we knew," said Logan, "we might be able to connect it to our search or at least eliminate it."

"Maybe she'll tell us on her own." I shrugged. "We're helping her out, after all."

I sat back at the table, cut off a sliver of the "beef," and popped it in my mouth. The delicious umami of real meat flooded my taste buds, reminding me of the very best and most expensive steaks I'd ever had. But I'd never eaten anything close to this in space. The resource cost of animal farming was so crazily high that substitutes were usually all you saw.

"Real beef?" I lifted up another piece.

An automated drinks dispenser circled the table, and Moriaby waved it over to him. The boxy device trundled up and delivered a large glass of red wine at the touch of a button. He took a mouthful and swallowed, then sighed. "Not quite. It's Geneered. Specially adapted for growth inside nutrient vats."

We had cultured meat on Earth, but it didn't taste anything like this. It was mostly used in mid-grade products with delusions of grandeur and mixed with real meat or soy-based products. I'd not tried it in its pure form, but from what I understood it was almost impossible to fully replicate natural flavorings. And with livestock farming hit hard by climate change, people had gotten used to the alternatives, saving the real thing for special occasions.

"The quality is amazing," I said. "Perhaps you'd be willing to share the secret?"

Moriaby grinned. "I wouldn't know the details. If you contact the Atoll agricultural bureau, I'm sure they'd be willing to share their secrets."

"I'll pass that along." Then again, I probably wouldn't. I could well imagine the response such a query would receive.

The conversation was muted as everybody tucked into the food, and I also spotted the MilSec team making liberal use of the drinks dispenser. "Watch out for those Atoll wines, Hernandez. They have quite a kick, remember?"

Hernandez rubbed his finger along the edge of his nose, surreptitiously flipping me the bird.

Moriaby was taking in most of his daily calorie allotment in liquid form, and as the meal progressed, his voice grew louder. "My grandfather was a *scroff*—sorry, I mean an *Earther*." He called for the dispenser again, refilling his over-large glass. "I've no idea what my grandmother saw in him. He seemed a beastly man from what I heard. One of the last Earthers to join an Atoll I believe. Addison was his name."

"Guy Addison?" Aurore looked shocked.

"That's him." Moriaby turned to her, slopping a significant amount of wine on the floor. "You've heard of him?"

"My great-grandmother worked with him. He was a shuttle pilot, saved an Atoll from a terrorist attack."

"Well, well. That's absolutely correct. My grandfather, the hero. May his name rot in the depths of history."

McDole took her plate over to the recycler. "Perhaps we should end this visit now."

"No, no, no. We're only getting started. We don't have a great deal of opportunity to entertain guests out here, not even"—he burped—"Earthers."

The wine was getting to him, and I wondered if his guard had dropped enough to wheedle some more information out of him. "If you don't like it here, why do you stay?"

Moriaby's face darkened. "My mongrel grandfather, of course. He's the reason I'm stuck in this cursed spot. Isn't that right, Commander?"

McDole was waiting by the food rails, unable to mask her disapproval. "I have no idea what you mean."

"My family has *tainted blood.* Yes, that's it." He took a drink that half-emptied his glass. "I've been marked since the day I was born. That was why I was always marked down when I was a child. Why I didn't place highly at the academy."

"All academic and military gradings are carried out by computer," McDole snapped. "No one can influence them, except yourself."

"Then finally... I make one small mistake. A minor infraction of the rules. A misdemeanor at best. And I'm summarily banished to this...place."

"You were—" McDole cut herself off.

"I'm sorry to hear that, Flight Lieutenant." Logan raised his glass. "Many of us know all too well how it feels to be overlooked and unfairly punished."

"Exactly." Moriaby had refilled his drink and turned to McDole. "Incredible. I get more understanding and sympathy from *scro*—Earthers—than I do my own kind."

"Could I ask a question?" Logan was playing him perfectly with his deferential tone. "Have you seen anything unusual out here?"

"Unusual?" Moriaby studied his wine glass for a moment then took another gulp. "No. Not a damn thing. It's a hellhole, I tell you. Nothing happens here."

Logan gave out a small sigh. "Thank y—"

"Well... apart from the ghosts."

A shiver crawled up my spine.

"Ghosts?" I said it the same time as Logan.

"Yes. Ghost ships. They're so bloody... *inconsiderate.*"

Logan lifted his eyebrows, and I nodded and sat back. He was doing well enough on his own without me screwing things up.

"What kind of ships?" Logan said.

"Flight Lieutenant, this conversation should end right now," McDole barked.

"What are you going to do, *Commander?* Have me exiled even farther?" Moriaby slammed his glass down, the contents splashing across the table.

"Are these Earth ships?" Logan cut in.

"What? Oh no... That is, we don't know. That's the crazy thing about it. We detect them on our scanners. We know they're coming through. Never message us or respond to our signals. Just come and go, here and gone, as though they weren't really there. Almost like... ghosts." His hand slapped the table on each point, sending up a shower of spilled wine each time.

"What about their transponders? Don't they identify the ships?"

"I wondered that too." Moriaby stared into the distance. "But I asked for the logs to be analyzed, and they told me there were no trapsonders...tran-sponders recorded."

That's unusual," said Logan. "And disappointing."

"It's a ghastly mystery." Moriaby leaned back in his chair. "I ordered the station to be put on high alert. Maximum scans of all incoming ship signatures. I thought we might identify them using secondary detections—thermal patterns, mass profiles, and the like."

"That was smart thinking," Logan said.

"I thought so." Moriaby waved at the drinks dispenser and refilled his glass.

"And...?"

"And nothing. That's the damnedest part. The signatures matched no known ship configuration—Atoll or Earther." He slurped his wine. "As I said, ghost ships. Don't tell anyone, but sometimes I wonder if they're real or not. Perhaps they're just artifacts from deep space. Being out here does strange things to the mind. *Hell Is Empty and All the Devils Are Here.*"

Giotto and Sullivan snickered, and Logan looked around.

"Perhaps it's time we were heading back," he said. "Thank you for your hospitality and the wonderful food. It would be impossible not to appreciate such an unexpected luxury all the way out here."

"Think nothing of it. We could feed half of Earth's population."

And yet you don't, I thought. "One last thing, Flight Lieutenant." I said out loud. "Do you think you could share your sensor logs of these unidentified ships? It may help us with our search."

Moriaby looked across at McDole, and I spotted the slight shake of her head.

"The logs? Well..." His fleshy lips curved into a smile. "Why not? We have nothing to hide, do we, Commander?"

McDole's words were labored. "No. Nothing at all."

"In that case, I'll have them sent over to you right away." He clambered unsteadily to his feet. "If you'll excuse me, I have duties

161

to perform. You can stay if you like—we have plenty of room. Or the robots can escort you to the airlock."

"We should get back to our ship." Logan also stood. "Some of our people remained onboard and might get nervous if we don't return."

"As you wish." Moriaby turned, lurching toward a door in the far wall.

A robot approached McDole, and they spoke privately for a few moments.

"Follow me," she said.

The trip back was uneventful, but everyone was more subdued than on the way out. McDole was silent and kept her eyes straight ahead, avoiding eye contact. Once back on the *Shokasta*, she was quick to remove her suit but didn't leave.

She placed her hand on my arm. "Could we talk? Privately?"

I was tired, even though I'd resisted the urge to sample the wine, but she might have something useful to tell me. "Where?"

"Is my cabin acceptable?"

Everyone's eyes were on me. "Give me five minutes to check on the ship."

McDole nodded and hurried away.

"So, you're going pump her for info after all?" Aurore said.

Everyone broke into laughter except Giotto, who looked like she'd sat on a firecracker.

"I expect she wants to discuss Moriaby or the ghost ships," I said.

Aurore's laugh was throaty. "Uh huh."

At the controls, I ran a simple diagnostic check. I'd been worried about leaving Dan onboard and wanted to make sure everything was in order. It didn't seem possible he could have accessed anything—the control systems were locked—but it had nagged at the back of my mind. After a few moments, the results came back green.

I stopped at Dan's cabin on my way to McDole's to see how he was doing—my guilty conscience playing up, no doubt. He'd made the decision to stay—no one had forced him.

He opened the door partway when I knocked, peering through the narrow gap. "Everything okay?"

"They had some good food. You'd have enjoyed it."

He gave a faltering smile. "Probably. I know they're not all bad. I just... I dunno. I get nightmares sometimes, where I'm, you know, tied up in a box and they're all poking at me and laughing."

Sometimes it's difficult to come to terms with how much one human being can screw up another, whether deliberately or not. "Don't worry. You're one of us now."

Dan had a bashful expression that reminding me so much of Charlie. "Thanks, Joe. But I feel more like an intruder, even here. No one wants to talk to me, not even you."

I remembered his harsh words when we first met on the Atoll, but his accusation hit home. We'd done little to make him feel welcome since bringing him onboard. "Let's change that."

After chatting a little longer with Dan, I made my excuses and headed to McDole's quarters. The door slid open when I knocked, and she gestured for me to enter.

"I'm sorry about Moriaby." Her chin dropped several centimeters. "I seem to be saying that a lot these days, especially to you. I don't know why I should care so much about your opinion. But I do."

"Why are you apologizing? I don't recall you forcing drinks into him."

"I know, but his language was appalling." McDole stepped closer and reached out to me. "It seems every time we're together, you see the worst displays of Atoll society."

Her hand was ridiculously small in mine, but the heat from her skin seemed to burn. "As you've said before, not all Atollers are the same."

She let go of me and sat down at the small desk. "Have you any idea about the ghost ships he mentioned?"

"I'm outside the loop on such things. Logan may know more, but I doubt it." I stood awkwardly by her bed. The second chair had vanished—maybe the rental period was up. "How about a trade?"

McDole's eyebrow formed an attractive arch. "What do you

mean? Information?"

"What happened to the Wright Atoll?"

"We don't know."

I took a step toward the door. "Play it your way."

She grabbed my wrist, pulling me around to face her. "Wait, Joe. I mean it, we *don't* know what happened. The *Yukawa* found almost nothing left. They identified some debris and found one of the station's data recorders."

"That didn't reveal anything?"

McDole shook her head. "It was from the Wright's traffic control system—routine monitoring information."

"Did it show any unusual traffic?"

"Everything it recorded was genuine. But..."

I finished off her thought. "But it wouldn't have detected a ghost ship?"

"The traffic systems key off a ship's transponder signal. Without one, a ship would be effectively invisible unless someone specifically scanned for it."

I still couldn't see how the loss of the station and the *Sacagawea* were related. "Some people think the U'Gani are behind the disappearance of the ship. Do you think they destroyed the Atoll?"

She pulled a face. "Unlikely. No one's had any contact with them that I know of, and why would they bother us out here? There are large distances between us and their territory according to the Ananta data."

"Possibly, but we're pushing outward fast," I said. "Anything else I should know?"

McDole bit her lip. "Whatever happened to the Atoll was rapid but not instantaneous. The recorder showed a definite series of events where it lost connections to other systems throughout the station. Our specialists hadn't finished the analysis when I left, but whatever happened, it took several hours."

My brain raced as I thought about what could cause such an effect. "That would rule out something like an explosion."

She nodded, her face grim. "It also means the people onboard would have seen their deaths coming."

That was a hard picture to get out of your head—to see doom

approaching but being unable to escape, and even worse knowing the only chance of rescue was literally light-years away.

McDole pulled me back to her. She seemed somehow delicate, in contrast to her usual determined strength. "I've never been scared of space," she said. "But I am now."

I didn't know what to say, so I put my arms around her hesitantly, holding her gently as if that could relieve her fears. McDole relaxed against my chest, and I felt her breathing, slow and regular. For a moment, it was nothing but two people sharing a moment of comfort, almost at a primitive level. Then I felt guilty and stiffened in her embrace.

She smiled at me sadly. "It's okay, Joe. I understand."

We moved apart awkwardly. "I'll ask Logan if he knows anything about the ghost ships, but I'm fairly sure his answer will be a negative."

She nodded and I left, my head swimming with crazy thoughts. Nothing seemed stable or clear. Dan was so screwed up he had nightmares. The Atolls knew no more about what had happened to their station than we did to the *Sacagawea*, and now we had ghost ships to worry about too. For a moment, even my feelings about Dollie paled into insignificance.

.

Chapter Fifteen

After some much needed sleep, I was ready for us to move on. Logan confirmed he had no idea what the ghost ships were, which didn't necessarily mean they weren't from Earth. McDole arranged for more supplies to be shipped over from Geller Station. It took several hours, but when we'd finished, every spare cubic meter was crammed to bursting point. By my calculations, this gave us about three weeks to search at each Jump. Not very long, but the systems with stations would require less time—if the *Sacagawea* had reached them, they'd almost certainly know about it.

Now we had no reason to linger—we wouldn't find out more by staying. Moriaby was noticeably "unavailable" while the supplies were shipped over but did make a brief appearance to wish us on our way.

I moved the ship away from the Atoll, wondering what would happen to it. If what Moriaby had said was true, and the Atolls had no real interest in expanding outside our solar system, perhaps they weren't the threat we thought they were. Though this idea conflicted with McDole's assertion that timing was the issue.

Our next destination was Procyon, another binary star system with its two stars separated by an average of twenty A.U.—about the same as the distance between the Sun and Uranus. I played around with the Jump programming, not sure how to set the target. If I set the Jump to come out close to Procyon A, we could also be too near to the second star. From the data we had, Procyon was a bust in terms of planets. There were two, in tight orbits, and neither was interesting to anyone but astronomers. Beyond that, there were several debris fields and belts, which were probably planets that had either been torn apart by the gravitational forces or had never got going for the same reason.

The trip was a little over five light-years. Which meant we'd have energy reserves to Jump again if necessary without having to allow time for the Casimir system to recharge. That was what convinced me, and I set the destination to the outskirts of the system, well away from both stars. We weren't near enough to Sirius' gravity well for it to worry us and cleared the station in a few hours. I broadcast a warning to everyone before triggering the Jump. Hernandez didn't bother showing up for this one—the excitement of his first two "dates" so great that he'd promptly thrown away my number.

I still felt the thrill as the countdown ticked away, then there was that momentary disorientation and we were there, floating on the edge of the Procyon system. It looked remarkably similar to Sirius, another bright star accompanied by a much smaller companion. Procyon was larger than Sirius, but cooler and dimmer, its light more yellow than blue-white. I held my breath at the sight. The trip might not have been under ideal circumstances but was ticking plenty of boxes on my space explorer's wish list.

"There's so much desolation out here." Logan studied the screens in front of him. "Hard to imagine we'll ever find decent planets."

"Maybe that's not a bad thing." Aurore set up a broad-spectrum scan to look for any traces that could be the *Sacagawea*.

"How come? Earth isn't exactly prime real-estate these days." I watched the instruments as the sensor data started coming in.

"Habitable planets are rare. But we know we can live in constructed habitats. If we build them big enough, like the Atolls, they'd be as good as a planet in most respects. And in some ways better."

"Why better?" It was Logan who asked, but I wondered the same thing.

"You can position a habitat wherever you want relative to a star, and if something disastrous happens you can move it."

"That would be a tricky maneuver with a large station," I said.

"Especially one with people onboard."

"Difficult, but not impossible. The Atollers did it with Fardosh-Baird." Aurore's brow furrowed. "And if you have a community of habitats, they're more efficient environmentally. You can use sunlight in an almost pure form for energy generation, and transportation costs between them would be virtually nil, so you could easily set up trade and passenger networks."

Aurore was as smart as they come—I could understand why Logan was attracted to her. "That's true. But they're also a lot more vulnerable."

"You're thinking too small, Joe. I'm talking about O'Neill setups even bigger than the Atolls use. They'd be robust and protected from hazards. And let's face it, we've shown how easy it is to screw up a planet—there are no guarantees."

"Sure, but would you want to raise your kids on some—" Logan stopped, his face flushing. "Talking hypothetically, that is."

"The inside could be landscaped." I was thinking about the PAC ambitions. "The Taikong Gaogu project is looking into that. It wouldn't seem much different from Earth."

Logan drummed his fingers against the arms of his chair. "I think we're better off keeping up the search. I'm not convinced people would choose a station over a planet."

Aurore grinned at him. "Don't worry. I'm not ready for kids eith—"

A series of high-pitched bleeps bounced around the room. I checked the diagnostic systems, but they didn't show any problems.

"There's a contact on the sensor feeds." Aurore tapped on her console. "It could be... no, it *is* a ship."

"Is it them?" Logan reached to unbuckle his straps.

"Need more data," Aurore said.

I brought up the system map, tagging the ship's location. Its position was a long way out from both stars and looked to be just inside the closest of the asteroid belts. If it *was* the *Sacagawea*, it had a strange orbit. As a survey ship, it should have been focusing on the planetary system.

Whatever its identity, the ship was about two and a half A.U. from us, so any sensor data we were picking up was over twenty minutes old. A prickle of excitement tingled across my neck. Could

169

this be one of the ghost ships Moriaby had talked about?

The ship's clock seemed to be frozen but eventually ticked over. Logan breathed deeply, and I heard Aurore's foot tapping against her chair.

"Any signs of a transponder?" I asked.

"Too soon," Aurore said.

"Should I take us closer?" I looked over at Logan.

The creases on Logan's forehead deepened, and I thought he hadn't heard me. "Not yet. Too risky," he finally replied.

I shuffled in my seat. It was hard to believe but only a few minutes had passed since the first detection. We wouldn't get any further information from our active sensors for another half hour.

"Should I activate the weapons?" My hand was over the controls, ready.

"No." Logan almost hissed. "Not before we know who it is."

McDole came in, pushed herself over to a spare console, and strapped herself in.

I switched the sensor information and system map to be broadcast around the ship. There was no point keeping them in the dark and risking everyone crowding the room to see what was happening. The sensor data stream rippled as more information was collected.

"Something strange here." Aurore fed the data through the analysis systems and flipped through several screens I was only partly familiar with.

"Is it them?" Logan repeated, his voice tight.

"It's a transponder signal, but—" Aurore switched to another data view. "No. It's *two* signals. Neither matches the *Sacagawea*."

"Who the hell is it then?" I snapped, though I knew I shouldn't. Aurore was at the mercy of the sensor information.

"One identifies as the CSS *Ayn Rand*, the other is the CSS *Independence III*."

"What are the Corporates doing out here?" Logan said.

I shrugged. "Beats me. I thought all they were interested in was searching for resources and habitable planets. And you'd have more chance of finding a copy of the *Rocket Ranger* lost pilot episode in this system."

170

Logan pointed to the map on the large display. "Can you get us closer?"

I was setting up another Jump even as I answered. "Should be possible."

"Then do it."

I used the second Jump to take us to within eight-million kilometers again. I figured that should be good enough for relatively easy communication, while not being so close we'd appear threatening—not to mention keeping enough room between us so we could respond if things turned sour.

I was securing the ship when the comm system beeped, and a transmission opened up on our screens.

"*USN Shokasta*, this is Captain Charles Trent of the Corporate ship *Ayn Rand*. Do not approach any nearer or we will consider it an unfriendly act. The Procyon star system has been claimed for development by the Commerce Executive. We have deployed a standard habitat module that is in the last stages of expansion. We will protect it at all costs."

"What?" Logan looked around. "That's ridiculous. Put me through."

I toggled the transmit button.

"Captain Trent, this is Captain Twofeathers commanding the *Shokasta*. We're on a peaceful mission in search of one of our ships that is overdue. I'm surprised to hear you claim the Procyon star system belongs to the Corporates. There are no precedents for this. We will, however, hold station at our current location. As I said, our mission is a peaceful one."

It took almost a minute for the response to reach us. Trent's square face had frozen with the lag and now jerked back to life.

"Your information appears to be out of date, Captain Twofeathers. Under the latest rulings in the World Congress, a nation state can lay claim to a system as long as they have fulfilled residency requirements or shown they are the first to visit and have lodged detailed commercial development plans."

Logan accessed the controls, bringing up historical data on Procyon. "According to my records, Procyon has been visited by ships from all nation states on multiple occasions. You're hardly the first ship here."

171

Trent's reply was brief. "Correct. Which is why we're establishing a colony. Our station will have a population of forty people, well above the minimum threshold demanded by the World Congress edicts. Now please depart this system, or I *will* take action."

"What do you think, Joe?" said Logan.

"Sensor data says he's bluffing. Their ship doesn't look heavily armed, though I'm basing that on configuration and power signatures. Looks like it's got a Jump drive with a bare minimum control setup. The habitat's an expanding one like he said. Could they be Jumping to star systems and dropping these off, hoping to get a claim to stick?"

"There were rumors about something like this happening," McDole said. "I didn't expect it so soon, though."

"What if the *Sacagawea* is somewhere in this system?" Aurore said. "We need time to survey it."

"Are there any signs of it yet?" Logan asked.

Aurore shook her head.

Logan turned to the frozen transmission. "Captain Trent, we're not in a position to validate your claim or otherwise. As I mentioned, we're looking for one of our ships. Have you picked up any signs of her? We'll transmit her identification code."

I broadcast the information, and we waited. It seemed to take far longer than fifty seconds to get a reply.

"I'm sorry to hear of your missing ship, but we have no information on her." He paused, and I thought his transmission had ended again then he jumped back to life. "Ships are lost in all sorts of circumstances. Our secondary mission out here is to look for traces of a Recon Discoverer class ship, the *RD-627*. She's been missing for six months. I don't imagine you've seen any trace of her, have you?"

I looked up the ship's classification—a Jump-enabled reconnaissance vessel with a crew of four. "Seems like we're getting careless out here. We're all losing ships or stations." I gripped the armrests. "Don't know what anyone else thinks, but it's looking to me like someone doesn't want us out here."

"We're not out here to start a fight." Logan looked at the main screen. "Can we Jump?"

The Casimir power levels were at the bottom of the scale. "Need a day to fully recharge."

"Take us away from the *Ayn Rand* and prepare to Jump as soon as possible." He floated out of his chair. "I need to think about things. Call me before the Jump."

I began setting up the departure, but before I was through, the transmission from the *Ayn Rand* reopened.

"Captain Twofeathers, I'm sorry if I sounded inhospitable. I have my orders, but there's no need for you to rush away. If you're interested, I'd be happy to share sensor information with you. That should help you remove Procyon from your list of potential locations for your lost ship. If you'd like to close further to facilitate data sharing, please do so."

Logan had turned back when the transmission came in. "Take us in, Joe. But stay alert. I don't trust them."

I reset the navigation system and plotted a route to take us closer to the Corporate ship. I also ran several basic weapons diagnostics. We needed to be ready for anything.

It took a day to reach a distance of two-million kilometers. That gave us a lag time of twelve seconds, which by spatial standards was practically real-time. We didn't stop our own sensor sweeps of the system during the approach. As we were staying longer, I thought we might as well gather as much data as we could.

I talked to Trent, while Logan met with Hernandez to discuss strategy. Once the captain understood we weren't looking for trouble, he seemed to relax but wasn't interested in getting close enough for a face-to-face meeting. "How long have you been out here?" I said.

"About a month. Took some time to work our way in from the outskirts of the system." He gestured around him. "These things aren't the fastest."

I'd dug out some information on the *Ayn Rand*'s design specifications. It was sketchy and largely speculative. The Corporates were almost as tight as the Atolls about releasing information and about as quick to steal anything useful they could get their hands on.

From the assumed data, the ship was an *Intent* class colonizer built by Xselsia Corporation and could hold up to seventy people, though from what Trent had shared with us, they only had forty onboard. Most of those were colonists with a skeleton crew of three.

We were close enough for the telescopic displays to give us a decent view of their ship. It looked similar to the back end of the *Shokasta* with a somewhat ridiculous-looking bulge that acted as the crew quarters. There were two long gantries running forward, and it took me a while to realize these were the field generators that would open the Bronikov fissure required to Jump. They extended out like giant insect antennae and looked as though they wrapped around the habitat when it was attached.

"Got family?" I remembered how lonely I'd felt when I was working away from Dollie. Even now after everything that had happened.

"Yeah." His voice was a mixture of annoyance and sadness. "You?"

"Yes, well… no." I still felt married even though my brain knew I wasn't.

Trent laughed. "Make up your mind there, buddy."

The Independence III Station was floating off the *Ayn Rand*'s port bow and looked like a floating white sausage. According to the sensors, it was barely thirty-five meters across—not much of a "colony."

"Is that as big as it gets?" I asked.

"Size isn't everything," Trent laughed. "It ain't an Interstellar Hotel, is it?"

That was an understatement. With forty people in it, that thing would be full to the point of bursting. What data I'd seen suggested they used a spin rate of four revolutions per minute to produce an apparent gravity similar to that of Mars. But with that rotation, nausea would be a distinct possibility. They could spin it slower, of course, but if they went much lower the pseudo-gravity wouldn't be enough to stop bone loss or other nasty side effects.

The *Ayn Rand*'s data showed nothing to indicate the *Sacagawea* had gotten that far. Though when I looked closer, the picture was less straightforward. I showed them the problem. "You see this here"—I pointed out the gaps in their logs—"and here."

"Any theories?" Logan asked.

"Their logging system could be flaky..." Aurore said.

I tapped the screen in front of me. "Or they've deleted entries they didn't want to share."

"Why would they do that?" Aurore peered closer at the display.

"Who knows?" I said. "But it means we can't trust them or their data."

"Did they share information on their missing ship?" said Logan. "Would that provide a clue?"

"Ask me another." I switched to the star map. "This is what they say was the planned itinerary."

The route was displayed as a dotted yellow line that slashed over to Tau Ceti then plunged down to a triple star system with the rather grand designation "EZ Aquarii." Despite the name, all three were red dwarf stars and showed considerable solar flare activity, making them poor choices for habitable worlds. Whatever the Corporates' ultimate plans, they certainly weren't obvious.

"I wonder if they reached that last system," said Aurore.

I considered the map. "If they did, they'd only have been a couple of Jumps from Wolf-1061."

Logan's eyes widened. "Wright Atoll?"

"Maybe." I plotted the route on the map, highlighting it in blue so it would stand out. "Or it could be coincidental. There are over a dozen systems within Jump distance of EZ Aquarii."

"Nothing seems to make sense, does it?" Logan sighed. "It's beginning to feel like a wild goose chase."

I nodded. I'd been here before.

It was enough for one day, and I headed to my cabin. Dan came out of his room as I passed by and jumped when he saw me. "Joe, you startled me, coming at me like that."

"Someone needs to invent something to make ZeeGee noisier."

Dan laughed—the first time I'd heard him do that—and it reminded me of Charlie's braying. "Getting some dinner," he said. "Wanna join me?"

My guilt over Charlie made me reluctant to spend time around Dan, and I also didn't want him to become a substitute for his brother. But I hadn't spent much time with him and needed to make good on my promise of making him more welcome. "Sure. I could do with some calories."

We headed to the wardroom and pulled some of the meal packs from the storage units. I'd chosen an Atoll meal—they were infinitely better—but Dan somewhat perversely grabbed a disgusting spicy fake-chicken one from Earth. As they say, there's no accounting for taste.

We sat and pressed the heating tabs on the packaging. A couple of minutes later, I smelled the rich aroma of something approximating beef bourguignon, unpleasantly mixing with the hot, spicy odor of Dan's food.

I sniffed dramatically. "We still have a lot to learn about living out here."

"You ain't wrong about that." Dan twirled his fork in his noodles, letting the bubbling mixture steam off some heat. "But after all this time, I'm kinda sick of eating that fancy 'Toller food."

"I'll be happy to trade my Earth provisions for your share of the Atoll ones." I peeled open the covering on the packaging and scooped up a small amount of stew. "You admit the Atolls are good at some things then?"

Dan chomped on his noodles then smacked his lips. "Yeah... they ain't all bad. I guess I wouldn't be here if it weren't for them."

I swallowed more of my food. It tasted so real, it would throw the average vegetarian into a spinning fit.

"Well, let's thank them for that at least." I held up my water in a toast. "I don't like them much either, but they're still human."

"You think we could work with them, Joe?" Dan ducked his head several times as he ate. "I mean, really? They've got so much and we got so little by comparison. Sometimes seems they don't even know how people on Earth live day-to-day."

"Could be. Sometimes I think all that's needed is to get people together for a while and learn from each other." It was refreshing to see Dan's change of attitude. But it made me curious. "What *did* they do to you?"

Dan chewed down three more mouthfuls of noodles and then washed them down with a big gulp of juice. "It's not... I mean... You're all so level. You and the others, and"—he jabbed his fork deep into his bowl, and his eyes seemed to lock on to something in the distance—"I can't talk about it."

"Sure. I didn't mean to pry." There was something about his response that I couldn't pin down.

He let out a long breath. "So, what are the Tigers' chances this year? Escarsega ain't pitching worth a damn."

"Same as the last few seasons." I finished my food and dropped my spoon in the bowl. "About as much chance of a MusCat preacher setting up a bordello."

Dan let out another braying laugh. "Sounds about right. Wanna make a bet on them reaching the playoffs?"

"I'm not that much of an optimist."

Grant came in, hesitated when he saw me, then dropped into a chair a few tables away. It seemed I was well and truly off his Christmas list. That didn't bother me as long as we could avoid further confrontation. With his Geneering, I'd have as much chance against him as I'd had with BRUCE.

"I'll see you later, Dan." I gathered up the debris from my food. "Time for some shut-eye."

"Sure." Dan's eyes flicked over to Grant almost imperceptibly. "I 'm gonna see what I can dig up for dessert."

Back in my cabin, my thoughts drifted to Dollie, but I dropped off without much delay—something that hadn't happened in a long time.

I woke with a start. The room was dark and quiet with no indication of what had roused me. I had only the vaguest memory of my dreams so I didn't know if they were responsible, but they often were.

My earlier discussion with Dan played on my mind. I hoped it meant that his loathing of the Atollers had gone down a notch, although both he and McDole avoided each other like a pair of plague victims. Even his animosity toward me seemed to have faded, so perhaps he'd accepted I wasn't to blame over Charlie. I was starting to drift back to sleep when it hit me.

How did Dan know I supported the Philadelphia Tigers?

Chapter Sixteen

I plotted a route to take us clear of the station the following day. Trent was expecting other ships to arrive, and although he didn't say as much, I got the impression he'd rather we weren't too close when they did. No doubt his orders were strict, and he'd ignored them to share information with us.

Dan's comment about the Tigers rattled around my head. Someone could have mentioned it, but Earth sports weren't a hot topic onboard, and I doubted it was included in my MilSec file. Logan and Aurore were the only ones who knew, but they hadn't had much to do with Dan as far as I knew. All I could imagine was that he'd looked it up. It was hardly a secret, yet something about him knowing made me uneasy.

After programming the departure and monitoring progress as the ship came to full acceleration, I made my way to the wardroom to grab something to eat. Dan was there again, chatting with Grant, Giotto, and Sullivan, the conversation louder than usual.

I sat next to them. "How're things going?"

Dan smiled, but it seemed a little too forced. "Joe, these ships are fantastic."

"The *Shokasta*?"

"Yeah. The Jump. Sustained acceleration. Cramazing."

Cramazing—crazy amazing—was a term that had gone out of fashion twenty years before I was born. "They're certainly changing things. I hope it's fast enough."

"Earth still bad, huh?"

That was an understatement. The equatorial Zone of Death

seemed to expand by the week, and extreme weather events were almost routine. There was already talk about how much longer until a mass uprising sprang up. Eventually people were going to demand what they couldn't have, and that could spell the end of humanity.

"It's not getting better." I sipped some coffee then took a mouthful of the bacon muffin I'd selected. "We need to get people off the planet wholesale. And soon."

"What's the story, Ballen?" Grant was next to Giotto, her knee over his, so their legs were half intertwined. "I thought there was supposed to be plenty of real estate out here."

It seemed that whatever had wound up Grant had been resolved in a mutually satisfactory way. I was happy to cross that off my worry list and couldn't say I was disappointed, though I suppose I should have been. Unlike McDole, Giotto was only interested in a recreational relationship, something that had never been my style. "There is. All of it bad."

I chewed more of the cardboard-like muffin. After the meal with Dan, I'd felt obliged to try more of the Earth supplies, but I'd have preferred to eat a discarded liner from a used p-suit instead of this garbage. I swigged some coffee, hoping to reincarnate my taste buds.

"No one's found anything habitable yet?" Dan sipped on a drinks tube filled with what looked like fruit juice.

I tried to ignore the rubbery residue in my mouth. "Not even close. That's why people are looking for alternatives."

"The 'Tollers could do something." Dan's words seemed to roll out of his mouth on ball bearings. "Hell, they could make a new Atoll just for Earth people if they wanted."

"That's right," Sullivan mumbled.

I looked closer. His eyes were a little glazed, his expression as blank as a baby's work record.

"They're not very helpful." I pointed to Sullivan with my fork. "Am I interrupting a private party here? I can eat in my cabin."

Grant grinned and shook his head. "Having a little fun. No harm in that, is there?"

Giotto pressed herself against Grant's muscular chest. "Ballen isn't big on fun. I think he likes jerking off too much."

"No worries. There are some real men around." Grant gave her a sloppy kiss.

Dan swallowed some of his drink then belched loudly, and I sniffed a distinct odor of alcohol.

"I know them better than you," he said. "If we worked with them, they'd help us out, for sure. They're not all assholes."

"Where'd the booze come from?"

Dan looked at the tube he was holding as if surprised, then grinned. "The army likes to keep its guys happy. Wanna try some? It's freeze-dried crap but does the job."

"Yeah, I've tried it. Didn't realize we had any onboard."

Dan leaned forward, lowering his voice to a fake whisper. "Talk to Grant. He'll fix you up. But don't tell the big guy, though. Those Indians like the joy juice a bit too much."

"Don't call him that." My teeth grated against each other, and I took a deep breath.

"Huh?" He puffed up his jowly cheeks then let the air escape with a whoosh. "What the hell should we call him then?"

"His name is Logan. You could start there. Or Mr. Twofeathers, if you want to show some respect. He's not an *Indian*—he's Coast Salish."

"Okay, sure. Whatever." Dan chugged from the bottle again then looked at Grant. "Why don't you let me have enough of this stuff to really tie one on? This journey sucks."

I was glad to hear Grant was showing some restraint. Unlike his brother, Dan didn't make for good company. Charlie once told me Dan was the "happy one," but there was precious little sign of it since we'd picked him up. I tried not to let my annoyance boil over. Maybe that's what a few years in an Atoll prison did to you.

"You need to keep your mind busy." Grant sipped from his own tube then let his hand run across Giotto's tight stomach. "And your body."

"Fat chance of that," Dan said.

"I used to go stargazing with my dad," Sullivan piped up. "When I was a kid. He made me draw all the consel... constanla...the star map things. He thought it was the best thing in the world."

"Do you enjoy drawing swans and all that shit, Sullivan?" Giotto

181

laughed hard, sounding like a lonely lighthouse's mating call.
"Naaahhh. It was more snakes and dragons. He'd tell me
stories...how they got their names." He hiccuped. "What do you
like to do in your downtime, Giotto?"

Her Geneered sapphire eyes locked with mine. "Screw."

Sullivan seemed to think that was hilarious and laughed so
much I thought he was going to choke. I imagined she was hoping
to make me jealous, but I wasn't—only relieved she had someone
else to keep her preoccupied.

Dan shot her a glance. "Any time you wanna kill some time,
baby..."

Giotto made a face and pulled back. "Not while there's breath
in this body, you wrinkly pervert. You couldn't even get it up."

Dan didn't seem to mind the insult and laughed. "You might
be surprised."

"Yeah?" she grunted. "Try Sullivan. He's probably more willing."

Grant emptied his tube and sat up a little. "Okay, folks. Bar's
closed."

Dan jumped in his seat. "You serious?"

"Always."

It was a good decision, given that the conversation was on the
brink of getting nasty. Grant wasn't stupid, though I didn't know
what Hernandez would think of him and Giotto practicing the
horizontal bop. On the other hand, perhaps he knew and wasn't
bothered as long as it didn't interfere with their mission. And
considering they'd had so little to do on this trip, there wasn't much
chance of that.

Dan leaned back, sipping on the last of his booze. "What about
you, Joe? How do you keep from going insane out here?"

His manner was odd. Initially, I'd thought he was drunk, but
now his voice was steady and he seemed in control of himself. For
some reason, I got the feeling there was something calculating
behind everything he said.

What *did* I do apart from miss Dollie or plan secret projects?
My head switched into job interview mode of its own free will.
"Catch up on engineering tech journals or learn a new skill." I shoved
the remnants of the muffin to one side. "Right now, I'm struggling

to wrap my head around Casimir tensor math. Not the practical stuff—theory."

"I'm too old for that." He drained the last drops from his drinking tube. "How about this bird? Do you think I could learn how to fly one of these?"

"The ship?"

"Yeah. I'm gonna need work when we get back. If I know more about these things, I might be able to land something with all the new activity out here."

At his age, I'd be surprised if he got medical clearance, but then again with the shortage of pilots he might be in luck. "I'm not sure about that."

"Why not?" Grant grunted. "This ain't your ship. You stole it."

"Yeah, Ballen. Stop being so uptight. Let the old man have a crack at it." Giotto's face broke into a grin. "Only crack he's gonna get around here."

Dan wasn't endearing himself to me. But he was still Charlie's brother, and a prickle of guilt brushed over my scalp. With his background, he'd likely have a strong work ethic, and what else would an old spaceman do? While I couldn't see any harm in him learning to operate the ship, I wasn't going to turn control over to him—but there were other options. "I'll give you access to the simulator. It's an alt-real interface, so it'll get you as close as possible without going hands-on."

"Thanks, Joe." He smiled. "Sorry if I was a jerk about Logan. Didn't mean anything by it. Been on my own so long, I forget my manners."

Giotto stood and wiggled her ass at Grant. "I think it's time for some relaxation."

Grant grinned and slapped her behind. "I'm right with you, *Private*."

I watched them walk away, giggling like a pair of teenagers, then looked back at Dan. He rubbed his face as though trying to wake himself up. "I'm gonna do some more catch-up. Lemme know when you set up the sim access."

Without Dan there to prop him up, Sullivan slid over sideways, his head slapping the bench. I thought about moving him but decided a cricked neck was partial payback for him leaving BRUCE activated. I was still sipping on my coffee when Hernandez walked in. His eyes went to Sullivan, slumped on the bench seat, half under the table. After checking on him, he sat down across from me.

"Grant messaged me. Said they'd been having a party and you'd showed up." He held his hands open, palms up. "I'm happy to let the kiddies enjoy themselves, if it doesn't go too far. Grant knows that. I trust him."

"How far?"

Hernandez eased into the chair opposite. "Enough to know I can count on him to save my life, which he's done more than once."

"It's your team." I finished the last of my coffee. "You don't need my approval."

His angle wasn't clear, then it dawned on me. "You're worried I'll tell Logan."

"You've been friends a long time."

I moved over to the recycler and happily threw the remains of my meal inside. "Long enough that I don't hide things from him."

"So you might feel you have to." Hernandez stared at me. "And he could give me a sad-looking Form Sixty when we get back."

I'd met enough of the military to know a Form Sixty was a mission evaluation report. A private document created by the person in charge, which could contain sensitive appraisals of all team members.

"If you're worried about it, you should talk to him. Logan's a reasonable man."

"So you're going to tell him about this?" He gestured at the drinks tubes littering the table.

"It's not my business." I moved toward the door. "But what makes you think he doesn't already know? Logan's a smart guy. He understands how crews work—and how to handle them."

"Ballen?"

I turned back around. Hernandez was holding up a small bag with some red powder in it. "Wanna drink?"

"Are you trying to bribe me, Sergeant?"

He didn't blink. "Absolutely."

"There's no need."

"Call it a gift then."

An intense hunger boiled up as my inner drunk fought to escape. The needy me wanted it so much I could almost taste the booze. I clamped down on the sensation, though I realized I was licking my lips unconsciously. "Thanks, I'm good."

Hernandez frowned. "You're not the guy I thought I knew from your profile. Mind a few questions?"

His comment might have been good or bad, but I didn't have anything to hide. I sat back down. "Fire away."

"Logan told me about the *RD-627*, the missing Corporate ship. Got any theories?"

That was the number one mystery, and I didn't have an answer. "Maybe it's one of Doctor Wingnut's diabolical schemes to cordon us to our own system. We have no idea. Ships are going missing, and the Atolls have lost a station. There's no evidence these are anything but malfunctions or accidents—although, some people think it might be the U'Gani."

"Those are the aliens, right?" Hernandez rubbed his fingers across his mouth. "The nearest, that is."

"Don't be fooled by that. The nearest U'Gani system we know of is over three-hundred and fifty light-years away. There's nothing that says we'd be of any interest to them."

He nodded. "It's goddamn strange all these things happening at the same time."

"Which is why we're searching for the *Sacagawea*. Hoping to get some answers."

"Do you think we'll find her?"

I hesitated. Hernandez should know the odds, but perhaps he didn't believe that one of our most advanced starships could simply vanish. "I think she's gone."

"Are we going to see any action on this trip?"

"Military action requiring your team?" I shook my head. "Very unlikely."

"So we don't know anything, do we?"

"Not unless you accept the Doctor Wingnut theory."

Hernandez played a tattoo of slaps on his legs. "Thanks, man. That's good to know—comforting."

A cold flush of surprise hit me, and my face must have betrayed that.

"I know. Sounds crazy, but at least you ain't bullshitting. I can deal with that." He tapped the bag of powder. "Think it's time for me to have a drink, though. Sure you don't wanna join me?"

I fought the rush his question triggered. "I'm your designated driver, remember?"

The control room was empty. I guessed the novelty of interstellar flight had worn off for Logan and Aurore too. It wasn't much of a surprise. There was little of interest to see and, without habitable worlds, almost nowhere to go. Though as a certified space nut, just thinking about it still sent a thrill through me.

The prospect of the next Jump was depressing. I had little confidence we'd find anything. Ross-614 was almost five light-years from Procyon and another binary. But both its stars were red dwarfs—the larger about one and a half times the size of Jupiter and the smaller about a third of that.

After the Jump, I brought them up on the screen. They cast a muddy orange light through the main display, with none of the brightness of either Sirius or Procyon. Aurore had left a sensor sweep setup in the system, and I triggered it to begin collecting information. But even before the data arrived, it appeared to have been a wasted trip. This system was so uninteresting nobody had bothered to rename it, even though several ships had visited according to our records.

I opened the system map, but it didn't help much. Both suns were flare stars, and the Habitable Zone was so close to the larger one that anything orbiting there would get fried at the first unusual solar activity—which considering the proximity of the second star was highly likely. There *were* several planet no-names and assorted orbital debris, but for the most part the system was as dead as a politician's promise.

I heard someone behind me and looked around. McDole was staring at the main screen, her angular face made harsher by her frown. "That doesn't look promising."

"It's not, but there's enough debris around that might hide signs of a ship, so we have to do a scan."

"I understand. I'd do the same." McDole sat next to me. "What type of search pattern are you running?"

I only knew one way to search. "Run the sensors until we get signals back. Why?"

"We're in a JumpShip."

"Thanks for reminding me..." I didn't see what difference that made.

"Program a series of Jumps forming a sphere around the system. Take a snapshot of sensor readings at each then merge the data. Any points of interest should stand out in the resulting data cloud."

I thought about it. The scans wouldn't happen any faster as such, but we could run them for shorter periods at each stop and effectively get the data back faster. "You're good. We'd need to allow time for the generators to re-energize between Jumps, but it would cut several days off the process."

McDole nodded. "You'd also get better triangulation, allowing you to narrow down any anomalous readings."

"I'm impressed."

"We're more experienced with operating in space than you. Besides"—she smiled—"I'd be as happy as everyone else to minimize the time out here."

"I can set up the Jumps, but I'll need to run it by the others. I can't see them objecting, though."

McDole patted my arm. "You see. I'm not the enemy."

Maybe she wasn't but someone was. "What happened to Dan?"

"What do you mean?"

I hesitated, not sure how to explain my uneasiness and with little confidence she'd answer truthfully anyway. "He was held on the Atoll all these years. I'd expect him to hate Atollers, but instead he seems scared. And he wanted to kill me, but now he seems to have changed his mind."

"He has?" McDole pursed her lips. "That's... strange."

"And you both avoid each other."

She laughed. "I don't like him, and I'm embarrassed that we kept him prisoner for so long. It's an uncomfortable combination."

I could almost accept that, if not for the fact that she'd avoided my question. "So, what *did* they do to him?"

The creases around her eyes seemed to tighten almost imperceptibly. "Standard physical and psychometric testing. Our scientists are curious about genetic drift and inherited diseases. We're your descendants, after all."

"That's all?" It didn't seem enough to trigger Dan's fears.

"Possibly some routine psychological therapy. He'd have been traumatized when he was picked up."

"You don't know?"

"Not in detail. I skimmed through his records after I was transferred there, but we were already processing him for release. It didn't seem important." She ran her hand through her hair. "There was no record of him being mistreated, if that's what you're thinking."

"By Atoll standards…"

"Yes, by *our* standards. I've told you before, we're not all the same. If it had been up to me, I'd have sent him back at the earliest opportunity."

McDole stood abruptly and headed for the door, almost colliding with Logan and Aurore. She pushed by them and disappeared down the passage, leaving them staring after her.

"Your seduction techniques slipping, Joe?" Aurore asked.

"Off the bottom of the scale."

I explained McDole's Jump idea, and Logan was happy to go along with it. An hour later, Aurore had made some refinements to my sequence, minimizing our recharge time. After that, it was only a matter of executing the sequence. I'd sent out a warning that we'd be in for a few rough days with the repeated Jumps. I also programmed an automatic countdown to broadcast around the ship so nobody would be caught by surprise.

As I was doing last-minute checks, I noticed a blip in systems use and expanded the display to show more details. Dan had been spending up to ten hours a day inside the simulator. It looked like he was running the same scenarios over and over, as though he was struggling to pick it up. It didn't seem healthy, but at least it was keeping him occupied.

When the Jump sequence began, it was like someone had jammed the pause button on activity onboard the ship. The physiological and psychological effects seemed to mount with each successive maneuver, and I was always on edge when we hit the final countdown. It was fortunate we needed breaks while the ship recharged—otherwise, I think we'd have lost the entire crew to nausea and starvation.

"Is this the last one?" Aurore was almost doubled over in a ball, her face puffy and streaked where tears had blotched her makeup. She looked ready to throw up again, and I felt the same.

"Yeah. After that, it's straightforward information processing." Logan sighed. "I'm ready for that."

The countdown ticked off the last second, and we hopped to the last point in our schedule. Several minutes later, the sensor signals kicked in and started finalizing the data set. It would take a while to get the last of the data back and process it, but was still faster and more thorough than doing it the way we'd been planning.

"Could you make a Ballen-ball to do this?" Aurore asked. "Program it to hop around the system to gather a data snapshot?"

I laughed at the nickname. "I suppose so. The real problem would be the Casimir generators. They're relatively large, so the unit wouldn't be any smaller than my communication drone. In fact, with the detection gear it might be even bigger."

Aurore shrugged. "Not very practical then."

"It depends. Technology has a habit of shrinking, so you never know." I gave her a thumbs-up. "Write it up and patent it. It might make you a fortune."

"I like that idea." Logan stretched his arms up, working knots from his shoulders. "I've nothing against being rich."

"Who said anything about you?" Aurore poked her tongue out at him.

Logan grinned. "Share and share alike."

Aurore made a show of thinking for a moment. "Okay. But only if I can have my own dance studio."

"You hate teaching."

"What's that got to do with it?" Aurore laughed.

When she was younger, Aurore had trained as a dancer, and for a long time had been torn between doing it professionally or continuing her science training. I'd seen her dance, and she was good enough to have gone pro.

"Never interfere with a woman's ambition." I waved a finger at

189

Logan in mock reproach.

Aurore chuckled. "Glad to see one man on this ship understands women—even if only partially."

I sighed. I wished that were true. Perhaps then I'd have been able to fix my relationship with Dollie. Instead, the gulf between us had grown even larger than the physical distance that now separated us.

"Do you think anything much has happened on Earth while we've been gone?" I said.

Aurore's expression turned serious. "What are you thinking of, Joe?"

Logan caught my eye, and I guessed he knew what I was thinking about.

"The All-Parties Conference. They might have already met and thrashed out some sort of strategic plan."

"You know better than that," said Logan. "When do politicians make progress quickly?"

"I know. But this is important. The whole world's at risk, and it's getting worse almost by the day."

"That's what they said a hundred and fifty years ago." Logan grimaced. "And look at what's happened."

McDole staggered in holding her stomach, looking as if she *had* thrown up. "That was the last?"

When I nodded, she seemed to relax. "When will the analysis be complete?"

I checked the progress of the data compilation. "Not long. We have around ninety percent coverage."

"Anything preliminary showing up?" she said.

I accessed the data cloud and transferred it to the large display volume. Everyone gathered around, peering at the nebula-like points.

"Filter for refined metals," Aurore said.

There were various blobs and traces around the area, but when I cross-referenced them they all proved to be false signals from asteroids and other space junk.

"Any traces of materials moving in trajectories from an explosion?" Logan asked.

I refined the display again, but everything appeared to be moving as nature intended. At least, at the resolution we had.

"Rogue EM signals?" suggested McDole.

There were some, but again they all tracked with natural sources. By the time the last sensor returns came back, there was only one conclusion.

"There's nothing here," I said.

My arms and legs felt like they weighed more than they did on Earth, even though we were at one-third of a g, and I leaned against the wall. I hadn't expected to find the ship that easily, but the farther we traveled the more it seemed pointless. For the first time, I wished I'd stayed on Earth. Maybe getting miserably drunk and programming asteroid mining robots was all I was good for anymore.

"I'm going to pay a visit to Corporal Grant, if anyone wants to join me. He has some powder that might help right about now."

"Hold on, Joe," said Logan.

I didn't want to have *that* conversation with others around.

He tried again. "We need to program the next Jump."

"Tomorrow's good enough." I didn't turn to face him. "We have to recharge anyway."

"I'd prefer to get it set up now so everyone has adequate time to prepare."

My muscles tightened, and my teeth ground against each other. "It's better to spread out disappointments, you know. Too many can kill you."

When he eventually replied, Logan's voice was softer. "Okay. Do what you feel is right."

I clambered down the passage, my limbs stiff. Nobody cared when the Jump was. It was a waste of time, like this whole mission. They knew it as much as I did. The only people who didn't were the stuffed-shirt politicos and paranoid military who'd insisted on a search against all good advice.

The wardroom was empty, so I headed toward Grant's quarters. I was about to knock on his door when something stopped me. I wasn't even sure what. I needed a drink. Needed it like a drowning man needs a gasp of air. It didn't matter anymore—none of it did. If that was the way out, then why the hell not—at least it was painless.

I lifted my hand again but froze. Then I spun around and climbed back up to my quarters, with no idea why I hadn't knocked. Something inside wouldn't let me, and it made me even angrier that I couldn't figure out what it was. I slammed my bad hand into the wall. It had closed up and the MediSkin had long washed away, but it still sometimes itched. Now it flared up angrily.

Leaning against the wall, I hammered my forehead against it. Maybe I should take a walk out the airlock without a p-suit. At least then I'd be out of mine and everybody else's misery. Logan could pilot the ship back—he didn't need me. Once I cleared my system locks, he could take the ship anywhere.

I opened the door to head to the bridge and almost tripped over McDole. She stepped back in surprise when she saw me.

"You startled me." She ran her hand through her hair, making it prickle out from her head. "I thought you were going to see Grant."

"That's not the direction I'm going," I said.

"You're bleeding."

I looked down. The wound had split open again, leaving blood trickling down my fingers. I hadn't even felt it. But it didn't matter anymore either. "No worries. I'm tough."

Her eyes searched my face. "Are you, Joe?"

"Sure. Meet me at the airlock in five, and I'll give you a ringside seat."

McDole's face suffused with blood, and her lips drew back in a snarl. Then her hand snapped out and cracked against my cheek, hard enough it felt like my jaw was dislocated.

"Don't you dare. Don't you *ever* say something like that."

Chapter Seventeen

Logan eyeballed me as I entered the control room the following day. After seeing what he needed to, his face split into a grin and he slapped my shoulder.

"You're doing okay, Joe."

I slipped into my seat. "Maybe."

I triggered the Jump countdown and sat back. My busted-up hand was covered with another MediSkin patch, but the split had torn so unevenly I'd backed it up with a roll of tape, making it feel like I was wearing a boxing glove. McDole had marched off after our encounter with no explanation, leaving me wondering what had made her react that way. That said, it seemed to have knocked some sense back into me, and I wasn't thinking about airlocks anymore. Or at least not for now.

GJ 3379, more recently and presumptuously renamed Buang's Star by an Atoller who'd surveyed it, was under five light-years away from our current position. It was another dwarf star with little to distinguish it, other than it happened to be the nearest star in the constellation of Orion as seen from Earth.

From a colonization perspective, dwarf stars weren't great candidates. But they were more numerous than sun-like ones, and nothing we knew precluded them from having habitable planets, which made surveying them important. And if nothing else, they were useful stepping stones to other systems.

But, following Aurore's logic, many of them would be good candidates for large-scale orbital or free-floating habitats. It also occurred to me that as binary stars tended to have large debris fields, they'd make for easier access to raw materials too. If you're already in space, moving resources around costs next to nothing—the expensive part is getting things in and out of a gravity well. And that was true even with the Elevators and the other orbital technology we had available.

I'd taken the opportunity to get a solid six hours of sleep, so not only did I feel more rested, the darkness that had surrounded me had lifted to an extent. I could still feel it lurking at the back of my mind, but at least it had dropped away enough to allow me to function somewhat normally.

By now, the Jump seemed almost routine, and after cruising for half a day to recharge, we executed the same pattern of Jumps we'd taken around Ross-614. With no secondary star to complicate matters, the process was shorter this time. Buang may have attached his name to it, but as far as star systems went it was about as welcoming as a seat in a cactus patch.

After the analysis came up empty again, it was time to move on. We jumped to GJ 3454 with at least some sense of optimism. Although this was another dwarf star, there was a PAC station located there. The system was known to have a number of planets and also held the most extensive debris belt yet found. Like Buang's Star, it had been labeled Learmonth by the Atolls, and the PAC had recognized this by naming their station after the new designation.

The Jump was short, so we had some power reserves, and I used them to bring us closer to the station. If the *Sacagawea* had gotten this far, the PAC would have almost certainly detected it. The star had a planetary system somewhat similar to Sol's with one substantial rocky planet, two small gas giants, and several smaller planetoids. Learmonth base was relatively close in, orbiting at around ninety-million kilometers in order to capture the star's feeble solar radiation. This also gave it easy access to the inner edge of the vast Etts debris field. As we approached, we picked up signals from a second source. It appeared the station had visitors already— a PAC vessel that identified as the *PTN Kunan*.

Most of the system was nestled within the one A.U. limit, which complicated our approach. I took the ship high above the equatorial region to find a route with less potential for debris then dropped back down once we were nearer to the station. By the time I'd finished we were close, but it wasn't what anyone would call convenient.

"Sixty-million kilometers. Comms lag about seven minutes round trip." I frowned at Logan. "Sorry, boss. Best I can do without risking a Jump problem."

Logan clasped his left hand around his fist. "Nature of the business. Send them a canned message that we intend to approach and will dock if they're willing."

He left with Hernandez, discussing other possible search strategies. I sent the message then set course at maximum speed and groaned when I saw the ETA.

"Three days." I shook my head.

"You'd think with all the power this ship has"—Aurore thumped the arm of her chair—"there'd be some way of getting around faster."

"If you think of something, be sure to let me know." I stood and stretched my back, feeling in need of another session with BRUCE. "I'm going to grab some food. Want to join me?"

"Might as well as my man seems to have abandoned me."

"He has a lot on his mind."

"Don't defend him, Joe. He's a big boy and can take care of himself." She grinned. "And so can I."

Sullivan and Dan were in the wardroom, sitting either side of the large display. They were playing a game of ZHexChess, and from the pieces left on the boards, Sullivan was losing badly.

He nodded at us, his concentration almost entirely focused on the chess board. After a pause, he moved one of his Marauders and leaned back with a confident glow on his face. But before his spine touched the seat, Dan worked his controls and one of his Reapers moved to lock onto Sullivan's Star Destroyer.

"Check and mate," Dan murmured. "That's another drink you owe me, kid."

"Damn it!" Sullivan slapped the table next to the screen. "You're impossible."

I waited while Aurore selected her meal and then grabbed one myself. She'd chosen some of the Atoll supplies, while I'd picked a laughingly named roast beef on rye sandwich that had never seen beef, and I was suspicious about the "rye" designation too.

Dan ambled out, leaving Sullivan with his head in his hands. "How does the old bastard do it?"

I opened my sandwich and waited for the steam to clear before taking a bite. "You on a losing streak?"

"Don't tease him, Joe." Aurore nibbled on her food.

"Every goddamn game. Whether it's chess, poker, or Jerundra Clash, he always does it." Sullivan slashed his hand at the controls to close the screen down. "I owe him a week's supply of booze now."

"Maybe you should challenge him at something you're good at," I said.

"Yeah, right." Sullivan clambered off his seat and headed for the door. "I was level seventy Jerundra during boot camp."

With that, he was gone too.

Aurore shrugged. "Sounds like a sore loser."

That might be true. But there was also something odd about it. I could see Dan winning at poker and maybe even chess—if you give credence to the idea that old age and treachery always beats youth and enthusiasm—but Jerundra was an alt-real twitch combat game. "If Sullivan's level seventy, then he's in the upper ten percent from what I know."

Aurore pursed her lips. "You're right. That's pretty much a semi-pro rating."

"How could someone Dan's age touch him?"

"Maybe Dan got lucky or the kid had a bad night." Aurore sipped on a tube of juice. "It happens."

I finished off my unsatisfactory sandwich and washed it down with some water. I wanted to be well hydrated for my intended workout, not riding a caffeine buzz.

"Time for me to do a robot beatdown," I said.

Aurore sipped from a tube of herbal tea. "Do you *ever* manage that?"

"Don't tell anyone, but I'm hoping to work up to a draw someday."

I was almost at the wardroom door when the main alarm sounded. I glanced at Aurore, then we both bolted up the corridor to the control room.

I dropped into my chair and checked the diagnostic screens as

Aurore slid into her own seat. There was no sign of damage or malfunction.

Logan barreled in with Hernandez only steps behind him.

"What have we got?" Logan said, pulling up his own displays.

"Everything's in the green," I said. "Not even a power fluctuation."

"Check tactical," said Aurore. "I think there's something there."

"Huh?" I activated the display and everything looked normal at first glance. Then I saw it—a blip on the edge of the screen, barely inside our sensor range. "Is that a ship?"

"I think so." Aurore manipulated the sensor data. "No. Make that two."

"Transponder signals?"

I overlaid the sensor information on the main screen, combining it with the system map. The star was highlighted, surrounded by the glowing orbital paths of the planets and brighter tracks showing the location of the station and *Kunan*. Our position was at the center of the volume, while off to our starboard at long range two dots flashed red, with the designation "No-ID."

"I don't like this." Logan rubbed his jaw. "Light 'em up, Joe. Just in case."

I flipped several controls, arming the weapons and point-defense systems, then opened the ship-wide comms. "All hands, battle stations. Strap down for high-g and unpredictable maneuvers."

Logan looked at Aurore. "Anything?"

"Picking up transponder IDs." She hesitated. "They're showing Atoll designation numbers. No names, only serial numbers."

"Atoll ships? That's crazy, why would—" He turned to Hernandez. "Get downstairs and make sure your people are ready, and send McDole up here. If she doesn't want to come, bring her."

The ID information transferred to the screen and tagged the two distant ships. They were AF-11 type cruisers—the same as the *Yukawa*. "Definitely returning Atoll IDs, and from what other data we have so far they match the profile," I said. "But they don't look like they're collecting for the Red Cross."

"Any orbital information?" Logan said, his eyes fixed on the screen.

"Too soon," Aurore said.

"Comm lag?"

I checked the distance. "Four minutes round trip."

"Send a signal."

He faced the main optical pick-up, and I opened a transmission. "Unidentified Atoll ships, this is Captain Twofeathers of the *USN Shokasta*. We are searching for a missing vessel and plan to dock with Learmonth Base. We are on a peaceful mission, but we *are* armed. Please inform us of your intentions."

"Anything on their trajectory yet?" Logan said.

"Still too early. One may be heading toward us, the other to the station." Aurore slammed her hand into the console. "I need more data."

"This doesn't make any sense. Why would the Atolls send two warships here?" I stared at the system map. "Are they after us or the PAC station? They might not like *us* much, but the PAC is their main terrestrial supplier."

"Could the PAC be responsible for the loss of the Wright Atoll?" Aurore's words were almost a whisper. "Are we getting caught up in a war between them and the Atolls?"

"If that were the case, they'd be responsible for the *Sacagawea* and the *RD-627*." Logan tapped his fingers on the arm of his chair. "The PAC is ultra-competitive and desperate, but they're not crazy enough to start a war with everyone."

McDole hastily strapped herself into the starboard seat. I hadn't seen her since she'd slapped me, and she looked tired, but her face was a mask showing no emotion.

"There are Atoll ships out there?" she said, her voice flat.

"We think so," I said. "They're showing Atoll transponder IDs but no names and appear to be AF-11 cruisers."

McDole's eyes widened. "Can you put me through to them?"

"Broadcast only," I said. "Response time four minutes."

She nodded, and I opened the transmission again.

"This is Commander McDole of the Atoll Defense Force onboard the *USN Shokasta*. I order you to identify yourselves and make your intentions known. This is a special order—Priority One. Override all other orders. Identification Code: Papa Foxtrot Whiskey Delta Golf Kilo Juliet Five One One Nine."

I cut the transmission, and silence filled the control room like a sack full of marshmallows in a half-liter cup.

Logan pointed to the screen. "Any idea who they are, Commander?"

McDole shook her head. "We have no ships operating out here that I know of. And we don't have many AF-11s. Two running together like this is... curious."

The clock was ticking for a possible response, and I felt increasingly nervous. "Is there anything we should know about their capabilities? Armaments, defensive systems?"

"They can be configured in many different ways." McDole lifted her hand up to forestall any objections. "I'm not being awkward or hiding anything. I don't know how these particular ones have been loaded."

The transmission indicator lit up. I glanced at the timer. It couldn't be the Atoll ships—not enough time had passed. I played the transmission on a secondary screen. A long-faced man appeared, smiling like he'd found his long-lost teddy bear.

"This is Lieutenant Matsudo, commanding Learmonth Base. Welcome to Learmonth, *Shokasta*. It would be a pleasure to have you and your crew come aboard." He spoke with a refined accent that reminded me of an old-style British actor. "We're rather starved of visitors out here, so your visit is a pleasant surprise. It will be some time before you get here, I see. Once in easier communication range, we can agree the—"

Matsudo had paused his broadcast, and it didn't take much to guess why. "Looks like he cut off transmission. No idea why."

"Could they have been attacked already?" Logan asked.

"Not unless the Atoll ships have some kind of faster-than-light weapon."

"We don't," McDole said. "That would be impossible."

The transmission light flashed again, and Matsudo reappeared.

"Captain Chandra on the *PTN Kunan* has informed me that two more ships have entered the Learmonth system. Are these vessels with you? This is all highly irregular. The station isn't equipped to deal with large numbers of visitors.

"As a precautionary measure, the *Kunan* is going to make its way to a neutral stand-off position. I'm sure you will understand. I look forward to an explanation for your presence."

Matsudo and Chandra weren't fools. They'd recognized the potential threat and were taking action to strengthen their defensive options and minimize their risks. "Why would the Atolls attack the PAC?" I turned to McDole.

"We wouldn't. We don't start hostilities. We're not aggressive," she said, coldly.

"Tell that to Dan's shipmates," I snapped. "Those *are* Atoll ships, aren't they?"

"Circumstances have changed. At that point, we felt we needed to act to preserve peace for our communities. Now Earth has the Jump drive, there's no point in continuing hostilities." McDole's gaze was fixed on the screen. "And if we're the aggressors, who destroyed Wright Atoll?"

"We have to assume they're hostile for now." Logan nodded. "Send a signal to the station."

My hand hovered over the controls. "The cruisers will pick it up as well."

"I'm counting on it," Logan growled.

He waited for a moment. "Lieutenant Matsudo, this is Captain Twofeathers on the *Shokasta*. We have detected signatures from the other ships suggesting they are Atoll vessels. They are not related to our mission, and we have no information on their intent. We have a high-ranking Atoll official on board who has ordered them to stand down, but they have not yet acknowledged. We're ready to render assistance to both your station and the *Kunan* as required. We will, of course, defend ourselves from any belligerent acts. To this end, we will make a small Jump to place our ship between Learmonth base and the other vessels."

Logan gripped the arms of his seat. "Do it, Joe. Damn the risk."

I switched to the Jump controls, programming a position roughly equidistant between the station and the closing Atoll ships. It was difficult to set up a clean transition, and I had to tweak the destination to balance the space-time curvature. I hoped that would minimize any potential difficulties, but it was far from certain. We could as easily disappear into oblivion for all I knew. When finished, I fed the data to Aurore for a sanity check.

It didn't take her long to work through my solution. "Looks as good as it can be, Joe."

Logan nodded, and I activated a ship-wide broadcast. "Jump in thirty. Hang on—this one might be rough."

The engines built to peak energy, and when the countdown hit zero the Jump engaged. My stomach felt like it had wrapped itself around a high-speed gear, and a shock of purple-blackness ripped through my brain. I might have yelled, but my senses were so overwhelmed that I couldn't be sure. When my eyesight returned, bright streaks of distortion streamed from the edge of my field of view, adding to the wave of nausea that almost doubled me over in pain.

My hands shook as I reached for the controls to check our position. After confirming it, my head had cleared enough to attempt speech. "Everyone okay?"

McDole didn't respond, and I look across at her. She was hunched over in her seat, her body racked with spasms.

I reached for my harness buckle. "McDole?"

She drew in a wet breath. "M'okay..."

I turned to the controls. "We're right between the ships and the station."

Aurore's voice was shaky. "The *Kunan* is moving away from the station. It looks like they're heading for a defensive position."

Logan turned around to face McDole. "Is there anything else you'd like to try before I give the order to fire, Commander?"

Tears gleamed on McDole's cheeks. "They're not answering to my orders. Take whatever action you feel necessary."

"They're your ships." Logan held his hands open, palms up.

"They may be our designs, but that doesn't mean they're under our control. If they were commanded by ADF officers, I would know about it. Your duty is to protect your ship. I understand that."

"We're in missile range," I said. "It's extreme."

"Target both ships." Logan waited until I confirmed. "Fire."

My hand moved to press the button but never got there.

"Wait!" Aurore stabbed at her controls. "They're gone."

"They Jumped?" Logan said.

"I'm not sure." Aurore flipped through the sensor data. "They must have."

"Could they have recharged their Jump drives in that time?" I looked at McDole.

"I can't answer that," she said.

"Can't or won't?" barked Logan.

His tone told me he wouldn't have believed either. I kept my eyes fixed to the sensor information. The ships could have Jumped to another system, or perhaps they'd taken a strategic risk like we had and moved in closer. A few seconds later I saw a blip, but before the system could make any sense out of the data, it was gone.

"Never seen anything like that," Aurore said. "Sensor glitch?"

After another short delay, I saw another pulse. "Right... and there's its twin brother."

I waited and spotted another spike of seemingly random data from the sensors. I filtered out the best location estimates of each burst and threw them on screen. They formed a line carving ever nearer to us.

"Are they doing micro-Jumps to close on us?" My voice came out more of a whisper than I intended.

"Micro-Jumps?" Logan turned to me. "How can that—"

The lighting flashed red several times, and a warning siren cut him off. "Incoming missiles detected," I shouted.

"The Atoll ships are behind us," Aurora called out.

"Emergency maneuvers," said Logan.

I triggered a pre-programmed sequence of jinking movements designed to break a missile lock or make it difficult for ballistic weapons to track. The room spun and twisted around us as the CASTOR system triggered. I fought to keep my eyes on the screens, but the movements made it almost impossible.

Aurore's voice warbled unsteadily over the siren. "The missiles are heading for the station."

"Target the ships and fire," Logan ordered.

They were inside our weapons range now, and I launched missiles at both, followed by a stream of railgun fire. We had a slim chance of hitting them, but hopefully it would distract them if nothing else.

A faint vibration ran through the ship as the missiles launched and streaked toward their targets. The location of the missiles tracked on the screen. The scale of the display was so large they seemed to crawl, even though they were traveling at thousands of kilometers a second and still accelerating.

McDole took a sharp breath. "They are *not* Atoll ships. We would never fire on a research facility."

"The evidence doesn't support your claim." Logan kept his voice low and level. "Perhaps you should wait in your quarters, Commander."

I paused the ship's crazy movements. "You have five minutes."

"Am I to consider myself under arrest?" McDole unlocked her harness and stood awkwardly.

Logan didn't look around. "You're our guest. And for the purposes of this encounter a civilian. I'd hate to have things get discourteous."

McDole sniffed then turned abruptly and left.

"They've fired again," Aurore said. "Tracking shows two separate volleys. One targeted on us, one on the *Kunan*."

"Point defense is tracking." I watched the timer. McDole had three more minutes. "Holding position."

I killed the warnings, and a throbbing silence filled the control room. It was a risk, not re-engaging the avoidance routine, but if I triggered it before McDole was strapped in, she'd be dead on the next maneuver. A trickle of sweat ran down my temple and neck, soaking into my shirt collar. Logan stared at the large screen showing the incoming weapons tracks, the muscles in his neck as taut as cables.

The comm system beeped. "Secure."

It was McDole, and I slapped the buttons to restart the evasive maneuvers. The ship bucked, and my neck cricked from leaning forward. Lights flashed as the point defense system triggered, spraying a cloud of railgun rounds and small interceptor missiles to screen us from the incoming missiles.

"They're gone again," Aurore said.

I couldn't believe the enemy ships could recharge that fast. And the idea that they had such large power reserves made almost as little sense. Whoever they were, they were more than a step ahead of us. And I didn't think the PAC was in a better position to fight them.

I focused on the sensor displays, fighting to keep my eyes steady despite the roller coaster motions. "They're at long range again. Looks like they're going for the *Kunan*."

"They hit the station," Aurore said. "Looks like several missiles got through its defenses."

It wasn't too surprising. As a scientific establishment, Learmonth was likely equipped with minimal defenses. Who'd spend a fortune to defend a bunch of research scientists in the middle of nowhere?

"Survivors?" Logan whispered.

"Impossible to say." Aurore glanced across at him. "Unlikely."

"You got anything, Joe?" he said.

"Looks like they've damaged the *Kunan* too. I'm picking up uncontrolled energy leaks." I filtered the data to focus on the PAC ship. "They're showing an energy surge—could be about to blow. Or maybe Jump."

"The Atoll ships have Jumped again. They're closing on the *Kunan*." Aurore's voice became a rough croak. "And they've fired."

It was two against one—the PAC ship didn't stand a chance. I hoped they were on a build to a Jump—otherwise, they were dead. The screen flashed red with warnings, and I changed displays. The Atoll ships were within weapons range of us again.

"Incoming!" shouted Aurore.

I activated the next Jump, not knowing if we'd make it or not. The counter clicked up on screen and ticked down as the Casimir generators built to maximum power. The defense systems kicked in again, and volley after volley of railgun rounds blasted out at the missiles accelerating toward us.

"Prepare to Jump!" I yelled into the comm system.

The last seconds ticked down, the ship lurched, and the lights went out.

Chapter Eighteen

"What happened?" Logan was floating next to me, shaking my arm. "You okay?"

"I triggered the Jump." It felt like I'd plowed into a minor planet head-first, but I seemed to be in one piece. "How's Aurore?"

"Shook up, but she'll live." Logan had made it to his feet. "Where did we Jump?"

"The navigation was programmed for our next scheduled stop, GJ 1116." I brought up the display. "It'll take a while to confirm that."

Several warning lights flashed, and I shook my head to clear the fog. "We've got some hull breaches. Small, but we're venting atmosphere." I unbuckled my belt, grabbed a comm-set, and twisted out of my chair. "I'll need help."

"Check our location if you can." Logan kissed Aurore then pushed off to follow me.

The ship's outer hull had an impact-resistant shell, and inside that was a lining made up of layers of ballistic fluid and the new Astrogel. The gel was a heavier duty version of the VacSeal routinely used to close holes in an emergency but was built-in. If we had a hole so large the gel couldn't seal it automatically, we needed to get on it pronto.

The gel also provided conductive resistance, allowing us to trace the punctured areas. We tracked one to McDole's quarters, and I hesitated before entering. The door inched open when I pushed it, but I wasn't relishing what we might find.

The hole was less than the width of my finger, but to have

David M. Kelly

produced that much damage through all the protective layers meant a substantial hit on the outside. I blasted it with a spray of VacSeal and slapped on a patch to be doubly sure.

McDole was strapped to her couch with a large red mark on her forehead. It couldn't have been from whatever had penetrated the ship, or there'd have been nothing left of her skull. I guessed something loose had hit her, though it wasn't obvious what that might have been. She was unconscious, her breathing ragged and unsteady.

As we moved her, Logan tapped his comm-set. "Sullivan, we need you in the MedBay, right away."

We were almost there when a reply sounded in my ear. It was Hernandez. "Sullivan didn't make it."

I swore. "Anyone else who can help?"

A moment later he answered. "We've all got first aid. That's it."

"Okay, we've got it," Logan said.

We both had basic emergency training, but she didn't need two of us. I pointed down the corridor. "There's one more hole. Can you take care of McDole?"

"Sure. Go."

I helped him swing her in the door for the MedBay and headed toward the reactor area where the next leak was.

I wondered if Sullivan, like McDole, had been hit by something loose, or had he not been strapped in? Either way, it wasn't the glorious end to his first space outing he'd been hoping for. I hoped McDole wouldn't end up the same way. If she died, it would be harder to explain than Dante trying to talk his way out of hell. But more than that, I liked her despite our differences.

I followed the indicators on my Scroll. An electronic bread-crumb trail led me into the stores area, close to the main reactor. When I found it, the hole wasn't as big as the first, but that wasn't the real problem. Whatever had hit us had punctured the CASTOR water tanks, and they'd leaked over the main food supplies. Even though they were sealed individually, shrapnel had cut up a large number of packs.

"Better get ready to tighten those belts, folks," I muttered. "Gonna be a long time 'till supper."

"Logan? Joe?" Aurore's voice buzzed in my ear. "I found something."

"What is it?" said Logan over the comm-set.

She hesitated before answering. "It could be the *Sacagawea*—or what's left of her."

After stopping up the leak, I went to the control room. Logan and Hernandez were staring at the screen with dour expressions, while Aurore was at her station working on the sensor data.

"Who's with McDole?" I said.

Hernandez glanced around. "Giotto's taking care of her."

I sat and checked the data coming in. It didn't take long to find what had grabbed Aurore's attention.

GJ 1116 was another red dwarf binary, though in this case the two stars were almost identical, making almost a double star. It was also the most barren system we'd visited so far. There was one planet about the size of Mars and a few small planetoids, the largest only a few hundred kilometers across.

Nothing in the system was close to the twin stars, but about five A.U. out, the sensors had picked up the unmistakable signals of a debris field scattered over several thousand kilometers. I opened the scans. The early spectrometry readings matched the materials profile that you'd expect from a ship like ours.

"Can we get closer, Joe?" Logan's voice choked.

"I should be able to bring us to within ten-million kilometers. Closer than that, and we might get caught out by the debris."

He nodded, and I programmed the Jump. There wasn't anything of substance this far out to distort space-time, so the hop was smooth—which I think everyone was relieved about. When it completed, I brought us back up to full acceleration to give us some pseudo-gravity to work with.

Logan stared at the screen for a long time then lowered his head. He must have been as close to Captain Begay as he was to me, perhaps closer, and I felt his pain almost as much as I would have if it had been Logan who'd been commanding the *Sacagawea*. He mouthed something silently, and Aurore moved over, placing her hand on his arm.

I'd been running a high resolution scan, and the data popped up on the display.

"I've got a signal," I said.

Logan snapped to face me. "Someone is alive?"

The damage made that impossible. "More likely a flight data recorder."

Aurore had rushed to her console. "I see it. Joe's right." ⌐

"Can we pick it up?" Logan didn't sound hopeful.

"Not with the *Shokasta*." I changed our course to bring us closer to the origin of the signal. "But we could with an SMPT."

Logan looked at Hernandez. "Any objections?"

"None. As long as one of my team is along for the ride."

"Who's got the most ZeeGee experience?" I said.

"Other than me, that would be Grant." He nodded in Logan's direction. "I stay here with him."

I checked our ETA. "Have Grant meet me at the SMPTs."

The debris cloud looked dangerous on the scanner, but in reality it was spread as thin as an early morning mist. The signal from the flight recorder was faint but led us toward one of the denser clusters of wreckage. Once inside visual range, we could see a large portion of the front hull of the *Sacagawea* was relatively intact.

The ship was almost an identical copy of the *Shokasta*. Seeing it smashed made my scalp itch and the hairs on the back of my neck stand at attention. Originally, it had looked like a sword with the engines forming the hilt, but now only half the "blade" was left, with the rest missing or floating around us as scrap. "Could someone still be alive in there?" It seemed unlikely, but at a distance that section looked untouched apart from the torn end where it had once been attached to the rest.

Aurore shook her head. "There are no energy traces large enough to support life and no atmosphere I can detect. That section is cut off from the generators, so I can't see how anyone could survive."

"I know it's a long shot, but check anyway. Leonard had a son." Logan's eyes caught mine momentarily. "But only if you can do it without risking yourself."

"Got it."

"The priority is the flight recorder. No heroics, Joe." He squeezed my shoulder.

"Who do you think I am, the Rocket Ranger?"

I made my way to the payload bay. Grant was suiting up with Giotto's help. She glowered at me, and I ignored her. Why she was mad wasn't clear. She'd been looking for some ship-board fun and found it. That it wasn't with me seemed irrelevant.

I pulled on my suit and checked my tanks were full. The SMPTs had their own supply tanks that we could jack into to extend the duration of our EVA, but I wouldn't want to put all my trust in them—breathing vacuum wasn't my style. I clambered over to Grant. He waved Giotto away, and she headed through the inner door so we could depressurize.

"Equipment check?" I said.

He looked surprised but nodded in agreement. The first thing drilled into you when you take Suit Procedures: 101 is to have your EVA buddy check all your seals and connections. You quite literally put your life in their hands, and vice versa. So you'd better trust them one hundred percent.

I drifted around Grant, checking his suit for correct setup and double checking several areas where it was easy to overtighten. Everything looked good, and he did the same, showing his experience by his methodical inspection.

Clambering into the SMPT, I took the main pilot's position while Grant took the secondary seat on my left. I closed my visor and connected a hose to my auxiliary air-feed. The supply from my tanks cut off automatically, leaving me breathing from the onboard tanks.

After Grant did the same, I opened a comm channel. "Ballen and Grant here. We're ready."

"Opening payload bay." Aurore's voice filled my helmet. "Clear to launch in approximately one minute."

The roar of the atmosphere being pumped out faded, and the green go signal lit up on the instrument panel. The large doors swung out, leaving a dark square patch under us that was as inky black as a bottomless shaft.

I threw in an enhancement filter on the display screen and hit the controls to retract the clamps holding us to the cradle. A few blasts with the fine control thrusters nudged us away from the ship. Once outside, I engaged the main thrusters and sent us on a course skimming along the underneath of the ship. As though we were passing along the underbelly of a gigantic pale whale, its skin gleamed with a sickening orange color reflected from the distant stars.

I activated an open broadcast. "I've got a sensor fix on the transponder. Heading toward it. ETA seven minutes."

The remnant of the *Sacagawea* resembled a broken bottle tumbling lazily ahead of us, the torn-up end a dangerous mass of twisted shards of metal and broken composites that would end our journey in an instant if we got caught up in the reef-like tangle.

"Hey, Ballen." It was Grant on a private channel. "This thing with Giotto... we cool?"

It seemed like a strange time to discuss it, but exposure to the harshness of space does strange things to a person's mind.

"There's nothing to talk about."

Grant was quiet for a minute or so. "You shouldn't have come onto her so strong. Girl likes a little romance, you know."

I didn't know what he was talking about and could only imagine what Giotto had been telling him. "I'm happy for both of you, I really am, but right now we need to focus on the mission."

He paused again. "Sure. Just don't want you mad at me. Not out here."

I sighed, leaving my comm signal closed. Did he seriously think I'd use an EVA as an opportunity to get revenge? It was as crazy as I'd heard. I slapped his shoulder to get his attention through his bulky suit then gave him a thumbs-up. I saw him nodding through his visor, and he returned my gesture.

I slowed the SMPT as we approached the wreckage. I needed to estimate the center of spin so we could lock on safely. If we were too far out, we'd get tossed away uncontrollably by the lurching rotation. I switched back to the open comm channel. "Approaching target. Will stand off a few meters with the SMPT to avoid problems."

Aurore acknowledged, and I triggered a slowdown routine that would to leave us ten meters from the derelict. The retro-thrusters kicked in, and I was pressed against the restraining straps. Once we were stationary relative to the wreckage, I unstrapped and disconnected from the SMPTs air supply. Then grabbed a line gun and climbed out, holding on to the SMPT so I wouldn't drift.

I shivered as I stared at the fragment of ship—it could so easily have been the *Shokasta* floating there. Literally dead in space. I lifted the gun one-handed, aiming for the center of rotation. The sticky bolt flashed across the gap trailing the line behind it, and I tied it to a handhold on the hull of the SMPT.

"Use this as a guide," I said to Grant. "Don't try and jump across."

I grabbed the line and pushed off gently with my legs. I didn't know how experienced Grant was with EVAs, but it didn't matter. Using the line was a simpler and safer method.

I tumbled a little as I crossed the gap, not enough to stop my progress but enough to make my landing awkward. I scrambled to grab a handhold on the hull. Once I was secure, I signaled to Grant.

He pushed off straighter and didn't tumble as much but used too much force. When he hit the hull it was more of a crash landing, and with the wreckage spinning, he slid over the hull surface, clutching at handholds. Fortunately he skittered in my direction, and I grabbed him as he passed.

"You okay?" I said.

He was breathing heavily. "Yeah. Fine. Thanks, man."

I cut the line to the SMPT to stop the spinning wreckage from winding the small transport in, then switched to the open channel. "Ballen and Grant, we're on the *Sacagawea*."

"Take it slow." Logan's voice rattled in my ears. "And keep it safe."

I turned to Grant. "Do you know how to get that data recorder?"

"Panel on the belly near the front." His breathing was returning to normal.

"You get the recorder. I'm going to check inside the ship."

He started pulling himself along the surface while I headed toward the torn-up back end. It was maybe forty meters away, but even from where I was I spotted twisted shards sticking out from the hull like a mass of tangled thorns. I wasn't keen on getting close, but if I could sneak through the mess, I might gain access to the rooms inside.

211

As I neared the edge, the strain on my arms increased. We weren't spinning fast, but I was glad I'd been working out. "Grant? You coping with the spin-strain?"

"...too hard... looking out... sick."

His transmission was breaking up as we got further away from each other, perhaps as a result of local interference from the damaged ship. I'd kept my eyes on the hull rather than looking out at the stars to avoid dizziness. On Earth, motion sickness is unpleasant but usually harmless, no matter how much you feel like you want to die. In space, it could literally kill you.

"Focus on what's immediately in front of you," I said. "That's always your point of reference."

I was at the edge of the torn section and moved crabwise, looking for an open path to let me climb around and inside the ship itself. I tried a few places, but when I edged forward I saw nothing but clusters of deadly looking twisted superstructure. Not only that—the strain on my arms and legs made my muscles cramp.

"Can't get inside." I turned to climb back. "Too much debris."

"Ballen?" Grant's voice sounded cracked and strained."...too strong... can't... uch longer..."

"On my way."

I pulled myself back up the ship, my limbs complaining with each movement. It would have been so easy to let go and float, except I'd get catapulted off the ship by the rotation. After several minutes, I was at the point where we'd crossed to the ship. I risked looking further along the ship's hull and saw something in the distance that might have been Grant.

"Grant. You hear me?"

"I'm stuck, Ballen." The interference had cleared now we were closer.

"Did you find the recorder?"

Grant laughed. "Yeah. That's the problem."

I wasn't sure what he meant but worked my way along the hull in the direction he'd taken. "What's the situation?"

"Found the access panel. Got the recorder. But now I'm hanging on with one hand with the other one holding the box. Can't pull myself back without losing it."

"Drop the recorder." I edged along the hull. "It's not worth your life."

"That ain't part of my... mission. This could tell us what happened." Grant's voice crackled with strain. "Come and grab the damn thing before I fall off this junk pile."

His Geneering meant he was undoubtedly stronger than me. The strain was building on my arms and legs again, and I wasn't sure how much farther I could go.

"Joe?" It was Aurore. "There's something you—"

"I'm kinda busy..."

"I know but we—"

I gritted my teeth. "It can wait." I saw him clearly now, his bulky space-suited body flat against the hull, and messaged the ship. "Grant's about fifty meters from me. Not sure I can get that far."

"The Atoll ships have Jumped into this system, Joe." It was Logan. "At their current speed, they'll be in weapons range in an hour, possibly less."

There'd been plenty of moments in my life where my only response was complete incredulity, and this was one of them. "They followed us? That's impossible."

"I know." Logan sounded like he was about to explode.

I fought to push it from my mind. I needed to focus—otherwise, we were going to lose another soldier. I scrambled forward a few more meters, but my arms and legs trembled with the strain of holding on.

"Grant?" I stopped to take a breath. "I can't get to you. The rotation is too much."

He didn't answer for a minute, and when he did his words crawled out. "Thanks for trying. You're a good guy, Ballen."

A good guy who'd seen far too many people die needlessly. I couldn't let it happen. I wouldn't. I strained to move again but almost lost my grip, and the line gun slapped against my back.

"Hang on," I called out, bringing the gun around. "One minute."

"Hell, I'll give you two," Grant growled. "But that's it."

I scrabbled to load another sticky dart with one hand. Attaching the line was almost impossible, but somehow I got it to lock in place. My arm shook when I lifted it. I fought to steady the gun and aimed directly at Grant. My eyes watered inside my helmet, obliterating my vision, and I blinked hard to clear them.

"Ballen!" Grant's yell was loud in my ears.

The sights lined up, and I squeezed the trigger. The bolt shot out, hitting Grant on the shoulder. A yelp came over the comm channel. I couldn't hold on and tie the line, but I managed to jam the butt of the gun into a tear in the hull.

"I've got a line on you, Grant."

His hand slipped. Whether his strength had given way or it was deliberate wasn't clear. He rolled along the surface of the hull, acting like a pendulum on the end of the line, stopping a good ten meters from where he'd been holding on.

"Remind me to thank you for shooting me sometime," he grunted. "Now what?"

"Find a handhold. You pull, and I'll reel you in."

"Got it."

A few seconds later, the tension dropped on the line, and I used the motor on the gun's reel to take in the slack. A few moments of rest, then another loose line, and I did the same. It was a slow process, but eventually I could see he was getting closer.

"I've got him," I broadcast to the ship.

No one replied, and I concentrated on pulling and reeling, like a big game fisherman landing a marlin. Ten minutes later, he was level with me. He had the recorder box in one hand. I edged over to him to look through his visor. His broad face was split by a huge grin. "Man, you play every point for keeps, don't you?"

"We're not out of it yet. Come on."

We began climbing to the spin center, each handhold getting easier.

"Atoll ships in range in thirty minutes, Joe." Logan's voice buzzed in my ears.

That was barely enough time to build up to a Jump, but we could probably make it, if the sequence was activated immediately. The fly in that particular ointment was that because of a certain someone's brilliant security measures, the only person who could trigger it was several kilometers away, crawling up the side of a destroyed JumpShip.

"We'll need fifteen minutes to get back," I said.

"Make it sooner," Logan said.

I'd underestimated—it took ten minutes to get opposite where we'd parked the SMPT. Despite his Geneered strength, Grant was flagging. Holding on against the spin had taken it out of him.

The end of the line tied to the SMPT floated where we'd left it, though it had snaked away from the *Sacagawea*. I didn't want to risk Grant jumping across and fired another line from the gun. I missed the first shot, but with the second, I managed to tangle the lines together, the sticky end forming a bond strong enough to hold while crossing.

"Over you go." I slapped his shoulder. "Remember your soldier training and go hand-over-hand. And don't let go of the rope."

Grant laughed, but his breathing was harsh in my ears. "You go first. You're needed more—"

"No one is needed more than anyone else, Corporal. We haven't got time to argue. Get over there now. I'm a lot quicker than you."

He grabbed the rope and pulled himself across the gap. The thrusters on the SMPT flickered, painting momentary splashes of white against the blackness of the sky as the station-keeping system worked to keep it in position. I held the recorder so Grant could use both arms. A lumbering minute later, he was there and wriggling through the door.

"Your turn, Ballen."

I tucked the recorder under my arm and braced my knees to push off.

"Use the rope," Grant shouted.

It was too late. I pushed off, diving straight at the ship. It took less than thirty seconds and then I careened into the edge of the SMPT, grabbing desperately at the handholds. As soon as I had one in my grasp, I twisted through the door. I shoved the box into Grant's lap and fastened the belts around me.

"You crazy son of a—"

His transmission was cut off by Logan. "Joe, we're out of time."

I was already on the controls and turning the little ship. When we were lined up, I punched the main thrusters on full. It seemed slow at first, but in a couple of minutes I was hammering on the reverse thrust. The *Shokasta* rushed toward us, and I thought we were going to crack up against the inner bulkhead. We hit it with a heavy crunch and scraped along the wall losing more than a little paint.

"We're in," I called. "Close and cycle."

The doors folded shut, and the atmosphere indicator lights flashed green to show pressure was building. I tried to control my breathing but was failing badly. A quiet hissing built up to a thunderous roar as the compartment filled with atmosphere. I checked my helmet clock. I was beginning to think the airlock had broken. Then the lights turned solid green.

I jumped out of the SMPT and dived toward the inner hatch, throwing my suit off. Once inside, I skimmed along the passage toward the control room. I wasn't sure if there was a record for the microgravity one-hundred meters, but I guessed I was close. I shot into the room like a railgun projectile, and if Logan hadn't grabbed me, I'd have smacked headlong into the wall.

"Thanks," I gasped, fastening myself into the pilot's seat and hitting the ship-wide comm. "Standby for acceleration. Thirty seconds. Hold tight. Is McDole strapped in?"

"They've launched missiles," Aurore shouted. "Tracking."

Even before the thrusters kicked in, I was setting up a Jump and starting the energy build-up sequence. If we could avoid being hit long enough, we might be able to get away. The program was nothing fancy, only a simple maximum-range Jump. If it worked, we'd be around ten light-years away. If it didn't, we'd become an elongated part of the debris field.

The ship twisted underneath us as the main engines kicked in and jerked us in a random direction at high-g. The maneuver was a drunken walk, designed to bounce the ship around but always vectored away from the oncoming Atoll ships.

"Impact in ninety seconds," Aurore said.

I activated the point defense system, but we were jinking around so much that our weapons would struggle to lock onto anything, let alone high-speed missiles. We bucked again, and a metallic tearing squeal sounded from deep inside the ship. I hoped whatever had failed wasn't critical and breathed a sigh of relief when no more red lights flashed on my console. The yellow ones would have to wait.

"One hundred."

The maneuvers had gained us a few precious seconds, but not enough. The energy levels on the Jump drive were too low. The *Shokasta* twisted from side to side, like a horse stung by a wasp. The indicator lights for the railguns flashed as they let out a burst of fire at one of the missiles.

"Sixty seconds," said Aurore.

"Hang on!" I thumped the pause control on the flight system, followed by the stabilizer button. The ship damped its wild movements and settled. It was a reckless gamble but possibly our only hope. I glared at the point defense indicators, but they remained dark.

"Forty-five." Aurore glanced at Logan. "Thirty."

The railgun lights flashed into life. With the ship stable, they'd targeted the closest missile and were pouring everything they had at it. A few seconds later, the cabin lights flickered. The lasers had cut in as well. I hit the override switch on the proximity missiles, launching them all simultaneously. That would create a cloud around the ship that would only last minutes, but it was all we needed.

"Five. Four. Th—"

Aurore didn't finish her countdown as the ship lurched again. The lights flickered on and off several times, then the emergency lights came on. I glanced at the readouts. The Casimir reactors were still building power.

"Missile destroyed. Second impact in two minutes."

The Jump drive was almost at maximum. It would be close.

Chapter Nineteen

A harsh burning stench filled my nose, and I coughed. Not the comforting odor of woodsmoke and barbecues, but rather the acrid sharpness of fried electronics and blown circuits. The control panel showed we'd Jumped. I ran a number of diagnostics. Unlike earlier, there were enough red lights flickering to satisfy the once-famous New Year's crowd in Times Square.

"I think I killed the ship." I looked up to see Logan grinning. "Am I missing something? What's so funny?"

"You saved us *and* the ship." His laugh boomed out. "And you're complaining?"

Aurore joined in, her laugh higher in pitch but apparently no less heartfelt.

"I did what I had to."

Logan slapped me on the back. "You always do, Joe."

I tried the comm system, surprised to find it operative. "Check in. Everyone okay?"

"Grant's got a busted arm, I think." Hernandez sounded shaken up. "He wasn't strapped down on that first maneuver."

The comm beeped. "This is Giotto. I'm okay, and I think McDole is too… unfortunately."

"Is Dan with you, Hernandez?" I asked.

"Yeah, he's here." I heard some muffled talking. "He says you're the worst pilot he's ever met and should stick to engineering."

"I'll do that." I took a deep breath and sighed. "Looks like it's clean-up time. Again."

"I'll help," Logan said.

Aurore unstrapped, floated over to him, and kissed his cheek. I think you mean *we'll* help."

"How did the Atoll ships track us?" I said.

"I've no idea. From what I know that's theoretically impossible." Aurore frowned. "The Jump is discontinuous from our space-time perspective, so what could they track?"

"Maybe they didn't," said Logan. "We usually Jump inter-system. If we did that from GJ 1116, there'd only be a few possibilities. What if they made a lucky guess? At least this time they didn't seem to have the power reserves to use the micro-Jumps right away."

Logan's explanation might be right. I couldn't access the navigation system to verify, but I felt sure there were quite a high number of star systems within Jump radius of GJ 116. "I'll check when we've got things back online. We're dead in space until I can work out what's happened to the main power."

I headed toward the exit.

"Joe? *Where* did we Jump?" Aurore said.

I turned back, my chest tight. "I'm not sure. I programmed the Jump to take us on the most direct line to Sol. But there are no star systems here, so we're drifting in deep space." And if we couldn't get the ship working, no amount of paddles would get us out of this creek.

Logan looked grim, and Aurore seemed to shrink.

"Let's get to work." I grabbed three handheld diagnostic scanners from the emergency locker and tossed two of them to Aurore and Logan. "Everyone got a comm set? Okay, let's start tracing fried circuits."

We hadn't got too far before we ran into Giotto. She looked scuffed and bruised but otherwise okay and had a small black bag looped around her shoulder.

"Hernandez thought you could do with some help." She pulled a diagnostic scanner from the bag similar to the ones we were carrying. "I'm only a grade-three tech, but I can handle the basics."

"Join the party." I turned to face them all. "First priority—trace the power circuitry between the controls, the core systems, and the engines. Once we find out what's broken, we should be able to bring the main system back online and do a more detailed self-diagnostic. If we fan out, we can cover more ground. I'll work my way toward the reactors from here. Logan, you do the same on corridor B. Aurore, if you and Giotto can do the same moving the other way, I think we'll have it covered."

"Will do, Joe." Aurore forced a smile.

Logan was already crossing to the other corridor. As I turned to head toward the engines, there was a tap on my shoulder. Giotto was still there.

"Carlton told me what you did out there."

Carlton was Grant's first name. He didn't use it much, and I could guess why—it didn't hang well with the MilSec tough-guy image. "I didn't do a lot."

"Yeah? Well, I want you to know that we *both* appreciate it."

"That's good. I have a reputation to maintain."

"Seriously, Joe. You're a good guy." She hesitated then kissed my cheek. "And I'm sorry I acted like a bitch."

A flush hit me, but before I could answer, she turned and pushed off down the corridor.

It didn't take long to track down the circuit breaks. We'd burned out several power junctions and relays when the power surge went through the ship. There was other damage, but those systems needed immediate attention.

"I can patch things up. That's not a problem," I said to Logan when we all met up.

"Now I'm worried." He frowned. "There are *always* problems."

I grinned. "Not for me because it's your decision, my friend."

"I might have known," said Logan. "What do we have to lose?"

"To repair the main power linkages, I'll need to cannibalize from other systems. I can take them from the weapons system, the CASTOR controls, or life support. It's your choice."

"Not much of one."

"If it helps, the CASTOR boost system is out of water, and I think the external tanks are screwed from that close explosion. That won't be back online short of a space-dock. The weapons? We've got no proximity missiles left, one of the railguns looks like it shot its last, and targeting for the long-range missiles may be out too."

"Thanks for making it easier," Logan grumbled. "And the life support?"

"I figured you'd want to keep that…"

"Always the smart-ass." Logan thought for a while. "Okay, take what you need from the CASTOR system first. Leave us some weapons if you can."

"You think those AF-11s will follow us here?"

"Let's hope not."

A few hours later, the main systems were patched up, and I brought the ship's internal diagnostic tools online. The ship wasn't badly damaged for the most part, and after some work on the control systems, I brought the main engines online to give us pseudo-gravity once more. The tearing sound we'd heard turned out to be the SMPT we'd used to get to the *Sacagawea*. In my haste to get to the controls, I'd not cradled it properly, and the *Shokasta's* jerky movements had smashed it to pieces against the outer payload bay doors. The other SMPT was intact, but the payload doors would need work before we could launch it.

The Casimir controls were unresponsive, and on my way to check them I stopped off at the MedBay to look in on McDole. She was alone, her eyes open, and she smiled slightly when I entered. "I heard you saved the day, Joe. Once again."

"Yeah, me and Rocket Ranger are like that." I crossed my fingers and held them up. "How are you feeling?"

"Apart from a terrible headache, I'm fine." She flapped the sheet that covered her. "I'm not even sure why I'm here to be honest. I feel like I should be doing something to help."

"I doubt there's anything you *can* do right now."

She nodded. "How is the ship?"

"Not in the best of condition, but considering we've survived two attacks by your ships, we're not in bad shape."

"They're not *ours*." An edge entered her voice.

"The Atolls build their own ships, don't they?" I sat next to the bed.

"Normally." She took a breath. "The AF-11s are different, though."

I lifted an eyebrow. "Different how?"

McDole drew herself up into a sitting position and looked down at her lap. "The Archipelago Directorate was worried that with Jump technology widely available, Earth would make use of its resources and large workforce to build vessels at a faster rate than we could.

"There's so much fear in the Atoll community. People are worried we're going to be left behind with the new push to other star systems. Earth's population is bigger than ours, and Earthers are, well, so much more desperate because their lives are so bad. Sorry, that's the general opinion, not mine."

"It's a fair assumption. Earth is getting harder to live on almost by the year."

"Do you remember when we last talked?"

So much had happened I had to think for a moment. "When you tried to disassemble my jaw?"

"Yes." Her voice was almost a whisper. "Years ago, when I was in the academy, I met a man—Jasper James Feehan—he wasn't in the military. Actually, he was an astrophysicist, specializing in math. It was my first serious relationship, I suppose."

I didn't know where this was going and wanted to get back to work. "The Casimir controls are down, I should—"

"J.J. had a stunning mind, undoubtedly on the way to being awarded a Dafazio Prize." She sniffed. "He was working on Jump Field research. He knew Earth scientists were researching the same area and wanted us to have it first. He was terrified that if Earth got the secret before us, they'd overrun the universe, and we'd be nothing but a footnote in history."

Most scientists had been skeptical that the Jump technology would ever work. If it hadn't been for Harmon's obsession with escaping Earth, secretly pushing the Ananta's construction, it would never have happened. "I thought the Atolls were as doubting as us."

McDole nodded, a silvery wet trail rolling down her cheeks. "They were, and they laughed at J.J.'s work. He believed if we could learn how to manipulate yau-space, we could move ships or entire Atolls to other stars. Then the Atolls could leave Earth to its own devices, and we'd finally be free.

"He published several papers. At first, everyone said he was brilliant and his work was acclaimed. But when he couldn't turn his theoretical work into anything practical, the critics savaged him, and in the end no one would publish him.

"He sank into a depression, and I couldn't help him. I tried to persuade him to have therapy, but he refused. One day, he must have given up." McDole swallowed hard. "He walked into an airlock without a p-suit and opened the door."

I reached out and squeezed her shoulder. Now I understood.

She let out a small sob. "The thing is, everything he predicted is coming true. Your ships can Jump farther than ours. You're building them faster. We can't compete because there's so few of us,and we don't like risk."

"You can't expect Earth to sit back and not try to expand," I said. "The Atolls tried to confine us for decades, and people can't forget that."

"I don't blame you, but others see things differently." She brushed her tears away. "The Directorate outsourced construction of the AF-11s to the Huanshi Corporation."

Huanshi was one of the largest of the Corporate states and an influential member of the Commerce Executive, the central body that coordinated Corporate activities. "You think they built their own ships using your designs?"

She nodded. "They were only supposed to build them to order, but they could have made some for their own use. It doesn't make sense why they'd attack us or the station, though."

"It makes sense if you want to start a war."

She sat up suddenly. "If they attack Earth ships or stations using our ships, people will think we did it."

"With the All-Parties Conference, there's a chance that all sides might come together and agree to explore space cooperatively. If that happens, the Corporates would lose a huge weapons market. I imagine they'd be willing to risk a few deaths to ensure that didn't happen."

"They must have destroyed the Wright Atoll as well." McDole gasped. "We could be on the verge of the first interstellar war. We have to stop this."

"I agree, but first I have to fix this ship." I helped her off the bed.

"You wanted to help? Tell Logan everything."

I left the MedBay and found Dan in the corridor outside.

"The Corporates stole their ship design?" He spat out the words. "Shit, everyone's on the make, ain't they?"

"You were listening?" I stared at him in disbelief. The inner walls weren't soundproof, but to stand there and deliberately eavesdrop was something else.

"Happened to be passing." He looked around. "Sometimes I almost feel sorry for those 'Toller bastards. With all the changes going on, they don't stand a chance against us Earthers."

"We could work together for the benefit of everyone."

"You can't trust anyone. The USP, 'Tollers, PAC, or the Corporates." His black eyes locked with mine. "Everybody lies."

"You don't think the Corporates would benefit from a war?"

"Ain't saying that." Dan leaned closer. "But I'd sooner trust a 'Toller than one o' them. At least they ain't only mercenaries."

McDole came through the door and glared at Dan. "Thank you, Mr. Anderson. I'm glad your unpleasant experiences haven't completely prejudiced you."

She headed toward the control room, and I turned back to Dan. "We still don't know for sure what's going on here. But the Atolls are getting desperate for sure."

"More than you imagine."

"What does that mean? What do you know?"

Dan had a gleam in his eye put me on edge. I pushed past him, toward the generator area.

"We're in the middle of the biggest transformation in history," Dan called after me. "Who knows what anyone is capable of? They'd kill their own mothers if it served their purposes. Maybe the Atoll wasn't destroyed. We only have their word for it."

I stopped. "There were scientists on the station from all nation-states. If they're not dead, where are they?"

"Seriously?" Dan snorted. "How long did they bang *me* up for?"

I walked away, but he had me wondering. The Corporates had close ties with the Atolls. They often provided the research while the Corporates supplied the labor and manufacturing power to complete the projects. Would the Corporates risk that by attacking Wright Atoll? Was everything about the attack propaganda designed to throw Earth off the scent? It seemed impossible, but how well *did* I know McDole or any of the other Atollers? They'd attacked both Deimos and Helios bases, not to mention the *Sarac* and *Shokasta*. That wasn't a glowing pacifist track record.

And then there was Dan himself. Despite being held prisoner for years, he showed remarkably little hatred for the Atolls. What was his game in all of this? I couldn't piece together all the odd quirks about him. I tried to push it out of my mind, but it lingered on the fringes like Banquo's ghost.

Several of the signal processors on the Casimir controls had blown and needed replacing. The only parts that could handle the load were the ones on the remaining railgun. I suppose I should have checked with Logan, but I didn't want to bother him with more decisions. Besides, without the Casimir generators, we couldn't get home—unless we wanted to send our corpses back in a few million years' time.

It took several hours to disassemble the weapons system and pull the components. I was working on automatic, thinking about McDole and Dan. I tended to trust McDole—she'd always seemed to be on the level with me, but I couldn't say the same for Dan, and there were all those missing pieces in his personal jigsaw puzzle. But was that a valid assessment? I turned it around, working from the position that McDole was lying and Dan was genuine, but that made no sense either. And why was Dan in such a healthy state compared to the way his brother had been several years ago? It could be chance, but it bothered me.

After gathering the parts I needed, switching them over to the drive controls was time-consuming but routine. When all the self-check lights turned green, I headed back up to make sure my patching had worked. I grabbed a coffee and an intact meal pack on the way.

The control room was deserted. When I checked, it was well past midnight ship's time. I wasn't feeling my freshest and gulped half the coffee before opening the food. The sandwich was terrible, and I'd have thrown it in the garbage, but we couldn't afford to waste food now.

I dropped into the pilot's chair and opened the Jump controls.

The system was slow responding, which wasn't too surprising considering the amount of bypassing I'd had to do. Some of the components I'd swapped in weren't exact matches on performance, but at least it worked and the Jump system was online again.

I stretched and yawned, satisfied that we could get home and switched the main screen to an exterior view. There was nothing to see—a scattering of distant stars but none close. I activated the starmap and checked something that had been bothering me since my conversation with Logan. I was right— there were sixteen stars within Jump radius of Learmonth. That made it extremely unlikely that the AF-11s had guessed where we were headed. Somehow those ships had done the impossible—they'd been able to detect our Jump destination.

"Joe?"

I stirred and rubbed my face then opened my eyes. There was half a tube of cold coffee in my hand, and the remnants of the sandwich were on the floor where they deserved to be. My shoulders felt like I'd taken a pounding from BRUCE, and when I sat up, my spine seemed to lock into place in multiple stages.

Logan stared down at me. "You okay?"

"Yeah." My neck creaked as I looked up. "Must have fallen asleep."

"It was a long day." He looked down, a shadow seeming to drift over his features.

Aurore clambered in through the door holding several coffee tubes and several of the Atoll rations. "Breakfast," she said, sounding far too cheerful.

The supplies were welcome, and I squeezed the heating tab. A minute later, it popped open to reveal a delicious-smelling toasted scrambled egg sandwich. I picked half out and waved it at her. "You're a lifesaver."

"I try my best."

I took a bite then panted several times to stop it from burning my mouth. "The Jump drive is back online."

"Now who's the lifesaver?" Aurore said.

"I try my best." I swallowed a smaller piece of sandwich. "What's the plan?"

Logan sipped his coffee. "We've done our job. We found the ship. Hopefully the recorder will tell us what happened to her, but I think we already know."

"Did McDole tell you about the AF-11s?"

He nodded. "The Corporates could trigger a war pretty easily if we don't get this information back to Earth. There's enough tension on all sides."

Aurore was working at her console. "Guys… there's something out there." She switched to a secondary display "Not sure what, but it's big."

Logan dropped into his seat. "They followed us again?"

"It's possible. That last time wasn't a lucky guess." I looked over at Logan. "There were over a dozen systems we could have Jumped to from Learmonth, and they *happened* to pick the right one?"

I brought up the local navigation map on the main display and added in an overlay of the main sensor data. It took a few seconds for the data feeds to build up a picture on the screen, but when they finished, the object was a giant blob a little under nine-hundred thousand kilometers away.

"That's a planet," Aurore said.

"I thought we were in the middle of nowhere." Logan stared at the display as if he thought the planet might vanish at any moment.

"Rogue planets exist," Aurore said. "They spotted the first ones back in the early twenty-first. Some theories suggest they aren't especially uncommon, though they're difficult to detect."

I brought up a visual image of the planet on the screen. There wasn't much to see. Without a sun to illuminate it, the planet was a barely visible circle blotting out the stars, the rim dimly lit by the ghostly light of the Milky Way. I threw in some augmentation filters and there it was, a real-life exoplanet, and we were undoubtedly the first humans to see it.

I took a breath. There was something incredibly exciting about being the discoverers of an alien world, though it wasn't exactly a thrilling sight. I read off the data—approximate diameter nine-thousand kilometers, making it slightly smaller than Neptune.

According to the sensors, it had a solid surface composed of rock and ice. There was no detectable magnetic field, and it didn't appear to be spinning. Even with augmentation, the surface was dark and looked unwelcoming with a predicted surface temperature of minus one hundred and fifty degrees. Prime real-estate if you happened to be a Frost Giant, but even an outpost would be challenging for us with our available technology.

"We should check it out." Aurore broke the silence. "We could run a survey while we're waiting for the generators to recharge."

"This isn't a research mission," I said, still transfixed by the planet.

Logan's dark eyes gleamed as he stared at the display.

"Am I reading that right?" he said. "Does that thing have an ocean?"

"Out here?" I looked closer at the data.

Aurore changed the sensor filters, and the screen rippled through different color changes before taking on a deep blue appearance.

"An ocean of hydrogen," she said. "Picked up from interstellar space. Judging by the depth, it looks like this thing has been out here a long time. There could even be a water ocean underneath that."

It was theoretically possible—the hydrogen would act as a buffer and keep the water from boiling away in the vacuum of space. According to specialists, the planet's internal heat could even keep the water warm enough to support life, though that seemed like a long shot to me. And even if possible, there was undoubtedly much more welcoming and accessible places to live.

No matter how interesting it was, it didn't make me want to delay our Jump. While the idea of charting an undiscovered planet was appealing, scientific endeavors would have to wait. All I wanted was to get back to Earth, preferably before the mystery AF-11s attacked us again. "We're one Jump from home. Considering the shape we're in, we should head back before our luck runs out."

Logan nodded. "Record its location. Maybe they'll call it Planet Aurore." He smiled at her. "Set up a Jump for Earth, Joe. Take us home."

Aurore stood up. "Don't I get a say in this?"

Logan took a deep breath, as if expecting an argument, then let it out slowly. "Sure. You're involved as much as anyone."

Aurore turned away, staring at the instruments. The planet was undoubtedly as much of a pull for her as space was for me. If things were different, I'd have been happy to go along with the idea of exploring it. But the grim reality was all too evident in the smoke-stained panels and burned carpeting.

After several minutes, she turned back. She stared at Logan for a moment, the challenge clear in her eyes, then whispered, "Make the Jump, Joe."

I took a breath. "Before I do that, there's something more important I need to do."

"There is?" Logan's eyebrows lifted.

"I'm adding you and Aurore to the ship's biometric security." I switched the controls over. "My selfish paranoia nearly got everyone killed."

"Damn." Logan whistled. "You're growing up."

"Thanks… I think." I finished adding their biogenetic information to the security database. "Okay, you're in."

"Now, I feel like a Captain." Logan laughed.

"You want to take care of the Jump?"

"Good grief, no." He grinned. "You're still the taxi driver."

I began setting up the Jump settings. I thought about what Dan had said the day before. *Everyone lies.* I looked at my friends—Logan was deep in thought, and Aurore was monitoring my programming. My throat felt dry and itchy, and I coughed.

"Before we left Earth, I had a visit from Gabriella." A flush of anger and guilt prickled my skin. "She came onboard the *Shokasta*."

Logan's face hardened. "And you didn't tell me?"

"There's not much to tell. I thought she was one of the engineering crew until she took off her helmet."

"What did she want?" Aurore didn't sound any happier than Logan.

"She's been playing a game that she wants me for a long time. I've told her several times I'm not interested."

"Was that it?" Logan narrowed his eyes.

"She claimed she was looking for work. Wanted my help." I

paused. "She also said that the mission wasn't what I thought it was."

Logan rubbed his jaw. "What does that mean?"

"Don't ask me. I figured it was more of her crap. But now I'm wondering if she knew something specific."

Aurore turned away from her console to face us. "She's an assassin, isn't she? So who's she out to kill?"

"Assassin is a part of it. She does anything that pays well," I said. "The dirtier the job, the better she likes it. She said something about a transformation protocol."

Aurore shook her head. "That could mean anything. She was working for SecOps when you went to meet the *Ananta*, wasn't she?"

"She was," said Logan. "But that ended when she went into business on her own and tried to steal the ship data. She was supposed to go on trial alongside Delacort. That never happened. I don't know why."

"Sounds like she has low friends in high places," Aurore said. "Could she still be working for SecOps?"

"It's possible." Logan screwed up his face, his hand unconsciously sliding up to his chest. "If she is, no one told me."

"One thing I'm sure of—Gabriella isn't driven by altruism."

"Do you think she knows something?" Aurore said.

"Ask me another." I completed the Jump programming and locked in the settings.

"Gabriella *could* be working for the Corporates," said Logan. "It would suit her. They don't ask many questions as long as things get done the way they want. But if she is, why would she try to tip you off?"

"I've no idea." I started the Jump countdown. "But I'd love to find out."

Chapter Twenty

"Prepare to Jump in forty-five minutes. We're going home," I announced ship-wide.

As the countdown ticked down, I wondered what was happening back on Earth. We'd only been gone a few weeks, but it seemed longer somehow. Maybe the All-Parties Conference was over and humanity was now one big happy family working together. But it was more likely that the world was once again deeply engaged in its favorite international sport—warfare.

My thoughts returned to Dollie. Despite everything, she was never far from my mind. I wasn't angry anymore. I only hoped that whatever life she'd chosen, she could find happiness once again. Sure, I'd give my good arm to be with her, but somewhere along the line I'd become resigned to the fact that it was too late for us. Anyway, who was I kidding? It wasn't exactly my choice.

The Jump counter seemed to tick down as fast as an insurance company processing a claim, and I mentally urged it on to distract myself from my thoughts.

"Were you able to get anything from the flight recorder?" I said to Aurore. She'd hooked it up to a test harness to try and pull some information from it.

"No time." She shrugged. "The MilSec techs will do it easily when we get back. They have all the right gear.

"I'm curious." I checked the counter again. "How *did* the *Sacagawea* handle those long Jumps?"

Aurore nodded. "They must have hopped into deep space, like we did."

"I guess so."

"Joe, you have a lump of suspicion inside you as big as an asteroid. You can stop digging now," Logan said softly. "The job's done."

He looked in a bad way. I guessed he'd been working hard to hold things together, but now we were heading home, his grief seemed to be swallowing him. At least I had the comfort of knowing Dollie was alive and could pointlessly fantasize about getting back together with her. But Logan had to face his family and tell them Begay was lost. We didn't even have a body to take back. He was right, though—our mission was over.

I reached over and clapped my hand on his shoulder. "You doing okay, old friend?"

Logan was still for several minutes. Long enough that Aurore looked around to check on him. Finally, he sighed and wiped his hand across his eyes. I couldn't remember seeing Logan cry before.

"I'll be okay," he said quietly.

The timer clicked over, and I opened the comm. "Jump in thirty seconds."

The power built up to maximum, and a sickly twist churned my stomach.

"Are we home?" Aurore whispered.

According to the navigation system, everything was in the right place. The closest planet was Saturn, and I brought it up on the screen. We were over two A.U.s away, so it looked more like a large smudged star, but when I threw in some magnification we were treated to a beautiful shot of the crescent limb of the planet and the glorious rings backlit by the sun.

Nobody spoke for several minutes as we sat there gawking at the sight. Then a series of beeps interrupted the moment. I checked my screens. We were receiving all kinds of in-system transmissions. It had been quiet for so long that now I felt like a man lost in a desert when he first spied an oasis.

"We're home. At least, there are no apes on the broadcasts..." I said. "It'll take some time to filter through the garble, though."

"Anything from SecOps Central?" Logan said.

I ran a quick search. "You'll have to get your supersecret code ring out. It's all encrypted."

He nodded. "I better do that in my quarters."

"One thing." I studied the communication list. "They changed the All-Parties Conference location. It's going to be held on the Marduk Atoll instead of Luna."

"Somehow that doesn't surprise me," muttered Logan. "Atollers always want the advantage if they can get it. Anything else?"

"Personal transmissions keyed to individuals and lots of routine traffic information."

"How long until Earth?" Aurore asked. "My Oprallé shoes will be missing me."

"At this distance"—I glanced at the controls—"about fourteen days."

"Can we Jump closer?" Logan said.

"Once the generators regenerate. That last Jump was a long one, and we're running on fumes."

"Okay. Do it as soon as you can." He dragged himself to his feet. "I should check the coded transmissions."

They disappeared into the corridor, leaving me alone. I felt deflated and cold. We'd searched for the ship and apparently cleared up one mystery, but so much more seemed unanswered. We didn't really know what had happened to the *Sacagawea*, or Wright Atoll for that matter. The AF-11s may have been the ghost ships, or perhaps the ghosts were something else entirely. Then there was Gabriella's visit and Dan's strange behavior. I felt like something must tie it all together, but it was as much of a mystery as the inside of a woman's purse.

I heard footsteps and looked around. McDole was climbing up from the corridor. She looked tired but smiled as she clambered out. She was back in her uniform, something she hadn't worn since the day she'd first come onboard.

"That was an inspiring image of Saturn," she said. "Did you arrange it specially?"

"Sure, the great Ballen knows no bounds and arranges planetary systems on request. Eclipses done to special order—only a small extra surcharge applies."

"May I join you?" She was carrying a number of drinking tubes, and judging by the color, they weren't coffee.

I hesitated, not knowing if I wanted company or not. The

future seemed so uncertain. I gestured at the spare seat. "Why not."

She sat down and offered me a tube. "It's the Cabernet Sauvignon you refused before."

The contents of the tube looked like blood through the plastic skin, and it even moved like it in our low gravity. I hadn't touched a drop since we left Earth and realized I didn't need it anymore. It didn't appall me or make me feel ill to think of drinking, but I no longer had that burning deep down inside me to use it to find oblivion.

"Sure. Thanks." I took the tube and put the nipple to my lips squeezing it and sucking. The fruity liquid danced over my taste buds and slid gently down, warming my throat as it did. "Wow."

"It doesn't travel well, I'm afraid," McDole said. "I think it's a little bruised."

"Aren't we all?"

McDole nodded and looked around. "You seem at home here. What will you do now?"

That was a big question. I couldn't keep hold of the *Shokasta* forever, even if I wanted to. For one thing, I was sure that SecOps would lock me up on Earth again if I tried, and secondly, now I'd given security access to Logan, I didn't think he'd let me.

"Look for an engineering job I guess. I'm not cut out to play the hero—I like breathing too much." I lifted the tube of wine in a toast. "I'm better leaving that to the professionals."

"Your record doesn't support that."

I shrugged. "I have a good publicist."

She laughed. "Would you like to join the Atolls? I'm sure I could arrange it."

I almost spat out my wine. "You mean… with you?"

"Not necessarily, if you don't want that. But together would be nice." She cocked her head to one side. "Would that be so bad?"

I moved over to lean against the wall. "What could I possibly do on an Atoll?"

"Earth isn't alone in needing good engineers."

"What you people call engineering is more like magic to us *scroffers*."

She pursed her lips. "Don't use that term, Joe. You're unworthy of that."

"Sorry, I'm a little *bruised*, remember." I took another small sip of the wine.

McDole smiled, but it fluttered away."*Aren't we all?*"

I was intrigued. In many ways, the Atolls *were* massively ahead of us. I'd be the first Earth person to learn their secrets. I might be able to share them and use the opportunity to bring the two cultures closer together. A chance of a lifetime. And as for McDole, she wasn't unattractive either physically or personality-wise. Perhaps it could work, if it was on the basis of if and when rather than an expectation...

My thoughts skidded to a halt, and I realized it was impossible. It might be nice. It might even be good. For a while, perhaps, I'd be able to convince myself I was happy, but I'd be lying. Even if I'd accepted the situation with Dollie, I wasn't ready to simply move on and forget everything. Maybe I was crazy or dumb or too much of a loner, but I couldn't do it.

"Sorry," I mumbled.

"I thought that would be your answer, and I respect it." She laughed. "Actually, no, I don't. I think you're missing out on something incredible. But it's your choice."

"You're a good person, Carrie McDole." I took her hand. "One day you'll find someone. Someone much better than a broken-down tinkerer like me."

She nodded, and when she lifted her head, I saw a tear on her cheek. "Okay, Joe."

Neither of us said anything for a while. Then she sniffed and let my hand drop. "Could you route any encrypted Atoll communications to my cabin please? I should catch up with what's happening."

I watched her as she walked over to the exit and disappeared down the corridor. I hadn't done anything to be ashamed of. I hadn't misled her or led her on. But somehow I still managed to feel like a complete bastard.

It would take at least twelve hours for the power levels to recover. Unlike the others, I didn't have any reason to check messages. The only thing in my in-box would be commercial messages, and I was in no rush to pick up such gems as "Free round the world cruise and lose that toenail fungus at the same time!"

I headed toward the payload bay, intending to fill a few hours with repairs to the doors, but as I approached the crew quarters, Dan was coming the other way.

"Just the guy I'm looking for," he said.

"Oh?"

"I'm sick o' feeling like a useless, old fart. There must be something I can do to help—used to be pretty good at fixing things, before..."

"There's not much to do right now. We'll be back home in a few days."

Dan looked down, staring at the deck beneath his feet. "Okay. Sorry, I was kinda hoping..."

"Hoping?" The way his voice trailed off made me think there was more behind this.

"I'm gonna need a job." He shrugged his shoulders. "Gotta do something so as not to starve, ya know?"

I didn't know how long he'd been away from Earth, but it was possible he didn't know the details of how things worked now. "If you stay in the USP, you're eligible for Basic Universal Income. It won't give you a millionaire lifestyle, but it's enough to live on if you're careful."

"Yeah. I heard about the universal wag." He scowled and scratched his ear. "Not my sorta thing. Don't hold against people who take it, mind. But me? Too damn proud."

He'd mentioned job hunting before, but I still had doubts. "You know that'll be tough? There are guys out there a quarter of your age looking for a landing site."

Dan frowned. "Yeah, I know. That's why I was... well, I figured if I did some work for you, you might put in a good word for me."

Even with my help, I doubted he'd have any success, but I couldn't refuse considering. "I'm on my way to repair the bay doors. If you want to tag along and help, you're welcome."

A big grin split his wrinkled face. "You're a good guy, Joe. I can see why Charlie liked you."

I reached for my tool bag, but Dan got there first. "I got it. Lead on, Macduff."

As we approached the inner airlock, I heard sounds of someone inside. I clambered through the open lock and found Hernandez rummaging around by the remaining SMPT.

"Going somewhere?" I called out.

Hernandez jumped away from the SMPT and looked around. "You scared the hell out of me."

I gestured at the broken doors. "If you're trying to desert, I think you're out of luck."

He laughed. "I guess so. Figured with the other one smashed up, I should check this one in case we needed it. And you seemed too busy."

"You could have depressurized the whole ship." I pointed at the inner airlock door. "You forgot to seal it."

His mouth dropped open. "Jesus, what a mistake. Sorry, Ballen. That was stupid."

"Forget it. We're here to take care of the door. Dan wanted to do some hands-on work and came to help. Haven't you got secret messages and stuff to check?"

"You found me out." Hernandez grinned. "I was looking for an excuse to avoid them."

I nodded. No one likes red tape. "We've all got our responsibilities."

Hernandez gave me a lazy salute. "I'll leave it to the experts then."

After he left, I closed the airlock as a precaution and checked over the door with Dan. The structure was good—otherwise we'd have been dead by now—but the actuators were damaged and bent. Dan also pointed out a big dent on the cover of the control circuitry.

"What a mess." I pulled two mid-size pry bars out of my tool bag and handed them to Dan. "See if you can straighten those actuators. I'll take a look at the control panel."

Dan went to work, sliding the bars under the arms and pulling firmly but being careful not to damage the door surface. I grabbed a star-driver and worked on the panel. Some creative wit had applied thread-lock to the fasteners, and I struggled to turn them, even using the proper tools. I thought of applying some heat, but not knowing the sensitivity of the components inside I decided it was safer to use my muscles.

"This needs straightening." Dan stepped back. "You got a hammer and a bench block?"

The hammer was no problem, but the block was something I didn't have. Dan sorted through the wreckage of the smashed SMPT until he came up with a thick chunk of aluminum from the main thruster mounts.

"This should do." He moved to the actuator arm. "You wanna hold the block while I hammer?"

I took the aluminum from him, holding it against the back of the bent arm. As soon I was ready, Dan pounded the hammer against the rod. It didn't take him long.

"What *did* they do to you?" I examined the straightened rod. It looked almost perfect. "The Atolls."

Dan's face tightened. "Waddya mean?"

I waved at the hammer. "This. As far as I know, you're over ninety years old, but you're stronger than many people half your age—smarter too."

I saw his jaw set, and when the words came out they were hard-edged and compressed. "They did all kinda stuff. Geneering enhancements, drugs, infected me a few times with crap they wanted to test. They didn't care what it did to me. Some of it did me good. Made me stronger, cleared my mind. Mostly it made me sick.

"Didn't matter to them, though. They kept on poking and cutting, seemed like every day. Three, maybe four, years like that." He spat the next words. "They deserve to die for what they did to me."

"I know you've been through a lot, and the people who held you captive should pay. But not all Atollers are evil or even necessarily anti-Earth."

Dan was silent for several minutes. When he spoke, his voice was quiet.

"You sure about that, Joe?"

I concentrated on getting the remaining fasteners out of the panel and lifted it off. Several of the smaller components had burned out, but there didn't appear to be any other physical damage. After replacing the components, the power indicator came on to show the controller was live.

Dan had finished straightening the second actuator arm, and we were ready to check our work. We moved back through the inner lock and closed it, so we could do a full test. After depressurizing the bay, the doors lumbered open to their maximum.

"Good job." I gave Dan a high five. "Thanks for the help."

"It was fun—brought back good memories." He hesitated. "You know, that guy worries me."

"Who?"

"The sergeant. Hernandez." Dan wiped his hands on a rag.

"He seems okay to me. A bit casual, but I'll take that over the usual orders-in-triplicate types."

"He's always poking around with something. I mean stuff a soldier wouldn't be interested in."

I activated the atmospheric cycling. "Like what?"

"Like being in here just now." Dan shrugged. "And I seen him at it late into the sleep cycle too. Poking around the reactors."

"What were *you* doing by the reactors?"

"Checking the layout. Matching what I'd learned from the virtual training to the real ship." He laughed. "You know designs never line up with as-builts."

That was true enough. Design specs and reality never tallied one hundred percent. "What was he doing?"

"Ah, I couldn't see. I was worried more about getting my own head straight. Looked like he was checking the cooling system and heat exchangers, but I could be wrong."

"Maybe he's doing some learning too." What Dan said surprised me a little but wasn't necessarily a sign of anything sinister. "Plenty of military people work on skills they can transfer to civilian life in their down-time. Perhaps he's studying engineering."

Dan rubbed his hands and turned to the actuators. "Wouldn't he have mentioned it? He could learn a lot from you and Logan."

For all I knew Hernandez *had* talked to Logan. I wouldn't necessarily know about it unless they wanted to include me. "I doubt it's anything to worry about."

The recycling finished, and I swung the airlock door open. "I'll finish putting the panel back on."

Dan grinned. "Think I'll see if Grant has any of that hooch left.

241

Wanna join me?"

I wasn't enthusiastic about the idea, but given the flash of anger he'd shown, perhaps I should keep an eye on him. "I'll stick my head in the wardroom after I've tidied up."

Dan ambled off, and I went back inside the bay. It didn't take long to replace the panel. But there was something else I wanted to check.

I crossed to the SMPT and leaned in through the open sides. What had Hernandez been doing here? Everything looked normal, but my gut said he'd been up to something. Or did I feel that because of what Dan had said? There were several storage lockers in the craft, and I opened each one. They were all empty.

It was possible he'd hidden something behind the paneling surrounding the main thrusters, but to do that he'd have had to remove the covers, and they weren't off when we came in. I cursed my suspicious mind and Dan for planting the seeds of doubt. I'd been burned before, and now I was seeing bogeymen everywhere.

I sealed the bay behind me and headed to meet Dan. I wasn't in the mood for drinking, but I figured I could have one to be sociable. Then, when I reached the main corridor, I stopped. The wardroom was to the left but instead I turned right, heading toward the reactor area.

Now my gut instincts were screaming, and the rational part of my brain was pushing to quiet the jangles of doubt. Dan said he'd seen Hernandez near the heat exchangers, and I edged through the tight corridors to get there, my feet scraping on the metal walkways.

The walls in the heat exchanger area were hidden by a rat's nest of pipes and conduit. Nothing looked out of place, but that didn't necessarily mean anything. I moved to the closest wall, pushing my arm through the tangle of pipework and felt around. There was nothing unusual, and I tried again in a different spot. Again, all I felt was the back end of the pipes and the wall.

I moved further along and tried again. Third time lucky, perhaps? I laughed when once again I felt nothing but the cold metal.

"You've officially gone space-happy, Ballen," I muttered. I was seeing spies in every shadow.

I moved further along the corridor, which felt more and more claustrophobic as it narrowed directly under the main Casimir reactors. I pushed my hand through another gap in the pipes, and then I felt it—something plastic-coated lodged behind one of the splitter manifolds.

Whatever it was resisted as I pulled on it but finally popped out. *It* was a black plastic cylinder about the size of a beer can, with a red stripe around the middle. A small sensor at one end with a red light next to a readout said "Armed." Next to that was a round button about the size of the end of my thumb. I turned it over, and at the other end was a printed product code, some brief instructions, and a bold heading that said "SEMPEC MK IX 2P." Even someone as slow as me didn't need a copy of the Military Explosives Almanac to decode the designation. It was a bomb.

The corridor wasn't well lit, and I struggled to read the instructions. But after a few minutes, I'd deciphered enough to understand I could disarm it by pressing the switch on top. I turned it back over. My finger trembled as it approached the button. Finally, I pressed it, the click reverberating in the silence, and the red light went dark.

I put it down next to the wall and took a slow breath, then worked my way around the rest of the corridor, checking behind all the pipework in the area. By the time I'd finished, I had six of the beasties lined up along the wall like I was planning on doing some plinking.

Suddenly, I needed a drink.

But I needed something else more. I gathered up my treasures and headed to see Logan.

Chapter Twenty-One

I knocked on the door and waited impatiently. The bombs made me nervous, and I didn't want to be seen holding an armful of explosives—especially by Hernandez.

Logan slid the door open. "Joe? Everything oka—"

I shouldered my way into the room, and Aurore pulled her nightgown tighter.

"Sorry for intruding, but it's important." I spread the bombs out on the bed.

"I don't like the look of those things." Aurore peered closer. "What are they? Bombs?"

Logan turned one over several times. "These are the new multi-purpose explosives. Can be detonated using a timer, short-term countdown, or a remote signal. Each one has enough strength to punch through the hull. This is standard MilSec ordnance, part of the team's supplies. Where'd you get them?"

"Planted behind the cooling system, underneath the main generators."

Logan whistled. "They could have destroyed the whole ship."

I nodded. All the energy contained in the generators would have been released at once, like a giant flash-gun going off—vaporizing the ship and everything in it. "You didn't know about this, I take it?"

Logan swallowed hard. "That's a nasty accusation, Joe."

"How can you even ask that?" said Aurore.

There was no way to sugarcoat it. "This whole mission is SecOps. This is their equipment. And you're the senior SecOps person on the ship."

"In name only." Logan moved away from me. "Jesus, Joe. I'm nothing but a contractor who knows how to keep his mouth shut. Do you seriously think I'd risk Aurore or myself? And, in case you've forgotten, I try to look after you too."

My stomach knotted, and my chest tightened. I was seeing threats everywhere. "I should have known better. Sorry."

Logan looked at Aurore then back to me. "I don't suppose you know who planted them?"

I didn't know whether I should mention Dan or not, but I was sick of all the secrets. "Dan was up late a few nights ago and spotted Hernandez near the generators. That seemed odd to me, so I decided to scout around."

"Hernandez?" They both spoke at once.

"I also saw him monkeying with the SMPT."

After a long pause, Logan said, "How long until we can Jump again?"

I checked. "About four hours." I knew what he'd ask next. "We'll end up about one A.U. out, five days cruising from Earth."

"Can you make it closer?"

"It's a risk. But I did it before." I took a deep breath. "What do you want to shoot for?"

Logan gave a humorless grin. "I'll let you balance your optimism with your appetite for adventure."

I moved toward the door. "I'll reprogram the Jump."

Logan stopped me. "You don't need to apologize for being human, Joe. I understand why you asked. I might have done the same in your shoes."

"Your big feet wouldn't fit in my shoes," I joked. "You going to talk to Hernandez?"

Logan sighed. "Is that the best option?"

"How do we know there aren't more of those *things*." Aurore stabbed a finger toward the bombs. "We're flying around in a ticking time bomb."

"How long would it take to sweep the ship?" Logan said.

"Days." I shrugged. "They're easy to hide."

"And he still has the trigger." Logan placed the bomb on the table next to him. "I don't think we can risk locking him up. Can we?"

He was right. If Hernandez was willing to blow up the ship with himself on board, as soon as we tried to take him down, he'd trigger the explosives. "I could search under the pretense of maintenance work."

Logan nodded. "Do that. But I think the best thing we can do is get home fast."

We all agreed. I couldn't think of a reason why Hernandez would want to destroy the *Shokasta*, unless he was secretly working for someone else. Which made it better to head back and get rid of him—at least until we were sure we weren't in danger.

Back at the controls, I began programming the Jump. I wasn't sure how fine I should try to cut it. The guidance said one A.U., and I had no idea if that number had been refined. After a great deal of thought and double-thought, I decided to go with half that, which would leave us about three days from Earth. It wasn't as close as I'd managed previously, but Earth's mass made me nervous about cutting it closer.

While waiting for the countdown, I finally checked my general delivery messages. As expected, it was mostly junk. It was stupid, but I'd been half hoping for a message from Dollie. There wasn't one, and I rooted around some tech journal back issues in-between my "maintenance," but nothing I read inspired me. Even with everything that had happened, I wanted to work in space, but I didn't see much chance unless I could score a piloting gig.

An ad in the Help Wanted section of the Space Construction Gazette caught my eye. It was from the Nakaji-Wei Consortium— the group had been commissioned to build the first habitat based on the Taikong Gaogu project. They were looking for experienced space engineers and a head of engineering for the project. I double-checked the date. It had been posted over a month ago. According to the listed schedule, they should have completed the initial printing of the giant cylinders and be working on all the other details that would make it livable.

The project was going ahead in the Alpha Centauri B system, which wasn't too much of a surprise. It was the closest star to the sun, providing relatively easy access, plus we knew it had a rich solar system to provide plenty of raw materials. The idea of building a world was tantalizing and the engineering challenges mouth-watering. Not to mention the idea of permanently escaping the confines of Earth. What more amazing adventure could there be? Just thinking about it sent shivers across my skin.

I knew I had next to zero chance. I already had two strikes against me as a non-PAC citizen. But I sent my résumé anyway, specifying I'd take any engineering position they'd consider me for. I couldn't think of a better way to make a fresh start. Or perhaps it was nothing more than a lame attempt to escape the emptiness waiting for me back on Earth.

When the Jump kicked in, it was rough. Earth's proximity made the psychosomatic effects greater than most of the ones we'd taken. But after that it was plain sailing, and I put us on course direct to the High-Rig.

Despite our losses, the atmosphere onboard was more light-hearted than on our outward journey. Instead of facing an unknown and dangerous future, people were talking about plans for what they'd do back on Earth. Though they knew of Hernandez's planned sabotage, I even saw Logan and Aurore sharing a joke with the MilSec guys.

Somehow I felt more defeated and isolated than when Dollie had kicked me out, and again I buried my problems in work. Everyone else had people waiting for them to get back, but I had no one. My only friends were on the ship, and I'd lose them when they reunited with their own families. I tried not to feel resentment, but the more I thought about it, the more I retreated into my own little cave.

The CASTOR tanks were the next item on my list. It was a long and tiring job, but over the next few days, with Dan's help, I patched most of the tanks while surreptitiously checking for any further bombs. He certainly worked hard enough, often putting in longer days than I did. He was also meticulous in his attention to detail, something essential on a task like this. By the time we'd finished, I was pretty sure the tanks would hold water again, even though we had no real way of testing them.

As I was finishing off the last one, Logan showed up and examined the patches we'd made, tutting over my crappy welding. "That's a lot of work, Joe. Find anything *unusual?*"

I shook my head. "Nothing. But doing this is better than lying in my bunk counting rivets."

He nodded. "Any plans for when we get back?"

I hesitated. "I sent my details to the PAC habitat program. They're looking for engineers."

"The PAC? Do you think you have a chance?"

"Seems unlikely." I remembered my conversation with McDole. "I also had an offer to move to the Atolls, believe it or not."

"You considering it?"

"I don't think I could compromise my ideals that much."

"Glad to hear it." Logan's eyes were like x-ray lasers. "There's another option, if you're looking for one."

"Thanks, but I already applied for the clown position at Buffo MeatFree Burgers. I'm hoping to hear back soon."

Logan laughed. "Huffo Buffo is a demanding role. But seriously, you could get on board with the kind of work I'm doing. You're tough and smart. Experienced with ZeeGee and a passable pilot. They'd take you if I recommended it."

"Passable?"

"They wouldn't believe me if I made you sound too good."

"Thanks... I think." I leaned back against the wall of the tank. "Things are changing, aren't they? Out here, I mean."

Logan nodded. "It's a whole new can of worms, for sure. And there's going to be big demand for people with our skills and experience."

"Sometimes I wonder if this is right—humanity leaving Earth or the solar system. Maybe we're the species equivalent of cancer." I twisted an empty tube of VacSeal in my fingers. "We don't have a good record on dealing with *different*. Look how screwed up the world has been on simple variations within our own species, let alone anything more extreme."

"Perhaps this can be a new beginning. With the right people in place, we might be able to move forward together and make sure everybody gets a fair chance this time."

"With Atoll ships out there attacking Earth ships and stations?" I said.

Logan rubbed his jaw. "But we know who's really to blame."

Aurore had decided to work on the recorder from the *Sacagawea* while we cruised home, and although her findings were preliminary, she'd uncovered evidence that the ship had been attacked by someone using the same type of AF-11s we'd encountered. Again, with no transponder IDs.

"Maybe." I stood up. "But will anyone believe that?"

"It's down to us to make sure they do." Logan looked at me seriously. "Anyway, think about my suggestion."

"I'm not cut out to be that closely tied to the military," I said. "They make me nervous."

"Me too."

Once we were close enough to the High-Rig to make two-way communication practical, we picked up a flurry of comms activity. McDole would be transferring to an Atoll ship to return to her duties, and the MilSec team was being re-assigned now that we didn't warrant any protection. Logan had reported our findings to SecOps and handed over our sensor logs of the encounters with the two mystery AF-11s, along with the data from the flight recorder. He also informed them we'd be handing over the *Shokasta* when we docked, which they were no doubt happy to hear.

I'd made several calls to Dollie's number, but she'd ignored them and let the answering service pick up. I did my best to make my messages sound friendly but hopeful. I don't know if I succeeded—probably not.

As we approached the station, I spotted an Atoll AF-11 docked on one side and shivered at the sight, remembering our recent encounters.

"That's the new *Bethe II*." McDole looked sort of lost, as if she were expecting someone else to be there but me. "I hope Commander Brackeen is happy with his new command."

"Brackeen? How come you're not getting the first of the new ships?"

"I'm no longer on active flight status." McDole winced. "My position is an administrative and managerial one."

"They grounded you?" I checked our approach speed. "How come?"

"Politics." She shrugged. "Officially, I was *promoted*."

"Great."

I'd cleared our approach with traffic control and brought us in to docking port 31W. As we came around, another large ship slid into view. It had similar proportions to the *Shokasta* but was easily four times as large. I'd seen some news about this during our approach to Earth and the station.

"The USN *Zenith*," I said, zooming in on the ship. "Latest flagship of the USP space navy."

"I've seen the reports, including the secret ones. It's a warship, Joe. Not something to be proud of, is it?"

"Is the *Bethe II* unarmed?" Her silence answered my question. "Let's hope sense can prevail at the conference."

"I hope so," McDole said.

I brought the ship to a halt off the docking port, and a metallic *clang* boomed through the superstructure as the docking tube attached. A gust of air pulled at my skin as the pressures equalized when the airlocks opened.

"Docked and safe," I broadcast throughout the ship. "Thank you for flying Ballen Spaceways. Adventure is our middle name. If you enjoyed your flight, please tell your friends. If you didn't, keep your mouth shut or I'll hunt you down in your sleep."

"Goodbye, Joe." McDole gave me a short nod. "I'll get my things."

I turned to McDole and held out my hand. She took it then pulled herself close to kiss my cheek.

"My offer stands."

She walked away, and as she vanished from sight, there was a thud as the umbilicals connected, then the lights flickered as the ship switched to external power. I slumped back into the seat, closed my eyes, and took several deep breaths. What was I going to do? I didn't want to go back to my crappy shoebox apartment, but I didn't have a job or the funds to pay for anything better. Everybody else would be returning to their normal lives, but I didn't have much of one anymore. I'd thought while I was away I might find something to help me move on, but I hadn't. No matter how far you go, you can't leave yourself behind. I wondered if Grant had already left. Maybe I could liberate his powdered alcohol supply before he did.

"You okay, Joe?"

I looked around. It was Logan and Aurore. "Yeah, I'm fine. Just wondering where I'm going to sleep for the next fifty years. Would anyone notice if I hunkered down in a quiet corner and gathered dust?"

"I've got some news." Logan glanced at Aurore, then back to me. "About Dollie."

A chill rolled down my spine. "What's happened?"

"Well… I got a SecOps report on her."

My mind skidded to a halt. "Say again?"

Aurore squeezed Logan's hand and moved to one side.

He folded his arms. "Because of our relationship, any SecOps information related to either of you gets automatically relayed to my account."

"You've been spying on us? On Dollie?"

"Don't get even more paranoid on me, Joe. We're only talking security-related items." Logan shrugged. "It's not like they were bugging you."

"Would Dollie agree with you on that?"

"Dollie's not here anymore."

Again, I felt like the ship had twisted from under me. "Huh?"

"What my clumsy lover is trying to tell you," Aurore said, "is that Dollie has left Earth."

I mentally reviewed Aurore's words, but they buzzed around my head in a sea of nonsense. When Dollie had said she was going away, I thought she meant switching apartments or something. "She went back to Luna?"

Logan looked grim. "She enrolled in the space piloting program and qualified. The SecOps notification says she's taken a contract doing a Tau Ceti resupply run.

"She got a job as a pilot?" That didn't make sense. Dollie was never that into the idea of space travel, other than Luna or an orbital resort perhaps. I was the one with the explorer monkey on my back.

"According to the report, she's done three runs while we've been away."

That was a long drag. Tau Ceti was a double Jump from Earth so not the easiest route she could have picked up. "Do you know her schedule?" The thought that she might be on the High-Rig had my head spinning, as though I'd thrown back several shots of Strelka vodka. If she was on the station, perhaps we could get together, for old times' sake, or—

"I don't have that information," Logan said firmly.

I realized I'd been babbling. "But you can get it, can't you? You can wave that magic SecOps clearance at traffic control, and they'll roll over for a belly rub."

"I can't do th—"

"Of course you can, Logan," said Aurore. "Give the guy a break."

He stared at her then laughed. "Whose side are you on?"

At the secondary console, he logged into some mystery account, and a few seconds later a screen of transit information appeared. He transferred it over to mine.

"Go ahead."

I scrolled through the list and found Dollie's name. She'd been licensed several months ago—before we'd left on our search for the *Sacagawea*. How it had happened without me noticing bothered me. I opened up her record and checked the schedule. Her run took place every three weeks, and her next trip was in a few days.

"She must be on the High-Rig," I said. "If that timetable is right."

Her ship was listed as the *USN Star Angel*—similar to the *Shokasta* but modified to carry cargo. I punched up the details.

"That's strange," I murmured. "It's not here."

"What?" Aurore said.

"According to this, Dollie's ship has left, even though it's not supposed to for several days."

"She might have decided on an early departure," Logan said.

"Perhaps. But according to the manifest, the ship wasn't loaded."

Logan looked closer at the screen. "That doesn't make any sense."

I was as confused. There was no reason for her to head to Tau Ceti early, especially if she hadn't taken on the cargo and supplies.

It would be a wasted trip, and even with the Jump drive making it possible, that wasn't something done lightly. Then it hit me.

"When was the announcement made about the new location for the All-Parties Conference?"

"About a week ago," said Aurore. "But what has that got to do with anything?"

"Will Paek be there?"

Logan pulled the interface back onto his console, and his fingers bounced off the screen as he searched the data. "He's confirmed as attending on behalf of both Xselsia and the Executive. But how could Dollie know that? The list isn't widely distributed."

What he said was true, but I could think of one way Dollie could get around any security issues. I linked to the systems interface for the High-Rig and opened up a back door into the station's security system.

"Jesus, Joe, do you want to get us locked up?" Logan hissed.

"SecOps aren't the only ones with a few tricks up their sleeves."

I accessed the archives and ran a search on the security footage around the docking port where the *Star Angel* should have been. I rewound the recordings to before the ship had left, then shuffled them forward. It didn't take long to spot someone who could have been Dollie, and I stopped the recording. Then I replayed it at normal speed, zooming in on the display. Two figures came into view headed for the *Star Angel's* airlock. When they entered the enlarged area, I froze the image and threw in an enhancement filter.

"That's Dollie," Aurore whispered. "But who's with her?"

If it was who I thought it was, I'd only seen her once without her alt-real helmet, but Logan knew her better.

"Sigurd," he said.

"They're going after Paek," I whispered.

"Who's Sigurd?" Aurore peered at the screen.

"Ex-SecOps something..." I said. "You'd have to ask Logan for details."

Logan barked out a short laugh. "I don't know much more than you. She was part of SecOps several years ago. Did covert ops during the Corporate Breakaway Conflicts. I never knew the details, except one time when she got into trouble down in the Central

South Alliance. I was working on an irrigation job near Pasto, and she turned up one day in the mud at the construction site. We thought she was dead, but when we moved her, she opened her eyes. We cleaned her up, but she'd been tortured and beaten almost to death."

Aurore paled. "What happened then?"

"We were on the border with the MusCat south territories, and their Enforcers came searching the next day, even though that was technically an invasion of the CSA. I hid her, and when she'd recovered some of her strength, I put her on a truck heading for Quito. She said once she was there, she'd could take care of things herself. I didn't doubt her—she was one tough lady. Never saw her again, but when my contract finished and I returned to the USP, I was contacted by SecOps for a debrief. That's where my connection with them started."

"And Dollie's involved with her?" Aurore stared at me.

"They used to be... hell, I don't know the whole story, but at one time they were lovers. Dollie left, and Sigurd didn't take it well."

"And now?" Aurore said.

"All I can think is that Dollie must have gone to Sigurd for help getting to Paek. He certainly deserves it." My head dropped. "I had plans along those lines too, but I was trapped on Earth when I wouldn't hand over the *Shokasta*."

"And you knew it was suicide," Logan said.

I stared at him. "That wouldn't have stopped me."

"I know that, Joe. Which is one of the reasons they kept you out of space." He sighed. "It wasn't only the ship. You're smart, able, and more than willing to put it all on the line. You've shown that multiple times."

"I'm going after her."

The room went quiet. I wasn't one hundred percent sure Logan wouldn't call security. When he replied, his voice grated like a stone slab unlocking the entrance to hell.

"That doesn't surprise me." He glanced at Aurore. "If I was in your situation, I'd likely do the same."

I checked the docking services system to see when everything would be replenished and refilled. "I'm leaving in two hours. Better get your gear off. This is probably a one-way mission."

Aurore came over and rested her hand on mine. "Are you going to stop Dollie? Or help her?"

"I'll let you know... when I get back."

She shivered, hugging herself, and turned to Logan. "And you?"

I could see how torn Logan was and patted his thick shoulder. "Don't worry, I'm not asking you to come along."

"You don't have to. I'm coming." He took a big lungful of air and turned to face Aurore. "I'm sorry, I ca—"

"Don't even think it. If you're going with him, we both are."

Logan froze. "But—"

Aurore lifted her chin. "This ain't no debate, lover."

My stomach felt like it had fallen through the floor at the thought of putting my closest friends at risk. "I can't let you—"

"We're the only family you've got, Joe," Logan rumbled. "Family sticks together, remember?"

"Then you'll need me too." McDole was standing by the entrance.

"We can manage," I said. "Besides, from what you've told me, you should stay well away from this."

"You don't have a chance of getting inside Marduk without me." McDole spread her feet wide. "Security will be impenetrable."

Logan grunted. "She's right, Joe. We wouldn't get within ten-thousand kilometers on our own."

I checked the clock again. "Departure in one hour, forty-five. And bring your hard hats. It's not going to be gentle."

Chapter Twenty-Two

When the lights on the supply transfer showed green, I opened the docking controls and overrode the standard clearance protocols. At this point, all I needed to do was disconnect us from the High-Rig—I'd taken care of the Jump programming while we were waiting for the servicing to complete.

"Sealing airlocks. Disconnecting umbilicals. Releasing docking clamps in ten. All systems switching to internal." I felt the slight pressure change inside my ears as the ship sealed. "Initializing main thrusters for immediate departure."

"Wait a second, Joe. Aren't you—?"

Logan was cut off by a shrill klaxon that filled the room and bounced around the off-white walls.

"What's that?" Aurore had to shout over the noise before I disabled the alarm.

"We don't have flight clearance." I saw her face twist with worry. "Didn't think they'd be happy if I put in a request."

She didn't reply, and I turned to the controls. "Thrust in... Three. Two. One."

The acceleration pushed me down in my seat. It wasn't much, a one-tenth gee boost to clear the High-Rig and move us into free space.

"Can we move faster?" McDole bit her lip.

"With the traffic around the High-Rig these days, we need to be careful. Make that double without clearance."

We hadn't even passed the inner traffic perimeter before the comm system buzzed into life, and a bored voice came from the speakers.

"*Shokasta,* what in the hell are you doing? You have *no* clearance and just lit up every warning on the boards. Looks like Christmas in a shitbake in here."

"Is that you, Fats?" I had no idea who it was, but in my experience insulting someone always made for a good distraction. "I thought they weren't gonna let you back on flight control."

"This is Senior Flight Control Officer Lazlo. I don't know who *you* are, but you better put that ship back on Docking Port 31W right away. You'll find some friendly SecOps people ready and waiting—to arrest you."

I'd already accessed the Jump controls, and now I activated the build-up sequence as we picked up speed. The Casimir generators had the reserves brimming with available power. I triggered the comms again.

"Did they finally manage to cure that rash, Fats? The docs ever figure out where you picked it up? And did your wife find out?"

There was no immediate response, and I looked up. Aurore had a wide grin plastered over her face.

"That's Francois Lazlo. I swear he hits on every woman assigned to control duty."

I glanced at the Jump indicator. It was several minutes from zero. I looked back at Aurore. "Know any recent ones?"

She thought for a minute. "Keshia Ford. He was slobbering all over her. She had better taste, though."

I thumbed the transmit button again. "Hey, Fats. Heard you tried to nail that babe, Keshia, and she told you to shove it in a fusion coil, that true?"

An alarm trilled. Maybe I'd pushed too hard. Several missiles had locked onto us.

"Joe, this might not be a good idea" Logan gripped the arms of his seat.

"Don't worry. They're posturing. There's no way they'd fire on us."

Lazlo's voice came back on the comms. "*USN Shokasta.* You have no flight clearance and have committed an act of piracy. Power down your engines and await a MilSec boarding team. This will be your first and *only* warning."

The Jump counter told me we were still a minute away. "Come on, Lazlo. Is that any way to treat an old beer buddy?"

The Jump was locked in. I couldn't change it at that point, even if I wanted to. We were at full acceleration too, but that wasn't enough to outrun a missile.

The alarm changed, becoming more urgent, and the threat warning system lit up, dominating the main screen as it tracked an approaching missile. I cursed. Sometimes my mouth definitely wasn't my best friend. The impact predictor was counting down almost in sync with the Jump counter. While technically the ship was armed and armored, a missile would take us out if it hit us. At this range, we couldn't outrun or outmaneuver it.

The on-screen missile track intersected with the indicator in the screen center representing the ship. I brought up an external display. The missile streaked toward us then detonated, and the screen went white as the ship bucked.

A second later we Jumped, even though we were far too close to Earth's mass. I felt an internal wrench as if my stomach had been grabbed by some invisible fist then twisted into a knot and ripped out through my navel. My vision collapsed inward, the visible area shrinking to a minuscule dot as if I were looking down a long telescope the wrong way. I groaned then lost consciousness.

When I came around, I had to check the ship's clock to find out how much time had passed. It hadn't been long. Transparent worms seemed to be wriggling around inside my eyeballs, but they faded quickly.

"I thought you were trying to get us killed," Logan said.

"Sorry, I figured if I could get him angry, it would keep him off-balance."

"Next time, let Logan do the talking." Aurore breathed heavily.

"Where are we?" McDole was staring at the screen.

"On the outskirts of Alpha Centauri B, near the Uhrmacher Belt."

The belt was a vast debris field that floated between Alpha Centauri A and B with asteroids and icy planetoids swapping between the two gravitational systems frequently. It wasn't the safest place to be, but I'd Jumped high above the ecliptic plane to minimize the danger. I brought the ship up to cruising acceleration so we had gravity once more and checked the generators. The Jump had been short, leaving plenty in the power reserves.

"We'll need four hours to recharge."

"What then?" Logan said.

"I'm heading straight in. As close as I can get."

Marduk Atoll was around one-hundred and thirty A.U. away, deep into the star system and close to the Habitable Zone of the star. There was no planet in the HZ—the dynamics of the twin stars largely disrupted the planetary-forming process, resulting in three separate asteroid belts. It meant we were a long way from the station, but as it wasn't near a planet, I could risk taking a deep Jump to get closer. Marduk had been seeded there a few months after Jump drive technology became available to the Atolls and was the biggest of their exo-bases with a population already over seven thousand.

"What the hell's going on? I almost broke my neck."

Dan stood by the entrance, rubbing his bald head.

I groaned. "Why didn't you get off at the High-Rig?"

"Well..." He looked at the floor. "I didn't have nowhere to go. And no way of getting there either."

After Charlie's death, his ranch had been sold off, and with Dan presumed dead in the attack on Deimos, the proceeds had passed to the state's social fund. Dan could undoubtedly claim the return, but with lawyers involved, it was bound to be a drawn-out process.

"We're heading to Marduk Atoll around Alpha Centauri. I think my wife is there."

"I thought you were divorced?" Dan stepped closer. "You're nuts."

I ignored him and made sure there was nothing close enough to hurt us.

"How close are you going to Jump?" McDole sounded nervous.

"See the hairs on my head?" As usual, it was shaved clean. "That close."

I programmed the Jump for when the ship reached full energy levels.

"You might want to reset your ship's transponder," McDole said.

"You're not going to get close to the Atoll if Paek sees you coming."

"Any suggestions?"

"I can set it up so we look like an Atoll vessel. At least that way we'll be able to dock with Marduk. Once we're onboard, though, you're on your own."

"Sounds reasonable." I opened the controls. The *Shokasta* would have a different physical appearance to an Atoll ship, but in my experience everybody trusted the transponder signal, as it was available at ranges beyond visual identification.

"I suggest we grab something to eat," Aurore said. "This might be our last chance."

"A last supper?" Logan growled.

Aurore and Logan left, with Dan trailing behind them. I turned back to the console and made the changes, guided by McDole. Once we'd finished, we made our way to the wardroom. There wasn't much in the way of supplies, but there were a few of the more edible Atoll rations. We joined the others around a table, and for several minutes, the room was filled with the crackle of food wrappers being opened and munching sounds.

"Are you going to stop Dollie?" Logan asked.

As usual, he'd cut straight to the heart of the problem, but I didn't have a clear answer. "Paek deserves to die."

"You sure, Joe?" Logan took a deep breath. "Everybody follows their own path through life. It often seems right to them, but sometimes that crosses someone else's. It's the nature of the universe."

"You think he should live?"

He shook his head. "That's not my call, but you have to choose what road you're on."

"If it had happened to you and Aurore, what would you do?"

Logan grimaced. "I'd kill him."

McDole had been silent through this, and I said to her, "I imagine you see things differently."

"Because you think I feel a kinship with him?"

"He's an Atoller."

"Was." She sighed. "I've said before, not everyone in the Atoll community feels the same—we're not clones. In my opinion, Paek was never a good member of our society."

"So you won't cry over his corpse?"

"Killing is always easy. Finding a way to live with someone you disagree with is much harder." She pushed the food around her plate with her fork. "Considering what he did, I wouldn't blame you or your wife if you killed him. But the death of a human being is never something to relish."

Dan brushed his hands together in dismissal. "Let the 'Tollers sort out their own mess. He ain't a threat to me. So I say leave him alone. Then we can go home."

I finished my sandwich in silence, doubt gnawing at my stomach like a rabid rat. I'd convinced myself Paek deserved to die and had been prepared to take him out, but the thought of Dollie doing that and how it would affect her afterward had me questioning myself. There was something about Dan that was nagging at me too. Why was he so charitable toward the Atollers after what they'd done to him? He should have been braying for blood as much as me, but all too often he was talking in a much more placatory fashion. Was he that much more forgiving than me?

A thought grabbed me—what if part of his "treatment" was a form of brainwashing? Could he be a double-agent for the Atolls, where they pretended to hand him over only to milk whatever secrets he could get out of us? Could the apparent indifference between him and McDole be a pretense to throw us off?

Or possibly the conspiracy rabbits inside my head were freaking out again.

All too soon, the time to make the next Jump arrived, and I was no nearer to a decision over what I should do. My head said one thing, and my gut said something else. Maybe if I was lucky, Dollie would take that decision away from me. It was cowardly, but in some ways, I hoped we'd get there too late.

It was strange seeing two large stars on the display, and despite the fact that Alpha Centauri A and B were farther apart than the small red dwarf binaries we'd seen, their relative brightness made them seem more of a double star.

I slid into the pilot's seat and glanced at the power levels. We were at full power, and I activated the Jump sequence. The countdown was short. Then my stomach twinged as the ship translated through the Jump, passing through the rent the field generators tore in normal space before squeezing us out like a bullet at the other end as the Bronikov fissure collapsed.

I watched the readings as they came in on the sensors. "We're about four-hundred thousand kilometers from Marduk. We'll be there in about six hours. Communication lag a tad over a second."

"That's pretty fine shooting, Joe." Logan grinned. "I hope you don't cut things too close one day, and we end up seeing the inside of infinity."

I laughed. "Somebody has to research these things."

Aurore shivered. "But it doesn't have to be us, does it?"

"Most Atollers think Earthers take so many risks," McDole said, "because their lives are so limited and poor they have nothing to lose."

"Research is the act of going up alleys to see if they're blind." I smiled at her frown. "Risk is part of life."

The comms system beeped for attention, a routine message directing us to a docking bay on the central hub of the Atoll.

"Our deception is working. The welcoming party will be carrying garlands instead of assault weapons." I nodded at McDole. "Say *thank you* to the nice lady, everyone."

I brought the ship up to full acceleration again, and felt myself pushed more firmly into the seat. "Let's hope they don't have a fit when they *see* us."

"With the ID I've given the ship, they shouldn't react adversely whatever our appearance," McDole said stiffly.

Logan raised an eyebrow. I imagined McDole had tagged the *Shokasta* as a special ops ship, which was a little surprising. The Atolls had little use for such subterfuge until relatively recently after Earth had broken out from under their isolating policies. Mostly they'd relied on the domination of their position in space.

As we approached Marduk, I brought up a magnified view on the screen. So far, the station only consisted of the initial hub that formed the central region on the more well-established Atolls. It was still a drum structure beneath the outer protective skin, but unlike the larger ones, there was only one section. Usually they were built in pairs that counter-rotated to offset the gyroscopic effects, but this one had the counter-balancing spoke system at the one end, with the center being a non-rotating area to permit easy ship docking.

Even without any secondary arms, the scale was impressive. The sensors told me it was three kilometers across and almost as deep. I did some quick math based on what I knew of the internal deck arrangement of the typical Atoll and came up with an internal surface area of over two-thousand square kilometers—about ten times the size of Baltimore and more than enough room to get lost in.

"That's a lot of ships."

Logan was right. There were at least a dozen ships around the station, far more than the Atoll could berth internally. "Presumably the VIPs are unloaded then the ships moved out to holding positions."

"That would be standard practice," McDole confirmed.

"Every big leaguer going must be here," Dan whispered.

"I'm scanning the transponders to see if I can pick up any sign of Dollie's ship." Aurore worked her controls.

"You won't find it," Logan said, shaking his head. "Sigurd will make sure of that."

"I could set up a visual search," I said. "Feed the imagery through a pattern matcher to see if anything is a mismatch with its transponder."

"I wouldn't count on that working either. Sigurd was a deep cover specialist." He paused. "I wouldn't be confident you'd find that ship if you went around and inspected every single one personally."

"You can't hide a spaceship," said McDole.

I felt the same way. While we knew various tricks to mask a ship's physical signatures, nothing could hide them completely. Unless...

"The ship might not even be here." I looked around. "They could have Jumped in, left the ship, and programmed it to Jump away again. There could be nothing to look for."

"And lose their only way of escaping?" Aurore looked at me. "Could they set the ship to automatically return?"

"Maybe." It seemed unlikely. The local space-time curvature played such a part in a Jump that I couldn't see any way of doing it accurately enough. One rogue gravitational anomaly, and your ship could end up several A.U.s away—not much of an escape route. But I had a hunch Dollie wouldn't care about that. She'd be focused on getting Paek. And ruthless. She'd have planned this down to the last detail.

"Couldn't you hide a ship inside wherever the Jump goes?" Dan asked.

"You'd need an infinite amount of energy to hold open the fissure," Aurore said. "That's what limits the length of the Jumps. We can only generate and release so much energy in a short period."

McDole pulled a set of station plans from Marduk's computer systems, complete with overlays detailing conference rooms, informal discussion areas, and even sleeping quarters for the guests on board. I was hoping we might anticipate where Dollie would target Paek. The information showed that he was already there, along with everyone else expected to attend. Paek had shown up in the latest Corporate ship design, the *Defined Payback*, another militarized development based around the *Ananta* architecture. Seckinger and General Mkandla had arrived the day before us in the *Zenith*, which I thought was a strange choice but undoubtedly increased the type of saber-rattling potential Mkandla would enjoy. The pissing contest was about to begin.

I huddled around the screen, studying the plans with Logan and McDole. The rooms where the all-important discussions were scheduled looked impenetrable. The information said they'd be guarded by a combined force drawn from all the major players as well as BlackISE, the private security force favored by the Corporates. The conference organizers seemed to have thought of everything, or at least if there was a weakness, I couldn't see it.

"That place looks like it's sewn up tighter than Krystal Bliss's pre-nup," I said.

Aurore laughed. "Her marriage to Romney lasted less time than it took to negotiate."

"Wow, look at that…" Dan fiddled with an old Scroll he'd been using to help him update his skills. "Who's the dame?"

He held up the screen. It showed the opening ceremony meet

and greet with the various attendees. I scanned it, but Dollie wasn't there. Then I realized what—or rather who—he was referring to. Paek's group had arrived and was hobnobbing with the other representatives. With him was a rather familiar psycho-in-residence.

"I was trying to hack some of their systems. See if I could find anything useful," Dan said.

"Gabriella…" I whispered.

Logan snatched the Scroll from Dan's hand, the composite shell crunching as he gripped it tightly. "That's crazy. She's listed as Paek's *companion*."

Gabriella used sex the same way some people used paper tissues, as something temporary and disposable. If she was with Paek, there was something behind it. "She's not there because she's fascinated with him. And I doubt she's decided to go into the prostitution business," I said.

Logan nodded. "So who is she working for?" He tossed the Scroll back to Dan.

The main console beeped. We were entering the Atoll's traffic network, and they were asking for control of the *Shokasta's* guidance systems. I looked around. "If anyone wants to get off, now's your last chance."

No one moved, but I swear I could hear people's heartbeats in the silence.

"Okay. We're going in."

I put the forward view on screen as the Atoll's mottled surface grew closer. The control thrusts were minimal and handled the approach smoothly. When we were a few hundred meters from the surface, we stopped. A docking tube extended out to meet us, and we heard the thump as it connected with our main airlock.

I locked the ship controls and turned.

Dan lowered the Scroll. His hands trembled. "I don't want to go. I wouldn't be any good to you anyway."

"I thought you'd changed your mind about the Atollers?"

He shivered. "I thought I could handle it… sorry."

I was surprised but slapped his shoulder. "You can guard the home front."

A look of relief flooded his face. "I'll keep poking at their systems. If I find anything useful, I'll let you know."

"Okay." I turned around. "Everybody grab a comm-link. That way we can keep in touch. Use channel twenty-seven. Scramble pattern Gamma."

That would give us some privacy for any communications we made. Not that the Atolls or anyone else couldn't break it, but the configuration was commonly used for maintenance traffic so should be relatively unmonitored.

At the airlock, Logan opened a weapons locker and pulled out a service pistol. "Commander, will we have clearance for these?"

McDole hesitated and blew out a short breath. "I made sure everyone had a special-ops rating. I'd rather you didn't take them, though."

"Joe?" Logan looked at me with raised eyebrows.

"It would only tempt me to shoot Paek. I'll pass."

He looked at Aurore.

"I'd be more danger to myself than anyone else," she said.

Logan clipped the belt around his waist and added a spare magazine. He looked at McDole. "You?"

She shook her head.

I moved over to the airlock controls. The indicator showed there was pressure on the other side, and I punched the door release.

"Time to crash this party."

Chapter Twenty-Three

The door opened, and we clambered along the docking tube using guide-lines running along its length. At the far end, a circular airlock was waiting for us. The light was green, showing it was ready to be opened, and I pressed the controls. The door slid open, and we let McDole go first, not knowing what we'd find. Once we passed through the inner door, we were met by two guards in Atoll Defense Force uniforms. They looked smaller and less heavily Geneered than most MilSec personnel. But their frowns, along with the QuenchGuns they were carrying, suggested a confrontation was best avoided.

"Would you provide a biogenetic verification, Commander McDole?" One of the guards carried a portable bio-scanner.

She held out her arm and let the scanner take a small cell sample. After a few seconds, it beeped, and an indicator flashed green.

"Thank you, Commander. Welcome to Marduk." The guard looked at us suspiciously. "If you don't mind."

"These are covert operatives. I vouch for them," McDole said sharply. "No identification required."

The second guard moved his hand onto the grip of his pistol. "That's highly unusual, Commander. We have specific instructions to—"

"I'm well aware of your instructions, Sergeant. This is an unusual circumstance, and I am over-riding your standing orders."

"I will have to log this breach of protocol," he said.

"Understood," McDole said coldly. "Now go about your other duties."

"Yes, ma'am."

The pair backed off like a couple of scolded dogs, allowing us to enter the elevator-like transport tube that shot us to the habitat levels where we had gravity again. I leaned over and whispered to McDole. "I thought we were screwed before we'd got started."

She smiled. "They had no choice but to let us through. But some men try to play power games—even when it's pointless."

For some reason, Palmer, my ex-project manager, came to mind, and I snorted. "True in all cultures."

When the tube doors opened, we stepped out onto a wide avenue lined on both sides by rather clinical-looking, single-story buildings. I looked up automatically, but there was nothing except roof above us. We weren't at the central level where we'd have a view of the other side of the cylinder. That wasn't too surprising. As far as I knew, they set aside the center for landscaped parkways. Oddly enough, the blue ceiling did look a little like sky, with drifting light patches that almost resembled clouds. There even seemed to be a gentle breeze in the air, complete with slight variations in temperature, though the station was air-conditioned naturally. It seemed the Atollers liked the idea of open air despite their criticism of the poor planet-bound *scroffers*. Whatever the thinking behind it, it made the atmosphere seem brighter and more airy.

"If we split up," McDole said, "we can cover more ground."

"How about you two take a look around the residential quarters while we work our way toward the main conference room?" I said to Logan and Aurore. "Keep in touch, though."

"Will do," said Logan. They headed away, along the long axis of the level.

McDole grabbed my arm. "This way."

We passed several people as we walked, some in larger groups but most in twos and threes. Everyone seemed relaxed and unhurried, a marked contrast to the bustle of a typical Earth city. Despite their reported population and the conference visitors, Marduk wasn't crowded, and I asked McDole about that.

"Even the oldest Atolls have population densities far below those of Earth. And Marduk is in the early development phase. Even with all the VIPs, it's still well below what we'd call full capacity.

"This is the third Atoll I've stepped on in a few months." While I talked, my eyes scanned everyone we passed. I also checked every room and corridor I could see into, looking for anything out of place. "Do I qualify for a frequent visitor discount?"

"You're probably the first to visit so many since the first generation Atollers." McDole stopped. "Up ahead."

She gestured, and I struggled to pick out what she'd seen.

"Tall woman, silver hair. Wearing Earther clothing."

It could have been Dollie, or Sigurd for that matter, though at this distance I couldn't tell. She was with a man or possibly a woman dressed in what would usually be thought of as men's clothing. McDole reached inside her jacket, pulled out a short rod, and flicked it. It extended into a Shock-Wand, though I'd never seen one so compact before. She must have been hiding it all the time she was on the ship, and it was worrying that it hadn't triggered the *Shokasta's* internal sensors.

"I'll approach them from the front," I said. "You stay on their blind-side."

I marched toward the couple. They weren't walking fast, so I quickly overtook them. I passed them in a wide curve, then turned back to meet them face-to-face. McDole moved up behind them, the wand ready in her hand.

Even if Dollie had drastically changed her appearance, I felt sure I'd know her once I got within a few meters, and my heart pounded in my chest as I closed on them. Then as the distance between us shrank, I realized neither of them was her. I shook my head at McDole, who fell back. When I joined her, she'd put the wand away.

"This isn't going to be easy," she said.

"Especially with Sigurd involved."

We moved on, heading for the main conference area. It got busier the closer we approached, and it was then I spotted the first figures in robes. "Oh hell, I'd forgotten about them."

"Who?"

I pointed at a small group ahead of us. "Representatives from the self-flagellating misogynists union—otherwise known as the MusCat Council of Light." They were dressed in the heavy robes traditionally worn by members, including cowl-like hoods that hid their faces. "What do we do about them?"

"We can't force them to reveal themselves," McDole said. "It would create a political nightmare."

"If we don't, we could have a different kind of nightmare on our hands."

"Joe?" Dan's voice buzzed through my comm-set. "I found something."

"I'm kinda busy, Dan."

"I hacked into the *Defined Payback's* data systems."

"Paek's ship?" I turned to McDole, who'd raised her eyebrows. "How did you manage that?"

"I wanted to find out what was going on."

"Dan, this is Logan. What have you got?"

There was the slightest of pauses before Dan spoke again. "Communications logs. Between Paek's ship and others. Some of the transponder entries match those of the AF-11s that attacked us."

I stopped breathing for about a minute. "Are you sure?"

"I ain't stupid."

Logan spoke again. "Can you copy the records without getting caught?"

Dan hesitated again. "Maybe. Yeah, I think so."

"Grab everything you can." My head spun, both from Dan's discovery and the fact that he'd been able to hack their systems at all. Could he have done the same with ours? "We need to get this to SecOps, not to mention the other nation-states."

"I said they weren't Atoll ships," McDole grumbled. "You should have believed me."

I held up my hands. "I didn't *disbelieve* you. How would you have felt if circumstances were the other way around?" I tapped the send button on my comm-set. "Keep poking around, Dan. See what else you can find out."

McDole seemed to shiver. "He confuses me. It's like he's old and decrepit but young at the same time. And sometimes I think I see a deep-set hatred in his eyes, but then he hides it so thoroughly you'd almost say you'd never seen it."

I understood how she felt. "He told me what the Atollers did to him. It was bad."

"I know. I saw the records." Her jaw set angrily. "I didn't want to admit it before. It was monstrously wrong, and I understand why he hates us—but then why does he try to hide it?"

I tapped my comm-set again. "Logan, there are MusCat representatives here in full robes. Dollie and Sigurd might use that as a disguise. I've no idea how we check them, though."

"How about a random ID check? I'm sure the Commander could pull that off."

"Might be our only hope," I said. "But that won't help you."

"We'll try to come up with something."

The group of MusCats didn't take long to catch. They were ambling along as if out for a morning stroll. Given their lack of interest in space development, their only goal at the conference would be gaining access to new resources. McDole walked up to them, while I stayed back a little, ready to jump in if anything happened.

"Atoll Security." She held up her ID to the man nearest her. "I need to check your IDs."

He hesitated, perhaps because he was being addressed by a woman. Then after a few moments, he held out his wrist to show the security tag and lifted his cowl, so she could see his face.

McDole gestured him aside and repeated the same routine with the next three in the group. But the last one delayed for several minutes, not saying a word.

"Brother Phelps..." said the first man, rubbing and twisting his hands together. "Comply with the... Atoller's request. We have nothing to fear while we act in the service of the Absolute."

Phelps didn't seem to hear, though even through the thick robe he was visibly shaking. Was it panic? Fear? Anger?

"Show your ID, Brother Phelps," he repeated.

Phelps bolted from the others. Unluckily for him, he'd been so intent on McDole, he hadn't noticed me edging around him and tripped on my extended foot.

"Excuse me..." I said, dropping down as if to help him up but in fact uncovering his wrist and his face in the process.

McDole glanced down at him then shook her head, and I

helped him back to his feet, making a show of dusting him down. "My apologies."

"Curse all of you unbelievers." He spat the words. "May the Absolute smite you down in holy vengeance."

"I hope you're satisfied, Commander," the first man said, then they turned and marched away almost in unison.

"Not the most elegant of encounters." McDole frowned. "But hardly surprising with those people."

Her reaction was understandable. The MusCat alliance had a long history of human—and especially women's—rights abuses. It was the rise of such fundamentalism that led to the old United States schism and was part of the drive to form the Atolls themselves. Scientists wanted a place where they could carry out their research without interference, and when they couldn't find it on Earth, they made their own.

I viewed the map on my Scroll. The main conference room was about five-hundred meters ahead. "The next session starts in twenty minutes."

"Could you be wrong?" McDole said. "Perhaps Dollie and this Sigurd took the ship for other reasons."

So far there had been nothing to support my theory, but I still felt I was right. "Dollie wouldn't steal a ship to take a joyride. I know that." I tapped my comm-set. "Dan? Did you find anything else?"

There was a short silence, then he came on the line sounding out of breath. "Nah. Nothing important. But those necking Corporates have definitely been playing games. It's all in their logs."

"Joe. Logan here, I—"

The comm channel filled with static, and a moment later I heard several rumbles, like the distant thunder of a summer storm. "Logan? You okay?"

There was no reply, and I tried again. "Logan? Aurore?"

A rush of air hit us from behind, and I half-turned, then heard the far-away crackle of what had to be gunfire. "That's at the residential area. Let's go."

McDole hesitated. "Why would they attack there? As you said, the session starts in the main hall in twenty minutes. How many people would be in the residences?"

A shrill warble sounded, almost deafening me with its intensity and frequency. "A diversion?" I shouted, trying to be heard over the alarm.

McDole nodded.

"Dan? Can you access the Atoll security systems?" He didn't answer, but possibly it was too noisy for him to hear my question.

I took several steps back the way we'd come.

"*This* way, Joe," McDole yelled. "If Dollie's anywhere, she's up ahead."

I turned toward McDole and the conference rooms. But although my head said she was right, my heart was screaming at me to run back in case Dollie *was* in the other direction.

A heavy *krump* sounded from the conference room area, the siren stopped warbling, and I was thrown to the floor. The corridors filled with people running in every direction away from the conference rooms. Moments later, they were met with an army of security in a mixture of uniforms, battling to get through the crowd to reach the conference area. I picked myself up and realized the alarm might not have ended—rather my ears weren't picking it up. The shock wave of the explosions had killed my hearing. Temporarily, I hoped.

The first attack must have been staged to draw the security people toward the residences. Then Dollie, no doubt with Sigurd's help, had attacked the conference rooms. The corridors vanished as a thick cloud of smoke rolled toward me, and a minute later I was enveloped. Blind as well as deaf. Things were looking up.

The feeling of dull nothing in my ears faded, only to be replaced by a high-pitched whistling tone, which wasn't much more of a help. I staggered forward, hoping I hadn't gotten turned around when I hit the floor. I banged into several people, but they were all heading the opposite way and not interested in me in the slightest. The smoke had a damp oily smell to it that caught in my nose, making my eyes water.

Somebody grabbed me, and I looked around to see McDole. She had a small cut above her eye, and a sliver of blood ran down her cheek almost like a bloody tear. She pulled me from the throng, and after a few steps I saw the glow of an information screen. Most of it flashed with a large hazard warning sign, but as we got closer I realized there was something odd about the display. There were no pressure or fire warnings.

That *could* have been because whatever had happened had messed up the sensors, but it seemed unlikely. An explosion that big would have started fires or blown a hole in the Atoll walls and caused at least a temporary pressure breach… unless someone wanted us to think there was trouble here when there wasn't.

But that didn't make sense either. The other attack had been the diversion, to draw attention to the residences. Or was it? Why risk carrying out two?

I heard a distant voice, almost inaudible against the whistling in my ears. Then there was a tug at my sleeve. McDole was screaming, but I couldn't make out her words. The smoke thinned, and she pointed along the corridor. But all I saw were groups of panicking people moving in all directions.

I struggled to understand why there'd be two diversions. Why make a bigger, louder bang when a smaller one will do? Then it hit me. In a small incident, the security forces would try to secure the situation on-site with minimal disruption. But in a large attack? They'd be thinking of evacuation. I pulled out my Scroll and checked the layout again. The *Defined Payback* was docked at port seventy A and B of the stationary inner hub. If Paek thought there'd been a large-scale attack, he'd bolt back to his ship for sure.

And Dollie would be waiting.

I abandoned McDole and headed directly to the nearest transport tube.

The tube let me out at a broad walkway connecting several docking ports. The closest one was surrounded by a panic-stricken mob beating on the airlock door, and I headed for the one further along. Despite the extra distance it didn't take much longer. I zipped along in the ZeeGee, and without the crowds, my path was clear.

The lock stood open when I got there, and I edged into the corridor beyond. There was no one in sight, but I heard the noise of the rabble behind me. I glanced back and saw a similar throng of people swarming toward the airlock I'd come through. I thought I'd seen some of them heading for the other port, but they must have seen me enter this one and followed. I slammed the door closed, locking out the external override.

I examined the other airlock, and sure enough, the door was sealed. Someone wanted to limit how many people could get on board, and I had a good idea who that was. An information display on the wall told me that the main command room was several decks up and in the center of the ship, where it would be best protected. I guessed that Paek would head there, looking to leave the Atoll for safety. But if I was right, he'd be looking at a very different form of escape when he got there.

I cut through the ship, jumping in long leaps and steering myself with brief touches against the guides and handholds. The *Defined Payback* was big, even larger than the *Zenith*, and it took several minutes to reach a point where I could turn inboard. I swung around the corner and crashed face-first into a BlackISE security guard.

Luckily he was floating harmlessly, either unconscious or dead, but I didn't waste time checking closely. I did take the liberty of grabbing his heavy pistol, though, in case I had a run-in with any of his friends.

I passed several more guards on my way, but they were all distinctly inactive. As I neared the command room, I crept more cautiously around corners, not knowing what I'd find. Then I heard voices up ahead and stopped, pulling myself close to a bulkhead. The sound bounced around the hard walls of the passage, and with my still-impaired hearing, I couldn't make out the words clearly, or even identify the people speaking. But the conversation was heated—that much was certain.

I tapped the button on my comm-set several times, trying to get through to someone but without response, and I gave up. The weapon I'd picked up was a type of QuenchGun, and the magpack was fully charged. I'd used something similar before and dialed down the settings to throw the needles slow enough not to blow a hole in the hull. Cradling the gun in my arms, I pushed off the bulkhead and through the door into the gloomy command center, not sure who I'd find. But if Paek was waiting, there was a good chance neither one of us would come out alive.

Chapter Twenty-Four

The first thing I saw was Paek. He was on his knees, surrounded by three people in BlackISE uniforms. That might have put him in a strong position, if any of them had been standing, but they were sprawled in ungainly poses around him—whether dead or unconscious, I couldn't tell. My hand tightened on the grip of the gun, and I had to fight not to jerk the trigger back and finish him on the spot. I touched down on the floor, and my shoes stuck to the carpeting, allowing me to walk with some stability.

"Hi, honey, I'm home."

"Joe?" Dollie stepped out from the shadows. She wore a bulky, almost black, armored p-suit that hid her curves completely, and yet somehow she still managed to look beautiful. "What the hell are you doing here?"

"Nothing much. Saving the world, as usual."

"You're here to stop me?"

Paek looked relieved and let out a long breath.

"Don't get your hopes up," I said to him then stepped toward Dollie. "I can't stop you. And I've no reason to. He's a murderer and deserves everything he gets."

Dollie pointed a heavy pistol at me. "Don't come any closer, Joe. I swear, the only way you can save him is if you kill me."

"And I don't suggest you do that."

I looked around. It was Sigurd. She was dressed like Dollie's twin, and she also had a gun trained on me. And where I might hope Dollie would hesitate a little to shoot me, I had no doubt Sigurd would cut me into ribbons without blinking.

279

"Those are some suits you've got. Do you shop at Space Marine Surplus?"

"Tools of the trade." Sigurd stepped closer. "Now, hand me the gun. Grip first."

I activated the safety and turned the gun around, offering it to her the way she'd asked. If I'd been the Rocket Ranger, I'd have done a fancy gun flip as she reached out and killed her and Dollie in a single movement. But I didn't have camera tricks to help me and couldn't have shot Dollie any more than I could have stopped breathing.

"Why are you here?" Sigurd stuffed my pistol in her belt and pushed me toward a wall.

"I've never seen my wife execute anybody before. I thought it'd be fun to throw peanuts from the gallery."

"She's not your wife anymore."

"A technicality. And I already have the peanuts."

"You people are scum." Paek spat the words out. "And when my other BlackISE people get here, they'll execute you without drawing breath. I don't think you even have the guts to do what you came for."

Dollie's hand tightened around her gun. Paek wasn't enhancing his prospects of survivability, and I wouldn't have blamed her if she'd fired.

"Before you put a bullet in this pathetic excuse for a human being, there's something you should know. It may not change how you feel or what you do. And maybe it shouldn't." I looked at Dollie. "Want to hear it?"

She didn't respond for a minute or so. Her eyes were locked on Paek and burned with an intensity I'd never seen from her before. "Say whatever you want. It won't change anything."

"Dollie…"

Dollie cut Sigurd off with a shake of her head.

Okay, this was it. Time for me to use all my silver-tongued skills to save her. Though the truth was, I didn't care if someone put a bullet in Paek's brain or not. I just didn't want it to be Dollie.

"Paek's finished, no matter how this plays out. He's a war criminal. Responsible for thousands of deaths."

Paek jerked his head up, sending a spray of sweat into the air. "You have nothing on me."

"We have records of his communications with several ships that were pretending to be in the service of the Atolls. We also have records of those same ships attacking both USP and PAC ships and stations."

Paek's eyes widened, but he didn't say anything.

"I don't care about those people. I only care about one." Dollie still had her gun on him.

"I know. But don't you see? You don't have to do this." I took a breath to control my emotions. "If we hand over the evidence and Paek, he'll be punished. No one will argue against it now."

"Kill him, Dollie," Sigurd said. "Kill him now, while we still have a chance of getting away."

"You really think anything will happen to me?" Paek smirked, wiping some of the blood off his forehead. "You have no idea. There are far too many skeletons buried in far too many closets for that to happen."

"Unfortunately, he's right." Gabriella strutted in. She flounced deeper into the room, swaying elegantly even though she relied on the same sticky carpeting as the rest of us. She didn't look armed, but that didn't mean a thing with her.

Dollie's jaw tightened further. "I'll be happy to kill you both, believe me."

"Hello again, Joe. Hello, Samara."

I'd never heard anyone use any other name for Sigurd, not even Dollie, and I was surprised that Gabriella seemed to know who she was. My expression must have given me away because Gabriella turned her attention back to me.

"You'd be surprised at the things I know. Our paths have never crossed *professionally*, but I'd be stupid not to recognize the once-legendary Samara Gruden. Especially in association with your ex-wife."

"If you know anything about me, then you should know better than to stick your nose into my business." Sigurd pointed her gun at Gabriella. "Turn around and crawl back under your rock."

"Well, I can hardly do that, can I?" Gabriella reached the wall and leaned against it as though she were in a park taking in the view. "I'm here on duty. Protecting *Mr.* Paek."

For the first time since I'd walked in, Paek looked surprised. "I thought—"

"You thought I was enamored with your physical *prowess?* Please, darling, I've had far better specimens than you. I'm acting for the USP. They wanted the Contravalency Phage, and you could make that happen." Gabriella's voice deepened. "Quite frankly, it's been one of the most disgusting assignments I've ever taken."

She looked away from Paek. "I know what you all think of me, and I understand why. I've done things that all of you have cause to dislike. But that *man* is the most pathetic example I've ever had the misfortune to meet. He thinks he's smart, but he's allowed himself to be manipulated at every turn. First by Atoll extremists, then the Corporates, and finally by the USP through me."

"Are you trying to pretend you've found a conscience?" Dollie spat the words through clenched teeth.

"Of course not, darling." Gabriella smiled, but it was more of a grimace. "I finally found something more repulsive than I am. You really should have helped me, Joe."

I didn't believe a word she was saying, but I wanted to know more before I made up my mind. "What's this Contravalency Phage?"

"Say anything, and I'll have you gutted and thrown out of an airlock naked," Paek said.

"Don't make promises you can't keep," Gabriella said. "Your chances of getting out of this alive are around zero.

"We all know the history of conflict between the Earthers and Atolls, don't we, children? Atoll superiority lies in their access to space—their blockade of Earth—but, more importantly, the Atolls themselves. They can grow their crystalline lattice in a matter of weeks and create something it would take months or even years for Earth people to reproduce. You're the engineer, Joe. What's the relative rate of construction?"

"Shut up," Paek barked.

"At the moment, somewhere around thirty to one. Some of the new technologies coming online might bring that down by about half." I was thinking about the asteroid construction I'd worked on or the Taikong Gaogu project, but I had no idea where she was going with this.

"That takes some beating, doesn't it? The Atolls can complete a whole new habitat in about a tenth of the time of our best efforts. That was when the USP came up with the Transformation Protocol. Remember, Joe? I mentioned that when we met on the *Shokasta*. The idea was to find something that would change everything, something that could turn the Atoll's strength against them if they looked like they were getting the upper hand again. Speed of Atoll construction is their biggest strength—and that's where the Phage comes in, to turn that into a weakness. I don't claim to follow the boring details, darlings, but the USP wanted some way of taking out an Atoll without simply blowing it up. Something that could be done gradually, that would take away that advantage without arousing too many suspicions.

"The Contravalency Phage does that. It breaks down the physical structure of an Atoll. Anything built using their technology is vulnerable and, once exposed, will eventually fail. But even more delicious—the Phage acts like a virus. People can carry it from one habitat to another on their clothes or on their bodies, where it will infect a new lattice without further deployment."

It was an incredible idea, almost too fantastic to believe. The stability of the Atoll crystalline technology had been unassailable for a century. If a chemical agent had been created to attack it, then the game changed completely. But somehow even more frightening was the idea that the USP had been behind it. Of course, lies came to Gabriella as easily as killing.

"I told you to keep your mouth shut." Paek's scream was painful, and he hammered his fist against his thigh repeatedly.

Gabriella grinned at him. "Fuck you, *darling*."

Dollie had been silent, but now she spoke. "I don't care. About any of this. I came here to kill that *thing*."

Gabriella shrugged. "Go ahead. I'm happy to see the filthy toad get what he deserves."

I stayed quiet until Dollie raised her gun again. "I can't let you kill him."

A brief wash of relief washed over Paek's face then vanished when Dollie didn't lower her gun even a millimeter.

"You can't stop me," Dollie hissed through clenched teeth.

"Why would you even try? He took everything. Our daughter. You. Our future."

Her voice growled like the cry of a tortured spirit from the depths of Sheol, and a tear ran down her cheek. I'd been as ready to do what she was planning, but now the reality was upon us, I realized that nobody had the right to be judge, jury, and executioner. Not her or me. No matter the circumstances.

I edged closer. "There are dozens of BlackISE people outside—and god knows who else. If you kill him, you won't get a hundred meters."

"I don't care." Dollie sucked in a deep, shuddering breath, her knuckles whitening around the pistol.

I was close enough that I could have reached out and touched her. "But I do."

Dollie wouldn't look at me. Another tear crept from the corner of her eye and matted across the curve of her cheek. I dragged a breath in, but my ribs felt like a steel cage around my heart.

"Paek didn't split us up, Dollie. We did that on our own. And as for our daughter, it could have happened anyway. The doctors told us that, but we were so busy hurting each other neither of us was listening."

"Get back, Joe." Dollie sniffed, "I swear, I'll kill you if I have to."

I stepped in front of the gun. "Then you better do that."

I saw the barrel quiver, the muscles in her hand so tight they sent shivers of movement through the pistol. "You can kill me. You can kill Paek. But that won't change what happened. All it will do is kill a part of *you*. And if you do somehow manage to survive, you'll have to live with that forever. Is that what you want?"

"He deserves to die."

"Yes, he does. But you can't sacrifice what makes you so special to do that."

Her eyes finally caught mine. When she spoke, I could barely hear her.

"I've ruined everything. *Failed* at everything. I failed you. Failed our baby. I can't fail at this too."

My stomach knotted. "You haven't failed. You've succeeded at being human. And I want that to continue for a very long time.

Whether you're with me or not."

Dollie blinked several times. "Do you mean that?"

I nodded, and she lowered the gun.

I heard a roar and half-turned to see Paek pushing up from the floor. I caught a flash in his hand and, in an almost lazy moment of recognition, identified it as a composite-bladed knife. He charged toward us, drawing his arm back to strike. Whether I was the target or Dollie wasn't clear, but I threw myself forward. The knife bit deep into my upper arm, and a cloud of blood burst from it, floating like smoke in the ZeeGee.

I twisted further, lashing out with my good hand and slammed my fist into his nose. I heard the bone snap, and the force of the impact bounced us apart. We both lost our grip on the carpet and floated in opposite directions. I twisted in a somersault, bringing my legs behind me, ready to dive back at him as soon as I had solid footing. Paek spun toward Gabriella and reached out for her to stop his tumble.

She grabbed his arm then jerked him around. Her other hand tore the knife from his grip, and as her arm locked around his neck, she plunged the knife up into his stomach and underneath his ribs. Paek gurgled twice then his head slumped. Gabriella dropped him, letting his body tumble lazily away.

"That's one you owe me, Joe. Don't forget it," she said, then turned and vanished from sight.

A moment later, Dollie was next to me. "Joe? Are you okay?"

I'd crumpled against the wall, and the blood was pumping out of my arm, but somehow it felt as if a load had lifted from me. Almost as though I'd killed Paek myself. "Sure. Takes more than a shaving cut to put the great Joe Ballen down. I'm cold, though."

Sigurd came over. "Christ, I'm getting slow." She shook her head and tutted. "And you're insane, Ballen. Going up against a soldier with a knife barehanded? You're lucky he didn't decapitate you."

She leaned down and tore open my sleeve. "He's losing blood. If we don't stop it, we'll lose him. And we need to get out of here. The security people could be here any minute."

Sigurd scrunched up a piece of my shirt and wadded it against the hole in my arm. "Press here tightly," she said to Dollie, who grabbed my arm and squeezed.

Sigurd rooted around the command room and came back a minute later with a roll of sticky tape. She wound several loops of it around my arm, fastening the improvised bandage in place. "You're going to need surgery, but that's the best I can do unless you brought a MediSkin dispenser.

The pain was so intense my vision blurred. "Left it in my other pants," I gasped.

"Let's go, Dollie."

Dollie looked at her then turned back to me. "I'm not leaving. You get away."

"It's okay." I squeezed Dollie's arm. "I'll be fine."

"He's coming with us." Dollie looked at Sigurd.

"How? He doesn't have a suit, and we don't have time to look for one."

"Help me to an airlock, and I'll find him a suit. If I can't, I'll help you escape."

Sigurd looked doubtful. "Let's get him up."

It wasn't easy moving through corridors. The ZeeGee helped, but my right arm was frozen, and even with the make-shift bandage I was leaving a trail of bloody smudges on every other bulkhead. Sigurd moved ahead, while Dollie helped me the best she could.

"I can't believe you're here. Why did you come, Joe?"

"Logan roped me in to searching for the *Sacagawea*."

"That must have been a long way from here."

I winced. "We took a wrong turn at Sirius."

A smile danced over Dollie's face, but it fell away almost immediately. "You're a terrible liar."

"I'll try harder."

We turned left down a short corridor that ended in an airlock. Two black air tanks were sitting next to the door. "This where you came in?"

"I'll check the lockers," Dollie said.

I was drifting in and out, unable to focus, but I was vaguely aware of Dollie throwing open locker doors.

"This looks too big but will have to do," she said, holding up a large suit. "I also found some reserve tanks."

I heard shouting in the distance, slid my legs into the lower suit, and then edged the upper part over my arm to avoid catching the wound. As I closed the waist, Sigurd moved over and snapped something pungent under my nose. My mind cleared when I breathed it in. It was probably more of her military supplies and highly addictive, but for now it gave me the boost I needed.

I threw open the locker doors, hoping they'd provide at least a little cover, then pulled the helmet on. I struggled because the suit was too big, but eventually I locked the collar closed.

A metallic *zing* sounded, and sparks flashed off the locker doors. Someone was shooting at us. "Go," I shouted, grabbing the two reserve tanks and bundling myself inside the airlock.

Sigurd hit the cycle controls even as I was connecting the first of the auxiliary tanks. She obviously wasn't planning on hanging around. When the outer doors opened, I had air, though the tank readout only said twenty minutes. I hoped that would be enough.

"Where's the *Star Angel?*" I asked.

Dollie shrugged. "Gone."

I tried my comm-set again. "Dan. This is Joe. We're outside the Atoll, heading to the *Shokasta*. We'll have to come in through the payload bay." There was still no reply. "What did you do to the comms, I can't ge—"

"Joe, we'll meet you back at the ship." It was Logan, so whatever they'd done to interfere with communications had worn off—so where was Dan?

"If you get there before I do, warm her up. We'll have an entire posse on our tails."

"Will do." He hesitated, and when he continued his voice was icy. "We heard your transmission. And what Gabriella said about the Contravalency Phage."

I was about to ask him if he knew about it but stopped myself. Logan might have worked for SecOps, but there was no way I could see him having anything to do with something so appalling. The USP wasn't perfect—no society ever is—but I'd hoped we were better than that. How could we criticize the Atolls and their actions when our leaders were actively seeking genocide? And the fact that they were doing this while pretending to seek cooperation was sickening.

Sigurd took the lead and covered the ground easily, but her progress was hampered by my slowness. Dollie stayed close, but we were like ants crawling along the side of a water tower. We daren't try to cross open space as none of us had any maneuvering units. By the time we'd been at it for fifteen minutes, my right arm was as much use as a bread stick that's been left in the dip too long. I was favoring it, but at the same time had no choice but to use it. And the light-headed feeling was a warning sign I could only ignore so long.

I grabbed the next handhold and pulled myself across the hull. My air supplies were getting low, and I'd have to change to the second tank soon. We could see the *Shokasta* now, but it looked a long way off, and a wave of defeat flooded through me. I wasn't going to make it. "Dollie..."

She was a few meters ahead and scrambled back to me. She pressed her helmet against mine. "Don't say it, Joe. You're not giving up now. You hear?"

"We're divorced. You can't order me around any longer."

She didn't answer right away. "Then do what you always do. Be a stubborn bastard."

I nodded and reached for the next handhold, using the rungs at my feet to push against. Sweat pooled inside my suit visor. Normally I'd turn up the pressure to push the moisture into the drying unit, but I didn't dare risk using more of my precious oxygen than necessary.

Crawling over the Atoll's hull I repeated the same action over and over, my vision distorted like a set of fun house mirrors by the layer of sweat coating the visor. Then onto the next handhold and the next. A red light flashed on my tank. It was empty.

I locked off the internal valve by feel, fighting an edge of panic as the airflow died, and felt for the connector from the second tank. It gave me a little more hope, as it was full. The trouble was my fingers were numb, and I couldn't feel the connector well enough to guide it into the right port on my suit. I struggled with it for a while then felt it being pulled out of my hands. A second later, it clicked into place. I couldn't have said if it was Dollie or Sigurd, but whoever it was, I was grateful. I opened the internal valve and felt cool air flood back in, the faster airflow clearing my visor a little.

"I wish someone would let me know about this stuff at staff meetings," I said. "I'd have brought a line gun."

We continued our never-ending climb, the surface of the Atoll becoming increasingly less distinct with each movement. Finally, a shadow fell over us, and I looked up. We were under the belly of the *Shokasta*, the bay visible with a ring of lights around it. Maybe Dan *had* heard me. My eyes blurred, and I blinked hard to clear them. But it only seemed to make things worse, and everything around me dimmed. Then the shadow of the ship grew deeper, and I drifted into a black hole.

Chapter Twenty-Five

When I came to, we were in the payload bay, and I heard the rush of the air pressure building. I reached up to twist my helmet off, but my right arm sent spasms of pain through me when I moved it, and I couldn't manage the helmet one-handed.

Dollie came over to help. Her eyes were wet. "How do you feel?" she said.

"I need to get to the controls. Is Logan onboard?"

"You're badly hurt. You should—" She interrupted herself. "Never mind. Do what you feel you have to."

I managed to slide out of the p-suit. The lining was coated with blood, and my dressing had slipped almost completely off. "There'll be some MediSkin in the medical supplies. Could you bring me some?"

She looked pale but nodded.

I wanted to kiss her but decided not to. I was already dealing with enough injuries.

When I reached the control room, Aurore gasped at my blood-soaked arm.

"Paek's dead," I said.

Logan's eyes, widened. "Did you…?"

I wasn't surprised that he thought that. "Gabriella. She didn't like being assigned as his bed warmer." I flopped into the pilot's seat. Logan had brought the main power online, but we remained connected via the docking tube. "Did I miss anything?"

"The *Zenith* has left," Aurore said.

I started the undocking procedure then brought up the tactical display. Sure enough, the *Zenith* was powering away from the station, heading for deep space. "I'm surprised Mkandla would bail like that. I guess she's thinking about Seckinger's safety."

"I don't think that's it." Logan's voice sounded like pouring astrocrete. "If what we've heard is right, they're both still on Marduk."

"Huh?" was my eloquent response. "Then what's going on?"

"Dan's missing…"

I lowered my head for a few moments, hoping it would clear. I'd been too intent on getting to the controls, and my thoughts were muddy. "But… Dan?"

"That would be my guess."

"You think he stole the *Zenith*?"

"Do you have another explanation?"

Something stabbed my arm, and I jumped. Dollie tore at my shirt, and once the area was clear she sprayed a copious amount of MediSkin foam over my wound. "Best I can do until you stop this madness."

"Even if he'd learned enough to do that, why would he? I know he's flaky, but he often seemed scared of his own shadow."

"Or maybe he played you… us… really well," Logan growled.

McDole had talked about the hatred she'd sensed, but he'd kept that hidden almost perfectly from everyone but her. I had a nagging feeling I was missing something and couldn't place my finger on it. I checked the dock status. There'd been no response to my undock request, so I flicked the button to talk to the station.

"Marduk control, this is the *Shokasta* on docking port seventeen. I will be boosting in five minutes. Release the docking tube and clear the port. I'll not provide a second warning."

"*Shokasta*, this is Marduk control. Please hold while I get my supervisor."

"You heard me. Clear the port, or I'll not be responsible."

The MediSkin foam had jellified over the wound, and the anesthetics were working their magic. I glanced at Dollie. "Thanks."

The comms system beeped, and I stabbed the button. I sensed traffic control wasn't taking me seriously. "You have four minutes, Marduk control."

"Joe. It's McDole—I'm on the *Osheroff*. I heard your transmission. Was that woman telling the truth about the Phage?"

"I have no idea. Gabriella isn't the most reliable of people. But I don't know of a reason for her to lie about it. She killed Paek."

"She did?" McDole hesitated. "Sorry, Joe, I assumed you..."

"There's something else. Dan has taken the *Zenith*."

"Why?"

I opened the data systems. Dan had said he'd found communication logs, but I wasn't sure he was telling the truth. In less than a minute, I located the records and skimmed through them, but there were over thirty thousand entries. I set up a quick search for the IDs of the fake Atoll ships and retrieved them easily, then did the same thing for Contravalency Phage and found the records almost as quickly. My body felt like I'd been dipped in liquid helium, and it wasn't anything to do with the anesthetic or blood loss.

"The Phage is on the *Zenith*."

My words were almost a whisper, but McDole caught them well enough. "That lunatic has a weapon that could destroy the entire Atoll community?"

I did another check. "Around fifty kilograms, packaged in ten missiles."

"Where he's heading?" McDole asked.

It didn't take much figuring out, given his cargo. "My guess is he'd head straight for Sol. Target the biggest Atoll communities."

"And you think he knows how to make the Jump?"

I thought about all his studying and simulation work. "Unfortunately, he probably does."

The next signal from McDole was on an open frequency. "This is Commander McDole on the *Osheroff* to *USN Zenith*. Cut your boost and prepare to be boarded. If you comply, I guarantee your safety. Otherwise, we will attack. You have two minutes to respond."

The docking tube had been released, and I swung the ship around to follow the *Zenith*. I hit maximum acceleration using both the main engines and hit the CASTOR boost. We accelerated at one-third of a gee, and it was then I remembered I'd had to cannibalize the boost system. Despite that, we were catching the *Zenith* but only at a snail's pace, and Dan had a big lead.

"What's our weapons status?" Logan barked.

"Partial point defense. One missile launcher and a single laser—if we can get close enough to burn him. That's it."

"Target the *Zenith*."

"Can I try talking to him?" I wasn't sure what I'd say but I still felt obligated to try, if only for Charlie's sake.

Logan hesitated then nodded, and I opened a broadcast. "Dan, this is Joe. There's no way you'll escape. Let's talk things through. I'm sure we can find ways to help you."

The silence stretched out, and I thought he was ignoring me, but then the transmission light came on.

"You think I'm stupid?" His laugh was full of scorn. "Consider yourself lucky. I was gonna blow you and that 'Toller bitch up together."

So Hernandez hadn't planted the explosives. "Why didn't you?"

"You were so gullible I knew I could pull the wool over your eyes as long as I wanted. And I had a feeling that if I waited, something better might come up. I was right. Turns out Mkandla and Seckinger have been planning this all along—they're all dirty bastards, like I said—but now I'm the one holding the cards."

"He's ten-thousand kilometers away. Could we Jump closer?" Aurore said. "Get in range. He's inexperienced, so it may take him a while to react and give us a chance."

"I'm not sure I could program a Jump that fine. Plus, it would take time to figure out." The screen in front of me flashed. "The *Osheroff* has launched what looks like their entire missile complement. They're also firing lasers and railguns, but it's borderline in terms of range."

"Did you target his ship?" Logan asked.

"Missiles locked and tracking."

"Then fire."

I reached to launch the missiles, but as my finger neared the controls, the track on the *Zenith* flickered and vanished.

"He Jumped," Aurore said.

I couldn't see how he'd built-up power that fast, especially as he'd be unfamiliar with the ship.

"Did they take him out?" Logan said.

I stared at the screen. "I don't think so."

McDole sounded over the comm system. "Joe, did you get him?"

"We think he made a Jump. I'm guessing, but from the time he spent preparing, I'd say it was blind."

The screen flickered, and McDole's face appeared. She looked pale and drawn. "So we've no idea where he went? But he's got enough weaponry to commit genocide."

"Even if he didn't head straight for Sol, you can bet that's where he'll go eventually." I wondered again how the Corporate ships had tracked us through the Jump.

McDole's expression was cold, but fear sparked in her eyes. "We're setting up a Jump, regardless. We need to warn our people. You better send me what evidence you have."

"You need to see this," said Aurore. "I've been searching the data from Paek's ship." She moved what she'd found on to the main screen—a transmission between Paek and the AF-11s, detailing their next target.

Logan's eyes were as wide as plates. "They're going to attack Proxima Station?"

The station was the first established through a joint PAC-USP-UAD project and designed to set up a mining operation in the vast Anglada belt around Proxima. Destroying it would kill thousands from all three nation-states. It would also give the Corporates unobstructed access to exploit the belt.

"They may have already attacked," Aurore said. "It doesn't specify timing."

Logan waved at the controls. "How soon can we Jump?"

"How long to transmit this data to McDole?" I asked Aurore.

She checked the files again. "Twenty minutes."

"Then that's how long it will take."

Dollie had been quiet until now. "You need medical attention, Joe. Don't try to be a hero."

"If we go back to Earth for help, it might be too late," I said. "Our glorious leaders aren't the quickest of decision makers."

Her face was expressionless. "We might get killed."

"I thought that was the plan?"

She headed for the door, no doubt to see what had become of

Sigurd. I forced myself to look at the controls and set up a Jump to Proxima.

"You kids need to kiss and make up," Aurore said. "Don't be so rough on her, Joe."

"No chance of that." She'd never forgive me for stopping her from killing Paek.

Proxima and the two stars of Alpha Centauri were almost close enough to touch from an astronomical perspective. It was a triple star system more than anything, and the Jump to Proxima was only a fifth of a light-year, so it wouldn't take much energy to get there. And as Proxima was so small, it gave us the chance to Jump close to the station.

As soon as the transmission was complete, I broadcast a warning and triggered the Jump.

Proxima was a bright orange blob off to the left of the screen. I'd brought us high above the ecliptic to avoid the majority of the debris that formed the Anglada asteroid field. The instruments said we were five-million kilometers from Proxima Station, and I set up an approach on full thrust. We were a day away, but we knew we were too late by the lack of response to our comm signals.

It wasn't hard to Jump in closer, and we had a good reserve of power to make it possible. I set up the programming and took us to within ten-thousand kilometers. The station was a ring-and-hub design similar to the High-Rig but was smaller and not as solidly built as it didn't have to support a Space Elevator.

I brought it up on the screen and let out a long breath. "Looks like the cavalry's too late."

The main hub showed signs of several blow-outs that were likely the result of missile strikes, and two-thirds of the ring was missing. The relatively intact sections were clustered around where the spokes connected it to the hub. It was still spinning, but off-center and not the way it was designed to. There'd been over twenty-five hundred people based on the station, but we'd be lucky if we found a single person alive.

Logan stared at the wreckage on the screen. "Any signals?"

"There's something. But it's unclear," said Aurore. "It could be a low-level transmitter, like a comm-set. Or possibly just electrical noise."

"Possibly flare radiation from the star. Besides, I wouldn't recommend going over there to check. That structure looks ready to fail at almost any second." Looking at the tumbling remains of the station made me feel sick in my stomach. "And with the off-kilter spin, it would be almost impossible to search it safely."

"All those people dead," Logan whispered. "I always hoped when we got away from Earth it would end the killing. There's room enough for everyone. Why fight over it?"

"Humanity has a limitless talent for creating conflict," I said. "No matter how difficult it is."

Dollie had returned with Sigurd, and they sat along the wall to my right. Sigurd studied the screen, but Dollie had her head down looking miserable and defeated, something I'd never seen through all the years I'd known her. It tore at me, and I wanted to find some way to comfort her—to see her smile again. But I'd be about as welcome as a beef-farmer at a vegan lunch.

"I've got another signal," Aurore said. "Definitely artificial but not from the station."

I brought up the system map on the screen and checked the coordinates. "Navigation beacon. It's listed as an asteroid—designation 1174-AG. Does that mean anything to anyone?" I waited, but nobody spoke up. "We should check it out."

"An outpost?" Logan said.

"Hard to know without getting closer."

I plotted the new course and headed toward the asteroid. It wasn't far away, and the orbit didn't match the ones of the Anglada belt objects. It looked as if it had been moved into position deliberately, possibly as a training facility—or perhaps it was simply a larger rock they were actively mining.

It would take us a few hours to get there, so I grabbed some food. I felt weak, and my arm was making me feel wretched and more than a little crabby. I could have used some of Sullivan's NanoBiotics, but that thought only reminded me we'd lost the young soldier and made me feel even worse. I didn't want to inflict my mood on anyone so stayed out of the way.

When I returned, the asteroid was visible on the screen. It was larger than I'd expected, around thirty-five kilometers across, with the usual rocky surface. Its gray appearance tinged orange by the light of Proxima. From our viewpoint, a large airlock was visible on the right side of the surface. There was some sort of facility there, which meant someone might have survived the attack on the station.

There were no transmissions coming from the asteroid. If anyone was on this rock, they were understandably keeping quiet. I matched orbits so the ship was stationary fifty kilometers from the surface. That was close enough. It might have been a relatively small asteroid but still plenty big enough to crush us if we got too close.

My mind was unsettled. At first, I thought it was the side-effects of the injury, but my gut told me it was something else. Proxima, along with its two bigger sibling stars, was altogether strange. Their mutual gravitational attraction pretty much screwed up planetary formation and created the extensive debris fields around us. This made them uncomfortable places for humans used to the relatively benign area around Sol, but that didn't fully explain my nervousness. It felt as though the star and the entire system were polluted by a sense of death, made real by the destruction of the station.

I pushed the feeling out of my head and refocused on the asteroid. "I'll need the SMPT to check it out."

Logan raised an eyebrow. "You sure you can manage?"

"Sure." I grinned ruefully. "As you keep telling me—I'm the better pilot."

Logan nodded. "We'll keep an eye out up here."

I left, not daring to look at Dollie, but I could feel her eyes digging into my back. She was no doubt hoping I'd simplify things by not making it back.

At the inner airlock, I pulled on my p-suit but not before checking the MediSkin patch. It had sealed well, but it was hard to say how much damage there was. The puncture was almost on the scarring from my Regen therapy, a problematic area at the best of times. I swallowed a bunch of nerve-tranqs to be on the safe side, hoping they'd deal with any messed-up signals that might show their ugly heads.

I was closing the suit when I heard someone coming. It was Dollie. She was dressed in the black p-suit she'd been wearing on Paek's ship and holding her helmet in her hands.

She spoke before I could. "First rule of EVA operations..."

"No buddy. No EVA..." I shook my head. "Not this time. If there's anyone on that rock, I'll need room for passengers."

"Logan sent me. Said I wasn't to let you go on your own."

I should have known she wouldn't be here for her own reasons. I shrugged. "Okay. Step inside."

We jammed ourselves into the airlock, and her natural scent tingled inside my nostrils. Talk about the wrong place and the wrong time for that memory. It didn't take long to prep the SMPT, then I called up to Logan to cycle the main airlock. As the doors opened, we could see the asteroid surface below us, a tumble of rough shards and shattered rocks that looked about as inviting as racing barefoot over broken glass.

I released the SMPT from its cradle and nudged us out of the *Shokasta*, clearing us from the payload bay before bringing up the thrust and increasing our velocity to sixty meters per second. We could have gone faster but we'd have used more fuel and had a harder time slowing down. Besides, that was plenty fast enough to get into trouble.

"Joe...?" Dollie's voice sounded in my comm-set.

"What?" The word came out more harshly than I intended.

"Doesn't matter."

This friend/enemy thing confused me. I couldn't work out whether she was being nice or still pissed at me. To be honest, I was more comfortable when she clearly hated me. This in-between limbo was nothing but torment. I flipped the SMPT at the halfway point and countered the thrust. By the time we were done, we were floating a few meters from the asteroid's airlock. Someone had riveted a crude painted sign on one side of the doors that read "Fraioli's Folly" in reflective silver.

"Hotshot Ballen does it again," I muttered.

"Very good. And how does hotshot Ballen propose to open the airlock?" Dollie said.

I hadn't intended broadcasting my comment. "I thought I'd climb out and jump across. We don't have a remote opener for this thing."

"That's what I thought." Dollie was unlocking her belt. "But you can sit here, and *I'll* do it."

"Why would I do that?"

"Because I'm in better shape than you."

The dull ache in my arm told me she was right. "Okay, I'll exercise my manly privilege and sit on my ass."

Dollie clambered out on the edge of the SMPT. There were handholds to help stabilize her position, and when she kicked off, the movement caused the ship to spin slowly. I stabilized the motion and looked out. She was already at the airlock controls. Minutes later, the wide doors began to open, like a giant yellow mouth.

I nudged the SMPT forward, drifting through the open door. "*To each his own fear,*" I whispered.

Once inside, Dollie followed and triggered the airlock cycle. The slab-like doors closed, and the lights turned green to show the atmosphere was breathable. I hauled myself out, grabbed onto a railing, and pulled myself over to a walkway nearby. I kept my feet away from the floor, though—it was less strain to float.

The airlock was empty, and we made our way to the inner door. Inside was a circular tunnel, the borehole cut as straight as a laser and finished in astrocrete. There was something very familiar about the tunnel and how the fittings lining it were laid out. We moved down the corridor, past several side rooms, but they were all empty. I cracked open my helmet, and the atmosphere had the unmistakable acrid smell of newly cured 'crete.

I passed through another door and found myself in a much wider area. The room was mostly empty, but mounted against the far wall was an operations console, its boxy shape something I'd seen before. I moved over and flipped a few switches, bringing up a swathe of displays on the screens. "Well, I'll be damned."

Dollie came up behind me. "What is it?"

"That's Hardrock Harry." I pointed at the screens. "Blasting Bob and there's Mudslapper Moses."

"Are you feeling okay?"

"They're old friends of mine." I tested the circuits—inactive—but as far as I could tell fully functional. "I guess they decided to run some greenfield trials on my last project. They're designed to work autonomously but could never handle it. Which means there's probably no one here, but we should check, in case."

There were two doors in the room besides the one we'd come through, and Dollie pointed to the one on the right. "I'll take this one—you take the other."

"Meet back here in thirty minutes regardless. There's no telling how far the tunnels might run. If the robots have been busy, there could be kilometers to check. And check in every five on the comm-set."

My door led to another corridor. Like the one we'd come through initially, it was lined with empty rooms ready to be put to use. This was significantly better than anything we'd managed during my involvement with the project. Maybe Palmer had been right—I *was* the reason it never worked.

After searching a dozen rooms, I called Dollie. "Everything okay?"

Her reply came back almost immediately. "I'm fine. This place is deserted, though."

"Looks like it."

I carried on farther and came to another door. It led to a storage area, with a second airlock even bigger than the one we'd come in by. Down one side were drums of raw materials, mostly polymerizer for the final astrocrete finishing, but also large spools of wire. The bots were sitting on the other side of the room, looking like the guardians of a temple for ancient alien gods.

I looked them over. They appeared to be okay but were on a dormant cycle. They looked pretty beat up, suggesting they'd been busy.

Logan's voice came over the comm-set. "Joe! You need to get ba—"

A minute later, a sharp crack reverberated around the corridor, followed by a low rumble.

"Dollie? Are you okay?"

No answer. I pushed off against Blasting Bob, heading back the way I'd come. "Logan? What's happening?"

Aurore answered. "Joe. The AF-11s are here. We've had to pull away. Logan's trying to shake them before they get too close."

"I felt tremors just now."

She was slow answering. "They launched missiles. Some of them hit the asteroid."

"Get that ship out of here. Don't try anything—"

A deafening rip sounded above me, as if the heavens were opening, followed by a long, deep tearing sound. Clouds of astrocrete splinters filled the air as a long crack traveled the length of the corridor. By instinct, I snapped my helmet closed. Then the first chunks hit me, and I slammed against the wall of the tunnel.

Chapter Twenty-Six

Somebody had a campfire burning. I saw the flickering light in the darkness and smelled the woodsmoke. I hoped they had crackers and marshmallows. It was getting close to S'mores Day. I could share some with Dollie—she'd like them. I couldn't think why we hadn't done that before now.

"Joe?"

I could hear Dollie but couldn't see her. "Why've we never had s'mores?"

"You don't like marshmallows," whispered Dollie.

That was news to me. "Sure, I do. Let's cook some on the fire."

"I'll get you some when we get home."

The word "home" sent a skewer through my brain, and I tried to sit up but couldn't. My right arm wasn't working properly, and the left seemed trapped. I opened my eyes.

"Dollie?"

Her face floated into view above mine, partially hidden by her helmet, but visible enough through the visor to recognize her. "Beautiful."

"Pull out of it, Joe," she said. "I need you with me, okay?"

"I need you too."

"That's not—never mind."

I closed my eyes for a second as I remembered. The Corporate ships had attacked, and the tunnel had collapsed. "Are we okay?"

"Depends on your definition."

"The *Shokasta*? Logan?" I squirmed around, trying to get up.

"Jumped, or...."

I didn't want to think about that. "I can't move."

Dollie sniffed. "Your arm…"

"I know. That bastard stabbed me."

"It's worse than that."

My arm felt dead, as if there was nothing there. No sensation. Nothing but a dull numbness. The nerve-tranq wasn't strong enough to do that, and I realized that something must have triggered the trauma suppression system in my suit. "How bad?"

Dollie didn't answer.

"Can you help me up?"

"Why?"

"I want to get to the operations console. We can use it to see what's going on out there."

Dollie pulled away some of the rubble then lifted me. I weighed nothing in ZeeGee, but moving anything in those conditions was always a struggle. Her Geneered strength made it easier, though.

The corridor was illuminated by flickering lights and was filled with loose astrocrete. It looked like the main structure had held, but the inner finishing surface had given way catastrophically. Dollie dragged me through it, scrambling through the debris like a cat squirming through a construction site.

Once we reached the console, I had her move me close to it. My left arm was working now, so I reached down to operate the controls, bringing up a display from the external cameras placed around the asteroid's surface. After thirty minutes or so, I caught movement on the screen and zoomed in on it. It was an AF-11. I carried on searching, but couldn't see any sign of the other ship—or the *Shokasta*.

"Logan must have made a Jump," I said, convincing no one. "The weapons systems were damaged. They wouldn't have stood a chance against two ships."

"And if he didn't?"

I ignored her question, not wanting to consider the alternatives. Logan had pulled me through so much, I couldn't imagine life without him. "The atmosphere seems stable. If this thing is operating the way it was originally designed, there should be a solar array keeping everything powered. We might have enough atmosphere in here to last a week—maybe a couple, depending on the ice reserves.

"What do robots eat?" Dollie said, pointedly.

"There might be some supplies in the next level down. But I wouldn't hold my breath."

I'd set the optical system to track the AF-11, and it beeped.

"The ship has changed trajectory." I flipped through several camera views. "It looks like it's heading here."

"But why?"

I managed a one-shouldered shrug. "They could be being thorough. Or they may have picked up the signals from this console."

Dollie gasped. "Then stop using it."

"Too late." I pointed at the screen as two streaks of light flashed from the ship and appeared to head straight toward the camera. "Hold onto something."

The lights flashed as a violent vibration shook the walls and floor. Luckily the console was bolted in place, or we could have been eating computer circuits. When the rattling stopped, I checked the cameras again. The AF-11 was still there but had changed course again. Perhaps they were waiting to see if there was any change in the signals before making another attack."

"Can they hurt us in here?" Dollie inspected the walls and roof.

Asteroids varied in composition from icy to rock or a mix of both. If this one had been selected using the project parameters we'd been following back on Earth, it should be solid, and it would take a lot to put a dent in it. The support systems and infrastructure that had been added made it less resilient, though. Done right, we were probably safe, but it depended how determined the people on the AF-11s were. I thought of reassuring Dollie but realized there wasn't much point. She deserved to know the truth.

"If they hit us with enough explosives, they could rattle us to death. Or generate fissures in the rock and cause a major atmospheric breach. We could hunker down inside an internal airlock. At least until we use up the air."

"And sit and wait for them to deliver the final blow." Dollie spat the words out.

"Maybe." I fired up the control systems to see if the bots were accessible. "Maybe not."

"I know that tone, Joe Ballen," Dollie said. "You're about to do something crazy, improbable, and more than likely dangerous."

"Only to my metal friends."

I swapped screens, bringing up a list of ore drones. They delivered raw materials to the asteroid from the debris fields, which were used—along with supplies from Earth—to build the asteroid base. Unlike the excavation robots, they weren't very smart— basically dumb haulers designed to carry several tonnes of raw materials in low-fuel, efficient orbits. But now they were going to play a more vital role.

I was fading in and out, so it took a good forty-five minutes to re-program the drones. The AF-11 attacked several times, but nothing major had failed—so far. When I finished, I signaled two of them to leave the docking bay on a direct, but slow, path back toward what was left of Proxima Station. Then I switched over to programming the fleet of Muckout Mikes and sent them to nestle in close to the asteroid's surface. After that, I turned my attention to the mining bots.

Harry was the first online after his boot sequence completed. "Somebody woke me. But I'm supposed to be on shut-down for three more weeks."

"Sorry, Harry. Unexpected schedule shift. I have some new orders for you."

"Joe? Is that you?" He paused. "We thought you'd left the project. Mr. Palmer said you—"

"Mr. Palmer was confused. You know I'd never abandon you guys like that."

"That's what I said. But you know what Bob's like. He didn't think—"

"Hey, what gives here?" It was Bob. "We're supposed to be on some well-deserved downtime. There ain't no rest, I tell ya."

"Bob, Joe's back!"

"Yeah. What's that bum want?"

"Hey, Bobby. We're moving up the project schedule."

Dollie was staring at me as if I was one hundred percent certifiable.

"We've got another asteroid that needs mining, and it's got to be done fast."

"So ya need someone to make some big explosions, right?"

"You bet. Biggest explosions you've ever seen."

"Hey, I'm your man. I always believed in ya, Joe. That other guy was a creep."

I woke up Moses and Willie. They were less grouchy than the others but slower, so I had more time to analyze the situation. Once I had my figures nailed down, I fed them new coordinates and directed the video of the AF-11 to them. "That's our new target asteroid."

"That thing?" Bob sounded disappointed. "That's pretty small, Joe. Thought ya said it was a big job."

"Don't worry, Bob. It might look small, but it's a tough nut to crack. So load up with everything you can carry."

"I've never heard a robot so enthusiastic about blowing things up," Dollie said.

The AF-11 had taken the bait and gone after the two haulers, assuming they held escaping people. It would blow them out of the stars easily, and after that they'd be back at the asteroid, intent on finishing the job.

"I'm going to send you guys revised flight patterns. This new asteroid is going to take everything you have to mine, but it's vital to the colonizing effort."

"That asteroid's traveling mighty fast, Joe." It was Moses. "Are we gonna catch it?"

He sounded suspicious, but that was probably my imagination. "It'll be in range soon, Mose."

Dollie tapped me on the shoulder, and I killed the comms to the bots.

"What are you doing?" She sounded exhausted. "We should be trying to find a way out of here, not playing games with these damn robots."

"We're stuck here until someone rescues us. But if I don't stop that ship, we won't be around to meet them."

"Those bots have no chance against that thing."

"We'll see."

After that, all we could do was wait. The two haulers I'd sent toward the station had been turned to dust, and the AF-11 was heading back to our asteroid at top speed. I launched the remaining haulers and sent them flying in different directions, to make it look as though more people were fleeing. As the ship closed, I activated the Mikes and opened a comm line to the mining bots.

"Okay, guys, fall in behind the Mike's. Go do your duty. And let no asteroid remain un-mined."

The cruiser was targeting the other haulers, and several had been destroyed. They didn't realize that the haulers were nothing but sacrificial pawns.

"You're using the first ships as decoys, I get that." Dollie watched the readouts on the screens, following the battle. "But they'll destroy the others when they see them."

"That might not be so easy."

The ship was close now—a few hundred kilometers away and slowing. The bots and the Mikes were waiting on the far side of the asteroid. They wouldn't be visible and were too small and too close to the surface to be easily detectable. When I guessed the ship was at its slowest, I broadcast the command to "mine the asteroid."

I followed them on the cameras as they skimmed the surface, building up speed, switching between several of their inboard cameras to make sure they were functioning correctly. Once I was sure, I switched to a camera on one of the Mikes. The horizon of the asteroid's surface wasn't far, and it sped under the Mike, giving an incredible sensation of speed.

Finally, the AF-11 swam into sight. The timing was perfect, and I estimated they were no more than a hundred and fifty kilometers away. I rotated the camera. All the Mikes were there, forming a wall ahead of Harry, Bob, and the others as I'd planned.

I returned to the front view. I could only guess at the panic inside the AF-11 as a whole fleet of "ships" appeared out of nothing, but I'd lay money on it being nicely chaotic. Several missiles launched, and I saw flashes from railguns and laser fire directed at the swarm of approaching 'bots.

Muckout Mikes weren't armored in the same sense as a military vessel, but they *were* mining vehicles, designed to scoop out ore from drifts and survive the harshest conditions up to and including rockfalls. They were the nearest thing I could imagine to a floating tank. The first few shots rattled off their giant blades without slowing them any. I saw a flash of a missile explode as it hit one, but still they continued. Several more shots hit, and a couple of the Mikes tumbled. Then what I'd been hoping for happened.

The missile launches stopped.

Even a warship can only carry so much ordnance, and in a spaceship where room is at a premium, weaponry would always be limited. The missiles were the biggest threat to the Mikes. The other weapons were dangerous but not anywhere near as effective.

The AF-11 crew had been too confident. They'd slowed down expecting a few easily destroyed ships and a lightly armed ground base to defeat. They didn't think anything on the asteroid that could threaten them. But now they were turning to escape, but it was too late and the flock of heavy robot ships was bearing down on them.

"Hey, Joe?" It was Bob.

They were only a minute or so from impact. "What's wrong, Bob?"

"That ain't no asteroid, ya putz."

I was sweating from the pain ripping through my arm and didn't have time to discuss it. "You're right, Bob. It's not. See you on the other side."

Bob didn't say anything for a while, then, "Neck it, who cares? Ramming speed!"

I switched to the asteroid's external cameras as the first of the Mikes punched through the hull of the AF-11. Even that didn't seem to slow them. Seconds later, the shapes of Harry, Bob, and Willie followed them.

Bob's voice came over the comm-link. "Fire in the hole!"

"Sorry, guys," I whispered.

A massive explosion gutted the ship, rippling through it like a belch of fire and finally reaching the reactor area. Then a second flash appeared, even bigger than the first as the reactor exploded, vaporizing what was left of the ship. The pickup we were watching on flickered off as it overloaded, and I switched to another. All I saw were stars and the distant wreckage of the station. No sign of the AF-11 or the bots.

"You did it, Joe." Dollie sounded amazed. "You actually pulled it off."

"Thanks. I'd like to say it was nothing, but the truth was, it was pure genius at work. And now I'm ready for a nap."

I tried to move, but all I could do was curl into a ball. The trauma system was meant to last long enough to find medical help—not indefinitely.

"This should give you some more time." I coughed as a wave of sickness washed through me. "I hope it's enough."

"Joe?" Dollie moved over and grabbed me. That hurt too, even though she hadn't touched my bad arm. "Dammit, stay with me."

"I'm sorry, Dollie. For everything."

"Fight it, Joe. Stay with me, Soldier."

She hadn't called me that in several years. And it felt good. Then I felt a stab of pain in my thigh, which didn't. "I'll always be... your soldier..."

"Then stay with me."

"I don't think... I can." My vision dimmed and the pain faded.

Sometime later, I found I was strapped loosely against a table. My helmet was off, and I looked around, groaning as I moved. The pain wasn't as intense as it had been before I blacked out, but I could hardly say I felt comfortable.

"Dollie?"

"Right here, Joe." She squatted by the wall, about a meter away. "You passed out. I gave you a shot, but I was too late."

"You want to turn me into an addict now?" Whatever she'd given me must have been good, because it was keeping things numb after all this time. Then I realized I didn't know how much time had passed. "How long?"

"You've been out over six hours."

"Have you been busy working out a rescue plan?"

Dollie's eyes were locked onto the astrocrete floor. "No. Just thinking and feeling sorry for myself."

"Sounds like fun... Come to any conclusions?"

She lifted her head. "I didn't *want* to push you away, Joe."

"You did it rather well for a disinterested party."

"It was Samara—Sigurd's—idea."

"You do surprise me. And you fell for it—" I was going to add "and straight back into Sigurd's bed," but stopped myself. I was way past the point where it was worth arguing.

"We... I... knew that if I went after Paek, I probably wouldn't survive. You were trapped on Earth, so you couldn't go after him." She took a deep breath. "I knew if I died that you'd suffer, and I thought it would be easier if you hated me. And I wanted to save you from that guilt. You already blamed yourself too much."

I laughed, which turned into a cough. "So you did it all for my own good, huh?"

"It may be hard to believe, but credit me with some compassion."

"And now what? You want me to forgive you before it's too late? Forgive you, so we can die in peace?"

She looked hurt. "I thought... hoped, maybe, that one day you might understand."

"So you want me to forgive you because I understand?" I stared at her, my head whirling as though my oxygen was low. "Well, I don't. I can't. Deliberately hurting someone you claim to love is nothing but cruel."

Dollie jerked as if I'd slapped her. "I deserve that. I'm truly sorry, Joe."

"There are a thousand reasons why I can't forgive you." And I'd felt each of them like a bullet through my heart. "And only one against all of that."

When she finally replied, her voice was a blurred whisper. "What's that?"

"Because I love you and have never stopped. For that reason, and that alone, I *have* to forgive you."

She clambered up and moved across to me. Her lips pressed against mine, and that hurt too, but I didn't care.

"About Sigurd. I want to—"

I lifted my good hand and pressed a finger to her lips. "It's not important. Besides you weren't the only one at fault."

She nodded. "You can be a real asshole sometimes."

"But still cute, huh?"

Dollie shook her head. "I don't deserve you."

"You're right. You don't. But I don't deserve you either. Or perhaps we both deserve each other. Whatever the answer, you're stuck with me for a while longer."

She smiled even though there were pools of tears in her eyes. "Sounds good to me. How long do you think that will be?"

"I don't know." If I didn't get medical treatment soon, it might not be long. "Let's say—for the rest of my life."

She kissed me again, and I felt light-headed but not from the pain.

"So, what's the plan to get us out of here, oh mighty Ballen?"

"Logan's coming back for us."

Her eyes widened. "You think he's alive?"

"Don't ask me how or why. But my gut says he is."

"And your gut is never wrong, huh?"

"Not even when I think it is." A wave of nausea hit me, and a spasm tore at my shoulder. "How bad is that arm?"

"I'm not sure. I think it's smashed down to the bone."

"I feel cold. But I know I'm sweating." I used my good arm to slide over on the table. "Would you do something for me?"

"Anything, Joe."

"Come up here and hold me for a while."

It was a gesture. I couldn't feel her through the bulk of our suits, but it made me feel better to watch her breathing. Don't let anyone tell you anything different. The best things in life can't be bought with money but are infinitely precious.

Sometime later, the room started shaking. The damage from the missiles must have been worse than I thought. Dollie was asleep and I called her name, the word coming out in a staggered blur.

"What's wrong?"

Then I realized it wasn't the room that was shaking—it was me. The pain levels had crept back up until I quivered on the table and would have fallen off without the straps.

"Dollie reached inside a pouch in her suit and pulled out an emergency hypo. "This is it, Joe. One more left. After that, I've got nothing to help you."

I nodded, and she punched it against my thigh.

A cool draught seemed to blow through me, and the shaking eased a little. Whatever was in the hypo was potent for sure. Knowing Sigurd's past, I guessed it was some type of illegal military test drug and not meant to be administered to anyone who hadn't been Geneered with rhino DNA. But at that moment, I didn't care. I didn't want to sleep, but my eyes disagreed as the drug bit deep.

"Dollie? I lov—"

The next thing I knew, I was being manhandled. It seemed like several pairs of hands were tossing me around the room, and when I looked around, my head was so woozy that little made sense. I was in the corridor heading to the main airlock, that much I knew. I heard voices around me, but the words were a tangled jumble.

"Dollie?" I called out. They ignored me. "Don't leave Dollie behind."

I pushed up, but the hands held me in place, and I didn't have the strength to push them off. A deep panic stabbed inside my brain, and I called for Dollie again, but there was still no answer. Why had they left her? She should be with me. We were going to spend our lives together. She'd promised.

Then I was in a white space as though enveloped in a bright warm cloud. A deep voice sounded close to me.

"Damn it, his arm's a complete mess. I think he's going to lose it."

Screw the arm. I can't lose Dollie! I thought I screamed it, but maybe I didn't. Or if I did, it was ignored.

"It's not good." This was a second voice, lighter than the first. Possibly female, but everything was so distorted I wasn't sure.

"Do what you can for him." The first voice sounded again. "I need to set up a Jump."

Logan? Where's Dollie? I thought I yelled but wasn't sure. Something tore at my arm, and I screamed. Then nothing.

Chapter Twenty-Seven

The next time I woke, I seemed to be in the same place, enveloped in a cloud that bathed me in a pure light. But I felt like one of Dr. Frankenstein's failed experiments. There was a beep, and a few minutes later, voices. Something was peeled away from my eyes, and I blinked several times before seeing Logan. We were in a hospital room. His craggy face looked lined and tired, but he still seemed to fill the space with his powerful bulk.

"You came back for us," I croaked. "I knew you would."

His gaze dropped, and fear crashed through me. "What's wrong? Where's Dollie?"

"I've got some bad news."

"Dollie?" I felt like I knew what he was going to tell me and didn't want to hear it.

"Dollie was hurt too, but she'll be fine. Been here all the time. Trust you to wake up when she had to go to the powder room."

I heard ringing in my ears. I'd been sure something had happened to her, though I wasn't quite sure why. "Then nothing else matters."

The door opened, and I saw a flash of movement. Then Dollie had her arms around me. After several moments, she pulled back, tears running down her face. "We almost lost you."

"I always said you were careless. I've been right here all the time. Where is *here* by the way?"

"Your arm was smashed up when the tunnel failed. It went septic despite the MediSkin. They're not sure if it was the knife wound or the later damage that did it. We're on the High-Rig."

The fingers of my left hand trembled as they brushed against the sheets. When they reached where my other arm should be, I felt a stump fattened by dressings and nothing more.

"They took my arm?" I clenched my eyes tight. "Again?"

Dollie looked across to Logan then back to me.

"What's wrong? What aren't you telling me?" My heart pumped hard, and my temples throbbed. "They'll Regen me a new one."

Dollie shook her head slowly. "The damage was too extensive. I talked to the doctors here and Dr. Kinsella. There's nothing they can do."

It felt like someone had thrown an ocean of ice water over me. Fate was playing a cruel game, but who said the universe was fair? I stroked Dollie's hair with my good hand. "Did you mean what you said on the asteroid?"

Her eyes were like glittering sapphires. "Every word. Did you?"

I nodded. "Then I don't care. As long as you'll have me back."

She kissed me long and deep, only pulling back when Logan coughed theatrically. "Spoilsport!"

"He needs to recover." Logan came over and gripped my hand. "There's another option—Cynetics. It's something new I heard about through SecOps."

"A robot arm?" I hesitated. "I'm not sure I like the sound of that."

"It's more than that from what I understand."

"And they're willing to let me try this?"

"Willing might not be the most accurate word." He grinned. "But they owe you that much. And I'll make sure you get it if you want it."

Robotic prosthetics had been around for a while but hadn't worked well up till now. The mechanics and control interfaces were always clunky, leaving people clanking around like MechaFluxx, Professor Wingnut's robot henchman. But maybe this would be different.

"Give me a while to think about it. I need to get used to the idea." A thought popped into my head. "What about the Atolls? Did Dan resurface?"

Logan moved closer. "Not yet. McDole scrambled their fleet, and they haven't stood down. Dan is out there somewhere, planning who knows what."

I was sure he was right. Unless something had happened to him, Dan would be back, and when he resurfaced the Atolls would die—unless they could figure out a way of inoculating their structures against the phage. "I presume the USP is providing them with technical information."

Logan shook his head grimly.

The door opened, Aurore breezed in and dashed over to give me a kiss on the cheek.

"Don't get the big guy jealous," I said.

"Pooh. We owe you so much, and Logan knows it more than anyone. Besides he can stand to be a little jealous—it keeps him on his toes."

I looked at Logan. "You'll be heading back into space. What's SecOps got cooked up for you this time?"

Aurore glanced at Logan. "You didn't tell him yet?"

"I'm not active with SecOps anymore." He put his arm around Aurore's waist. "This thing with the Contravalency Phage sickens me. I used to think we were the good guys, but *we* developed that or had it developed. That's not the world I want to live in."

"Tell him!" Aurore laughed.

"What?" I had no idea what they were keeping from me, and perhaps I didn't want to know.

When he spoke again, Logan's voice was almost a whisper. "I did it, Joe. *We* did it."

"You and Aurore? That's not much of a surprise, you know. We all figured out that you two were—"

"We found a planet."

"Huh?" While interesting in an academic sense, that wasn't exactly amazing news. Planets were everywhere as far as we knew.

"A habitable planet!"

My head was spinning as if the High-Rig had flipped upside down in an impossible maneuver. A habitable planet within Jump distance of Earth would change everything. "You sure?"

"I could be wrong." Logan squeezed Aurore tighter. "But not my lady here—oxygen/nitrogen atmosphere, water, oceans, clouds, temperate."

"Life?"

"Vegetation detectable from orbit. Hell, it looked green and lush like a savanna. Animal life? Who knows. We need to do some surveys."

I wondered if I was dreaming. "They better call it Logan's World. That's fantastic."

He nodded. "We Jumped randomly several times, in case the AF-11s tried to follow us. That's when we found it."

"And we're going. Logan is heading up the first survey and development team, and I'm not about to let him wander around a strange planet on his own. Besides, I'm going to head up the first scientific mission." Aurore's face split in a wide smile. "And be the first to dance on a new world!"

I couldn't believe what I was hearing. It was an unbelievable opportunity and one they both deserved. "Don't forget to set up the RoboPony and send some postcards."

"You could come as well," Logan said. "Both of you."

I shifted in the bed, the loss of my arm suddenly all too real. I looked at Dollie, but she stared placidly back, giving no hint of what she was thinking.

"I think we're done with space," I said. "There are only so many limbs a guy can lose."

"Give him some time. He's tired," Dollie said. "And if anyone's going to tire him out, it's me."

Logan chuckled and led Aurore out. Dollie perched on the edge of the bed. "You know it's your choice, don't you? If you still want to space, I won't try and stop you."

"Thank you." I reached out to squeeze her hand. "No rush, though. Before that we should get remarried. If you want to."

Dollie grinned. "Already done. You're officially my man again, Joe Ballen."

She reached into her purse and pulled out a marriage license. It was freshly notarized.

"How? I wasn't even conscious."

"Remote application. I forged your signature and got a nurse to collect the DNA sample for verification."

"Oh."

"Are you complaining?"

"No. Well, yes... I missed out on the fun, romantic bit."

She leaned in and kissed me. "I'll let you make it up to me."

I kissed her back. "I'm sure I'll find a way of rising to the occasion."

"Someone's been trying to get a hold of you. They finally sent you an eFlimsy." She reached into a bag and pulled out the transparent sheet.

It had no markings on it other than the red circle for my thumbprint. "I'm surprised you didn't unlock it yourself."

Dollie laughed "I *did* consider it."

I pressed my thumb against the circle, which pulsed as it not only read the print but took a minute trace of my DNA. After several seconds, the plastic sheet flickered then filled with information. At the top of the page was a large heading that said "Nakaji-Wei Consortium" next to a bold red logo. I skimmed through the text, scrolling past several pages bristling with technical project details. I wanted to get an idea of the main message rather than the nitty-gritty.

"Are you going to tell me what it is?"

My excitement grew the more I read, but my heart fell. I knew how Dollie felt about me working in space. "I've been offered a job. Head of engineering for the Taikong Gaogu project."

"We're moving to the PAC? Fantastic—I need to go shopping."

I didn't answer. Dollie stopped bubbling in excitement, and her shoulders fell. "It's in space, not in the PAC?"

I nodded. "It's their new giant habitat project. I'd have to live there while the infrastructure is built, make sure everything's working, and keep a whole team of engineers busy."

"How long?"

"It doesn't matter. Something like that will take years."

"But you want it." It was a statement, not a question.

"Not if it means leaving you behind." I swallowed hard. "I lost you once. I can't go through that again."

When Dollie finally spoke again, her words were soft. "What if you didn't have to?"

"What do you mean?"

She took my hand in hers and looked me in the eyes. "They'll accommodate a married couple."

I didn't know if that was an option, but Dollie's tone said they'd have no choice in the matter, much like me. Maybe I was wrong, and sometimes things did get better. I pulled her close and kissed her passionately, only breaking away when I felt I might lose consciousness again.

"I better message Logan."

Dollie snuggled against me. "How come?"

"I think I'm going to need that steam-powered arm after all."

End

Also From David M. Kelly

Joe Ballen, book one

Meet former space engineer, Joe Ballen. These days, he's scraping a living flying cabs in flooded-out Baltimore. When one of his passengers suffers a grisly death, Joe is dragged into a dangerous web of ruthless academic rivalry centered on a prototype spaceship.

As the bodies pile up, Joe becomes suspect number one, and his enemies will stop at nothing to hide the truth. With the help of an enigmatic scientist, a senile survivalist, and the glamorous Ms Buntin, can Joe untangle the conspiracy and prove his innocence before it's too late?

Joe Ballen, book two

Joe Ballen is working on a new ore-processing platform in the harsh environment around Mercury. When a savage Atoll attack leaves him injured he returns to Earth to recover.

But vital JumpShip iles are missing, and Joe is bulldozed into the not-so-choice assignment. As Joe searches for the data, he gets tangled up in a high-stakes game of cat and mouse in the depths of space, where no one is quite what they seem.

Can old enemies ever make good allies? And can Joe trust even the people closest to him?

See all my books online: **davidmkelly.net/my-books/**

.

Acknowledgements

I hope you enjoyed reading this novel. This book would not have been possible without the help and support of my family, friends, and other members of the writing community. I'd like to thank them all. I would especially like to thank my wife, Hilary, for her constant love, support, and patience. Without that, this book would simply never have been written.

A special mention must go to my editor, Michelle Dunbar (michelledunbar.co.uk) who helped polish the raw manuscript into the masterpiece that lies before you. ;-)

The best way to help any writer, especially an indie like myself, is through sharing your enjoyment via word-of-mouth. Please consider leaving a rating and/or review on your preferred book retailer. Even if only a line or two, it's very much appreciated. Also, please look out for other independent authors. There are a lot of us out there who work hard to bring you stories that you would never see through commercial publishers.

For a complete list of my fiction, please visit my website (davidmkelly.net) and consider signing up for my free update newsletter. I won't share your information with anyone for any reason and won't bombard your mailbox either. Newsletter subscribers benefit from early release information as well as occasional free stories.

Thanks again.

David M. Kelly

About The Author

David M. Kelly writes fast-paced, near future sci-fi thrillers with engaging characters, cynical humor, and plausible science. He is the author of the Joe Ballen series (*Mathematics of Eternity, Perimeter, and Transformation Protocol*) as well as the short story collection *Dead Reckoning And Other Stories*.

Originally from the wild and woolly region of Yorkshire, England, David now lives in wild and rocky Northern Ontario, Canada, with his patient and long-suffering wife, Hilary. He's passionate about science, especially astronomy and physics, and is a rabid science news follower. When not writing, you can find him driving his own personal starship, a 1991 Corvette ZR-1, or exploring the local hiking trails.

Find out more at www.davidmkelly.net

To sign up for the mailing list, go to www.davidmkelly.net/contact

You can also follow David through the following channels:

Facebook: facebook.com/David.Kelly.SF

Twitter: twitter.com/David_Kelly_SF

Goodreads: goodreads.com/DavidMKelly

Manufactured by Amazon.ca
Bolton, ON